MW00475487

GERI GUILLAUME

Her Brother's KEEPER

ARABESQUE®

ISBN-13: 978-1-58314-805-1
ISBN-10:   1-58314-805-1

HER BROTHER'S KEEPER

www.kimanipress.com

Printed in U.S.A.

Chapter 1

Summer
White Wolf, Montana

"What'll it be, hon?"

It was too early for the lunchtime rush. So, Marjean grabbed a ticket book to serve the lanky fellow sitting all by his lonesome in a booth at the back of her café. Owner. Proprietor. Chief cook. Bottle washer. At various times, Marjean had worn all of those labels and wasn't too proud to haul herself from behind the counter when she needed to. Not when it came to money. Or, as she reminded herself watching that big fellow warily, a potential threat to her money.

Her daughter, Barbara Jean, had seated the man twenty minutes ago, moving him three times at his request. First by the front door. But that wasn't good enough. Then to a table in the middle of the restaurant. That wouldn't do, either.

"Well, why don'tcha tell me where ya wanna sit, mister?" Barbara Jean had demanded, impatience evident in her tone and in the way she planted one hand in the small of her back to support the weight of her very obvious late-term pregnancy. She didn't even try to hide her irritation. It wasn't as if she expected a large tip from him.

Nothing about that man said big tipper—from the faded blue baseball cap turned backward on his badly-in-need-of-a-touch-up cornrows, to his sweat-stained T-shirt beneath the open plaid button-down shirt, down to the raveled hems of his mud-splattered jeans. Barbara Jean almost turned up her nose, wondering what kind of health violations he'd committed by walking up there in those raggedy pants. They were seriously frayed at the hems, as if he'd stepped on them one too many times with the worn heels of his scuffed work boots.

"There," he said, indicating with a lift of his stubbled chin at the spot. "I'll take that table." He'd chosen the last booth seat, with his back against the wall.

"Fine," Barbara Jean snarled, slapping a tri-fold laminated menu on the tabletop, and pulling a paper-wrapped straw and napkin from her apron pocket. Being young, not yet thirty, and pregnant with her fourth child didn't help her disposition. Gone were the days when she could take the time to shoot the breeze with any of her customers. Flirting with some. Flattering others. She was getting too old and too tired for that. Now, it was all business.

"What do you want to drink?" she offered, with as little grace as she had patience.

"Water. Easy ice," he said simply. As she walked away, he called after her. "And make sure you put it in a clean glass."

She would have turned around and glared at him if her feet and back didn't ache so much. Who was he kidding? Clean glass? Something told her that if it weren't for the public restroom in the gas station a few miles down the road from where he'd come walking up, he probably wouldn't have had water to bathe himself. For somebody who looked as if he didn't have two nickels to rub together, he sure did sound as if he owned the world.

At least he doesn't stink, she thought gratefully. Though, her limited goodwill started to slip a notch when she heard him impatiently drumming his fingers along the tabletop.

It was a good thing for him that the café was still so empty, Barbara Jean thought. She probably wouldn't have put up with that nonsense if more of her regulars had come in—regulars who knew her and would reward her for any extra effort.

After she'd seated him, she went back behind the counter to fill a frosted white plastic tumbler with ice water. Still grumbling under her breath, she pressed the tumbler against the ice maker, partially filling the glass with shaved ice, shaking it to make the ice settle, then slammed the tumbler against the lever to start the water flowing.

Without a word, she returned to her customer, set the glass on the table. Barbara Jean didn't speak, but the way the plastic tumbler hit the table with a noticeable *thump* spoke volumes. Her lack of friendly conversation wasn't even noticed. She might as well be invisible. He didn't bother to speak, either. Not even to acknowledge her for her prompt service.

Barbara Jean stood there for a few minutes, waiting expectantly for him to order. When he didn't speak, she prompted, "Ready to order, mister?"

"I'll let you know when I'm ready," he returned. Again, avoiding the eye contact.

"Fine," she said snippily. It wasn't as if she had all day to wait on him. She joined her mother back at the counter. When the man wasn't looking, Barbara Jean leaned over and muttered to Marjean, "Check him out, Mama. Got us another one. A real class-A jerk."

Barbara Jean flashed the secret sign at her mother to warn her that this one might be a skipper. There was barely enough meat on the man's bones to keep his clothes hanging on him. Barbara Jean could easily imagine him ordering up a huge meal, eating some, stashing the rest in that duffel bag that he'd dumped on the seat across from him, then making a dash for the door as soon as the lunch crowd came in. He would probably get away with it, too. She was too pregnant to stop him. And Mama was certainly in no condition to go running down the street after what might amount to only twenty dollars' worth of food.

While Marjean wiped down Formica countertops and refilled ketchup bottles, she watched him out of the corner of her eye as he opened up the menu and stared at it for a very long time. Too long of a time.

Yep, he's a skipper, all right, Marjean figured.

The most expensive item on the lunch menu wasn't more than eight dollars. And that's if you supersized the fries. Not that her place, Marjean's Café, was known around White Wolf for the most gourmet meals; but it didn't come cheap, either. Every time one of those—how could she say it with political correctness—roving nonresidents came into her place, she ran the risk of having to foot the bill for one of their eat-and-runs.

Marjean figured that she'd better keep an eye on this one herself. She couldn't afford to let one patron skip out without paying. She had expenses to pay. Lordy, she still hadn't paid off her loan from having to rebuild her place when that tornado had blown through near about seven years back.

"Let me deal with him," Marjean offered. "You go on in the back, B.J., and check that we've got enough patties in the freezer to handle the rush. If there ain't, make sure you push yesterday's special today. We've still got plenty of that left over."

"Yesterday's chicken-fried steak, two sides, and a roll." Barbara Jean rattled off the menu from memory.

"You got it."

Marjean gave an inaudible grunt as she eased her nearly two-hundred-eighty-pound frame off the stool and moved with more agility than her large frame should have allowed past the rows of tables with a smattering of customers, past the vinyl-and-cloth booths and the vintage Wurlitzer jukebox to where her customer still sat, drumming his fingers on the tabletop. Now, he'd added a knee bounce to the mix. Several times, his knee hit the table underneath, causing the metal containers of condiments to rattle. A bundle of nerves, that one. She wondered if he was high on something, then figured not. If he couldn't afford to eat, he probably couldn't afford the kind of habit that would keep him hopped up like that.

"You made up your mind yet?" she addressed the young man with slightly more patience, though with no less suspicion, than her daughter had.

"Another glass of water," he said, pushing the empty tumbler across the table at her.

The closer Marjean got to him, the more she observed him, the less inclined she was to believe that he was on something. His speech wasn't slurred. His eyes weren't blurred. His hands were steady and even.

Marjean picked up the glass. "It's awful hot out there, hon. Sure I can't interest you in a glass of iced tea? Refills are free."

"Just water," he repeated, picking up the menu again.

"And?" she prompted. She wasn't going to let him sit here all day, sucking up ice water *and* her air-conditioning when there were others, possibly better-paying customers, waiting to take up that seat.

"And..." he repeated, slowly folding the menu closed, "a grilled-cheese sandwich."

"Anything else?" Marjean asked, her pen poised over the order pad.

"All I want is the sandwich and the water," he said, passing the menu back to her. When he did so, Marjean noticed his hands. Rough, calloused, each one with their share of scars. Some healed. Some not. Dirty fingernails. A laborer's hands. You didn't get hands like that always bumming food. Somewhere along the way, he'd worked for it.

Marjean's attitude softened. She had no problem with folks not having money. More often than not, money always ran short in her household. Especially with Barbara Jean popping out babies like bubbles from Lawrence Welk's bubble machine. Anyone trying to make their way would always be given a chance in her book.

He was thin, but not emaciated. Nothing, Marjean mused, a few steak-and-potato meals under his belt wouldn't fix. The muscles in his arms were lean, sinewy, but looked as though he could lift his weight, if he had to. Judging from the bulk of his duffel bag, maybe he had. He gave the appearance of a man traveling light, with his few earthly possessions bundled up in that ratty green army duffel.

"Maybe you'd be interested in our special," she suggested sympathetically. "Double-patty cheeseburger, fries, a side of chicken-fried steak, rolls, veggies, and a large iced tea. Pecan pie for dessert."

When he looked up at her, his expression wavered between stubborn pride and undeniable hunger. The smell of grilled onions and flame-kissed beef patties hovered in the air. It was only 10:30 a.m. Yet, within thirty minutes, smoke rising from the grills' exhaust vents to the open air outside would lure the lunchtime crowd to her place like the Pied Piper of Hamlin. He shook his head no.

"I can't pay for any of that."

When she saw that he'd made up his mind, pride winning the tug-of-war, she insisted. "All that comes with the grilled-cheese sandwich," she insisted.

"No, thank you. Just bring me what I asked for."

"I told you. It's the special."

When he turned back to face her, he smiled at Marjean. Not so much a smile, she mentally corrected, but an upward turn of his mouth. The humor of the ridiculousness of her claim never reached his dark eyes.

"I don't remember seeing it on the menu." Though his logic was irrefutable, Marjean took a certain pride in not letting anyone get anything over on her in her place.

"We don't print those up every day," she said, tapping her pencil twice against the plastic-covered menu. "So, do you want the special or not?"

"Sure. Give me the special," he relented, his tone clipped. The audible rumbling of his stomach killed any opportunity for a proud refusal of her offer. "Burger well done. No gravy on the chicken-fried steak. Unsweetened tea. Extra lemons."

"Be right up," Marjean promised.

When she set the plate in front of him ten minutes later, he attacked the meal as if there had never been any debate. He grabbed the bottles of ketchup and mustard, liberally spreading them over the sizzling, dripping burger patties as if it had been exactly what he'd ordered. Marjean set the tall glass of amber-colored tea in front of him, stepping back to watch as he tapped his fingers against the bright yellow sweetener packets, ripping them open and sprinkling them into the glass.

As he stirred the crystals before they sank to the bottom, he asked in a subdued tone, "Are you hiring?"

"Me? No," Marjean said. "Got all the help I need between my daughter, B.J., and her husband, Waydell."

"How else am I going to pay for all of this?" he asked, waving his hand over the platter.

"I told you—"

"The special, I know," he interrupted her. "Only, I don't see the grilled-cheese sandwich here."

Marjean pursed her lips, reaching for the plate. "I could take it back, if it's not to your liking, hon."

"That's all right. It'll do." He lifted the burger, took a healthy bite out of it, barely chewed before swallowing and gulping down almost half the glass of iced tea.

"Whoa there. Slow down now, son," Marjean said. Without asking permission, she eased herself on the opposite side of the booth, folded her hands on top of the table. "You'll make yourself sick eating so fast."

She watched him close his eyes, come back to himself. He pushed the plate away from him, spread his hands out on the table. This time he did smile. Not an unpleasant one, Marjean noted. It almost made him look passable for a human being, rather than the surly bear that had come in here half an hour ago. Amazing what a little food in the belly did for his disposition.

"I'll tell you what…Marjean," he said, his eyes shifting to

her name badge. "You let me bus tables for the afternoon. Enough to earn tips to pay for my meal."

"Oh, you don't have to do that." She started to dismiss his offer.

"Yeah, I do," he said, picking up a dill pickle wedge and munching on it.

"I told you, I'm not hiring," she stressed. With Barbara Jean in her third trimester, her daughter needed all the tips she could pick up before the baby was born. Her generosity was only going to go so far. Her bleeding heart let him have the meal. She wouldn't take the food from her baby's mouth by denying her the opportunity to earn those tips.

"I heard you the first time," he said sharply. He had the look of a man who didn't like repeating himself. As hastily as the mask of frustration settled over his face, he recomposed himself. "I only want to earn back what I ate."

"If you're looking for work, I think I might know someone who is hiring."

He lifted his eyebrows in question. "Who?"

"There's a ranch outside of White Wolf called Hollings Way. They might not have a full crew yet. You ever do any ranching work, mister?"

"Some," he admitted, holding a lemon wedge against the spoon and squeezing the liquid into what was left of his iced tea. Again, Marjean noticed the hands. From the look of those calluses, she'd figured more than just *some*. The first thing he ought to do, once he started out there, was get himself a pair of good work gloves. She waved Barbara Jean over, pointing to his empty tea glass. She waited until Barbara Jean turned her attention to another customer before continuing.

"The pay may not be all that good," she warned him.

"Better than nothing," he said, more to himself than to Marjean.

"If you're willing to work, that's your best bet around here." She pulled out a napkin from her pocket and sketched out directions. "The man you want to see is named Leon Redmond. They call him Red Bone. He's the ranch foreman."

"He does the hiring?"

"Mostly. But the one who has the final say is Jon-Tyler Holling. He and his father Nate own the place."

"Then that's who I want to talk to. I'm not wasting my time with anyone else."

Marjean sat back, regarding him with a mixture of curiosity and amusement. Kind of a high-handed tone for someone who she figured before he came to her place had no other plans.

"You in a hurry to be somewhere, hon?"

Instead of responding to her taunt, he picked up his burger again and nodded at the door before taking another bite. "You've got customers, Marjean."

Marjean twisted around, looking over her shoulder. The regulars were starting to trickle in. They took their favorite seats around the restaurant, not waiting for her or her daughter to seat them. Marjean lifted her hand, waved to some, called out to others by name to acknowledge them.

When a couple of truckers unfamiliar with the café's routine, identifiable by the company logos on their caps and their bulging paunches, paused at the Please Wait to Be Seated sign posted at the entrance and waved her over, Marjean planted her hands on the table. She pushed herself up with a lament of *Oh, mercy!* then waved them over, indicating where they should sit.

One of the truckers sat at a booth in front of her, peered over and whistled appreciatively at what remained of that chicken-fried steak and pecan pie her customer was now shoveling into his mouth.

"*Whew-ee!* Boy, that sure looks good. I'll have what he's having."

"Be right with you, mister," Marjean promised.

The trucker laughed, reshaped the bill of his dingy brown cap, and winked broadly at Marjean and her customer with wide gray eyes. "I wasn't necessarily talking about the burger, sweet thing. Tell me, son, where does a man get him a taste of something like that?"

"You let him alone, now. Let a man eat his meal in peace without all of that nonsense."

"Is that what you want, son? A little peace?" he said, making it sound as if serenity were the last thing he'd intimated.

She made a shooing motion, making the trucker turn around. But her cheeks were flushed. Before her daughter had started having babies, she'd been the one getting all of the attention. Those rig jockeys who'd come in here must have been on the road a long time if *she* was starting to look more appealing to them than the lunch special.

Before she left, she turned back around.

"Gotta go earn my keep. Speaking of which, you take your time with that meal, hon. You can talk to me later about picking up an odd job around here, if you're determined. But you make sure you get your fill. Believe you me, mister, you'll have plenty of time to pay me after you start working out there at the Holling place."

Chapter 2

Six months later

"What do you think you're doing, mister?"

Sawyer Holling reached out with a gloved hand and squeezed the chubby cheeks of her six-year-old son, barely in time to keep him from sticking his tongue to the ice-covered chrome bumper of his father's truck.

"Not this time," she warned, giving his head a gentle shake. "How many times do I have to tell you, Jayden, not to stick your tongue where it doesn't belong?"

"But Thydney dared me!" Jayden lisped, trying to speak through his mother's viselike grip.

Sawyer cut her eyes at her daughter, who was sitting cross-legged on the bed of the truck. Her head was bent over one of her favorite Dav Pilkey books.

"Sydney Rose Holling." Sawyer voiced a dire warning in the calling of her daughter's full name. No wonder Jayden was constantly in trouble. Sydney took her cue from the fictional characters in those Captain Underpants books.

As much as she encouraged the twins to read, Sawyer had a good mind to take the boxed set of books that she had stashed in the top shelf of her closet back to the store. There was no sense in blaming her daughter if Sawyer was the one constantly giving her the ammunition she needed to torture her poor, impressionable son.

"Ma'am?" Sydney looked up; her wide eyes were guileless.

Sawyer wasn't taken in. She knew her daughter. Knew her oh-so-well. When she looked down at her, it was like peering into a looking glass. Sawyer could see more than simply physical similarities. Every lift of her daughter's fine dark eyebrows, every quirk of her tiny mouth, each time she batted those long, silky lashes, it was like stepping through a time machine. Every act of chaos, followed by every protest of innocence, was oh-so-familiar to Sawyer.

Sydney was a living, breathing testimony to all of the drama she'd put her own family through. Sawyer could not be fooled by that look of innocence. She'd mastered it. Even though she recognized that look, she couldn't resist it.

"Do you want Santa to pass up our house? I can't believe you're still torturing your brother this close to Christmas."

"But I didn't do anything!" Sydney insisted. "I was sitting right here. Reading. Being good. Like you told me to, Mommy."

Sawyer lowered her chin and narrowed her eyes. She didn't believe her daughter's claim of innocence, but didn't have the detailed proof to issue the kind of warning that would make her confess. She only had Jayden's word. And though the boy was as honest as he was impressionable, Sawyer couldn't help but wonder when Jayden would catch on to the fact that if he kept blaming his sister, his punishment wouldn't be as severe.

Sighing, she turned her attention back to her son.

"Jay-Jay, you should know better than to stick your tongue on something iced over from the last time Sydney talked you into doing it. Don't you remember the last time, son? Don't you remember how long you were stuck to that light pole?"

"Unh-huh." He tried to nod, despite his mother's grip on his round cheeks. Even she wasn't sure how long he'd been out there until one of the employees had heard him blubbering and rescued him from yet another one of Sydney's pranks.

"Then why in the world did you let Sydney talk you into trying it again?" Sawyer's voice was weary with parental confusion.

"I don't know!" Jayden exclaimed, bringing to Sawyer's mind an old Bill Cosby comedy routine. Something about all kids having brain damage. Catching that boy in the act of nearly having his tongue frozen to the bumper at his sister's needling, Sawyer was inclined to believe that beloved old Jell-O pudding pitchman.

"Come here, you little snot blossom." Sawyer reached into her coat pocket and pulled out a package of tissues. She dabbed around Jayden's mouth and swabbed at his runny nose for good measure.

"Blow," she instructed.

Jayden snuffled, drawing more viscous fluid back into his nose than out.

"The other way," Sawyer clarified.

He took a deep breath, filling her tissue.

"That's a good boy. Again," she prompted.

"That's so nasty," Sydney proclaimed, scrunching up her face at the wet, honking sound.

"You're next," Sawyer promised, folding up the used tissue and pressing it into Jayden's mittened hand. "You keep that and use it when you need to instead of your coat sleeve."

She pulled out a fresh wad and held it up to her daughter's nose.

"I can do it myself, Mommy. I'm not a baby anymore," Sydney complained, leaning her head away.

"You're right. You are a big girl now. I keep forgetting." Sawyer sighed again, her shoulders drooping.

Seven years. Lordy, where had the time gone? Wasn't it just yesterday that she was roaring into what she disdainfully thought was a Podunk little town, smack dab in the middle of Nowheresville, Montana.

Tired, angry and pregnant—Sawyer's stop had been a necessity. The stop into White Wolf hadn't been planned…and neither had her pregnancy. She'd pulled off the road from her three-day flight from Birmingham to stash her motorcycle under the shelter of Marjean's Café to get out of a summer storm.

The twister that had torn the town apart was the perfect metaphor for what had been her life. Wild. Unpredictable. Hell-bent on destruction. Seven years ago, she'd had every intention of breezing through this stoplight, doing whatever damage she was bound to do, and heading out before the dust settled. That had been her MO for as long as she could remember. She was a free spirit, accountable to no one.

Back in the day, she had been Sawyer Garth. Romance writer. Trust-fund baby. Spoiled brat. If it hadn't been for another force of nature, equally as strong, but a force of irresistible calm, Sawyer wasn't sure where she'd be right now.

Probably dead, she thought with morbid certainty. She'd been on the brink of total self-destruction. If it weren't for the love of a praying family and the unfailing, unconditional support and acceptance of a good man…

Sawyer shuddered, turning her face away from the thought of how her life could have gone if it weren't for Holling.

"What's wrong, Mama?" Sydney's voice broke into her thoughts.

Sawyer blinked, not realizing that tears had welled up in her eyes and were creating a cool river down her cheek. "Nothing, Syd. Nothing's wrong," Sawyer tried to assure her daughter.

Sydney reached out and touched her mother's cheek with her mittens. "Then why are you crying? Are you sad? I'm sorry, Mama. I promise I won't make Jay-Jay lick the ice again."

"Sometimes, baby, people cry when they're happy. And I'm so very happy today!" She leaned forward and clasped her daughter to her.

Then, leaning back, she tried to make her face stern as she warned, "But not about you trying to trick your brother. You know that's wrong, don't you, Sydney?"

"Yes, ma'am," Sydney replied dutifully, hanging her head with the right amount of contrition to make anyone less savvy believe that she was sorry for what she'd done.

"She's happy because it's Christmas and Santa's coming!" Jayden offered. "Santa's coming! Santa's coming!" Jayden bounced up and down, his boundless energy barely containable.

"Um…something like that," Sawyer hedged.

She'd debated long and hard about whether or not to tell the twins about the existence of Santa. She'd wanted them to hang on to their innocence for as long as they would.

Her belief in the mythical character had been dashed much too soon. With her mother dying in childbirth and an absentee father, Sawyer had never known what others called a typical

Christmas. Her holiday gifts had always come through special delivery, FedEx or UPS, packed in mountains of Styrofoam peanuts or bubble wrap, and had never been wrapped with festive paper or bows. If her father had been feeling especially generous, the gifts would come with a brief note, usually signed by her father's administrative assistant.

If Sawyer had wanted to "see" evidence of Santa's visits, she usually had to go to the homes of one of her cousins— Shiri or Brenda, or their play cousin Essence. Their mothers, Pam and Doris, and even their mothers, Lela Johnson and Rosie Kincaid, had made sure that no child coming into their home would leave without a gift.

Sawyer had learned early that Santa Claus, and waking to find the magic of gifts appearing mysteriously under the tree, were dreams other children were allowed to have. Not Sawyer Garth. It hadn't been until she was older, and would sometimes accompany her cousins on their holiday shopping sprees, that she'd realized how much it hurt her not to wake up to tinsel and toys in her own home.

It hadn't been about the gifts, really. She'd known that, thanks to her mother's investments and sharp business sense, she was comfortably well-off. It was the sharing of joy that she'd missed. Even with all of the shopping, being dragged by her cousins from store to store to make sure that each and every family member would receive a small token of Johnson love, Sawyer had realized that the family had never failed to take the reason for the season to heart.

Still, Sawyer wouldn't take the wonder of Santa from her precious babies for anything in the world. She didn't want the reason for the season to get lost in her attempts to make each Christmas special for her own children. Which was one of the reasons why they were tramping around in the wooded acreage several miles from her house, having her husband search for the "perfect" tree.

Thoughts of her husband brought a warm flush to her cheeks and the kind of secret smile to her lips that made her want to turn her face away before her children could see her expression. The images running through her head at the thought of him weren't exactly of the G-rated variety. Forget any mischief that Sydney could stir up. The naughty-but-nice behavior that Sawyer and Holling conducted in behind closed bedroom doors would definitely give Santa good reason to consider bypassing her house.

Holling was the reason that she was still alive today. She was alive and well and living the life she'd never thought she deserved—right here in this same Podunk town. Raising her children. Loving her husband. Seven years later and still going strong.

"I'm cold, Mama," Sydney complained. "When are Daddy and Grandpa Nate gonna be done?"

She looked up on the hillside where Holling and his father Nate were applying a chain saw and tie line to the tree that the twins had picked out. In the spring, when the ground thawed, they would all return to this very spot, with a sapling to replant in its place.

The tree they'd selected, a blue spruce, was over fifteen feet tall and would look, Sawyer thought, absolutely heavenly decorated with holiday ribbons, twinkling lights and enough ornaments to weigh the spruce's branches down. She'd already picked out the perfect spot for it. She wanted it right in the middle of the foyer so that it was the first thing anyone would notice when they walked into the bed-and-breakfast inn that the Holling family owned and managed. If she could have found a bigger tree, she would have, until Holling had reminded her that anything bigger wouldn't fit through the door.

Most of their seasonal decorations were already in place. Mantels and staircases decked with greenery and ribbon. Lights strung. Wreathes hung. The only thing missing was the tree. The glorious tree for which Sawyer had designed a theme and concept for four weeks. The tree that they'd selected was so tall, Sawyer imagined that she would have to stand on the second-level balcony of the bed-and-breakfast to reach over and add the star to the top.

"Here it comes, darlin'!"

Sawyer plugged her ears as Holling revved up the chain saw. He adjusted the choke, throttling it back to be heard as he shouted down to Sawyer and his kids. She blew him a kiss as he waved away the plume of blueish-gray smoke coming from the exhaust of the chainsaw, readjusted his safety goggles, and swiped aside the accumulation of frost and sawdust.

"Better start the truck up, Sawyer, gal. We'll be hauling this tree off before you can say Jack Frost."

Holling's father, Nate, took another step back, tugging at the safety tie line. Sawyer saw the top of the tree dip and sway toward him.

"Be careful, Nate!" She cupped her hands to her lips and called out a warning. "You don't want to spend your Christmas picking pine needles out of your head."

"I've been felling trees since you were a twinkle in your daddy's eye, gal!" Nate yelled back. "Here we go! Almost got it. Whoa, Nelly!"

"You're supposed to say, 'Timber!', Grandpa Nate!" Sydney stood up in the bed of the truck and advised him.

Nate maneuvered himself behind two trees that had grown closely together. Their trunks jutted from the ground, forming a twenty-foot-tall V. As Holling cut through the trunk of the tree they'd selected, Nate tugged on the safety line, bending the tree so that it would fall and wedge between the two trees.

Sawyer watched as Holling shifted his stance, turned his back to them, bringing the whirring, grinding blade of the chainsaw through the blue spruce's trunk. Nate worked his arms back and forth, giving another tug and trying to force the spruce in the direction he wanted it to go.

It might have been her imagination, she couldn't be sure over the near-deafening racket of the chainsaw, but she thought she heard a whip crack as Nate tugged on the line, bending the blue spruce almost parallel to the ground.

"Timber!" Jayden and Sydney shouted in unison.

"Holling!" Nate shouted. But it wasn't a cry of triumph. It was a cry of warning. "Get out of the way!"

He'd tugged on the tie line as they'd planned to guide it toward them; but neither one of them had planned on the safety line snapping as the full weight of the tree bore down on it.

"Oh, my God!" Sawyer's hands flew to her mouth. "Holling!"

Scrambling to get out of the way, Holling backpedaled, slipping and stumbling on the frozen ground as the heavy trunk end of the tree skidded and rolled away from them. He grabbed his left knee, grimacing in pain as he yanked the goggles from his face. As the trunk of the tree took an unpredictable turn, he scuttled along the ground, trying to get out of the way.

"Move, son!" Nate shouted from behind the relative safety of the two trees.

Sawyer froze for what seemed like a lifetime for her. Too much to process at once. Her husband. Her children. Her tree! That gorgeous tree! It was sliding down the hill, barreling toward them.

"Mama!"

It was Jayden's voice, strident and full of terror, that snapped Sawyer out of her paralysis and set her priorities for her.

"Jayden, get in the truck!" she ordered, using the universal, I-mean-business tone that he would recognize and obey without question. Sawyer then scooped Sydney in her arms and shoved her into the crew cab seat next to her brother. She looked over her shoulder, gauging the speed and the distance of the runaway tree from the truck. In a matter of seconds, it would be down on them. She slid into the driver's seat, barely bothering to shut the door as she turned the key and yanked on the gearshift almost simultaneously. Sawyer cursed under her breath as she had to scrunch down in the seat in order to reach the pedals. The seat had been adjusted for Holling's height and comfort. At five foot eleven, her husband was a good seven inches taller than she was.

"Oooooo-whee!" Sydney whispered in awe, her face plastered to the rear side window.

"Timber!" Jayden shouted enthusiastically.

Sawyer glanced out the window. A few more feet and the tree would smash broadside into them. She stomped on the gas pedal, causing the huge diesel-engine truck to surge forward. A few feet. That was all she needed. Enough to get out of its path. She wasn't going to go far. She'd taken a solemn oath seven years ago that she would never leave Holling's side. Never. She wasn't leaving him now. She was only going far enough to get the kids out of harm's way.

Sawyer slammed on the brakes, skidding in the snow for a few more yards. Glancing in the rearview, she watched as the blue spruce needles plummeted down the hill. Rolling. Twisting. Sliding. Gaining speed as it drove up a cloud of powdery snow and needles in its wake. She watched it until it passed completely from sight. Only then, when she felt that it was safe to leave the kids, did she turn off the engine and shove the keys into her coat pocket.

"Jayden, Sydney, you two stay here. I mean it. Don't you leave this truck." There was no room for debate or questioning in her tone.

"Yes, ma'am." Their voices were small and earnest-sounding enough. She gave an extra warning glance to her daughter, pointing to her, as she climbed out of the truck.

Sawyer scrambled midway up the hill to where Nate was supporting Holling as he hobbled down to meet her.

"Holling?" Sawyer asked, moving to the other side of him, draping his arm around her shoulder to give him extra support. "Baby, are you all right?"

Tenderly, she swiped at his face to remove the mixture of frozen mud, snow and sawdust covering his bronze skin.

"Yeah, I'm all right, darlin'." His tone was strained, his jaws clamping down hard as he spoke as if he could clamp down on his pain. "It's not bad. I only strained my knee."

"Don't try to walk," Sawyer advised. "I'll go and get the truck."

"I can make it," Holling insisted, taking another step forward. He lifted his chin, assessing the damage to the tree by the score marks left in the ground. "I guess that tree is a total loss."

"Don't worry about that now, boy," Nate admonished. "We'd better get that knee looked at."

"I'm fine," he insisted, trying to take another step on his own. His ill-timed bravado caused him to double over in pain, biting his lip against the impulse to swear.

"How bad is it?" Nate asked.

"Oh, it's bad." Holling grimaced.

Nate and Sawyer exchanged concerned glances. Holling wasn't one to complain.

"I'm so sorry, Holling." Sawyer tried to soothe him. "This is all my fault. Wanting that stupid tree. I should have been like all of the other smart shoppers and picked a tree from a lot or a tree farm like everybody else in White Wolf."

"It's not stupid," Holling contradicted. "Not getting out of the way of a falling tree, now that was stupid."

"You got that right, boy," Nate admonished.

Sawyer's concern turned to anger at her father-in-law. "Don't call him *stupid*. You were the one holding the safety line, Nate. What went wrong? Didn't you check it?"

"Of course I checked it," Nate said indignantly. "I'm not an idiot, little missy."

Sawyer grimaced at the nickname. She hadn't liked it when he'd called her that the first time he'd met her, sitting on the edge of the hospital gurney, about to puke her guts out from morning sickness. Seven years later, she hadn't grown to like that nickname.

"Hey!" Holling called out sharply. "Do you think we can table this discussion? I really need to get off my feet now."

"I'll go get the truck," Sawyer offered, throwing an apologetic glance over her shoulder at her father-in-law. She loved Nate. He was closer to her than her own father had been. She didn't mean to jump down his throat. But, when Holling hurt, she hurt. It was as simple as that. They were tied together—mind, body and spirit. Anything that threatened that bond threatened her, too. And she wouldn't take that kind of threat lying down.

Chapter 3

"Here, baby. Let me get you another pillow."

Sawyer eased another support to prop up Holling's foot. Though she tried to be careful, she still managed to jostle his leg. His entire left leg, from ankle to midthigh, was covered in a thick plaster cast and would remain that way for the next eight weeks.

"Easy...easy there now..."

Holling groaned, bracing his back against the headboard and gouging his fingers into the blankets to keep from letting Sawyer know that the pain medication prescribed by the doctor had not yet kicked in. Instead of pills, the doctor had given him a prescription for a patch that was supposed to continuously release pain medication into his system. Holling had his doubts. For all the good that it was doing, he might as well have slapped a swatch of masking tape on his skin.

"Do you want me to massage your foot for you, Holling?" Sawyer asked solicitously.

When she reached for his exposed heel and toes, Holling flinched. The slightest touch sent pain shooting up and down his leg.

"No. Maybe later." He panted, beads of perspiration popping out on his forehead. The mixture of medications he'd taken was making his stomach turn the kind of flips that would even impress the Cirque du Soleil acrobats. He lay his head back, closing his eyes. The subtle swirl pattern in the muted cream wallpaper was making his head swim. Each time he opened his eyes, he couldn't help following the eggplant-and-gold-trimmed border paper around and around and around the room. Holling groaned, grabbing a pillow. He wanted to press it to his face. What he really wanted to do was ask Sawyer to press it to his face. Press hard enough to put him peacefully to sleep. On second thought, she probably wouldn't go for that. Holling retracted the thought. She'd probably think that he was suddenly into some kinky sex thing and would start to question why he suddenly wanted it that way.

He reached up to grab one of the metal bars of the headboard.

"Ouch! That hurts!" Holling exclaimed when he jabbed his palm with one of the pointed ends of the fleur-de-lis accents running through the frame of their bed. He was frustrated. Sawyer had insisted on changing out his old oak furniture for this feminine contraption of "distressed" metal, delicately carved iron, and purple silk bed skirts with matching draperies and frilly, flouncy table covers. No, not purple, she had to repeatedly remind him. Eggplant. He didn't see what was the matter with his old bed. His old quilts. Now that he was going to have to stay in this bed, he was even less inclined to be comfortable here.

"How about some hot cocoa? I bought the little colored marshmallows. And picked out all of the green ones for you.

Your favorite kind." She sat down on the bed, causing Holling's leg to slide off the pillow and onto the bed with the tiniest of bounces. For the ripples of pain that shot up his leg and back, she might as well have been using the bed as a trampoline.

"No…I don't want any cocoa!" Holling said sharply, reaching for the plaster-covered knee and massaging the area. It didn't help. He couldn't feel his hand through the plaster.

"Are you hungry? Chale made a huge pot of turkey chili especially for you. Extra spicy."

The thought of food made Holling want to retch. "Maybe later."

"Or I could—"

"Sawyer! Please…I know you want to help, baby. I just want to rest. Okay?"

Holling was completely exhausted. He didn't remember having to work so hard simply to relax. It had been a journey, getting from the truck, into the wheelchair, up the access ramp and into his bedroom. The trek had been made all the more difficult by Jayden and Sydney scampering all around him, shouting at the top of their lungs, with Sawyer's smothering care, and his father Nate's constant chatter. By the time he'd made it to his bedroom, he'd been wishing that he had stayed another couple of days in the hospital. His reconstructive knee surgery had gone better than expected. The doctor had assured him that with plenty of rest and scheduled physical therapy, he would be back to work in no time. Couldn't be soon enough. This was not the time of year to be flat on his backside, relying heavily on hired help and family to do what he'd expected to have done himself.

He was more than angry with himself. Holling was furious. Furious at his own carelessness. Though, he had to count his blessings that his injury wasn't worse than it was. He'd been lucky. That tree could have come down on his head...or worse. Completely gotten away from him and come crashing down on Sawyer and the kids. As painful as it had been when he'd felt his knee give out from under him, nothing could have hurt him more than knowing that his family was in harm's way.

Frustration also made him grind his teeth together. He was frustrated at his helplessness. Granted, everyone needed help sometimes. But he, Jon-Tyler Holling, was usually the helper. Not the helpee. He hated being so dependent, so useless. He could feel his frustration growing like a cancer in his stomach. It was eating him up, from the inside out, to have to sit there and let others do for him.

"Okay, Holling," Sawyer said, trying to sound cheerful for his benefit. She wasn't cut out to play nursemaid. She'd told him that a long time ago. She'd already shooed the kids out of the room and had sent Nate on an errand to keep him out of the way.

"You try to rest. I've got some things to take care of this afternoon."

"What kind of things?"

"Well, I still haven't finished wrapping the individual gifts for the employees." Sawyer counted off on one finger. "I promised Chale I would help with some of the holiday baking." She held up another finger. "Sydney needs her hair washed and braided. And Nate said something about me going with him over to Sam and Felicity's place to help them sort and box up donations for the women's shelter. After I finish all of that, I want to freshen up that room before Aidan gets here."

"Aidan? Who said she could come home?"

"Holling, we talked about this." Sawyer's reminder was more chastising than she intended. "She's been calling almost every day for the past two weeks hinting that she wants to come home."

"She'll keep on hinting until someone offers to pay for the plane ticket," Holling said ungraciously.

"I'm going online and making a reservation now before all of the flights are booked and it costs a small fortune for her to fly in. You know, if you'd just told her back in October that you wanted her home, we could have made the reservation and saved a lot of money."

"She wasn't hinting then that she wanted to come back home."

"Well, now she has," Sawyer said with finality. "Whether you like it or not, your sister's spending time with us for the holidays."

"It's not like I've got a choice. You and Pops have already made up your minds that you want her here."

"There's no reason why she shouldn't be, Holling."

"You mean other than the fact that she hasn't had anything to do with this family for ten years?"

"That's exactly the reason why we need to make every effort to make sure she feels welcome, baby. Don't you see? People look to the holidays to give them reasons to reach out, to repair what was broken in their lives. Aidan's reaching."

"Into our pockets," he complained.

"Your pockets are deep enough," Sawyer retorted. "And if I go reaching in there and you hand me nothing but lint, then I'll reach into mine. One way or another, we're getting her here. Until then, I've got more than enough to do than sit here and coddle you, Jon-Tyler Holling. So, I'll let you get some rest. If you need me, all you have to do is sing out."

"Thanks, darlin'. And…uh…I didn't mean to bark at you…okay? It's just…"

"I know." Her smile was less forced now. Tenderly, she

smoothed her hand over his forehead, wiping away the furrow lines and the thin bead of perspiration. She sat beside him for several moments. Not speaking. Barely moving. The only motion was the caress of her hand across his forehead.

When Holling's breathing deepened, and his eyelids fluttered closed, she carefully eased off the bed and backed away.

Before she'd taken three steps back, Holling's eyes popped open, his expression anxious and confused. "Sawyer?!"

"I'm here, Holling," Sawyer called out to him soothingly. "I'm not going anywhere."

"Sorry…sorry…I must have dozed off. I was having this crazy dream."

"About what?"

He gave her a half-crooked smile. "You remember that night we explored Weeko Canyon?"

"That's not all we explored that night, Jon-Tyler Holling," Sawyer reminded him. How could she forget? One of her children had been conceived that night.

Holling chuckled. "I was dreaming that we were being chased. Only, it wasn't that hellhound after us…"

"What was it, then?"

Holling gave a pained expression as if he didn't want to own up to the thoughts running around in his head.

"Holling?" Sawyer prompted him.

"Trees," he finally confessed. "We were being chased out of the canyon by giant trees with glowing red eyes and long, sharp, green fangs."

Sawyer bit the inside of her cheek to keep from laughing out loud. *Trees?*

"I knew you'd laugh at me," he accused her.

"I'm not laughing," Sawyer immediately denied, shaking her head back and forth. "Really I'm not. Trees chasing you...well, that sounds like something right out of one of those fantasy *Lord of the Rings* movies."

"It's my knee cracked up, not my head," Holling grumbled.

"I know, Holling. I expect it's that medicine making you dream those crazy things," she soothed.

Holling sighed. "I wasn't afraid for myself, Sawyer. It was for you and the kids."

"We were fine, baby," Sawyer soothed him. "We weren't in danger. Not really."

"Thanks to you and your quick thinking, getting out of the way."

"Call it a mother's instinct for self-preservation and more than our share of divine intervention."

"A mother's love and divine intervention," Holling echoed. He took Sawyer's hand and squeezed it, then raised it to his lips.

"It's true," she insisted. "We've been very blessed over the years, Holling, with nothing more serious than a scrape or a bruise on those two. And heaven knows that Sydney and Jayden certainly have tested all the grace we've been granted."

Holling laughed. "If grace were a fast-food restaurant's side dish, we're the type of family that always has to super-size! As much trouble as those two have gotten into, I know somebody up there has to be keeping watch out for those bad-assed kids of ours."

"You know what it is, don't you?" Sawyer offered an explanation.

"What?"

"Don't you remember your folks ever putting that old curse on you? Wishing you had kids just like you were when you were one?"

Holling groaned. "Oh, Lordy. And this is only the beginning. Makes me wish that old Luce was still around. We could use her special knack for getting you and me out of trouble with our kids."

"They might even be too much for her," Sawyer offered. "Maybe that's why she doesn't come around anymore."

Seven years had passed since that old woman had come into their lives. For a time, it had seemed as though she was always around. And then, just like that, nothing. No goodbyes. No good-lucks. No see-you-laters. No phone calls. No letters. No casual stop bys. Simply gone.

As much as she missed her, there were times when Sawyer fully expected to turn a corner and find that old woman, with the iron-gray hair and the mushroom-colored leisure suit, standing there. Especially when she and Holling had been going through a difficult time, as all married couples sometimes did. She could have used Luce's steadfast assurances that everything was going to work out.

When she was at her angriest with Holling, when the same qualities that attracted her threatened to drive her crazy, Sawyer often wished for Luce. Yet, she never came. And as the years passed and the warmth of her friendship started to fade, Sawyer started to wonder if there ever had been a Luce in her life. Maybe she was a figment of her overstressed imagination. Maybe she'd dreamed her up to compensate for not having a mother to confide in and to guide her. As soon as Sawyer convinced herself that Luce was only a crutch she used to escape the pain and difficulties of her life, Holling would dredge up a memory of how Luce had touched them.

Remember that time Luce helped you find me when that tornado struck White Wolf?

Or, *remember that time Luce stopped those looters from tracking us down with that attack dog?*

Do you remember that time Luce kept you from miscarrying the twins?

How about that time Luce stopped me from being a damned fool and convinced me to ask you to marry me?

Despite the woman not being around in body, she was certainly there in spirit. The fact that Sawyer and Holling were together, still desperately in love, still committed to one another despite the statistics that bode ill for short-courtship relationships, was a testimony to Luce's existence. In all fairness, she and Holling shouldn't be together. Not with the way their relationship had started. Rocky. Filled with stress, chaos and haters who hadn't believed a self-proclaimed lifelong bachelor and a knocked up biker chick on the run could make it work.

"You go on back to sleep, baby," Sawyer said tenderly. "I'll check in on you in a while."

He took a deep breath, settling himself. "Who can go to sleep after a dream like that?"

"I know it's hard, but try. You need to rest."

"I've got plenty of time to lie back here in this bed. I'm starting to go stir-crazy. Is Darry still downstairs?"

Sawyer blew out a huffy, impatient breath. "Now, what do you want with him?"

She'd admonished her husband not to think about ranch business. He should trust her or Nate to handle anything to come up while he was recuperating. But as soon as they'd made it home from the hospital, he'd insisted on calling Darion Haddock, Holling's right-hand man, up to the house.

Darion had shown up six months ago, with nothing more than a battered olive-green army surplus duffel bag, and a map and note scrawled in Marjean's handwriting.

The fact that a drifter had shown up on the property wasn't a surprise to Sawyer. The Holling ranch was a magnet for drifters, transients and day laborers—people looking to pick up some cash before moving on to their next stop. The Holling name was well-known in the area for providing a fair day's wages for a fair day's work.

What did interest Sawyer was how easily the man was able to gain the confidence and trust of her husband. Within a month, Darion had gone from doing odd jobs around the place to Holling's most indispensable employee—right up there alongside Chale, their family cook for twenty years, and Red Bone, the ranch foreman.

Holling wasn't an easy man to impress. Yet, somehow, Darion had done it. And now, you could hardly find one without the other. Sawyer had once joked that if she weren't careful, she'd wake up to find Darion Haddock had taken up residence in their bedroom. To which Holling had promptly quipped that she should keep those sexual fantasies confined to the pages of her next romance novel.

"I think he's still down there. Why do you want him?"

"Would you get him up here? I need to have a word with him…to go over some things before this pain medication really knocks me off my feet."

"Are you sure, Holling? If you're too tired, why don't I tell him to come back later? Whatever it is, it'll keep, won't it? Until you're feeling better?"

"No. I'm all right, darlin'. Send him on up."

"Holling," Sawyer said, her tone scolding, "you need to rest. Anything Darion has to tell you can wait."

"All I need is a few minutes with him, Sawyer. Darion's gonna have to be my eyes and ears…especially since I'm stuck here in this bed."

Sawyer waggled her eyebrows at him. "Maybe being stuck here won't be such a bad thing."

"I don't see how you figure that," Holling grumbled, reaching for his knee again.

She gave him a long, slow smile before responding. "The doctor told me that I have to give you a sponge bath. At least once a day. Does that make your time confined to bed any less torturous?"

Holling's lopsided grin eased the tension in his face. "I'll make sure to think extra dirty thoughts until you get back."

Laughing and blowing him a kiss, Sawyer stepped out of the room, closing the door behind her. She left the family quarters, containing several bedrooms with private bathroom suites, a secondary kitchen and common room, and passed through a set a double oak doors leading to the grand entrance of the bed-and-breakfast. Off to the left was the main sitting room.

She peeked in on Darion, debating whether or not to overrule Holling's request to see him. If she waited long enough, the medication would work its magic. Holling would fall asleep. By the time he woke up, she or Nate or even Darion himself would have handled any pressing issues that concerned him.

She bit her lip in indecision. Then again, maybe she should go ahead and let the young man in. Holling was irritable enough as it was. She didn't want that irritation to turn into open anger. Nobody wanted to be around Holling when he was angry. Including her. Besides, Darion had been waiting to speak with his boss for an hour. When she saw him sitting in the common room, she made up her mind.

Sitting was such a loose term when it came to Darion Haddock. That man was a ball of nervous energy. She wondered if he even realized that his right knee was continuously bouncing up and down so dramatically that it made the antique hurricane lamp sitting on the end table beside him precariously rattle. The fingers of his right hand drummed along the ornately carved wooden arm of the couch, tapping out an unrecognizable tune. His left leg was stretched out in front of him, exposing the worn-down boot heels and the frayed hem of Wrangler jeans that had seen, Sawyer was certain, better days. She clucked her tongue in mild irritation as clumps of dried ice and mud flaked onto the area rug that she'd had steam cleaned last week for the holidays.

"I'm so sorry to keep you waiting, Darion," Sawyer apologized, turning on her sweet Southern charm as she entered the room.

"Ms. Holling." Darion shot to his feet. The faded blue baseball cap that he'd rested on the couch beside him fell to the floor, causing him to bend his long, lean frame to scoop it up.

"How's the big boss man doing?" he asked, twirling, shaping and remolding the cap in his hands as he faced Sawyer.

"Very cranky," Sawyer admitted. "You know Holling. The idea of not being able to move around is driving him absolutely bananas."

"You know, you might have to strap him down for his own good, Ms. Holling." Darion flashed her one of his rare smiles.

In the six months that he'd worked for them, Sawyer was certain that she'd only seen Darion smile a handful of times. Not that he wasn't a pleasant man. He was always polite and respectful toward her.

Yet, it seemed to her that Darion was especially reserved. For someone who was around most of the time, Sawyer knew so little about him. Where was he from? she wondered. Did he have any family? Was he married? What was he doing with his money? Was he sending it home? He obviously didn't spend it on himself. From what she saw, his wardrobe con-

sisted of three pairs of jeans and a handful of plain T-shirts—
black, white and gray.

As near as she could tell, Darion didn't own a car. Or a
truck. Or a bicycle, for that matter. He either walked most
places he wanted to go or caught rides from some of the
other hands. Lately, Holling had been letting him use the
ranch truck for getting around. Even though he sometimes
let him keep the truck through the weekend, Darion was
careful to use it only on ranch business. If anyone needed
him to make pickups or deliveries or to get the vehicle
serviced, he was the first one into the driver seat. Let anyone
suggest that he use the truck to do something other than
work—like go out on a date—you'd think from his reaction
that they'd asked him to use the vehicle to commit a felony
crime. Sawyer found that behavior odd. What red-blooded
male, in his prime, with a pocketful of cash and free use of
a vehicle didn't want to blow it all on an equally hot-
blooded female? Especially if what she was offering him
came free and easy?

Holling had even let him use the business credit card. If
anything said how much Holling trusted him to Sawyer, that
did. So far, Darion had not done anything to make them
believe that trust was misplaced. Each time he used the credit
card, he brought back the receipt. And, if any of the purchases on the card were not company business, but were
personal, Darion always brought the cash to cover the
purchase as soon as he could. Every purchase every
time…even for items as small as a pack of gum.

He was no slouch; yet, she'd never seen Darion spruce up.
Not even for church. As always, he wore jeans and a T-shirt.
He took the trouble to clean and press his clothes. That was
the limit. She'd never seen him go out with some of the other

hands. No clubbing. No drinking. No women. Though, on days that he was scheduled off, he was usually nowhere to be seen around the place. So, where did he go?

Darion never volunteered any details about himself. If asked openly, he always courteously, but insistently, turned any inquiries into his life aside. He'd made it clear from day one that he wasn't there to win any popularity contests. He didn't chat or socialize with the other hands. He came to work. And work hard he did. Sometimes, long after others had quit for the evening. Probably one of the reasons why Holling had quickly elevated him to favored-worker status. Darion's stamina and work ethic were matched only by Holling's.

Wanting his privacy was Darion's only fault that Holling could see. So, he'd encouraged Sawyer to let the matter drop. After all, hadn't she, when she'd first come to White Wolf, put up her barriers, not even wanting to tell him her true name?

Still, she had to wonder about the hardworking, quick-witted and—she had to admit—good-looking man who spent all of his time in his own company, shunning even the most enticing offers. Sawyer had once seen him nearly break his neck trying to get away from one of the guests who'd cornered him in the stables under the pretext of wanting riding lessons.

There was something compelling about Darion Haddock. He presented a challenge that any female with eyes could see. What woman wouldn't be attracted to a man like Darion? She was happily married, but that didn't stop her from sneaking a peak at him every now and then. He had the kind of face she would love to describe in one of her novels—if she weren't concerned that Holling would get the wrong idea.

From the moment she'd met Darion, she'd been instantly

intrigued by him. Not attracted. She had to immediately draw the distinction in her mind. There was no one for her but Holling. But even she had to recognize the appeal Darion had. Who wouldn't be drawn to the strong lines of his face, his high cheekbones? Hooded, dark eyes…so dark, she wasn't sure where the irises ended and the pupils began. Those ebony eyes were framed by well-shaped eyebrows and his closely trimmed shadow of a beard. He wore his hair in cornrows or in an unevenly trimmed natural cut, thick enough for any woman to want to get her fingers in. He had that bohemian quality working for him. Raw, sensual, in a Lenny Kravitz kind of way—complete with tattoos up and down his sculpted arms. If he knew the effect that he had on the women, he didn't acknowledge it…let alone try to act on it.

"Is it true that a twenty-foot tree fell on him, Ms. Holling?" Darion asked, his deep voice rumbling above her head.

"You've been listening to Nate," Sawyer accused, staring up at him. "Every time he tells that story, the tree gets bigger and the damage to Holling gets more severe. No, the tree didn't fall on him. And it wasn't twenty feet tall."

Darion's tone was wry. "I guess that means that it didn't smash off his leg, from the hip down, either."

"That would be a safe bet," Sawyer said, making a "follow me" gesture.

"Grizzly bear?"

"Never happened."

"And the avalanche?"

"A figment of Nate's imagination."

"Too bad. All of that made for a helluva story…pardon my French, ma'am."

"Forgiven," Sawyer replied, knowing full well that Darion had heard her use stronger language than that when she was upset. Really upset. A private joke between her and Holling was that one day he would buy a case of soap-on-a-rope to wear around her neck for those moments when the epithets flew as fast as her temper flared.

Sawyer had to congratulate herself. Her language had gotten better, cleaner, since becoming a mother. Still, when the twins pushed her to the limit, there was more than a time or two when she'd had to excuse herself to her room or her office, push her face into a pillow and vent her feelings until the moment had passed.

She pushed open the door. "Holling? Are you awake?"

Holling had leaned his head back against the oak headboard, his eyes closed.

"I should come back later," Darion suggested.

"No," Holling said, lowering his chin and wiping his hands over his eyes to clear them. The painkillers had finally started to do their job. "Come on in, Darry."

"How are you feeling, boss?" Darion asked.

"Like a tree fell on me," Holling said with a grunt.

Sawyer then stepped back, allowing the tall man to enter. "Don't keep him up too long, Darion. He needs his rest."

"No, ma'am. I won't," Darion promised.

"Can I get you anything before I go, Holling?" Sawyer offered.

"No, darlin'. I'm all right. You go on and do what you gotta do."

"Darion?"

"No, ma'am. I'm just fine."

Sawyer pulled the door closed behind her. But not before she saw Darion's jeans mold to his rear as he turned the straight-back chair around and straddled it.

Just fine.

An understatement. Sawyer sucked in an impressed breath.
The man wasn't lying. It ought to be illegal for a man to look
so *just fine* in a pair of thrift-store jeans.

Chapter 4

Darion scooted his chair closer to the bed, folded his arms and rested them on the back of the chair. He looked Holling up and down, giving a low whistle of commiseration.

"Yeah," Holling said in agreement. "I jacked myself up really bad this time."

Darion reached over and picked up several bottles of medication from the nightstand. Painkillers. Anti-inflammatories. Antibiotics. He shook one of the bottles, making the large pills inside rattle around.

"Are you thinking about opening your own pharmacy?" he asked, raising his eyebrows. "You know, boss man, if you wanted to take a break, all you had to do was say so. You didn't have to get yourself all busted up."

"Not the best timing to be laid up in bed."

"Never is," Darion agreed.

Holling cursed in frustration, staring at the ceiling. "I can't be sitting up here on my backside like this. I've got too much to do." He shifted, tried to sit up as if he could will his leg to work for him.

When he grimaced in pain, breathing harshly, Darion held out his hand, laid it gently but insistently on his shoulder and held Holling down.

"Easy, now, boss man. Whatever it is you're trying to haul yourself out of bed to do, it can wait. Unless, of course, it's another kind of business you're trying to take care of."

He looked over, indicating the open door to the bathroom.

Holling snorted in derision and pointed to the plastic, handheld urinal sitting within easy reach on the opposite nightstand. "The doctor says that I shouldn't even be moving around to do that. Not yet."

"If you don't mind me asking, how did it happen?"

Holling shook his head. "An accident. A stupid accident. That's all I can say for sure. One minute I was laying in the cuts to take down that blue spruce that Sawyer wanted for the guest parlor. The next thing I know, I'm scrambling, trying to get out of the way of a runaway tree. I'm glad that I had Sawyer and the kids waiting by the truck instead of by me like I wanted… If I'd taken them up there with me to stay by that tree, there's no telling what would have happened." Holling put his hand over his eyes, massaging his eyelids, rubbing out the image of his worst nightmare—the loss of his family.

"Don't get yourself worked up, boss man. No sense in thinking about what might have been. Just be grateful. Your family's okay."

"Thank God for that," Holling murmured.

"And your good sense."

"I don't know how good it is. I got myself run down by a damned tree, didn't I?"

Darion stood up, moved to the center of the room. "Don't you worry about it, boss. I came to tell you that me and the boys have got your back. When we heard what happened, we went out and found the tree, hauled it back here, and stripped it down."

He pantomimed with his hands, demonstrated the tug on the chains when they wrapped them around the tree.

"Chale, Mrs. Holling, and some of the other volunteers at the homeless shelter took the loose branches and made them into holiday wreathes. I think they're going to sell them and donate the money back to the shelter. Yesterday, they had us delivering the ones on order. Anything that wasn't made into a wreath was chopped and is now sitting in the wood bin, just waiting for the opportunity to be tossed into a Holling fireplace. We're saving the best piece for you...the part of the trunk that you took the chain saw to."

Holling threw back his head and laughed. "Well, the next time I'm attacked by a forest full of trees, I'll know who to come to." He paused and said, "On the for real, Darion...since I'm laid up like this, I'm gonna have to rely on you to handle things until I'm back on my feet."

"You don't even have to ask, boss man."

"I know that I don't. But I didn't want to make any assumptions. It's the holiday season. In a few days, this place is going to clear out. Everyone who put in for vacation time to be with their families is going to be itching to leave. I'm not going to ask them to postpone their trips because I was too clumsy to get out of the way of a damned tree."

"I wasn't planning on leaving," Darion reminded him.

"I thought maybe you would have changed your mind."

Darion shook his head. "No, sir. I haven't. You tell me what you need done and I'll take care of it."

"For starters, Jillian Malveaux has an Appaloosa mare that

she had put up for sale. Said that she was going to give me first look at her before she put in the announcement in the trades or showed her off at the auction. Now, I've already seen pictures of it. But pictures don't always do justice to the animal. I want you to go out there with Pops and Red Bone and let me know if she's worth the price Jillian's asking."

"Got it," Darion said. "Anything else, boss?"

Holling paused for a moment, regarding the younger man. "There is something…."

"Name it."

"Sawyer hasn't finished the last of her shopping. And I know she's still delivering items to those charities where she volunteers. I heard on the news that there have been a couple of carjackings around the mall. Folks bold enough, in broad daylight, snatching purses, breaking into vehicles."

"'Tis the season to be greedy and trifling."

"I don't want Sawyer out there by herself," Holling said, his voice strained. "I know her. I know that she'll be so focused on doing for others that she won't be thinking about herself."

"I'll watch out for her, sir."

"You do and I'll make sure there's a little something extra in your paycheck envelope."

Darion shook his head. "You don't have to do that, Mr. Holling. All I want is for you to pay me what I'm due. That's all I'm asking."

Holling turned his head, looking at Darion out of the corner of narrowed eyes. "Sometimes, Darion, I don't get you."

"What's there to get?"

"You came up in here, not a penny to your name, just the clothes on your back. You work hard enough for three men, but when someone tries to reward you for it, you turn it down. You bucking for sainthood or something?"

"I'm nobody's saint, Mr. Holling. I've done some things—"

"As have we all," Holling abruptly interjected.

He'd never asked Darion about his past. Of course, he'd checked his references when he'd walked onto the ranch. But he hadn't dug any deeper than he had for any of the others seeking employment. It was no secret that Holling's Way ranch was a haven for those running away from personal demons. If they worked hard, didn't cause trouble, they were welcome to stay as long as they wanted. Some stayed days. Some for years. Holling had become at expert at judging which category his employees would fall into.

From the very beginning, he'd known that Darion was a stayer—despite his deceptive appearances. His lack of attachment to any of the other employees, his lack of personal possessions, his habit of disappearing on weekends, pushing the curfew to the limit before showing back up at his bunk—all of it said runner. Yet, Holling looked past all of it and took an extra-special interest in the younger man. Training him. Guiding him. Trusting him.

There were only a few times in his life when he'd had such an immediate affinity for an individual. The last time he'd trusted so easily, so completely, he'd wound up marrying that individual. Since he was already happily committed, Holling didn't think that he was subconsciously grooming Darion for himself.

Chapter 5

It had been a while since Aidan Holling had had to put on thermal underwear along with her jeans. A very long time. In fact, she couldn't even buy thermal underwear in Fort Lauderdale, Florida, where she'd been living. Instead, she'd used the layover at Denver International Airport to rush out and buy a pair after she'd seen the forecast on one of the overhead monitors in the airport waiting area. She'd bought two pairs of thermals, an extra pair of socks and several sticks of moisturizing lip balm.

Tonight, the temperature in White Wolf threatened to dip into the teens. Well below freezing. As much as she trusted and looked forward to riding back home in the comfort of her brother's new truck, mentally, she would feel better with an extra layer of insulation between her and the weather.

She knelt in one of the stalls in the airport bathroom, digging through her carry-on bag, trying to find an extra sweater to toss on before going outside to the pickup lane where her father, Nate, would be waiting to take her home.

"You come on home, Aida Beth," Nate had insisted when she'd called him a few weeks ago and told him that she was only *considering* coming back to White Wolf for the holidays. *Considering.* That had been her secret code word meaning she could be swayed if he offered to purchase her ticket home.

Home.

Funny that she was still calling it that, even though she hadn't lived there in ten years. Five and a half of those years had been spent at a traditional four-year college while she'd remained consistently undecided about settling on a major. Taking her time, trying different curricula, picking and choosing her classes with all of the precision of someone who had absolutely no idea what they were doing or what they wanted. Another three years had slipped by her in a blur while she'd attended graduate school and thought about earning a master's degree. Another two years of trying to find the right profession that would allow her to use her amalgam education. Somehow, she didn't think her present job, seasonal help working the cosmetics counter at a department store, did all of that education justice.

Not that she minded working in the department store. The sales-associate discount she received as a job perk almost made it worth dealing with the pushy, impatient, demanding or—even worse—indecisive customers who came to her counter, looking for that miracle cosmetic that would take the years off their appearance, or make them look like some supermodel or television star. She'd gotten pretty good at sales. The floor manager often incorporated her ideas for spicing up the display cases.

Yet, cosmetic sales weren't what she wanted for her career.

She couldn't imagine herself pushing polishes, spritzing fragrances or matching foundations for the next ten years. She hadn't quite figured out what she wanted out of her life yet. She knew that this wasn't it. So, after only three weeks, barely out of trainee status, Aidan had turned in her name badge, collected her first and last paycheck, and had hopped on the plane with the e-ticket stub that her big brother Holling had purchased for her.

Aidan suspected that her homecoming had more to do with her sister-in-law's influence than Holling's generous nature. Holling was well-known to pinch a penny or two.

Face it, Aidan thought. The man was downright stingy. His pint-size bride, Sawyer, used all of her persuasive skills to get the money from him. And, from what Nate had told her of Sawyer's own healthy financial balance sheet with her access to a trust fund, even if Holling had refused to pay for the ticket, Sawyer would have seen to it that Aidan made it home.

Sawyer had always been kind to her, Aidan reflected, with a twinge of guilt. She was always warm and welcoming whenever she called. Aidan could always count on Sawyer to fill her in on all of the family gossip when Holling was too tight-lipped or busy running the business to talk to her.

Every now and then, Sawyer let it slip that everyone in the family was concerned about Aidan's lack of direction in her life. She didn't think the accidental slips of the lip were as accidental as Sawyer wanted her to believe. She was only being diplomatic. In her own well-meaning way, she wanted Aidan to know that everyone was curious to know when Aidan would settle down. That didn't necessarily mean get married and have babies. It meant settling on something—anything—rather than the aimless drifting through life she'd adopted. Get herself a man. Get herself a career. Get herself a focus. A direction. Do one. Do all. But do something!

The pressure to be "something" was one of the reasons she'd stayed away for so long. Her strained relationship with Holling was another reason for her long absence. She had a better relationship being several states away than she did being close to him. That didn't stop Aidan, however, from wanting to know what was going on in the lives of her well-meaning but manipulative family. It was why she called so often, even at the risk of Sawyer's hints dropped as gracefully as bowling balls.

"If you want to know what's going on here, why don't you come back and find out for yourself," Holling had admonished her on more than one occasion. "And stop calling collect!"

"I'll come back," Aidan had always promised. But she seldom had, not even for her own brother's wedding. Which was, Aidan suspected, one of the reasons why her brother was sometimes insensitive toward her. She knew that he'd never understand that as pleased as she was that he'd found happiness, she didn't want to be around all of those people who would wonder and whisper about her.

As beautiful as she knew the ceremony would be, she hadn't wanted to sit there, in God's house, pretending that she was happy and content when she really wasn't. She didn't want to sit at a table of near strangers at the reception, smiling so that her face hurt, and wondering what was wrong with her that she couldn't find the kind of peace that Holling seemed to have found in Sawyer.

She loved her brother dearly, and supported his decision to settle down with a good woman. But Holling had always known the kind of woman he wanted. It was only a matter of finding her. She had no such inkling about what she wanted or needed in a life partner. She was just starting to figure out what to expect from herself.

Aidan had faith that once she found peace with herself, then she would be willing to share part of herself with someone else. Until that time, she didn't want to be reminded how far she had to go. She didn't want to be reminded by all of the blessings brought into Holling's life, the blessings she didn't have…or might not ever be meant to have, for that matter. That didn't mean she couldn't rejoice in his happiness. It meant, for her own sanity, she had to do it from afar.

The support of family was always such a big deal for Holling. He never could understand that support didn't mean you had to be there, under foot, every blessed day. To make matters worse, he'd married a woman who was equally as tied to her family. From what Sawyer told her about that Johnson clan, they were always in each other's business.

Aidan was convinced that you could support your family in other ways. Didn't she show how pleased and proud she was when Holling had told her that Sawyer had given birth to twins, a boy and a girl, when she'd sent that lovely fruit basket and bouquet of balloons? If that didn't show emotional support, she didn't know what did. She'd even paid for it herself. Hadn't asked her family for a single dime to have the gifts delivered to the hospital.

And now, here she was back home. No more certain of her future than she had been ten years ago when she'd left.

"It's now or never, Aida Beth." She addressed herself with the family nickname given to her by her father, Nate. She may not know what her future held, but through those doors was her past. A past she'd run from for too long. Time to stop running. Time to come home for a much needed rest.

Aidan slipped her arms into her black leather jacket, pulled her woolen cap over her ears and picked up the handles of her bags. Lifting her chin and holding up her head with renewed determination, she pushed on the ladies' room door and headed straight for the moving walkway that would take her past the airport terminals to the baggage-claim area.

Even though the drive from the ranch to the airport would take him nearly two hours, she figured Nate should be outside by now. When she'd called from the pay phone to say that her plane had touched down, Sawyer had informed her that Nate had already gone. If he was not already at the airport, he would be there soon. Her flight's descent had been delayed a half hour due to the accumulation of ice and snow on the ground. From outside her window seat on the plane, Aidan could see the swirl of storm clouds and snow flurries. For a moment, she'd had doubts about whether or not the plane would be allowed to land.

"This is not an omen," Aidan had tried to convince herself. This was not a message from above telling her that she should have stayed away. She was *supposed* to be home now. She'd been out on her own long enough and needed the comfort and familiarity of the people and places she'd always known to help her get her life's bearings.

Weaving her way in and out of a steady stream of travelers, Aidan followed the overhead signs, past the airport restaurants, the newspaper kiosks and the banks of airport monitors flashing like Christmas-tree lights as flight after flight was either canceled or delayed. Shaking her head, she heaved a sigh of relief.

Thank God! She'd barely made it. In another half hour or so, this place would become a hotbed of controversy, despite the freezing temperatures outside.

As realization swept through the airport, passengers would soon begin the desperate, chaotic song and dance of the stranded. The search for remaining flights out on alternate airlines, jockeying for position on padded waiting-area seats or the floor in preparation of a camp out, or calls to nearby hotels to reserve rooms. The fact that she was on the ground, and would soon be on her way home was offered as proof that her timing was right. She was meant to be home.

As she approached them, the automatic exit doors slid open, causing a gust of wind to blow through the baggage-claim area. Tucking her head down close to her chin, Aidan braced herself then stepped out onto the pavement. To her left, airport attendants were waving the next cabbies in the queue to the pickup point. To her right, private cars were carefully navigating the drive. Like watching a choreographed performance, Aidan noted trunks popping open. Bags tossed in. Brief hugs of greeting. Bodies hurriedly filling vehicles before the cold and the wind sucked away their warmth. Turn signals indicated the merge into oncoming traffic. A puff of exhaust, a flash of brake lights, and vehicles disappeared, heading to points unknown. More travelers filed out and the odd performance began again.

Aidan looked up and down the drive, fully expecting at any moment for Nate to pull up soon…to allow her a chance to participate in the departure ritual. Five minutes. Ten minutes. She shivered and stomped her booted feet. They were starting to go numb. She ducked back inside for five minutes, but stayed close to the door to keep an eye out for him. Being inside didn't help much. Each time another passenger left the baggage-claim area, Aidan felt the sting of the weather, even through her extra layers of clothing.

Twenty minutes. Half an hour. Even with the worsening weather, her father should have been there by now. She stepped outside for another ten minutes, blinking rapidly as the wind caused her eyes to tear up. She told herself that the tears were caused by the wind, and not by fatigue and frustration. She was so ready to be home now. She hadn't realized how homesick she really was until she got this close and was still not allowed to enjoy it.

Back inside for another ten minutes. Enough time to watch most of the passengers who'd gotten off the plane with her collect their bags and meet up with their parties.

"Lovely," Aidan muttered. Some homecoming. She hadn't been home in ten years and this was how they showed their support? She dug into her pocket for some change and found a nearby pay phone. It was almost ten o'clock. She'd been waiting for nearly an hour. She dialed the number to the family quarters.

"Hello?" a young voice answered after several rings.

"Hello? Who is this? Is this Sydney?" Aidan was surprised the child would still be up at this hour.

"Who is this?" The child on the other end was suspicious. And well-trained. Aidan remembered when she was about Sydney's age Nate instructing her never to give her name out over the phone.

"Sydney, this is your Aunt Aidan."

"Hi, Aunt Aida Beth! Mommy! It's Aunt Aida Beth on the phone!"

Aidan held the phone away from her ear, protecting it against the high-pitched screech. Moments later, Sawyer's concerned voice came over the line.

"Aidan? Where are you?"

"I'm still at the airport, that's where I am. The question of the night is where's my father?"

"You mean Nate's not there? He should have been there by now," Sawyer said. "He left over two hours ago."

"Well, he's not here," Aidan said, trying not to let her irritation come through the phone. Irritation and concern.

"I've been trying to reach him. I got worried when I hadn't heard from him or from you. Either he didn't take his cell phone with him or it's turned off."

"So, what am I supposed to do now?"

"Hold on a minute, Aidan." Sawyer's words were calming. "We'll figure something out."

The next few words were muffled. Aidan could tell that Sawyer had placed her hand over the receiver. A moment later, Holling's voice came on the line. He sounded groggy, disoriented as he mumbled, "Yeah… Who is this?

"Holling? It's me. It's Aidan."

"Aida Beth? What's up with you, gal?"

"I'm still at the airport, Holling. Dad's not here."

"What do you mean he's not there?"

Aidan huffed into the phone. "I got off the plane, picked up my bags, and went to the passenger pickup area. When I called earlier, Sawyer said that he'd be in your new truck, right, Holling? A big red, crew-cab dually with chrome grill, chrome running board, and fog lights. Right?"

"That's the one."

"He never came through. I watched and I waited for him."

"You sound pissed." Holling chuckled.

"I am," Aidan openly admitted. "But more than that, I'm really worried, Holling. Shouldn't he have been here by now? Do you think something could've happened to him?"

"Don't go borrowing trouble, now, gal."

"Gal?" Aidan's tone rose in pitch. "Why are you still calling me *gal?* I thought Sawyer would have broken you out of those chauvinistic expressions of yours by now."

"Oh, *excuse me.* I suppose you're too grown to be called *gal* anymore. Is that it, Ms. Independent Woman?"

"Some independence," Aidan retorted. "These days, the

only thing I'm good at is borrowing money. And I'm almost fresh out of coins. So, whatever you have to say to me, Holling, you'd better say it fast. Or I'll be calling you collect again."

"If Dad doesn't show up at the airport, or back here, in twenty minutes, I'm sending someone out there to get you, Aida Beth. One of the hands. What are you wearing so he'll recognize you."

"Jeans. A dark blue sweater and a black leather jacket."

"Like you and all the other passengers roaming around the airport. That oughta help him pick you out in a crowd."

"I'm way too tired to deal with your sarcasm, Holling. What do you want me to do? Slap a sign on my forehead that says Long-lost Holling Sibling?"

"If it'll get you out of the cold that much sooner," Holling quipped.

"Blond," Aidan snapped back.

"Excuse me?"

"I've gone blond, Holling. Long blond locks. Does that help the description any?"

A pause, then a blatant snicker. Holling didn't even try to cover the phone. "Did you say *blond,* Aida Beth?"

"That's right," Aidan said crisply. "Go ahead and get out all of your laughing right now. If you've got any blonde jokes, get them over with now. Believe you me, I've heard them all. Say what you want. Truth is, big brother, I look hot and I know it."

"Ohhhhh-kaaayyyy," Holling drew the word out.

"And what about your hired man? The one who's coming for me?"

"Well, he ain't blond, that's for damn sure." Holling was openly laughing now.

"Holling!" Sawyer's voice admonished in the background.

"Please deposit thirty-five cents…" A feminine, mechanical warning came over the phone line.

"Holling? Hello? Are you still there?" Aidan called anxiously into the phone. She spoke rapidly before the call was cut off. "How am I going to know your man? Is he gonna carry a sign or something?"

"Don't you worry, Aida Beth. With a description like that, he's *gotta* find you."

Chapter 6

Darion coasted up to the entrance to the parking garage and then rolled down the window. He stabbed at the button to eject a parking ticket. When the security arm lifted, he stepped on the gas and eased up the ramp. Around and around he circled, his fingers tapping out the beat on the steering wheel to the music on the radio.

As a courtesy, he'd turned the volume down before he'd rolled down the window to get the parking stub. During the drive out to the Billings airport, he hadn't had to be so considerate. Out on the open road, there hadn't been as single car for long stretches at a time. Nobody to object to his taste in music or his singing ability. So, he'd cranked up the volume to keep his mind alert.

As soon as he had his ticket and could roll up the windows, he turned the music up again. The strains of the heavy bass thumping made several car alarms go off as the compact truck rolled on.

By the time he'd reached the second level, the station had switched disc jockeys. And with the changeover came a switch in musical styles. No more rhythm and blues. No more hip-hop. This late in the day, it was all about the mellow and the smooth. Darion's mouth twisted in a grimace of dissatisfaction as he reached for the buttons to change stations. Too slow. Much too slow. Some young, prepubescent boy band, not even old enough to shave, had come on the air whining and crying into the microphones about how they'd given up the *playa* lifestyle after finding that one true love.

Darion didn't particularly care for the song so he called up another station, thankful for the satellite receiver that the boss had installed in the truck. Plenty of selection to keep him from drifting off to sleep as he made the two-and-a-half-hour drive.

He drove on, taking left turns as directed by the parking arrows, until he found a spot on the roof to park. There were so many cars still in the garage. No big surprise. The local news station reported that the airport was practically on shutdown, no more flights allowed to take off or land until this storm cleared. Darion imagined that half of the owners of these vehicles were either camping out in the airport or were still circling in jets overhead, waiting for the go-ahead to land from the control tower. Everybody was staying put. Everybody but him, that is. He was the only knucklehead out here in this weather.

By now, it was 2:15 a.m. Yet, he waited in the car a few more moments, singing to himself, his shoulders pulsing to the beat, as the last song ended. Only when the last note faded and the DJ began reciting the last few songs played did he reach behind him and grab his sheepskin-lined denim jacket from the bench seat. Adjusting his cap to settle firmly on his head, the bill pulled low over his eyes, Darion opened the door and stepped from the shelter of the truck. The moment he got out, the wind hit him hard, making him brace himself. A few seconds of the icy onslaught and then it was still.

Whew! He let out a low whistle, watching the puffs of air hovering in front of him as his breath crystallized before his very eyes. It was so cold, with the kind of wind that could cut right through you as it whipped through the open-sided garage. The ranch foreman, Red Bone, often referred to a wind like this one as *the hawk*.

You'd get no argument from him, Darion mused. As the wind swept over him, he imagined icy talons ripping into his skin and drawing out all warmth from his body. He turned up the collar of his jacket, aimed the key remote at the truck. Lights flashed and the horn sounded once as the doors locked and the security system engaged. He thrust his hands deeply into his pockets and lowered his head, making sure to check the painted sign identifying the section of the parking garage. As tired as he was, he didn't want to make the mistake of wandering around lost, not remembering where he'd parked.

As he walked briskly toward the elevators, his booted feet echoed on the concrete and occasionally crunched on driven snow. After he pushed the button, he counted the chilly seconds until the light overhead came on and the double doors slid open. Inside the elevator wasn't much warmer. Darion stood in place, but shifted his weight from one foot to the other to keep his blood flowing. Another stop on the third floor and a couple, heavily bundled in leather and fur, hustled into the elevator.

Darion moved to the back right corner of the elevator, mindful of the furtive glances the elderly couple gave him when they stepped inside. Darion couldn't blame them for their misgivings. If he'd stepped into a dark closed-in box in the middle of the night with a big, scowling hulk of a man inside, he'd have had second thoughts about going in, as well. Nobody had any business being out this time of night, in this kind of weather. He counted himself in that number. But the boss man had asked to him go. He'd trusted him to go after his only sister.

He couldn't go, with that busted leg. And Mrs. H. had to stay and nurse the twins through those bad colds. Darion supposed that it was another vote of confidence in him that Mr. H. would trust his only sister to him. For one brief moment while he'd splashed water on his face to snap himself awake and had stared bleary-eyed at his own reflection in the mirror, he'd wished that Mr. H. didn't trust him so damned much. Blind trust like that could get a man into trouble.

The elevator lurched and then chimed when it reached the ground floor. When the doors opened, the couple hunkered even lower and stepped into the pedestrian crossing leading to the airport passenger pickup area. Darion followed, but at a noticeable distance. He suspected that the hasty pace of the couple had about as much to do with him following behind them as it did the icy weather.

Darion looked up, checking the posted signs. The red-and-blue logo of United Airlines was affixed to the wall beside the entryway. This was the place. He'd made it. He'd barely approached the door when the cellular phone clipped to his belt started to vibrate. He reached under his coat and slid the phone from its clip. The caller ID was from the ranch.

He pressed the button, using the two-way radio feature. "Yes, sir."

"Darion. It's Mrs. Holling."

"Yes, ma'am. What can I do for you?"

"Have you found her yet?"

Darion was thankful that he was able to keep his tone even as he said, "No, ma'am. Not yet. I just made it to the airport."

"Just got there!" He could hear the surprise in her voice. "It's that bad out there, Darion?"

"The roads are icing over pretty fast," he reminded her. "I took my time."

"I'm sorry we had to drag you out in the middle of the night like this, Darion."

Her tone mollified him. But not by much.

"No problem," Darion said convincingly. *That's why I get paid the big bucks. Babysitting the boss's baby sister.*

"I called to let you know that Mr. Nate finally made it back."

"Is everything all right? Did he say why he couldn't find Miss Holling?"

"He said that she never showed up."

"Never showed up?" Darion echoed, stopping in his tracks. "Is he sure?"

"This wouldn't be the first time her trip was unexpectedly canceled. Aidan isn't always the most..." The phone went silent. Darion wasn't sure if he'd momentarily lost the signal or if Mrs. H. hadn't completed her sentence.

He took a cursory glance around the baggage-claim area. "But she did call and say that she was at the airport now?"

How could there have been a miscommunication? There was no way to misinterpret the words, *My plane has landed.*

The corners of his mouth turned down as he rubbed his fingers over tired eyes. *If I've driven out all this way for nothing...*

"Yes, she did call. I don't know why Nate said she wasn't there. Maybe she got tired of waiting for him. Maybe she got another ride...or something," Sawyer finished lamely.

"If that were true, wouldn't she have called to let you know that she was leaving?"

Silence on the other end was the response. Darion shook his head. This time he was certain that he hadn't lost the signal. Mrs. H. was sending out some very clear signals. Gradually, a very clear of impression of the boss's sister was starting to form in his head. Unlike the other Hollings he'd come to know over the past few months, this Aidan Holling must be one irresponsible flake.

"If she's still here, I'll find her. I'll have her paged or something." He looked up and down the sidewalk, checking out the stops for the shuttle buses and the cabs to make certain she wasn't one of the few pulling away from the airport. "What's she wearing?"

"Jeans, a sweater and a leather jacket." Sawyer relayed the same description that Aidan had given Holling. Her voice lowered considerably, sounding almost hesitant as she whispered, "Aidan will probably be the only two-hundred-pound, five-foot-eight, blond black woman in the airport…if you understand what I'm saying."

"Yes, ma'am. I…uh…I think I do," Darion said carefully. He'd never met the boss man's sister. He'd heard some of the other employees speak about her, though. The questionably kinder comments hinted that the lady had plenty of junk in her trunk.

"How about if I give you a call back when I find her," he suggested carefully.

Sawyer laughed in response to his diplomatic request. "Okay, okay. I can take a hint. In other words, stop bugging you and let you do your job! Before you hang up, let me give you this one last piece of advice. If the weather is still bad by the time you start back, don't take any chances. I mean that,

Darion. Do what you have to do. Camp out at the airport or get them to put you up for the night."

"I don't think that'll be necessary, but I'll keep it in mind."

He'd heard how Mrs. H. had once taken a chance on the weather, and had been almost carried away by a summer storm. How she'd ridden her motorcycle right in front of Marjean's Café was the stuff of legends around White Wolf. The boss never got tired of telling that story. Though, each time he told it, her stunt-riding skills grew more fantastic. Somehow, knowing Mrs. H. as the epitome of motherly devotion, he couldn't see her burning rubber in the parking lot and popping wheelies along the sidewalk.

He paused, several steps from the entry door—staying far enough away to keep the sensors from making the door whoosh open. As he stood, his eyes scanned the baggage-claim area. Over to his right, a family of four had taken up positions around the baggage carousel, snatching off luggage.

Beside them, the elderly couple that had ridden down the elevator with him from the parking lot was making huge displays of affection.

A security guard patrolled the area. His two-way radio squawked as he paused to give Darion a perfunctory nod before moving on.

Darion figured that he'd better find the boss's sister fast. He had probably five or ten more minutes of obvious loitering before he either had to use the courtesy phone to have Aidan Holling paged...or suffer through the polite, but no-nonsense interrogation from the security guard wondering about his business there.

He picked a direction, heading off to his right. It was as good as any, he assumed, as he strolled around the area, trying to study the faces of the remaining passengers in the area.

Plenty of blondes to be found. Darion figured that must be the new color in all the beauty parlors and barbershops. There were as many men wearing the color as women—everything from dirty, dishwater blond to ultra-bleached like that Hilton gal splattered all over the television and glamour magazines these days. Darion searched, but there wasn't a single tall, heavyset, blond black woman matching Ms. Holling's description.

Darion doubled back, heading down the opposite end of the baggage-claim area. Midway between the entry door and the escalators, he thought he'd found a likely candidate. He paused, unsure whether he should try to approach the blond woman sleeping on one of the benches against the wall. She was partially obscured from view as a man pushing a large airport luggage cart passed in front of him.

That might be her, he thought.

The woman lay in a fetal position with her knees tucked almost to her stomach. One hand rested under her cheek, cushioning it from the hard bench. The other hand was draped across her luggage, sitting on the floor beneath her, as if, even in sleep, she was keeping the airport-mandated careful watch on her luggage. One of the luggage clips, meant to hold the shoulder strap, was tucked loosely through a silver charm bracelet on her wrist.

Darion took another step toward her, eyeing her critically. Black. Blond. Big boned. Mrs. Holling's words echoed in his mind, making him uncertain as to whether he should risk disturbing the sleeper. The more he studied her, the less certain he became. She only fit two of the criteria.

He also thought back to the reaction of the couple in the elevator when they'd taken one look at him. He could almost read their thoughts—automatic responses of fear and distrust brought on by generations of prejudices and misunderstandings. He was a black man walking around in the middle of the night. What else could he be about than to do them harm?

What if he woke this woman and she wasn't the one?

"It could be the boss man's sister." He talked himself into the possibility.

She had the Hollings' same copper-colored skin. And she was very obviously blond. Her tight coils of bright blond hair, almost the color of lemon custard, tumbled over her shoulder and covered part of her face. When she shifted, trying to find a more comfortable position, she brushed her hand across her face, revealing the sharp, high cheekbones that were a prominent feature in the Holling family.

Darion grew more encouraged the closer he got to her. Black and blond. Two out of three Bs. Yet, as he stood almost directly over her, he felt his confidence slip a notch. Something didn't feel right. Something about this woman didn't match the last remaining B.

The description of Holling's sister being bigboned was off. Way off. By at least sixty or seventy pounds, Darion calculated. The woman lying in front of him couldn't have been more than a hundred and forty pounds. Maybe less than that. It was hard to tell under the bulk of her winter clothing. Some qualities, however, couldn't be hidden.

Her fashion sense was all about comfort. Comfort and function. This deep into winter, he knew the multiple layers were meant for warmth. Yet, Darion couldn't help but wonder if there wasn't a certain sassiness in her dress, as well. A kind of sexy chic that could make a man want to look past all of the similarly dressed women and zero exclusively in on her.

Darion didn't have any trouble at all following the curve of her generous hips. Suddenly, his eyes didn't feel quite so tired, observing the way her jeans hugged every line of her calves and thighs. The stretchable material was tested to the limit over her derriere by her sleeping pose.

He made an involuntary sound of appreciation. Um…Um…Um… If this was Aidan Holling, then Nate Holling and the lady's mama needed to be slapped. Shame on them for bringing a woman with a body like that into this world. It was cruel. Unjust. What kind of a parent could create the kind of body that said *look all you want, but don't touch?* No, sir. He'd better not touch. Not if he wanted to keep his job.

He had yet to find out the limit of his boss's trust. This was not the time to test it. Unemployment was down by three percent. Or so the local pundits said. He'd be a fool for testing those statistics by letting his hands roam freely. Darion felt the palms of his hands grow warm, almost tingly, as if in anticipation of cupping the firm, round rear hovering right in front of him.

I could send someone else. But I trust you.

The boss's words echoed in his mind. It was one of the last things that he'd said to him after Darion had expressed concerns that another worker, one more familiar to Aidan Holling, would be a better a choice for picking her up from the airport.

I trust you.

Darion wouldn't betray that trust. Not for anything. Certainly not for anything as foolish as trying to sneak a quick thrill by feeling her up while she slept. So, he shoved his hands deep into his pockets to squash the temptation. Yet, his eyes continued to follow the faded blue line of her jeans all the way to her booted feet. Size eight and a half…maybe size nine.

No, she was not a petite woman. Black. Blond. Big boned. They'd forgotten one B, Darion mused, with a wry sense of irony. The joke was on him. In all Mrs. Holling's careful, politically correct descriptions, she'd neglected to add *beautiful*. Because that was certainly one beautiful black woman lying in front of him now. This had to be her. This had to be Aidan Holling. A true sister, in every sense of the word.

He leaned forward, one hand reaching out, inches away from gently tapping her on her shoulder. But before he could do so—

"Can I help you, sir?" A voice directly behind him interrupted.

The security guard had made his rounds again and came up behind him unannounced. The abruptness of the question startled Darion, making him jerk his hand back and take a discreet step away.

Maybe it was the security guard's question or his own sudden movement that woke the woman. She shot up, one hand raised to give a stinging slap to the waking offender. Confusion and confrontation registered on her face, her head swiveling back and forth, as if deciding which one to strike first.

The presence of the guard in the crisp uniform as an authority figure won out over her trusting the man badly in need of a shave, wearing the battered baseball cap and secondhand clothes. When her gaze finally settled on him, she sat there for several seconds, her expression pure irritation, before her hand slowly relaxed. Instead of slapping him, she changed the motion in midswing and pushed her hair over her shoulder.

"Ma'am, is everything all right?" The security guard's attention shifted. He moved to position himself between Darion and the woman.

Darion didn't respond to the security guard, but addressed the woman instead.

"Aidan Holling."

It wasn't a question. He spoke with certainty, defusing the

situation with his confidence. This was the one. He didn't need to call back to Mrs. Holling for confirmation. She was the boss man's sister and he knew it.

She lifted her chin and asked without answering Darion's question, "And you are?"

"My name's Darion Haddock. I work for your brother. He sent me here to pick you up and bring you home."

"Do you have some identification, Mr. Haddock?" Aidan asked, swinging her long legs off the bench. She reached down and unclipped her bracelet from the luggage. As Darion reached into his inside jacket pocket for his wallet, she arched her back, rotating her head in slow circles to ease the cramp in her neck.

He flipped open the battered leather wallet, holding it out toward her for her closer inspection.

She took a moment to study it then gave a dismissive tilt of her head to the security guard.

"Ma'am." The security guard nodded, moving away, but remained within hearing distance for a few moments more.

Aidan handed the wallet back to Darion. "Looks like a freakin' mug shot," she observed.

"It was taken right after I woke up," he said crisply. "I wasn't at my best, either."

Cranky when she wakes up. Better add another B *to that list,* Darion thought. This B wasn't as complimentary as when he'd marveled at her beauty.

His comment brought an involuntary smile to her lips. Darion's eyes instantly focused on her full lips. If she wore any makeup at all, it was sheer, of the barely there variety. A light sheen added more accent than color, strangely reminding him of the apricot glaze that Chale made to spread over his homemade buttermilk biscuits.

Aidan stood up from the bench, massaging a cramp in her side. Darion used the excuse of lowering his eyes, reaching for her luggage, to avoid noticing how her sweater tugged and strained across her body in all of the hard-not-to-notice places.

"Is this all the luggage you've got, Miss Holling?" he asked.

Aidan nodded. "Yeah, that's it."

"This way, then." Darion indicated with a dip of his head toward the door. "We can be on our way."

"Hold up there a minute, Slim." She reached out and grabbed his elbow. "Not so fast. Do you have any change on you?"

"Excuse me?"

"Change," she repeated distinctly. "Coins. For the pay phone. Before I head off into the middle of the night with a perfect stranger, I'd like to call my brother to make sure you are who you claim to be."

"You can use my cell phone," he offered, shifting her bags to the other hand and reaching for his belt clip.

"No thank you. Haven't you heard? Those things give you brain cancer. All of those electromagnetic waves." She waved her hands in the air above her head, as if the motion could dispel the invisible tumor-causing rays.

"A pay phone?" Darion echoed. "You don't want to use my cell phone, but you're perfectly willing to use a public phone with who knows what kinds of germs swarming over it?"

"That's what disinfectant wipes are for," she said, reaching into her bag and pulling out a travel-sized package of tissue wipes.

Her behavior reminded him of a television show that some of the hands had been watching tonight. Something about a quirky but brilliant police detective whose obsessive-compulsive behavior wouldn't let him function without disinfecting anything human hands had touched.

"Here you go." Acquiescing, Darion dug deep into his pocket and pulled out several coins.

"Thanks," she said, starting for the phone kiosk. "You wait here. I'll be right back."

Darion looked at her, looked down at her luggage, then raised his eyes ever so slightly. Just enough to let her know what was on his mind. How long did she expect him to stand there and play babysitter to her bags?

"It won't take me but a hot minute to find out if you are who you say you are, Mr. Haddock. If you're some kind of sleazy airport con artist, trying to get your hands on my luggage, there's nothing in those bags that I can't replace given time and—" she balled up her hand into a fist and jingled his coins in her hand "—a little money."

Chapter 7

Aidan self-consciously adjusted her clothing, patted the matted side of her hair where she'd slept, then strolled with a nonchalance she didn't really have past Darion.

"Be right back," she promised him.

"Sure thing, Ms. Holling. You go right on ahead and take your time. Me and your bags will wait right here. Right here." He pointed to a spot on the floor.

Was he being facetious? Aidan couldn't tell by his tone or his expression. She didn't quite trust this Darion Haddock. Common sense told her not to trust him. Statistics were staggering about the women who were abducted because they'd let their guard down. As desperate as she was to get out of this airport, she wasn't going to take a step out that door until she'd verified his identity.

As she edged past him, she avoided his piercing gaze by opening her palm and counting out the coins that he'd given her. Though Aidan couldn't see him as she headed for the pay phone, she had the distinct feeling that, as she strode away, he was still tracking her with his eyes.

Those eyes! Those incredibly hypnotic eyes.

She drew in a deep breath to steady herself at the memory of them. They were the first things that she'd noticed when she'd woken up—the sight of those eyes staring down at her. Deep. Liquid. Bottomless.

The feeling strangely reminded her of the shivers of terror she received when watching actors from classic horror movies. Bela Lugosi. Lon Chaney. Christopher Lee. The feelings those actors invoked were intensified by the camera's dramatic focus on their piercing eyes. No wonder she'd awakened with a self-preservative instinct to lash out. She felt as if the intense color could draw her in and, like Dracula's cape, cover her until she was completely lost.

"Come on, Aida Beth," she admonished herself. "Get a grip. That man isn't going to hurt you." Though she and Holling didn't exactly see eye to eye on all things, she knew that her brother was no fool. On business matters, she trusted her brother. If he'd sent this Darion Haddock out to get her from point A to point B, it was because he trusted the man implicitly. She relied on her brother's good sense. Yet, she had a little common sense of her own. And that little voice inside was telling her to not take this man at his word without question. Before she went anywhere with him, she was going to get the full story.

Aidan picked up the telephone receiver, gave it a cursory cleaning with the disinfectant wipes, and turned around to wave the tissue in the air to show Darion Haddock, if that was his real name, that she wasn't kidding about her germ-fighting efforts. She pushed his coins into the slot, listening for the dial tone before stabbing at the silver buttons to call home.

Someone picked up immediately after the second ring. But the grogginess was evident by the creaky-voiced greeting.

Sawyer cleared her throat before speaking. "Hello?"

Aidan winced. It was so late. She hated having to wake her.

"Sawyer, it's Aidan again. I'm so sorry to be calling this late. I hated to wake you up, but—"

"It's all right," Sawyer interrupted, stifling a yawn. "I was getting up anyway to check on the twins." Her tone perked up. "Is everything all right? Did Darion find you?"

Aidan turned to look behind her. Darion was standing vigil over her luggage as she'd instructed. Not really standing, but pacing back and forth, circling around it, looking as if he would carve a trench into the floor before long.

"Darion Haddock. He wouldn't happen to be a long, lanky son of a gun? Cornrows? Hasn't seen a razor in days? Full of nervous energy? Looks like he's about to bounce right out of his skin? Is that the man you sent to get me?"

"Yes, that would be him."

"Then, yes. He's made it. I was calling to check in and to make sure that he was the one you sent. A girl can't be too careful, you know…running off with the wrong man."

"*Ooo*, girl, I know what you mean," Sawyer said with exaggerated emotion. She was wide-awake now. Now that she knew that Aidan wasn't missing, and would soon be safely home, she was finding more humor in Aidan's predicament than she should have. "I've made plenty of those kinds of mistakes before I met your brother. There was this one guy I went out with who had this thing about ladies shoes—"

"Sawyer," Aidan interrupted before she could go on. "Sweetheart, that's not exactly what I meant."

"I know what you meant. I was only teasing you, Aida Beth Holling. You know, trying to find a little warmth and humor on a cold winter's night. I'm so glad you called and that everything's all right. We were really worried when Nate came back without you, saying that he couldn't find you."

"He said that he couldn't find me?" Aidan exclaimed. "What's up with that? I've been right here the whole time! I was out of my mind with worry thinking that something terrible had happened to him when he was the one who didn't show up."

"I think there was some miscommunication going on, Aidan."

"I hate that a so-called little miscommunication made you send that poor man to drive all the way out here. Anyway, now that I know that he's the one you sent for me, I'll get off this phone before I run out of minutes."

"Run out of minutes? What are you talking about?"

"On my change for the pay phone."

"Pay phone? Why are you calling from a pay phone? I gave Darion a fully charged cell phone."

"I hate those things, Sawyer."

"We gave Darion that cell phone so that we could stay in touch. Though," Sawyer said admittedly, "the plan didn't work for Nate. We tried calling him when he didn't come back here when he should have."

"He probably got tired of the stupid thing ringing, so he turned it off."

"Well, the important thing is that Darion's there now. Everything's going to be all right."

Aidan checked back over her shoulder. "I'd better end this call and head out before your man wears a groove in the floor."

"If you're heading out now, I'd like to say a couple of words to Darion before you go. Is he close by?"

"Sure. Hold on a moment, Sawyer." Aidan turned back around and waved Darion over to her.

At her beckoning, Darion pointed to himself and mouthed, "Me?"

"Yes, you!" Aidan mouthed back, whistled and made another impatient come-over-here gesture.

He scooped up her luggage and joined her at the phone booth, but not before Aidan saw a look that crossed his face. A look that said he didn't necessarily care to be beckoned to like a dog. By the time he walked up to her, he'd composed his face into that same bland willing-to-serve-you expression.

"It's my sister-in-law," she said as she held the receiver out to him and took a step back. "She wants to talk to you."

"Ms. Holling," he addressed Sawyer, then paused before continuing. "No, I wouldn't say she was being paranoid. Just being careful about the company she keeps." He looked directly at Aidan, making sure she knew that she was the topic of their conversation.

"Paranoid? Did Sawyer say that I was paranoid? I am *not* paranoid," Aidan denied emphatically. "I am very particular."

Substitute the word *particular* for *picky*. That was what Holling had always said about her. If she had a dollar for every time he'd said that she could have been settled a long time ago if she wasn't so damned picky.

Cradling the phone between his ear and shoulder, Darion pushed back his jacket sleeve to check his watch. "We're heading out now, Ms. Holling. I should have her back home in a couple of hours."

Aidan lifted her eyebrow, noting the platinum band on his watch. Somehow, it didn't match the rest of his attire. If he was as down on his luck as his dress made him appear, he could have pawned that trinket and at least bought himself a few things that didn't look as if they'd been passed around a couple of times.

She wasn't a snob; working in that department store had taught her that you couldn't always tell a person's net worth by the clothes they wore. But she'd also gained some observational skills that helped her pick up on potential problem customers. This Darion Haddock was giving her that vibe. He seemed pleasant enough. Willing to please. Yet, there was something about him, something that she couldn't quite figure out, that kept her on edge.

Aidan stood on tiptoe, placing her hand against his other shoulder for balance as she called loudly into the phone, "Thanks for sending the lift, Sawyer. I promise I won't wake you again until I'm home."

"Be safe, Aidan," Sawyer's voice came back over the line.

"Anything else you want to add?" Darion covered the receiver with his hand and asked her.

Aidan shook her head, indicating that it was okay to hang up the phone.

Darion placed the phone back into the cradle. "Ready to go?"

"I was ready *hours* ago. Lead the way, Slim." Aidan gestured for him to precede her.

They crossed the baggage-claim area one last time, heading for the exit. As the doors slid open, a swift, icy blast of air struck her. Aidan gave an involuntary gasp, dipping her head and hunching her shoulders against the wind.

"We must be hitting record temperatures," she said through clenched teeth. She didn't think it was possible, but it was even colder now than it had been when she'd first arrived. Automatically, instinctively, she moved closer to Darion, walking so that her shoulder pressed against his arm.

He looked down at her, but didn't say a word.

"Sorry about that, Slim," she murmured, clenching her teeth to keep them from chattering. "I don't mean to crowd you. But,

I've been in south Florida the past three years. My blood's thinned since the last time I was back here for the winter."

"Do you want to wait inside where it's warmer? I can bring the truck around," he offered.

She shook her head definitively. "No, thank you! I've had about all I can stand of waiting in the airport. Please! Let's get out of here. Just get me home."

Without asking for her permission, he shifted her luggage to his left shoulder and linked his arm with Aidan's, drawing her close to his side. Together, they stepped into the crosswalk, walking almost in perfect sync from the passenger pickup to the adjoining parking garage.

Aidan pushed the elevator call button and sent up a prayer of thanks when the doors immediately opened. She breathed through her nose, trying not to complain as every breath seemed to sting her nostrils.

"Now I remember why I transplanted myself to Florida," she said with a shaky laugh. "I never could get used to playing the snow bunny."

Darion selected the floor level and took the lead again when the doors opened. Aidan followed with her hands tucked inside the shallow pockets of her leather jacket.

"Are you all right?" Hearing her still complaining against the cold, Darion stopped and looked back over his shoulder.

Aidan bobbed her head up and down and tried to give him a reassuring smile. "I'll feel a lot better when I'm home." It was hard to sound upbeat with her teeth chattering.

He slowed down. Only this time, he didn't take her arm. This time, he draped his arm around her shoulders and drew her close to his side to shield her from the wind. "It won't be long," he promised.

"Two hours." She reminded him of what he'd told Sawyer

on the phone. "I know in the grand scheme of things it's only a little while. But it's been torture, being this close to home and not being able to take that final step through the door."

"You could always go back to sleep," he suggested. "It'll make the time go by faster."

"Oh yeah? And what happens when you finally pull up in our drive? You saw how mean I was when I woke up. You'd risk trying to wake me again and having your teeth knocked down your throat, Slim?" she challenged.

"Trust me. I'm not gonna gamble with my life. Next time I wake you up, Miss Holling, I'll make sure to keep a teeth-saving distance away from you."

He'd said it in all seriousness—with the same deadpan expression and flat tone that he'd used when he'd made the joke about his mug shot-looking driver's license picture. But somehow, it didn't quite come across as the joke he meant it to be.

Rather than putting her off, something in the joke had an underlying hint of intimacy that Aidan couldn't ignore. Something in his tone turned his words into a private joke to be shared between the two of them. Aidan imagined that it was the kind of joke they could make vague references to in a crowded room and only they would get it. A secret connecting point.

On the surface the banter seemed benign enough. It was all idle chatter to pass the time as they walked to the garage. She'd shared the same meaningless conversation with the stranger in the seat beside her as their plane's landing had been delayed. As soon as the passengers had disembarked and everyone had gone their separate ways, each concern, each attempt at humor was forgotten. But not this time. She could not easily shrug off Darion's mild humor. Aidan had a hard time figuring out why.

Maybe it was the way his arm was draped possessively around her shoulder. Or maybe it was the subtle squeeze she felt through the layers of her clothing as he drew her closer to his side. It didn't escape Aidan's attention that Darion hadn't said *if* I have to wake you up again." He'd said "next time."

"It's your own fault, you know, for creeping up on me like that. Don't you know you can't come up on a woman traveling alone? Especially one that's asleep. One that's left herself vulnerable and exposed. That's asking for trouble."

"I wasn't creeping," he said, taking objection to the suggestion. "I was only doing what I was told. Just looking."

"Just looking. Sure you were," she murmured. "Hope you got an eyeful, Slim."

Her tone implied that, if given the chance, he probably would have touched her. Yet, Aidan knew that if she ever had to swear to his actions in court, she would never be able to convict him of having done otherwise. The truth was that he'd been only looking. Looking for her, and at her, with those incredible eyes. Those incredibly sexy eyes.

She must have felt the power of them even in her sleep. What else could have made her jump up from a dead sleep? What else could have jolted her senses to full alert status? She didn't think it had been a noise that had disturbed her. To get any rest at all, she had to be able to drown out the typical airport noises. The announcements over the PA system, the warning sirens of employees on go-carts moving from terminal to terminal, tired, crying, cranky babies, even ringing cell phones—all had faded to the background as fatigue had taken over.

No, it wasn't anything that she'd heard that had woken her. It was something that she'd sensed. Something that she'd felt, even if he hadn't touched her. The feeling of his eyes on her did more to unsettle her than any hand he could have laid on her.

"You know, Slim, we used to have this saying when we were kids," Aidan began.

"Look with your eyes, not with your hands," Darion supplied.

"Yeah, we used to say it, too. And my name's Darion. Not *Slim*."

He aimed the key remote at the truck, unlocking the door. Darion moved to the passenger's side first, holding the door open for her.

"Thanks," she acknowledged the gesture. "So you'll know, back there at the baggage-claim area, I really wouldn't have slapped you," Aidan said as she eased into the passenger's seat.

"Very hard," he completed the sentence for her, closing the door with a solid thud.

Aidan raised her hand to smother her laughter as Darion circled around to the driver's side. She had to admit, he had a point. As tired and, at the same time, as wired as she was, there was no telling what she would have done if that airport security guard hadn't stopped Darion from reaching out to touch her. She shook her head at the thought of her abrupt awakening and wondered what *would* she have done to him if he had touched her? Maybe nothing at all.

The more she thought about it, the more she realized that it wasn't the *idea* of his touching her that she objected to. She hadn't uttered a single word when he'd put his arm around her to shield her from the wind as they'd walked to the truck. Deep down inside, she secretly welcomed the gesture.

At first she tried to blame it on the cold. Cuddling close to Darion Haddock was a matter of comfort and convenience. Like her clothes. He was the one source of warmth while they were out there and she was eager to take it.

That line of reasoning didn't last too long.

Yeah, right, Aida Beth. Who are you trying to fool? Blame it on the cold.

She admonished herself. Yes, it was cold outside. And, yes, she was glad that he had the kind of chivalrous compassion to want to shield her from the weather. With some of the dates she'd had, she was starting to believe that not only was chivalry dead…it had long since turned to dust.

Yet the tiny, illuminating voice of truth inside of her head, and in her heart, reminded her that she probably would have allowed him to hold her even if it wasn't *that* cold outside. There was something about having a tall, good-looking man at her side that gave her self-esteem the kind of boost she hadn't had in a good long while. Darion was eye candy…and she hadn't indulged her sweet tooth in a very long time. Granted, he looked like a piece of candy that had been dropped on the floor a couple of times, or left forgotten in the bottom of her purse, covered in fuzz, wrapper all smudged and crinkled…a smooshed chocolate drop. But he had potential. More than potential. A powerful sex appeal that she responded to, despite warnings to herself not to do so.

She pointedly did not look at him as he tossed her bags into the back seat, removed his jacket and added it to the pile.

"Are you all right?" he asked again as he climbed behind the wheel.

"I will be," she assured him. "I'm so tired. You must be, too, after driving all this way out to pick me up. I know I didn't sound very grateful when I first met you, but I am. Very grateful."

He shrugged, placing the key in the ignition. "Just doing the boss man a favor."

"Did my big brother Holling make you do it?"

"He didn't *make* me," Darion corrected with an edge to his voice that bordered on irritation. "He asked me to."

"*Make* was a wrong choice of words," she immediately retracted. Nope, he definitely didn't like taking orders. "Nobody can make a grown man do what he really doesn't want to do. I said what I said because I know my brother. And the funny thing about my big brother is that even when he asks, it's not really a request. He has a way of putting things that makes it clear that he isn't going to take no for an answer. It's hard to stand up to him. If you work for him, you already know that."

"Your brother's a good man," Darion defended his boss.

"I didn't say that he wasn't. He's a good boss. And a very good man. He's also a very hard man. He makes it hard on everyone else who isn't as…um…good as he is."

Aidan bit her lip, as if she'd said too much, then turned to stare out of the window. She reached up and folded her arms across her chest, squeezing her upper arms. "I must be tired. I'm starting to talk too much. That happens when I'm really tired."

"Still cold?" Darion took her defensive body language as an unspoken request for him to adjust the heat. He turned a couple of knobs on the dashboard, adjusting the temperature.

She rearranged the air vents so that they were blowing comfortably from head to foot. Then Aidan pulled off her gloves and warmed her hands from the sudden rush of heat.

"You're being so nice to me. I have to ask. What kind of a bonus do you get for coming out on a night like this?"

"Bonus? What do you mean?"

"Come on now, Slim. I may be loopy from lack of sleep, but I'm not stupid. To come all the way out here, in the middle of the night, you have to be getting something out of this."

"You mean, other than the obvious pleasure of your company, Miss Holling," Darion replied smoothly.

"Is that supposed to be funny?" Aidan bristled.

"Was it funny?"

"No," she said bluntly.

Darion shrugged again. "Then I guess it wasn't supposed

to be." He pulled up to the paying station, handing the attendant his parking ticket.

"No, really. I'm serious. I want to know." Aidan turned an open, interested expression to him. "How much was it worth to you?"

The garage attendant swiped the parking ticket through the reader and called out the fee. "Twelve-fifty, please."

"I don't mean to be rude, Miss Holling, but it's really none of your business," Darion said politely but firmly.

"I know it isn't," she conceded, but chose to ignore the quiet warning in his tone. "But I'm asking anyway."

"Why do you care so much?"

"Everybody has a price. I want to know yours."

"Why?"

"I'm a student of human nature. It'll give me some kind of insight on what kind of person you are."

"It won't."

Aidan tapped her index finger to her chin and said thoughtfully, "I think it will."

"You sound like one of those women who thinks they can tell the way a man is by the quality of his shoes. It's not always about money, you know."

As if to make a point, he handed the attendant a crisp fifty-dollar bill. The bill was new. Yet, the wallet it came from was worn and battered, as if it had unwillingly coughed up its last dollar.

"That's where you're wrong, Slim. It's always about money," Aidan returned offhandedly. "Holling knows that he can make anyone do just about whatever he wants them to do…. All he has to do is whip out the old checkbook and, boy, everybody is supposed to fall over themselves doing whatever he wants. All I wanted to know is are you one of his whipping boys?"

"No," Darion returned.

"Maybe you're not. But, even if you were, it wouldn't be such a bad thing. I've been one of my brother's whipping boys for as long as he could sign a check. And look how well-adjusted I turned out."

Darion didn't respond, but kept his eyes trained on the road as he pulled out from the shelter of the garage. He reached for the radio, turning it back to the station that was playing the soft rock and rhythm and blues. A song similar to the one he'd changed in disgust before meeting Aidan had started to play. When he reached for the radio to change it back, Aidan exclaimed, "Ooh! Holling's got satellite radio in this rig?"

She leaned back against the headrest, closed her eyes and hummed to the tune.

"I could find a better station if you want," he said, reaching for the radio.

"Leave it there. I love that song!"

"But—"

"Sh!" she quieted him. "Listen to that four-part harmony. Those boys sound tight!"

Darion ground his teeth, suffering through the boy band's declaration of love and devotion to all of their many ladies. He'd picked the station with the intention of letting the music lull her to sleep. His irritation with the music was a small price to pay for a long, quiet ride where he wouldn't have to keep his end of the conversation up. Instead of calming her, the music seemed to have the opposite effect.

Chapter 8

She's exhausted, Darion thought sympathetically. He stole occasional glances at Aidan as she slept and couldn't help thinking how much more at peace she looked than when she was awake. When she was awake, she was tense. Uptight. So ready to show her displeasure with him. She didn't even try to hide it.

But, as she rested, the worry creases between her eyebrows smoothed away. The deep etched lines around the corners of her mouth relaxed, as if the cares of the world no longer weighed her down. She looked younger. So much younger.

On looks alone, Darion couldn't determine her actual age. He knew that she was the youngest of the three Holling siblings. Mr. H. was the oldest. His brother Shane was the middle child. And Aidan was the baby of the family. Because she was the baby and the only girl, Darion figured that the Holling men had spoiled her rotten. It was probably why she was allowed such leniency in her life's choices.

Listening to the boss man complain with both adoration and irritation about her, Darion often heard how Holling's baby sister was out there doing pretty much whatever she wanted, whenever she wanted. Accountable to no one. He'd even once heard Holling admit that she was too much like her mother. Too much like Janeen Holling. Some folks would call that kind of behavior free-spirited. Holling would take exception to that.

"Ain't nothing free about those Holling women," he was often quoted saying. "Especially when it's us soft-hearted, soft-headed Holling men who keep writing the checks to keep them out of trouble."

Is that why she'd chosen to come home now? Was Aidan Holling in some kind of trouble? According to the gossip around the bunkhouse, she hadn't set foot in her family's home in ten years—choosing to stay away from all of the events that should have brought her running home.

Darion wasn't the kind of man who had the time to sit around all day and flap his gums about something that wasn't any of his business. Yet, it was hard not to listen when it came to tales of the prodigal daughter. Whether the boss man knew or not, whether he liked it or not, little sister's name was on the lips of almost every man on the ranch. Speculation about her odd behavior helped pass the time when the jobs were tedious and the days were long.

Those who'd known her nearly all her life, like Chale, would not talk about her as she was now. He would only refer to her in past tenses. She was always such a beautiful child, but disobedient. So, so disobedient. Yet, no one could punish her. How could they, with that smile, that genuine promise to do better? Mischief without malice. She'd gotten away with everything short of murder in the Holling household.

There were plenty of the boss man's hired hands who hadn't known Aidan when she'd been a little girl. That didn't stop them from talking about her. In fact, the younger the hired help, the juicier the gossip. All of them giving their opinion on what they could do for her…and with her…or *to* her if she ever showed up on the ranch.

Yet, with each passing season, Aidan Holling was always a no-show. Never giving her family a good enough reason why. Never giving those young studs a chance to strut their stuff in front of her. Some moved on, either tired of the work or tired of the waiting for her. Those that remained kept the fires of mystery surrounding that woman burning.

Why wasn't she there for her brother Holling's wedding? Or for the birth of his twins? When her brother ran for city council and lost, why wasn't she there during that hard-fought campaign? Though, she wasn't without some degree of decency and familial responsibility. To her credit, she had tried to console her sister-in-law, to help her through her time of sorrow, when Sawyer's father had passed away. Once, Darion had gotten caught up in the *As the Aidan Turns,* drama as it was known around the bunkhouse, and had let it slip that he himself had signed for the floral arrangements that she'd sent to express her condolences. The final slap in the face, everyone had decided, was her boycott last summer. She hadn't even been there to share in her family's joy when the Holling homestead celebrated its bicentennial.

So many family memories. The kinds of memories that ought to bind a family together. And yet, she'd chosen to stay away. No one could fathom why. Now that he'd met her, he was starting to get an inkling into her personality. Maybe she wasn't joking when she'd said that living in Florida had thinned her blood. Through all that her family had gone through, she'd been absent. Blood ties had not been strong enough to bring her back.

Maybe the big boss man was right. Maybe the only time the Holling women popped back into their men's lives was when they were desperate. When they were in need. If she couldn't tear herself away from Florida's fun in the sun for the sake of family and friends, then he could only surmise that she'd come back because she couldn't keep living that lifestyle. Aidan Holling must have been flat broke. Barely enough change in her pockets to make a phone call to get herself home. Did Aidan Holling have issues? Yeah, he believed that she did. Though, he'd never say so to her face. His job was to drive the truck. That was it. Just drive the truck.

Darion turned off the main four-lane highway, taking the exit that would lead him to White Wolf. He followed behind a huge tanker truck carrying diesel fuel. When Darion realized that he was following too closely to the truck, he backed off. Way off. The pull home toward his warm, soft bed was making him a little reckless. Sure he wanted to get home. Sure he could hardly wait to feel the warmth of his covers pulled up to his chin. If he wasn't careful, he'd be stretched out in the back of an ambulance. Or worse, having the coroner zip him up to his chin, and beyond, in a body bag.

He slowed down enough to keep the tanker truck in clear sight, using the glowing amber lights outlining the truck as additional visual road cues. Flashing brake lights warned him to hazards ahead that he could not see.

As he took a gradual curve in the road, Aidan's head lolled over to the side. It bobbed back and forth several times, keeping in almost perfect time with the turns, until she finally came to rest against his shoulder.

Darion glanced down, catching a whiff of the scent of wild

jasmine. Was it her shampoo? Or maybe it was her perfume. Whatever it was, it was doing crazy things to his senses. Making him see and hear things that weren't really there. He'd heard it said that scent was a powerful stimulant. The faintest whiff could bring back memories long forgotten. Only, this was no memory he was experiencing. This was pure fantasy.

He shook his head, a guilty grin on his face. He couldn't remember the last time he'd fantasized about a woman. The perfect car. The perfect house. Even the perfect sandwich when he was really hungry…and he'd been hungry a time or two, moving from job to job as he had. But to fantasize about a woman. He'd almost forgotten how to.

Despite the heavy winter clothing, Aidan's essence was tropical. Exotic. She took his thoughts away from the scenes of the winter wasteland rolling by outside. Snow-capped mountains gave way to rolling seas, frothing with crashing waves and sea foam. Wavering before his eyes, frozen prairie gave way to images of steamy summers on lush islands. The southernmost tip of Florida, maybe. He had Florida on his mind now that Aidan was back. Or maybe he dreamed of points beyond. As tired as he was and as bleak as it was outside, imagining that he was anywhere but there was an improvement.

If he listened carefully, the rhythm of the wipers *swooshing* across the windshield could easily be the creak of a hammock large enough for two, rocking back and forth, as he lounged in the shade between two palm trees. It wasn't the frigid, howling wind whistling around them, wasn't slamming a mixture of ice and snow against the glass. Instead tropical breezes swept crystal-white sands across his own private beach. The peppering of pea-size sleet and hail on the truck turned magically to the sound of steel drums, rumbling out a rich island tune.

Though only her head rested on his shoulder, the entire right side of Darion's body tingled. As she lay against him, he wasn't worried about her cutting off the circulation to his shoulder and arm. More like the opposite. He was concerned about her closeness stirring his senses, increasing his heart rate, making him breathe a little faster. A little harder. Again, Darion found himself fighting the impulse to reach out to Aidan and smooth his hand over her hair to push back honeyed curls. He'd felt this same way while he'd watched her sleep in the airport.

This time, there was no airport security guard to encourage him to keep his hands at his sides. Caught in the confines of the small truck, this time there was only his strength of will and the assurance that his boss trusted him.

Get a grip on yourself, fool! Darion admonished himself. This wasn't a fairy tale. She wasn't Sleeping Beauty and he was no Prince Charming…or whichever one of those fictional stories that made everything turn out all right with a chaste kiss. This was reality. Harsh reality. And if he acted in a moment of weakness, he could lose his job. More devastating than the loss of the paycheck, he could lose the big boss man's respect. He wasn't about to do that. Not after all of the hard work he'd put in to gain it.

Instead of caressing her, Darion lifted his arm and positioned it along the back of the headrest.

Look at you, he thought in a mixture of tender amusement and jealous annoyance. *Sleeping like you don't have a thing to worry about.*

And that's exactly the way it should be. It was his job to make sure that the boss man's sister didn't have to worry. He didn't want to wake her up. He understood about being bone-tired and needing to sleep. He felt that way himself. In fact, he'd be asleep right now if it weren't for her. Still, he couldn't let the situation go on like this. Somehow, he had to put a little distance between them. The slight movement shouldn't have been enough to wake her. In hindsight, Darion wished that it had. His readjustment was enough to encourage Aidan to snuggle closer. She did so, muttering something about skimpy airplane pillows before drawing another contented breath and falling deeper into sleep.

Just as she'd done on the bench back at the airport, Aidan slept with one hand resting under her cheek. The other she let fall limply as she shifted over to him.

Oh, hell. This can't be happening! I'm not going out like this....

Darion mentally cursed himself. This must be what old-timers called temptation of the worst kind. She was close. So close. All he had to do was reach out and—

No! No, he wouldn't. He couldn't.

I shouldn't, should I?

The fact that he could even ask himself the question was enough to let him know that he was getting in over his head. There shouldn't be any question. The answer was simple. The answer was no.

Or was it?

Like a character in a cartoon, Darion could almost feel the angel in the white robe on his right shoulder and the devil in a blazing red jumpsuit on his left shoulder playing tug-of-war with his conscience. He was trying to do the right thing. The noble thing. How could he have made the situation worse?

Or, much better?

Darion's attitude shifted, resigning himself to the fact that there wasn't much else he could have done to extricate himself. It all depended on how he wanted to look at it. He could curse his luck for the untimely fall of Aidan's hand on his thigh or thank his lucky stars. It only added to his fantasy of lying next to her.

The image of Aidan's scantily clad body, swinging in the hammock next to him, coiled sensuously around him, drifted before his eyes. He thought he felt her long, lean body next to him, with little more than a two-piece bikini and a gauzy shawl slung loosely around her waist to cover her as they swayed back and forth.

I trust you, Darion.

Darion blinked and shook his head, forcing his mind back to concentrating on the road. It wasn't easy. In fact it was damned hard…made even more so when Aidan slid her other arm through his. She slept, linking arms with him as they'd done when they'd left the airport. She snuggled her face closer to his arm and snaked her other hand around his inner thigh as if gripping a comfortable pillow.

He tensed, gripping the steering wheel. Funny not in the ha-ha way how rapidly a situation could change. Who was the uptight one now? Not Aidan Holling. He was the one stressing. It would have been oh-so-easy to let his hand accidentally stray and brush against her breast. Oh-so-easy. She was *sooo* tired. No one would ever know.

For a moment, he tossed around the idea that she wasn't asleep. Maybe she was doing this to him on purpose—to mess with his mind. Maybe she was the kind of person who enjoyed manipulating men. What if she was the type who enjoyed grabbing them by the proverbial privates and watching them squirm? Maybe she'd get back home with her old girlfriends and have a really good laugh at his expense. He imagined her getting together with the boss's wife, sitting out on the front porch, watching him as he worked, giggling behind her hands every time he walked by. She could be a tease. How would he know? He didn't know much about this Aidan Holling.

But then he heard her mumble lazily in her sleep. "Pass the sunscreen, baby," she muttered. "Too hot out here."

A light sheen of perspiration shimmered on Aidan's face, trickled down her cheek and trailed down the hollow of her neck.

"Do you want me to turn down the heat?" Darion asked, loud enough to show that he'd made the effort, yet quietly enough not to disturb her as she slept.

"So hot… Hit me up on one of those refills of that banana daiquiri," she continued, licking her lips as if wiping away the last drops of the fruity drink.

No, Darion concluded, she wasn't deliberately trying to bait him. She wasn't using her sexuality to mess with his mind. In her mind, she was somewhere else, too. Certainly not Montana, if she was asking for banana daiquiris. Florida, maybe? Or some other tropical locale?

Surprised that their thoughts could be so closely in tune with each other, Darion looked down at her again, taking his eyes off the road. His distraction lasted for a second. Only a second. But it was more than enough time for the unthinkable to happen. Darion cut his eyes back to the road barely in time to see the tanker truck in front of him suddenly slam on the brakes.

Immediately, instinctively, Darion lifted his foot from the gas and started to steer to the side of the road. Any other day, he would have reacted by tapping on the brakes as well. Not today. Not with all of that ice covering the road.

He didn't know what had caused the truck ahead of him to try to come to a sudden stop. It really didn't matter. His only concern was putting more distance between him and the tanker as brake lights flashed their warning.

"This is not good," Darion predicted when it didn't appear as if the tanker was going to stop. Not the way it should have. It had been traveling too fast. The roads were too slick. He could only watch in awful fascination as the tanker's rear end started to shift, sliding toward the right edge of the road, even as the front end continued to plow forward.

"What is it? What's happening? Are we there yet?" Aidan mumbled, lifting her head from Darion's shoulder to stare with bleary eyes up at him. Their sudden deceleration had jolted her awake as the safety belt tightened across her chest and waist.

Darion didn't take the time to answer, but concentrated on keeping them from sliding on the icy road.

Aidan started to stretch, arching her back. Only then did it register where she'd had her hands.

"What's the matter with you? Why didn't you wake me up?" she exclaimed, jerking her hand from between Darion's thighs and then unlinking her other arm. As she edged away from him, she reoriented herself so that she was facing the windshield.

"Had…other…things…on my…mind!" he gritted, working the steering wheel to keep them from running completely off the road.

She swallowed back a strangled cry and pressed her hands against the dashboard as if she could stop their forward motion with a wish.

"Stop!" she called out stridently.

"The thought *had* occurred to me," he retorted.

"We're six feet away from slamming into the back of that diesel truck and lighting up the night sky like Roman candles, and you've got jokes?"

"Twelve feet," he corrected. He'd backed off when he realized that he was following too closely. Even that wasn't enough. It wasn't a question of his driving ability or the effectiveness of the brakes. If he gave in to the impulse and slammed on the brakes to stop them immediately, they would still slide several more yards before they came to a complete stop.

The rear end of the tanker fishtailed, swerving from the right side of the road to the left. For a moment, it seemed to balance on the tires on its right side as it tipped precariously going into a curve. On the two-lane road, there was no room to pass. Darion couldn't go around it. He couldn't stay behind it. As he saw it, he had only one option. Take his foot off the gas and let the law of physics have its way with them. As the tanker shot away from them, they coasted to a complete stop.

In shocked silence, they sat and watched in horror as a series of unthinkable events all converged at that one place and time. The tanker took one last turn too sharply. It was too much. High speed, icy roads and gravity converged and brought the full brunt of cruel nature on the truck. The lights that had been so much of a help to Darion, keeping him safely on the road, suddenly spun out of sight, crashing through a guardrail and plummeting down the embankment in a deafening screech of torn metal.

Chapter 9

Aidan sat with her trembling hands pressed against her mouth, her eyes wide open.

"Oh, my God," she moaned, turning her stricken expression to Darion. "Did you see that? I don't believe this is happening. This can't be happening!"

Her lament broke Darion out of his momentary paralysis. He seemed to move in several directions all at once—shutting off the engine, throwing open the door, reaching toward the back seat to grab his coat and slapping his cellular phone in Aidan's hand all at the same time.

"Call 9-1-1," he ordered. He climbed out of the truck, shoving his arms into his coat and wriggling his fingers into his leather gloves.

"Where do you think you're going?" Aidan leaned across the seat and called out to him as he walked briskly away from her.

"Tell them what's happened and give them our location!" Darion cupped his hands to his mouth and shouted at her.

"I can't do that!" Aidan protested, clutching the phone to her chest.

Darion took a menacing step toward her, pointing at her. "Don't you give me any crap about brain cancer and not wanting to use the cell phone," he snapped. "The driver might have made it out of there. I'm going to go take a look. I need you to make that call." Then he spun around and sprinted for the side of the road where the tanker had gone over.

"Tell them where we are? How am I going to do that? *I* don't even know where we are!" Aidan shouted after him.

He didn't hear her. Even if he had, she didn't think it would make a difference. Darion Haddock had that look on his face. The same look that her brother Holling would get once he'd made up his mind about something. Stubborn. Unstoppable. Never willing to let the little details get in the way of him doing what he wanted to do.

She threw up her hands in frustration and then pulled the door closed. Where was she, anyway? She'd been asleep almost the entire drive. In hindsight, it probably wasn't a smart idea to put her trust in a complete stranger so willingly. Even if he did work for her brother, that didn't mean she should have completely let herself become so complacent. To let someone she'd recently met drive off with her into the night, without her paying attention to road signs, was plain foolish.

Having to call 9-1-1 and give the dispatcher her location illuminated the recklessness of her behavior with startling clarity. What if it had been her, instead of the tanker-truck driver, who needed help? What if Darion Haddock wasn't as trustworthy as he appeared? What if she was the one whose life depended on being able to tell someone where she was? For all she knew, he could have been taking her off to some dark, wild place never to be seen again…all because she didn't have the good sense to keep her eyes open and her wits about her.

With trembling fingers and a grateful heart for the grace that had spared her from her own foolishness, she dialed the emergency number. The voice coming over the line was prompt, efficient.

"9-1-1 Emergency. Can I have your location?"

"I…I'm not sure," Aidan stammered. "On the outskirts of White Wolf…Montana. We're on some kind of two-lane road…It's dark. No streetlights. I don't see any road signs or mile markers. I don't know where I am!" Her strident tone conveyed her panic.

"Ma'am, I'm gonna need you to keep calm. We're gonna find you, but I need you to help me. What can you see from where you are?"

"I'm in a freakin' snowstorm! I see mountains and snow and ice from where I am!"

"Ma'am…ma'am, keep calm, now. What's your emergency?"

"A tanker truck just went off the road in front of us!"

"Can you tell me in which direction you were heading?" the dispatcher requested.

"Umm…I don't know…oh…wait!" Aidan drew in a breath to settle herself, and then looked around for visual clues. The corner of the rearview mirror glowed faintly green, giving the temperature outside and the direction they were headed.

"Northeast," she relayed to the dispatcher. "The compass in the truck says we're headed northeast."

"That's good. I want you to stay on the line if you can. Don't hang up. We're going to locate you by the cell phone with a tower and GPS."

"A global positioning system?"

"Yes, ma'am. That's right. If you've got a signal, there's a tower nearby. We should be able to find you."

Perfect, Aidan thought wryly. She envisioned hundreds of satellites floating above the planet, zeroing in on her position. One more invisible beam cutting through the stratosphere to push brain cancer upon her. She pulled the phone away from her ear, resisting the urge to hurl it out the window.

"Ma'am? Ma'am, are you still there? You have to stay on the line," the dispatcher urged.

Aidan could hear tapping on a keyboard, muted voices in the background.

"We're going to find you," the dispatcher continued to assure her. "Can you confirm some information? We've got this phone registered to a Jon T. Holling."

"Yes, that's my brother!" Aidan said excitedly. "I'm his sister, Aidan. We were on our way back from the airport...almost home...when this truck just started swerving all over the road. It crashed through the guardrail and went over the side! It was unbelievable. I've never seen anything like that before!"

The more she talked, the higher her pitch climbed, letting the dispatcher know that she was starting to panic again.

"Listen to me, Ms. Holling, we've got a fix on your location. We're sending out some rescue units right now. How many other vehicles are in the area? Any others involved in the accident?"

"I'm not sure. I was asleep when it all started. My brother's employee was driving us back to the ranch...Darion Haddock."

"Is Mr. Haddock there with you now?"

"No...he's not. He's out trying to see if he can find the driver of that tanker truck."

"Ms. Holling, I advise you to stay away from the vehicle

until the rescue units arrive. Do you hear me? Keep clear of the vehicle."

"Don't tell me. Tell him. He's the one running off like some kind of lunatic with delusions of heroics…leaving me out here all by my damn self…cold…hungry…tired…you're not taping this conversation, are you? I don't want this played back on the six o'clock news. Make me sound like some kind of whining, pathetic, can't-do-for-herself female."

Aidan thought she could hear the trained professionalism of the dispatcher slip a notch as she answered with a smile in her voice, "Yes, ma'am. You are being recorded. It's policy."

"How long until the rescue units get here?"

"One unit has been dispatched from White Wolf. Depending on the condition of the roads and your exact location, the ETA is forty-five minutes to an hour. A hazardous materials team is on its way from Billings."

"An hour!" Aidan exclaimed. "We need that haz mat team out here now. Please! You've got to do something. The tanker could explode."

"Ma'am, we're doing everything that we can."

"I can't sit here for an hour and do nothing," Aidan said, more to herself than to the dispatcher.

"Listen to me, Ms. Holling…the best thing you can do right now is stay in your truck. Stay out of the weather and away from the tanker. Is that understood?"

"I understand," she returned, responding to the voice of authority. Her instinct for self-preservation told her to listen to the dispatcher. She'd made good sense. Inside the truck, she was warm and dry. Why should she go running off into the night, in a snowstorm, down an icy, rocky, probably diesel-soaked mountainside? What made her think that she could do anything? The driver of the truck was probably dead before he'd hit the bottom of the chasm. If the unthinkable happened, if the tanker truck did explode, she had the keys. She had her brother's truck. She could crank up the engine and get herself out of there. Away from the threat of an explosion. Staying put was the rational thing to do.

Only, Aidan reminded herself, nothing about this return home so far was rational. There was no reason why she should leave her friends, her easy, no-stress job and her comfortable summer Florida life to risk coming home in the dead of winter to a family that would probably only judge her and give her grief. No reason why she should have accepted the word of a total stranger, trusted his driving in treacherous road conditions. She'd willingly put her life into the hands of a man she'd never laid eyes on before. This wasn't like trusting in an airplane pilot, or a taxicab driver…or any other person who made their living ferrying people from one place to another. Where was her instinct for self-preservation when she'd curled up next to Darion, as contented as a kitten, deep in blissful slumber while he'd taken her on unfamiliar back roads. No…there was no reasonable or rational explanation for what she had done. Or, she thought with sudden determination, for what she was *about* to do.

"He's still out there," she murmured, more to herself than to the dispatcher.

"Ma'am?"

"My brother's employee," Aidan said louder. "Mr. Haddock. He's still out there somewhere looking for the driver of that tanker truck."

She reached behind the seat and grabbed her own coat. "He should have been back by now…either to tell me that the driver was gone or that he can still be saved. Something's not right. He's been out there for too long."

"Ms. Holling…you're not thinking about—"

"Not thinking about," Aidan interrupted the dispatcher. "Doing."

She set the phone on the seat behind her for a moment while she pulled on her jacket and adjusted her woolen cap over her ears. Aidan ignored the insistent call of the dispatcher as she checked the gas gauge. Even after all of that driving, there was well over three-quarters of a tank left.

"Holling," she murmured. Wasn't it like her brother to get the kind of low-cost, high-comfort, fuel-efficient work-horse of a truck that he could get every cent of his money's worth out of?

Aidan slid over to the driver's side, made sure the vehicle was still in Park, set the emergency brake and then cranked up the engine. She stepped on the gas, revving the engine to make sure that it would not cut off, and then turned on the emergency flashers and the high-beam headlights. Only then did she pick up the phone and speak firmly into it.

"My truck is parked on the side of the road with the emergency flashers on. When the rescue units get here, you can't miss me."

"Ms. Holling…" The dispatcher's voice was filled with warning and disapproval.

"I know…I know…you want me to stay in the truck. Believe me, lady, I want to stay in here, too. And as soon as I can, I'm getting my frozen tail back in here. But I have to go and check on my brother's employee. I *have* to. I can't leave him stuck out there like that. I promise I'll stay on the phone as long as I can…but I *am* going out there."

She opened the door. As soon as the wind hit her, it sucked the air out of her lungs. Aidan felt as if her courage was snatched from her very breath and scattered to the wind.

"Some big-time heroine you are, Aida Beth," she muttered.

"First sign of a little wind and you're ready to climb your scary behind back into the truck."

She lowered her head and ground her teeth together to keep them from chattering. Carefully, she stepped onto the ice-covered ground to walk around the front and gave the dispatcher the make and model of the truck and the license-plate number.

"Ms. Holling? Are you still there?"

"Yeah, I'm still out here. Against my better judgment and yours."

As she spoke into the phone, Aidan had one more flash of inspiration. She pressed the button to open the utility box bolted onto the bed of the truck and rummaged until she found what she knew had to be there. She knew her brother. Mr. Boy Scout. Always prepared. Plenty of truck maintenance supplies.

"Can't use this," she muttered, shoving aside a couple of cans of Fix-A-Flat. "Or this." Three quarts of oil and a bottle of antifreeze were also moved out of her way.

"Now, we're talking!" she exclaimed in triumph, clutching a basic first-aid kit to her.

Aidan hurried around to the other side of the box. When she lifted the lid on the opposite side, she rummaged some more. Next to a tackle box filled with maintenance tools, she found a small blanket, halter and bit, and a coil of lead rope. She pushed them aside until she found an extra set of work gloves and several battery-powered roadside emergency lights.

"Please." She sent up a fervent prayer. "Please let these lights be bright enough, and last long enough to keep some fool from running into the back of me."

Aidan turned three of the emergency flashers on, leaving them several feet away from the truck so that anyone approaching the accident site would see them and take the proper precautions. The fourth light she stuck down in her jacket. There had also been a few roadside flares in the truck utility box.

"I found a few things that they can use until you get here." She directed her comments into the phone to the dispatcher. "But it's probably not a good idea to be igniting road flares around the site where diesel fuel might have spilled, huh?"

"No, probably not."

"I didn't think so. Okay...here we go. I'm standing about twelve feet from where the truck went over off the road. When the truck tipped, it left a huge scrape in the road, but it's all starting to be covered over by the snow."

Her voice dropped in awe. She'd been a beach bunny for far too long. She'd forgotten how beautiful the winters in Montana could be.

"It's...incredible. In a few minutes, you won't be able to tell that anything happened here at all...except for that huge gaping hole in the guardrail... Everything's covered over with snow...like a fairy winter wonderland. If it wasn't all so terrible...seeing the truck go over the side like that...it would be beautiful...."

Under different circumstances, this could be a picture-perfect postcard moment—with the mountains to the right of her and the valley where White Wolf was nestled to the left. She'd been in Florida for so long, she'd almost forgotten how a true white Christmas could be. Somehow, the crystal-white sands of the beach outside of her apartment didn't quite put her in the mood of the season. Draping tinsel and lights over the potted palms wasn't the same.

She'd forgotten what it was like to wake up in the morning with the season's first snow, rush outside and hold out her tongue to catch drifting flakes. And as winter wore on, she and her brothers had pelted each other with snowballs or sneaked clothes from her father's closet to dress their snow-men…every year from the time she could walk to the time she had walked away from them ten years ago. She'd missed the crisp nights, wrapped in her favorite throw, sitting beside the fireplace, trading tales with her brothers or curled up with a good book. Falling asleep to the crackle and hiss of the logs on the fire was a nightly occurrence. As regular as clock-work. As soon as Holling and her father, Nate, had started arguing about who was the worst cheater at dominoes, her head would begin to nod.

Aidan only took a moment, as memories rushed in on her. But even that was enough to remind her of the deceptiveness of the winters here. While she stood reminiscing, snow was driven against her, settling on her head, shoulders and booted feet. The wind swirled, creating minicyclones of snow. Even with the headlights' high beams on, she couldn't pick up Darion's trail. His footsteps had been completely obscured.

She walked a few steps in the direction she thought he'd gone, looking back over her shoulder to make sure that she could still see the truck's flashers. Aidan pulled the phone away from her mouth and called out, "Haddock! Can you hear me? Where are you?!"

She listened for a moment, hoping to catch the sound of his voice over the wind whistling in her ears.

"Come on, Slim! Give me a shout out if you can hear me!"

Nothing. She checked over her shoulder one last time. Then, taking a few more steps away from the truck, Aidan cautiously approached the guardrail, keeping a healthy distance from the opening where jagged metal and the remnants of reflective direction arrows along the retaining wall jutted into the open air.

"I'm going to set you down now," she told the dispatcher.

"I'll leave the phone on as long as I can. But I'm gonna have to shut it down to save the battery. Whatever you're doing to find us, you'd better put a hurry on it."

She set the phone next to one of the rail support posts and clutched the guardrail with both hands. As she leaned over the edge, she felt the wind shift directions. Instead of coming head-on, making her bow her head against it, it suddenly came at her from behind. Aidan felt as if someone had suddenly shoved her with a pair of massive, icy hands. She gasped and held on with all of her strength, feeling as if the wind would suck her over the edge and send her tumbling down the mountainside.

Are you crazy? Have you completely lost your last good brain cell, Aida Beth Holling? What do you think you're doing? You're no superwoman. You can barely balance your checkbook and now you want to balance your tail on the side of a mountain. This is crazy. This is insane. You can't do anything to help them. You did your part. You called 9-1-1. So why don't you just go back and wait in the truck until someone who knows what they're doing shows up.

She almost talked herself into going back. Why didn't she listen to the dispatcher? Why didn't she keep her crazy behind in the truck?

Darion Haddock, that was why. He was still out there. But he hadn't answered her. Why hadn't he answered her? Why hadn't he shown himself by now?

"Haddock? Can you hear me?" she called out, her worst fears swirling before her eyes, dancing like the snow flurries.

On inspiration, she took out the last emergency beacon, turned it on and held it out as far as she dared over the opening.

"Answer me, Darion, if you can see this!"

"Aidan?" A voice echoed faintly on the wind. Breathless. Strained. "Is that you?"

Aidan still couldn't see him, not from where she was.

"Yeah, it's me. Where are you, Haddock? I can't see you." She moved closer to the edge. One hand held on to the last support post. The other hand held the flashing beacon out so that Darion could see it better. Trying to see, she stepped too close to the edge.

Aidan cried out sharply when her foot slid out from under her, sending a chunk of ice and cracked asphalt skittering over the side. She dropped to her knees, clutching the rail with both arms wrapped around it, breathing hard and fighting the overwhelming sense of vertigo making her head swim. As she sat there, she thought she heard the voice of the dispatcher coming from the tiny speaker of the cell phone.

"Ms. Holling? Are you all right? What's happened?"

"I'm all right." She turned her head and talked to the phone. "My stupid foot decided to go skating without me. Trust me, it won't happen again." She then looked down at her offending foot. "Try that again, you stupid size nine and a half and I'll be squeezing you into size sevens for the rest of the year. See how you deal with that."

Aidan tried to stand again, sending more loose rock raining down on Darion.

"What do you think you're doing, woman? I thought I told you to stay in the truck!" Darion's voice was filled with concern and irritation that she'd disregarded his instructions.

"Fine. I'll go back to the truck and leave you down there until help comes. About an hour from now, if you think you'll last that long."

When he didn't respond immediately, Aidan had the distinct impression that realization of how desperate their situation really was sank in.

"What's taking them so long?" Darion called up to her.

"What do you think? It's this weather," Aidan told him. "They've got units coming out of White Wolf, Cut Bank and Billings. But it'll take time. For now, I'm all you've got, Slim. So, you'd better check your attitude. Where exactly are you? I can hear you but I can't see you." She craned her neck as far as she dared. Hooking one arm around the rail, she stretched her arm out, holding the emergency flasher.

"We can see you," Darion assured her. "If that's you with the light. We're down here. On a ledge about fifteen feet or so off to your left."

"You said *we!*" Aidan said excitedly. "Does that mean you've found the driver?"

"Yeah… he's got a busted leg and his face is all cut up…. Either he jumped out of the truck or was thrown out when it tipped over…but we're both down here."

"Oh, thank God!" Aidan's voice flooded with relief.

"What are you thanking Him for?" Darion retorted. "It's not as if we're in any better shape. I don't think the driver has the strength to climb out on his own. What good is it saving yourself from a fiery crash if you're going to freeze to death before help can get here?"

"Hold on, then. I'm coming down. I'll help you get him out of there."

"No, you won't!" Darion's command was immediate. "You stay up there where it's safe."

"You need my help," she insisted. "If you stay down there, you could freeze before the rescue units get there."

"I'd rather freeze my butt off than have your brother stomping all over it if anything happened to you," Darion warned her. "He trusted me to get you back home safe and sound."

"And how are you going to do that stuck down there?" she pointedly reminded him.

"I'll figure something out. Give me a minute."

"You've got sixty of them. Can you think that fast?" Aidan taunted.

More silence.

"Yeah, that's what I thought. I'm not leaving you down there, Slim."

"You don't have a choice. You have to stay. I'm telling you to get back in the truck."

"Hey! My family pays *you*. Or have you forgotten that? We do the telling around here, Mr. Haddock. And right now, I'm telling you that you're getting my help—whether you like it or not!"

"Don't, Aidan…don't do it. Stay up there… Please…"

"You'd better listen to him, ma'am." Another voice joined in the conversation. Not as strong as Darion's, but equally as insistent. It had to be the tanker driver. "It's not safe for you to risk it. The sides are all slick with ice. Loose gravel could give way at any time. And the wind is something fierce. If you aren't careful, it'll pick you right up and carry you off the side of the mountain like a slip of paper. Do like the man says and go back inside where you're warm and safe. It'll be all right. I promise you."

"You're just saying that!" Aidan accused. Yet, she bit her lip in indecision. "What should I do?" she whispered to herself, closing her eyes and trying to visualize the possible outcomes.

If she went against Darion's wishes and tried to reach them, what was the worst that could happen? She could help them out of their predicament and have to deal with Darion's wounded pride for her having disobeyed his orders. Or, as the tanker driver had warned her, she could end up as a bloody frozen pulp at the bottom of the mountain.

If she followed Darion's directions and waited in the truck, if she did nothing to help them, the rescue units *might* get there in time. Then again, they might not and those two could die from exposure. Would she be able to live with herself, knowing that she could have done something to help them and hadn't?

Aidan knew the answer to that question even before she asked it of herself. She would not be able to handle the guilt and the self-recrimination. It didn't matter where she chose to live. Back in Florida. Here in Montana. It would be the same. Her life would be intolerable. She didn't know how, but somehow she had to find the means to do something to help them.

When Aidan didn't speak for several minutes, Darion queried, "Aidan? Are you still there?" His voice was filled with concern.

"I'm still here, Slim," she affirmed. "Don't worry. I won't try to climb down if you don't want me to."

"Definitely not one of those wishing-you-were-here moments," he agreed.

Aidan had no trouble picking up the sarcasm in his tone, even despite the wind.

"You're about to become one life-sized, chocolate Popsicle and you've got jokes," she returned.

"Well, Ms. Holling, if they have to find me frozen stiff, I'd rather have gone with a smile on my face," Darion returned.

"No, sir!" Aidan said adamantly. "You get thoughts like that out of your head. I'm not letting you ruin *my* Christmas by making me go to your funeral, Mr. Haddock!"

"Too bad we didn't stop right in front of a Starbucks or something before we got on the road. I could really use a cup of coffee right now to take off some of this chill."

"The closest thing we've got is a bottle of antifreeze back in Holling's utility box."

"Now who's the one with the jokes?" was his rejoinder.

Aidan paused, mentally going through all of the items in her brother's truck utility box.

"You two hold on, Slim! I've got something better for you than jokes!"

Chapter 10

"Where did she go? She wouldn't leave us, would she?" the tanker truck driver asked. He sat with his back pressed against the cliff wall. One leg, bound a few inches below the knee with Darion's bandanna, was stretched out in front of him. The other leg was drawn up so that he could rest his forehead on his knee.

Darion stood with his face turned up to the sky, staring at what had been the one bright spot in this entire night. Now that Aidan had gone, she'd taken the emergency beacon with her.

"No," Darion said with all certainty. "She wouldn't."

"Then she must be as nutty as you are, mister. If I was that gal, I woulda hauled ass out of here. The fuel in the tanker could still go, you know. If we don't get off this rock…"

"Don't worry. We're getting out of here. Aidan said that they're sending out rescue units from all over."

"So I heard. They're at least an hour away, if we're lucky. By the time they get here…" The driver took a deep breath, squaring his shoulders. "Look, mister, there's no reason for you to be stuck out with me. There's still time. You can climb up outta here. Save your own behind."

Darion shook his head resolutely. "Ain't nothin' happening. We're both getting out of here."

"Don't be a fool, man. You go and get that gal outta here. You know she doesn't need to be out here in this storm."

"You heard the lady," Darion reminded him, twisting his mouth into a reluctant smile. "I don't give the orders around here. She does. And she's not going anywhere. I can't make her go, even if I wanted to."

"Both of you are nutty as the proverbial Christmas fruitcake. But I sure am grateful that you two happened along. As bad as it was out there, I didn't expect anybody to be out on the road."

"You were out here."

The driver grinned at him. "That's my job. I was trying to finish my haul and get back before Christmas. An extra bonus in it for me if I got the load delivered early."

"You risked your neck for a check?"

"It wasn't only about the money. I wanted to get back so I could see my family for Christmas. Four children, three girls and a boy. They've given me nine strapping grandchildren and one great-grandchild. That's why I was on the road. What about you?"

"Coming back from the airport. My boss man is laid up with a busted leg so he asked me to pick up his sister."

"You mean you risked your neck for a check?" the driver repeated Darion's own words.

Darion shook his head, grinning at him. "Touché. We were on our way back to White Wolf when—"

"Let me guess." The driver gave a dry, humorless chuckle. "By crashin' my rig, I made you take an unexpected detour."

"We were doing fine following behind you for a while. You were making good time, making a way, keeping the road clear for us, until that last turn. If you don't mind me asking, what happened? What made you go off the road like that?"

"Crazy deer in the road. Three of them, popped up from outta nowhere and crossed right in front of me. I couldn't stop. Couldn't turn. Couldn't run into them. I know from experience what running into a fully grown buck could do to my rig. Tore up my front grill and sent my insurance sky high when I made the claim. Before I knew it, my tank was sliding east and my cab was rolling west."

"How'd you make it out of there?"

"It wasn't planned, I'll tell you that much. I wasn't doing much thinking when I started to roll. Plenty of cursin', though…and when the cursin' stopped, plenty of prayin'…and I ain't usually a prayin' man. You know what I mean, don't you? You're not much of a prayin' man yourself. Are you?"

Darion didn't respond, but looked up into the night sky again, looking for signs of Aidan's return. "I used to be," he said somberly. "But after a while, a man gets tired of talking when it's obvious nobody's listening."

"I never get tired of hearing myself talk," the driver said. "But I can listen, too, when I have to."

After a few minutes, Darion sat down next to the tanker driver and held out his hand.

"Darion Haddock," he introduced himself.

"Lucas Mackenzie. My friends call me Luke."

"Don't take this the wrong way, Mr. Mackenzie. But any other time, I'd say it was a pleasure to meet you."

"Seeing that you scrambled down a mountain in the dead of night, in the middle of a blizzard to find me, I'd be a fool for taking it as an insult. So, given the situation, I figure you earned the right to call me Luke."

"Luke," Darion said agreeably. He paused, staring curiously at the driver. "Do I know you?"

"I don't think so. Why?"

Darion narrowed his eyes, as if trying to remember. "Something about you seems familiar."

"I've got that kind of face, I suppose," Luke said. He reached up, pulled his faded brown trucker's cap from his head, ran this fingers through a shock of snowy white hair, then settled the cap on his head again. "It's possible you know me. Anything's possible. In my line of work, I meet a lot of people. I never know whose path I'll cross. Sometimes more than once. That's why, in my book, it pays to treat people right the first time. You never know when you'll have occasion to see them again."

Darion nodded, accepting the explanation.

"I sure am glad our paths crossed tonight, Darion," Luke said enthusiastically, and squeezed his hand briefly, then withdrew his hand to fold his arms across his chest and tuck them under his armpits.

"Good Lord! Must be nearly twenty below. Cold enough to freeze the balls off a—"

He didn't get the opportunity to finish his sentence before Aidan's voice echoed down to them.

"Yo, Slim! Are you still with me? You're still hanging in there, aren't you?"

"Yeah, we're still here!" Darion stood up and turned his face to the night sky again. Luke didn't have to finish his sentence. Darion knew exactly what he was thinking and was in total agreement. Exposed as they were, the cold cut through his coat, making his entire body tighten and stiffen against it.

Still, he was grateful for the feeling—as miserable as it was. The time to start worrying was when he couldn't feel anything at all. If frostbite set in, he wouldn't be able to complain against the cold. "Where did you go, Aidan?"

"I went back to the truck for a minute."

"Seemed like longer than a minute to me," Darion observed.

"You'd better be glad that I came back at all. I've kept the engine running with the heat cranked up in the truck. It felt *so* good. You don't know how hard it was to get back out here."

"Trust me," Darion said, not minding that his teeth were chattering as he spoke, "we've got a pretty good idea!"

"Listen, Slim. If you can't come up and you won't let me come down, then there's only one other way I can think of to help you. I'm sending something down to you."

"If it isn't that double shot of mocha latte, then I don't need it. And you don't need to be dangling yourself over the edge. Get back to the truck, Aidan, and wait for the rescue units."

"There you go, giving the orders again," she chastised. "I thought we'd established an understanding about that. I'm the one giving the orders. I've got a blanket tied to a rope and bundled up with one of my brother's halters that he had stashed in the utility box. I think the rope is long enough to reach you."

"Did you say you had a blanket?"

"I thought that might get your attention." Her tone was both pleasant and smug. "Yes, I have a blanket with a first-aid kit and one of those emergency flashers wrapped up in it. The blanket isn't very big…and it's got a few moth holes in it. I don't know what good the first-aid kit will do…but I'm sending it all down anyway."

"You'll get no more complaints from us. Don't try to toss

the rope out, Aidan. The wind will snatch it out of reach. Can you come over to your left a few feet and let the length out slowly?" Darion directed. "Lie down on the ground when you lower the rope. You'll have better control."

"Lie down on the ground! Do you know how cold that ground is?" she quibbled.

"I've got a general idea," Darion said sarcastically.

"Fine! I'll lie down on the ground. Let me know when you can see the care package," she prompted.

Darion kept his face trained toward the top of the ridge. It was still too dark to make out anything, so he listened for the sound of Aidan's bundle sliding across the cliff face.

"Letting out the slack," she informed him. "About two feet now…three…going on four."

"How long is that rope?" he wanted to know.

"I'm not sure. It could be eight feet. It could be ten. Will that be enough to reach you?"

"Can't say. Keep letting it out until I say stop."

"Five feet," she counted aloud. "I'm about halfway out of rope, Slim. See anything yet?"

"Not yet. Keep going."

"I think I see something," Luke said excitedly, pointing overhead. "Over there. But it's too far over for you to reach it."

"Aidan—" Darion cupped his hands to his mouth "—come back over to your right some more. That's it. Keep going."

"I'm almost out of rope. Can you reach the blanket yet? If you can reach it, give it a couple of good yanks."

"Not yet. Just a little bit more."

"I can't go much more without letting go of the rope. Maybe if I tie it to the rail…it'll be…long enough to reach…"

"Don't try anything crazy. Don't get too close to the edge, either," he warned.

"Who's doing this? You or me?"

"Does wanting to be the big boss run in your family?" Darion wanted to know. "You sound exactly like your brother."

"If Holling were here, he'd tell you to show a little gratitude while you're being rescued."

Don't worry, Darion thought. If he got out of this jam, he'd show more than a little gratitude.

"Got it!" he alerted her by tugging twice on the rope. "Now you get yourself back into that truck and wait for the rescue units."

"You've twisted my arm," she called down to him. "I'm going. Slim?"

"Yeah?"

"You watch yourself down there. Okay?"

"Like a hawk," he promised. "Go on. Get going, Aidan. We'll be all right."

"You'd better be all right. Because I don't want to hear my brother's mouth when I tell him that I've lost his blanket and his bridle."

"Your concern overwhelms me," Darion muttered as he untied the knot and unrolled the blanket. He knelt on the ledge and stuffed the first-aid kit and the emergency beacon in his coat pocket.

"Here you go, Luke." Darion snapped the dirt and ice from the blanket and held it out to the tanker driver. "I'm not your mama, so you'll have to tuck your own self in."

"What about you?"

"What about me?"

The driver lifted his eyebrow meaningfully at the corner of the blanket.

"I know you don't expect me to snuggle in next to you, do you?"

"It's mighty cold out here, mister. This little strip of cloth might mean the difference between your living and dying."

"Don't think because I've saved your skin that we're a couple now. I'm all right, right over here. I'll take my chances with the rescue units getting here before it comes to us adopting a personal, community property policy. It ain't that kind of a party."

Luke grinned at him. "What's the matter? You think snuggling next to me will make your gal jealous?"

Darion shook his head. "No. It's not like that."

"What do you mean?"

"I told you, never met her, never talked to her before tonight. I'm only the driver…sent out on a three-dog night to pick up the boss man's sister. It's strictly business."

Tucking the bottom of the blanket under his legs, Luke pulled the corner up to his chin and regarded Darion with crinkling gray eyes. "Seems to me that there's more to it than that."

Darion avoided Luke's eyes, pulling out the first-aid kit and searching for antiseptic and bandages. There was only the kind of supplies to treat superficial wounds. He opened up an alcohol-soaked swab and dabbed at the cuts on Luke's face. When he got to the bandages, he had to laugh. He could tell this was a kit meant for kids. He couldn't imagine any of the hands walking around with bright purple dinosaurs stuck to their injuries.

"Take two of these," Darion directed, handing Luke a couple of aspirin.

He popped them in his mouth and ground them between his teeth. "You and your lady make a really fine team."

"I told you," Darion said wearily, "she's not my lady."

"Say what you want. But I can feel the heat between you two."

"What makes you think—" Darion began.

"That there's something between you?" Luke asked, leaning forward and whispering conspiratorially.

"Yeah. Tell me," Darion said as if he were humoring him.

Luke shrugged. "Something in her voice, son. Like the lady said, she could have gotten in the truck and driven away. Left us here, stuck like Chuck, out here on this ledge. But she didn't. She stayed. She stayed when most other folks would've put the pedal to the metal and taken off. Especially with the threat of that tanker going up. Why would she do that if there wasn't something in it for her to stick around for?"

"I guess she's hanging in there because she believes that's what she's supposed to do."

"You don't believe that?"

"It doesn't matter what I believe. My job is to do my job and collect my paycheck."

"Aha! So, it's all about the money, then," Luke said, running his index finger and thumb together in a circular motion, pantomiming the feel of paper money between his fingertips.

Laughing, Darion closed the first-aid kid. "Trust me, Luke. I don't get paid enough for this. It's not about the money. I keep telling folks, it's not always about the money."

"Is she pretty?" Luke asked.

"Excuse me?"

"That lady up there…warming her buns in your truck. Is she good-looking?"

Darion shrugged, feigning nonchalance. "I guess she looks all right."

Luke gave a low whistle. "I think you're full of it. You know she looks better than all right. If you ask me, she sounds like she's hot enough to melt ice!"

Darion's eyes narrowed, clamping down on an emotion that he couldn't quite place yet—couldn't quite accept that he was feeling. It had been a while since he'd felt this way about anything. Let alone a woman. He didn't know Aidan Holling. Still, that didn't stop him from experiencing an unexplainable surge of jealousy. Jealousy, of all the ridiculous things. What was he doing feeling possessive about a woman he didn't have?

Darion sat with his back against the mountain face, his knees drawn up and his forehead resting on top of them. He wrapped his arms around his knees, trying to conserve as much body heat as he could. When he didn't speak for several minutes, Luke called out. "You asleep, boy?"

"No," Darion said, proud of the way he was able to keep his teeth from chattering.

"Don't go to sleep on me, boy. Talk to me."

"I don't feel much like talking, Luke," Darion confessed.

"Either you're going to talk to me or I'm gonna start shouting for that lady friend of yours to talk to me. I'll bet she'll have some conversation for me."

"Like what?" Darion lifted his head and fixed Luke with a less-than-friendly stare.

"I don't know. I don't care. She can recite her ABCs for all the difference it makes to me. I just like the sound of her voice…sorta husky. Sounds like a fully grown woman. Nothing sexier in the world, don't you think?"

"If you say so," Darion acquiesced.

"I *do* say so," Luke insisted. "I can't stand the sound of a woman who wants to sound like a baby. Gets on my damn nerves. I like a woman who speaks with confidence. Like she knows what she wants and ain't ashamed to tell me."

Luke sucked in air through the gap in his two front teeth and shook his head back and forth, as if reliving one of those private moments. "Umm…umm…umm…. I always love it when they tell me what they want."

Darion ground his teeth against Luke's free exchange of information. They might have been trapped together there on that rock, but that didn't mean he had to put up with his innuendos and insinuations. It didn't matter that he barely knew Aidan Holling. He didn't want Luke talking about her that way. He didn't even want him *thinking* about her in that way.

"Does she have a good body?"

"Why are you so interested?" Darion asked, not because he particularly wanted Luke's opinion.

"Gotta do something to take my mind off the cold," he said, giving a shiver that he didn't have to exaggerate.

"I suggest you put your mind on other things, Luke," Darion said, his tone about as frigid as the air swirling around him.

"No offense. I didn't mean to strike a nerve. I was curious as to what would make you want to throw yourself down the face of a mountain. Sometimes the way a woman looks, umm…umm…umm…even the way she smells… can make a man do some real crazy things…like scaling a mountain to impress her. Is that why you came after me…what's that she calls you…Slim?"

"Listen, Luke. The last time I tried to pull a crazy stunt to impress a woman, I was nine years old. I wound up falling out of a tree and needing twenty-one stitches. The only thing that impressed her was my level of stupidity." Darion self-consciously reached up and touched the spot on his scalp where his unbraided hair hid most of the scar. "I told you, I was trying only to help you. And if you want to get off this mountain without a busted jaw, you won't call me Slim again."

Luke laughed. "Sorry, *Mr.* Haddock. I'll leave that one alone. That must be her own special pet name for you. Another thing a pretty woman could do to you that you'd never let another man do… call you by a goofy name. She must be a real beauty. I had this woman in Tulsa once with a set of—" he didn't finish his sentence, but held his hands out in front of him as if palming basketballs. "That girl up there…she got those kinda assets?"

This time, Darion did grin. "You don't give up, do you?"

"Giving up never gets you anywhere, Darion. You spend half of your life giving up and you wind up with half of your life with nothing in it."

"That isn't always such a bad thing," Darion said convincingly. "Some of us would be a lot better off if we didn't have half the crap we have in our lives now. So much wasted time chasing after things…things that don't mean a damn. And once you get them, then what? You're never satisfied. Just looking for ways to collect more junk."

"I wasn't necessarily talking about material things, son," Luke said soothingly. "I'm talking about giving up on people."

"I could do without half the people in my life, too," Darion said sourly.

"You didn't give up on me. And I thank you for it."

"Just taking a page from the book of Holling," Darion said, shrugging.

"Like that gal up there?"

"Yeah, like that gal up there," Darion echoed, staring up at where Aidan had been.

"Don't worry, son. She'll be all right," Luke assured him.

"I hope so…because it'll be my ass if she isn't."

"What kind of ass has she got?" Luke wanted to know.

Darion's laughter rang out. He avoided answering the question by posing one of his own. "You like blondes, Luke?"

"Blondes. Redheads. Brunettes. I'm not picky." Luke sighed and lowered his head against his knee.

"She's blond. I didn't think I liked blondes, either. Not before tonight."

"You do like her, then."

Darion shrugged again. "I have to admit, I'm attracted to her. Even though I'd never met her, I'd heard things about her."

"What kind of things?"

"You know. Things," Darion said evasively. He thought about the topics of conversation. Bunkhouse boys, talking trash knowing good and well that they were never going to get the chance to act out any of those fantasies.

"The kinds of things that are said about a woman when it's just us guys around. Small minds. Small talk. I had this impression of her, so that by the time I picked her up at the airport…everything was all turned upside down. She's not exactly what I expected…if you know what I mean."

"I think I do."

"I'm attracted to her," Darion repeated, as if making himself comfortable with the idea. "And I'm grateful. I'm glad that she stuck around. Who knows what would have happened to us if she didn't."

"Sounds like you've got more than simple attraction on your mind," Luke observed.

"Like what?"

He shrugged. "I don't know. She's your friend. Maybe something along the lines of something more permanent."

"Whoa now! Hold up," Darion said, putting his hands out in front of him. "I wouldn't say that much."

"Why not?"

"Because it takes more than a simple case of gratitude and a tug on my crotch to make a relationship."

"I know of some marriages that have started with less and lasted a lifetime."

"And I know a helluva lot a guys who confused lust with love and got themselves into a worse jam than we're in now. I'm not going out like that."

"I'll tell you what, son, if we do get out of this, I don't care what your gal looks like…for sticking around and sticking her neck out for me…somebody she ain't never met and barely even knows, when I get up there, I'm gonna give that gal a big, sloppy wet kiss." He winked at Darion. "Since she ain't your gal, you won't mind, will you, now?"

Chapter 11

"Now, where in the world are they?"

Sawyer picked up the phone and held it pressed against her ear with her shoulder as she spooned cocoa mix into a mug of steaming milk. Her other hand counted out marshmallows, dropping them one by one into an oversize mug. Her movements were careless, distracted as she paid more attention to the phone than she did to the steaming liquid sitting on the tray in her lap.

"Sawyer…baby…are you trying to make cocoa or pothole-patching tar?" Holling gently clamped his hand over his wife's to stop her from spooning more of the powdered mixture into the mug. She'd kept pace with each unanswered ring on the telephone. One ring. One spoon of powder. Holling figured he'd counted at least ten heaping spoonfuls before he got her attention.

"Sorry, Holling," she murmured hastily, then frowned

when she realized that she'd put so many marshmallows into the mug, they'd swollen and absorbed most of the milk. She used the spoon to poke at the soggy, sticky mess, trying to squeeze some of the milk back into the mug. "I'm worried. This is the third time I've tried to call Darion. And there's still no answer."

When she only succeeded in making the cocoa worse, she leaned over and set the tray on the floor beside the bed.

"Maybe you should wait longer than five minutes before trying to call him again," Holling suggested.

"That's *your* sister out there, Holling," Sawyer reminded him testily. "I'm worried because I haven't heard from them. Why hasn't your sister called us by now? Why hasn't she called me? She should have called me."

"Sawyer, I'm glad that you and my sister are getting along. She's a grown woman. She doesn't need to check in with us."

"Have you looked outside lately, Holling! It's awful. There must be ice three inches thick on the windows and walkways. I'd think you'd show a little more concern. What if something has happened to them?"

"Something like what?"

"I don't know…let me think. Icy roads. Dark night. Sleepy employee behind the wheel. What do you think could happen given those conditions?" Sawyer said, her sarcasm as thick as the ice covering the windows.

"Don't let that active imagination of yours run away with you, Sawyer. Save the drama for your novels. I'm sure they're fine."

"What makes you so sure?" she demanded.

Holling shrugged. "Maybe it's a general sense of goodwill from all of these happy drugs that I'm taking."

"That's not funny, Holling!"

Sawyer threw back the covers, draped her robe over her shoulders and paced in agitation alongside the bed.

"Sawyer…sweetie…calm down. I trust Darion. I wouldn't have sent him out there to get Aida Beth if I didn't. He's a good driver and knows these roads."

"But he sounded so exhausted on the phone at the airport."

"I'm not surprised. That's because after ten minutes with my sister, he probably felt like he'd run a marathon, trying to keep up with all of that crazy talk of hers. She wears me out, too."

"Aha! There you go!" Sawyer pointed at him like a television-drama prosecuting attorney, catching the defendant in an obvious lie.

"Maybe he and Aida Beth started talking. Maybe he got distracted and ran off the road. They could be wrapped around a tree at this very moment…bleeding…unconscious…with no way to contact us. The cell phone is out of arm's reach. Their last breaths puffing out into the winter air…their eyes rolled back into their heads and clouding over…scavengers circling the wreckage, waiting for the flames to die down before they move in to pick their flesh from their broken bones."

She held her hands out in front of her, her thumbs perpendicular to the rest of her fingers as if she were framing the image in her mind's eye.

"Would you listen to what you're saying? You sound like you could use a happy pill or two yourself," Holling observed.

"Oh, you're just grouchy because I ruined your cocoa," she said, poking at the mug with her big toe.

"Lack of cocoa isn't what's got me grouchy," Holling muttered under his breath.

"What's that? What did you say?"

"Nuthin'. Could you hand me that prescription over there?

One more of those little yellow pills and this grouchy mood will pass in a minute or two."

"Holling, I'm serious. If you don't stop talking like that, I'm gonna cut your dosage in half. The doctor said those painkillers weren't addictive. But I have to wonder. Maybe I should forget about reducing your dosage and cut you off altogether!"

"I'm only kidding you, baby." He held out his arms to her in invitation. Sawyer eased back into bed next to him, snaking her arms around his waist.

Lowering his chin on the top of her head, Holling murmured, partly in jest, "With as much lovin' as I'm getting from you these days, a man can sure feel like he's being cut off."

"The doctor said no extreme physical exertion," she reminded him.

"I promise I won't exert myself. Let me lie back and moan a little bit."

"Not being able to participate? That can't be any fun for you," she cooed.

"Oh, yeah. Sure. Having you touch me in all the right places is definitely torture."

"I don't know how you can even think about making love when your sister is out there…missing…no one having heard from them in hours."

Holling sighed through his nose, tilted his head back so that it rested against the headboard. "I was trying to take my mind off of that fact, Sawyer."

"Then you are worried about them?" she insisted.

"No," he said firmly. "No, I'm not."

When Sawyer gave him a disbelieving look, he amended, "But I am curious… What's taking them so long? They should have been here by now. You think the MDT's shut down the roads around White Wolf again?"

Again, Holling lifted his shoulders. "Could be, if it's that bad out there. Turn on the television. Let's see if we can catch the early news."

Sawyer reached for the remote control, flipped past movie channels and infomercials. She stopped flipping, her eyes trained intently on the screen.

"That doesn't look like the news to me," Holling observed.

"Shh!" she quieted him, reaching inside of the nightstand drawer for a pencil and paper. "I've been trying to get the order number of that miniature deep fryer for days."

"For what? You don't cook," he pointedly reminded her.

"I know," she came back, without one iota of embarrassment. "And neither do you. From what Nate and Chale tell me, you've been banned from the kitchen."

"That was only that one time," Holling said defensively.

"I'm not buying this for me. I'm buying it for your father and Chale. This will be the perfect gift for them…and look at that price. For the next ten minutes, it's on sale. I could—"

"You could give me that remote," Holling retorted, reaching out for it. Sawyer held it out of reach, knowing that he couldn't move his leg without some difficulty to reach after her.

"I knew you were more worried about Aidan than you were putting on," she said triumphantly, waving it in front of him, taunting him. "I was pulling your leg, Holling. And yes, the pun was intended. Besides, I ordered those fryers three weeks ago. They're sitting in my closet, already wrapped."

"I know," he retorted with an equally smug grin. "I had the twins poking around in there looking for my Christmas gift. Check the back rear corner of that gift where they pulled aside the wrapping paper. I don't know how well of a retaping job they did."

"Holling!" Sawyer exclaimed. "You're not supposed to be peeking."

"A man's gotta do something, darlin', to occupy his time while he's laid up in bed."

"I can see that, left to your own devices, you'll only get yourself and the twins into trouble. We have to do something about those idle hands of yours."

"I'm open to suggestions," he said, waggling his eyebrows up and down at her.

"Uh-huh," Sawyer said, unmoved by this comic display of affection. As she aimed the remote at the television again, she made a mental note to find a better hiding spot for all of her presents.

She flipped through a few more channels, ignoring the documentary she'd been trying to find the time to watch, the movie she'd already seen a thousand times and several more shopping channels, until she found a station that was showing the news.

"Turn that up!" Holling said excitedly, even as Sawyer's thumb was poised above the volume button.

"Hey, isn't that—" she began, recognizing the on-the-scene reporter. It was the same reporter who had been sent to cover the devastation to Holling's town after a tornado had struck White Wolf over seven years ago. It was the very same tornado that had literally blown Sawyer into town and into the arms of what would become her husband.

"It certainly is…that's my truck!" Holling declared, pointing at the screen to the snow-covered vehicle parked along the side of the road. Emergency flashers were still blinking, yet they were barely visible through the swirl of snow, and the red-and-blue emergency flashers of the rescue vehicles and the hazardous-materials unit parked all around it.

Sawyer and Holling exchanged glances. The expression in her wide green eyes clearly said, *I told you so!*

"I knew it," she said in a breathy whisper. "I could feel it. I knew something was wrong."

Holling grimaced. "Remind me never to make fun of your female intuition again."

"There's your truck," she said, wishing that the camera would pan and cover the entire area. "But I don't see Aidan."

"Or Darion," Holling added.

They sat and watched anxiously as the reporter continued to describe the scene, moving from official to official to get an assessment of the situation. All they would give was twenty-second sound bites that were crafted to be cautiously optimistic. Enough to give sketchy details and still leave the impression that the situation was under control.

"Come on…come on…" Sawyer urged. "Stop all of that chatter and get to the part about the survivors. They have to be there somewhere!"

"More of your female intuition?" Holling said, squeezing her hand in encouragement.

"More like faith," she said.

Chapter 12

"What's happening?" Aidan demanded to know. "Have they pulled them up yet?" She waited behind the bright yellow caution tape as long as she could, anxiously trying to edge her way around the highway patrol officer.

The officer held up her hand, managing to keep Aidan back without putting her hand on her.

"They're working on it, ma'am. I'm gonna have to ask you to stay back behind the line, please." The female patrol officer was several inches shorter than Aidan, but still managed to exude a solid wall of impenetrability. No one was going to get past her until the rescue units told her that it was safe to do so. Not the reporters. Not the curious and crazy onlookers who'd gotten into their vehicles and braved the winter storm to see the wreck for themselves. And certainly not that Amazon towering over her, swinging emotionally from deep concern to irate bitchiness for having been held here against her wishes.

The officer's expression was as frosty as the snow and ice collecting on the rounded brim of her hat. She lowered her head and her steely gaze at Aidan, sending her back behind the line.

Aidan paced back and forth behind the caution tape strung from one patrol car to another. Several times the tape ripped, came free, whipped in the wind. The patrol officer had finished double looping the tape to secure it tightly when she caught Aidan trying to take advantage of her preoccupation by slipping through the line.

"I'm going, I'm going," Aidan muttered. "Instead of hassling me, you should be thanking me. I'm the one who called the accident in, you know."

"And we're all grateful for your civic duty." The patrol's tone was barely a note above sarcasm. "I'm still gonna ask you to wait over there."

She pointed to a spot on the far side of the road. Far away from the other patrol officer, directing traffic away from the accident. Far away from the hazardous-materials team, taking samples of the soil and snow for evidence of chemical spillage.

Aidan was asked to move far enough away so that she could barely see the rescue workers lowering the rope and harness down to Darion and the tanker driver. She was sent away from the camera crews and the reporters, more than one station now, all jockeying for the best position. Portable halogen lights and satellite uplinks and several power cords snaked in and around the parked vehicles.

Aidan backpedaled. And she didn't stop until she was out of hearing range of those driven out from the safety and comfort of their homes to be eyewitnesses to a local disaster. Gawking. Pointing. Waiting for something momentous to happen. Horrendous, even. Aidan shuddered. The image of circling vultures came to her mind. The crowd was waiting—just waiting—for something to happen. Their concerned, hushed voices were a silent scream in her ears as they proclaimed to others waiting along with them that they *hoped* the tanker didn't explode. They *prayed* that the driver was found alive.

Aidan wanted to shout at them that they were all hypocrites. Stupid, two-faced, lying hypocrites. They wanted something terrible to happen. Of course they did. Why else would they drag themselves out there? They wanted to be able to share the tale with those who weren't here.

She stood with her hands thrust deeply in her pockets, shifting her weight from one foot to the other, trying to keep warm.

"You are such an idiot!" she said aloud. Part of her berated Darion Haddock for his misguided heroics. The other insult was directed at herself. Why was she standing out there, suffering miserably in the cold? Why couldn't she go back to the truck and wait inside?

Aidan had remembered to turn off the engine as soon as the emergency crews had started to arrive. Yet, she imagined that even if she couldn't have the heater blowing, at least she'd be out of the weather.

Suddenly, a shout went up from the rescuers hovering around the gap in the highway guardrail. As the winch on one of the emergency trucks continued to grind, shortening the rope attached to a body harness, a sense of urgency collectively clamped down on the rescue crew. They'd been moving with a practiced sense of urgency before. Yet, something had changed. Something wasn't right. Aidan knew it before the first shouts faded in the air.

"Get 'em up! Now!"

"Move it! Move it!"

"Get another tie line on that basket or we'll lose it to the wind."

Something inside Aidan's stomach clenched, like a soda

can in a trash compactor. She pressed her fists to her mouth, keeping herself from crying out.

"No…please, no! Don't let anything happen to him…to them…"

The onlookers collectively surged forward, barely restrained by the patrol officer's sharply barked command. "Stay back!"

"Somebody get those cameras the hell away from here!"

One of the rescuers gestured at a camera operator—who'd somehow worked his way around the caution tape and was aiming his equipment over the chasm to capture those oh-so-crucial, gritty, raw, live moments.

More shouting as two highway patrol officers physically removed the eager journalist from the scene. Accusations and counteraccusations. Protests of the rights of the press and an equally heated suggestion for what that camera operator could do with those rights.

By the time the patrol officers cleared the area of non-rescue personnel, Aidan counted as many as ten workers gathered around the two trucks with their front-mounted winches. They were frantically trying to send down additional support lines, even as one of the winches whined in critical strain, pushed to its speed and safety limit.

A hush fell over the area. Even the howling winds ceased. Aidan thought with an eerie shudder that it was quiet enough for a single shout to be heard over the commotion.

"What the hell is he doing? Get another line on him!"

"We're gonna lose him! Mister, wait! Keep those safety lines on."

Aidan leaned back against the truck for support as she felt her knees give way. One hand clenched against her stomach. She hadn't eaten in several hours. That didn't stop the sick feeling in the pit of her stomach from making her want to retch. "No…"

Closing her eyes, Aidan went into a mental spiral of denial. This wasn't happening. It couldn't be happening. She was dreaming. Maybe she was still on the plane. At any moment, she would wake up. The flight attendant would come by, offer her another undersize pillow or something to drink…and then she'd wake up…and everything would be all right.

Even better than that scenario, maybe she'd never even left Florida. She was at home and in her bed. The one with the luxurious comforter set and matching valance and sheers. She'd fallen asleep, curled beneath the covers and the down pillows with the television on. Some strange drama was playing and somehow infiltrated her dreams. That was it. That had to be it. This nightmare playing out before her couldn't be real.

Part of her wanted to climb into her brother's truck, gun the engine and keep on driving until the memory of tonight's accident faded with the spring thaw. Yet, something kept her rooted to the spot and kept her from bolting. Something stronger than habit. More forceful than her fear. She edged closer to the caution tape as soon as it became clear that one of those rescue baskets was nearing the top. Somebody was going to come out of that ordeal alive.

"Ma'am…ma'am, you'll have to stay back." The patrol officer held her hand out again, speaking in that same professional, clipped tone.

Aidan's gaze swung from the officer's outstretched hand to her severe face.

"Officer," she said slowly, distinctly, keeping her tone low and even. "I know you've got a job to do. And I'm not trying to interfere with that. But that's my friend down there. In a minute, they're going to be pulling those baskets from the ledge. Maybe he's going to be in one of them. Maybe he isn't. Either way, I'm going to be there to see for myself. To stop me, you're either going to have to handcuff me... or shoot me."

There was no threat in Aidan's tone. No belligerence. No malice. She spoke in truth. Plain and simple truth. The officer could hear it in her voice. See it in her face. It didn't matter to Aidan that she'd barely known Darion a few hours. Only a few hours. It didn't seem possible that she could be so emotionally invested in someone that she'd just met. Yet, there she was. Fearing for him, praying for him, as if she'd known him for years.

By the look on her face, the officer would not be able to tell the difference. Aidan's feelings were the same. Her words were proof of the intensity of those feelings. She had to be there. Had to be! And if she had to make a scene in front of witnesses and the camera to do it, she would.

The patrol officer looked up at Aidan, hesitating a moment, before giving a curt nod of her head past the caution tape. To the casual observer, it might appear as if the officer was merely shaking an accumulation of snow and ice from the brim of her hat. Aidan took the ambiguous gesture as permission to proceed. She ducked under the tape, mouthing a grateful *thank you* to the officer before walking rapidly, with purpose and determination, toward the rescue team.

She was several feet away when shouts from the rescuers called out a warning. The team that they'd sent down to strap Darion and the tanker driver to the safety harnesses were on their way up with their survivor. The anchor men guided the rope, grabbed their hands as they hauled them up over the edge.

Aidan felt some of the spring in her step leave her as she approached the scene. She took a few hesitant steps forward. Then a few more. She was close enough to tell that whomever they'd grabbed, they were working with him, still in the basket lying on the pavement. Yet, she was still far enough away that she couldn't quite tell who it was.

"Please be him…please be him…" she whispered to the open air.

Did she feel a twinge of guilt for selfishly wishing that it was Darion who'd been spared? A twinge, yes. But not enough to want to call back her prayers. She didn't know that tanker driver. Hadn't had the opportunity to talk to him. To touch him. And to be touched by him.

That tanker driver hadn't woken in the middle of the night to come after her when her own family had failed. She hadn't felt the tanker driver's arm around her, sheltering her from the cold night. He hadn't worked his way into her dreams, stirring feelings in her that she hadn't felt in a long time.

Only one would be in that rescue basket.

"Please, Lord…please let him be the one." She clasped her hands in front of her, clutching so tightly that her knuckles ached.

"Easy…now! Get that line off of him."

"Help him up out of there."

"Here's that spare blanket, chief. Put that around his shoulders."

"Somebody get a gurney over here!"

Orders were flying from all around her. Aidan's head swiveled back and forth, watching the rescue team in action. They darted in front of her. Behind her. All around her. She stood still, frozen to the spot, as if by not drawing attention to herself, no one would bother to send her back behind the police line. She took a few more steps and found herself less than ten feet away from the huddle of bodies gathered around the basket.

"Help him stand up… Take it easy now… Lean on us, mister, until you get the feeling back in your limbs."

She could see them reach for his arms to help him to a

standing position. Just who *he* was, Aidan still couldn't see. Was it the flurry of snow still swirling all around her? Or was it the sudden misting of her eyes?

"You pull yourself together now, Aida Beth," she chastised herself. "Don't fall apart now." When she blinked, tears of fear and agonizing anticipation pooled behind her eyelids and drizzled down her cheeks. She wiped her nose on her jacket sleeve. Her heart pounded so loudly in her chest, she was certain that she shook the ground she stood on. Aidan imagined that somewhere, some egghead seismologists were taking notes and wondering why they were getting rumblings way off the Richter scale.

Finally, when she could stand the wait no more, the press of bodies around the basket cleared and the first rescuee appeared before her.

"Darion!" Aidan cried out and took off at a full-tilt run toward him. She launched herself into Darion's arms, flinging her arms around his neck.

Sawyer jumped up and pointed at the television as the camera panned over the scene.

"There she is! Oh…oh, my…"

Her excited cry dropped to a surprised murmur as the camera focused on Aidan, clasped in what appeared, at first, to be an enthusiastic embrace. But as the camera zoomed closer, Sawyer raised her eyebrows. More than enthusiastic. More than an embrace. She looked back at Holling, biting her lip as if she didn't know whether to laugh or cry in relief. "I guess I shouldn't have worried. She looks like she's doing all right."

"All right, my foot." Holling snorted. "She'd better be *better* than all right by the time I get my hands on her…making me worry like that."

"What are you complaining about? You said that Darion was a good man, didn't you? You said that you trusted him. Looks to me like your sister is in very good hands."

Holling turned and glared at his wife.

"That's not what I meant when I asked him to pick up my sister!"

Chapter 13

"Somebody had better catch me," Darion warned.

He'd been so cold for what seemed like so long that he could barely feel his legs under him. He didn't know how he found the strength to keep from falling backward as Aidan clung to him. As she rushed forward to embrace him, her momentum had been enough to send them both tumbling back over the side of the mountain.

"Darion!"

She'd launched her body at him, flinging her arms around his neck. At first, Darion had thought that he would fall flat on his backside, dragging Aidan with him. Yet, the longer she held on to him, Darion found a reserve of strength that he hadn't believed he had. He wrapped his arms around her waist, hugged her so tightly that her feet lifted from the ground.

All around him, the snow still swirled. At his back, he could feel the icy wind pounding him. Yet, the feeling rushed back into his arms, warmed by Aidan's presence. All around him there was chaos and confusion. But as he stood there in the center of it all, holding Aidan to him, he wasn't aware of any of it. For now, there was only him and Aidan. With the entire length of her body molded to his, he felt her trembling. Crying and trembling…and trying to speak through gulping gasps.

"When I heard them say they were going to lose one of you…I th-thought you wuh-wuh-were…"

Darion placed an index finger against her lips, stopping her distressed prediction. "I'm all right," he assured. "I'm okay."

He set her on her feet again, brushing away the mingling of snow and tears on her face. Aidan closed her eyes, letting him wipe over her eyelids and cheeks. Then she leaned her forehead on his chest.

"I'm thankful that you're all right, Slim."

"I am…I am all right. Thanks to you." He massaged her shoulders, feeling her trembles subside under his caress.

"You sure you're all right?" she insisted. She reached up, cupped his chin in her hand and turned his face left, then right, checking out his multiple scrapes and bruises. "Those look nasty. You'd better let the paramedics take care of those."

"I'm fine," he assured her. "Trust me. I'm so cold, I don't even feel my face."

Aidan's expression suddenly turned hard. "Good!"

Without warning, she drew back her fist and punched him soundly on the arm.

"What the—!" Darion exclaimed, massaging his biceps where her fist had connected. It hurt more than he'd thought it would through the layers of winter clothing. "What's the matter with you? What did you do that for?"

"That's for leaving me all alone up here, you big jerk!" she explained, stabbing him in the chest with an accusing index finger. "What's the matter with *you,* taking off like that and leaving me all alone? Anything could have happened. Anything!"

"But it didn't, did it?" Darion said through clenched teeth. "You're fine. I'm fine. You're still here, aren't you? You're still alive."

"Don't you know you could have been killed?" She reached up, grabbed two fistfuls of his jacket and shook him. "Don't you ever, ever, ever do anything that stupid again. You hear me?" With some of her fear and anger vented, Aidan rested her forehead against his chest once again.

"I won't," he promised. "I'm sorry I had to do that. But I couldn't sit by and do nothing."

"I understand," she said. "That doesn't mean I have to like it."

"Well, you get your brownie points for being the Good Samaritan, anyway. Thanks to you, Luke's going to be—"

He looked around, confused by the sight of the rescue workers breaking down equipment, storing it back in their vehicles. "What…what's going on?"

"What do you mean?" Aidan asked.

"What do you mean what do I mean? They're packing up and clearing out." He spun around, taking in the activity. "What's taking so long? Why haven't they gotten Luke off the ledge?"

Aidan was at a loss for words. She was so relieved to see Darion that she'd almost forgotten about the reason he'd left her in the first place.

"I don't know," she responded. "Maybe they—" She didn't get the opportunity to finish her sentence.

Darion broke away from her and grabbed one of the EMTs, who was storing away several reflective triangles that had been placed around the critical zone. She was young, barely in her twenties.

"Ma'am, excuse me, can you tell me what's going on here?"

"Sir, you really should see a paramedic about those cuts." She looked up, and almost did a double take at the gash along Darion's forehead. Dried blood was barely contained by the two strips of adhesive cartoon dinosaur bandages.

"Never mind about me." Darion tossed concern for himself aside. "I want to know, why haven't you taken care of Luke?"

"Come on, just let me get you over to the ambulance." When she reached for Darion's arm, he jerked away from her.

"I'm not the one who's hurt!" he insisted. "Luke's the one with the busted leg."

She stared at him for a minute, then turned her gaze on Aidan.

"Maybe you can get him to seek some medical aid."

"Let's go, Slim," Aidan said, linking her arm through his and starting to tug. "She doesn't know."

"Wait a minute, now! Why isn't anyone going after Luke? Luke Mackenzie. Remember him?" Darion stalked away from her.

"Hold up, Slim!" Aidan called out, jogging to keep up with his long strides. She caught up to him as he tracked down another emergency rescuer.

"Sir, wait a minute. Can you tell me, when are they going to get that driver out of there? He's still down there."

This one was a little older, seemed to be more of an authority figure. An older gentleman with a grizzled army buzz cut and weathered features reached out and clasped Darion on the shoulder. "Son, you'd better get that head wound taken care of. Cracks on the skull are nothing to play with."

Frustrated, Darion pointed back to the stretch of highway where the diesel truck had broken through the guardrail. The rescue team that had pulled him up had already left the area. Now, workers from the Montana Department of Transportation had arrived on the scene and were setting up large safety barrels filled with sand to cover the gap until the road could be fixed and signs placed warning of the damage to the guardrail.

"I…am…fine!" Darion enunciated each word distinctly, though a painful throbbing began in his head that he hadn't noticed before. "What I want to know is, why is everybody standing around like a bunch of statues? There's still a man down there!"

The worker shook his head, giving Darion an odd look. Finally, he said, "I'll tell you what. You get yourself over to the ambulance. Let them take care of you. I'll find out what's happened to your friend. Fair enough?"

Realizing that he wasn't going to get a better answer, Darion agreed.

"Fine. I'm going," he snapped. "But it doesn't make any damned sense. What kind of people are you? I stick out my neck to do *your* job and you all sit around with your thumbs up your asses!"

He turned away, making a follow-me motion with his head at Aidan. She looked over her shoulder at the rescuer, giving him an apologetic shrug.

"Ma'am," he called out to her, waving his hand to get her attention.

Aidan paused, then looked up at Darion. "Go on, Slim. Get yourself checked out. I'll see about Luke."

He nodded once, slowly, wearily, continued on, following the flashing emergency lights of the ambulance.

Aidan approached the worker. "I'm sorry about that, sir. I guess he's pretty shaken up. It was terrible watching that tanker go over the side of the mountain like that."

"I don't doubt it," he agreed. "But you should make sure that he gets proper medical attention. From the looks of that scalp, he's lost some blood. Might even have a concussion. Were you two involved in the accident?"

"No. Just the tanker driver. When Darion took off after him, he wasn't injured. That is, he didn't have a head wound. Though, I can't vouch that he wasn't a little touched in the head. I mean, what kind of a sane person would go charging off like that? I was so mad when he left me out here, all by myself. So dark and cold. Leaving me stranded in the middle of a freakin' blizzard! Maybe he got that injury going down the mountain after Luke. He did risk his life, you know. I guess Darion doesn't want that effort to be in vain. He wants to make sure that Luke gets taken care of. It was a miracle to find that he'd survived the crash and—"

"Ma'am…ma'am!" the worker interrupted her, holding up his hands, palm outward, making the slowdown motion. "I didn't want to be the one to tell your friend. That is, not in the condition that he's in."

"Tell…tell him what?" Aidan stammered, though she had a sinking feeling that she knew what that rescuer was so reluctant to say.

"That tanker driver, what did you say his name was?"

"Darion said that his name was Luke something. Macintosh… McManus… No, it was…um…Mackenzie." Aidan snapped a finger in remembrance. "Luke Mackenzie. That was it."

The rescuer shrugged fatalistically. "I'm sorry to be the one to tell you. But that driver didn't survive the crash."

"What?! Oh, no!" Aidan cried out. "Oh, that poor man. Is that why they didn't send down another rescue basket?"

"Wasn't any need. There was only one of them on that ledge, anyway."

"What? No…no, you're wrong. There were two of them…Darion and Luke. I heard them talk to me…call out to me…Maybe he…uh…got off the ledge somehow and made it back to his truck before you guys got here. I don't know. I wasn't with them the whole time. I was waiting back in my vehicle, trying not to freeze to death."

"Ma'am, I can't say what you heard or didn't hear. I've only been here a while. But I do know this. We sent a team down there to check out that diesel truck, to spray it down to make sure that it didn't go up in flames…and if my reports are right, the driver of that tanker truck never made it out of there alive. The coroner has been dispatched to come and retrieve the body."

"There has to be some kind of mistake," Aidan insisted.

"No mistake. The name you gave me matches with the driver's license and registration of the person that was pulled from the tanker. Luke Mackenzie."

"But Darion—"

"I told you, cracks on the head like the one he has are nothing nice. Couple that with the cold, near frostbite…"

"Darion's not crazy! And neither am I. I know what I heard. I heard Luke Mackenzie down there on that ledge."

The rescuer took a step back, holding up his hands again. "All I know is what my people told me. Maybe he was there. Maybe he wasn't. The fact is, he's not there now. Right now, he's probably on his way to the county morgue. I'm sorry, ma'am. I really am."

Aidan's shoulders slumped. What in the world was she going to tell Darion?

Slowly, she made her way through the maze of trucks and reporters and gawkers. Aidan was thankful that the patrol officers were still on their jobs. Still sealing off the area from the more persistent onlookers.

She came up to Darion as the paramedic was applying a strip of adhesive tape onto his head to seal the wound.

"Well?" Darion demanded. "What did he say? Did you find out anything about Luke?"

"Um…yes," she said hesitantly. "He said…uh…that Luke was…" She mentally scrambled around in her head for the right words. "He said that Luke was being taken care of," she finished lamely. "He said not to worry. And that everything's going to be all right."

The tension released from his body was almost visible. Aidan watched his shoulders slump, his head lower until his chin almost touched his chest.

When she walked up to him, Darion slowly lifted his arms, embraced her tentatively. When she didn't move, didn't shake him off, he sighed deeply, lowered his chin to rest on top of her head. Darion caressed her back, soothing her. Aidan responded immediately, squeezing him tighter, turning her face so that her cheek pressed against his chest.

"Take me home, Slim," she said, her voice strained. "I want to get off this mountain. I want to go home!"

"I'm trying, Aidan," he replied. "Believe me, I am."

"This must be what hell feels like," she complained. "Being so close to home, so close to warmth and rest…so close I can almost taste it…but I can't seem to get there!"

"You folks live in White Wolf?" the paramedic asked, removing his rubber gloves with a snap and disposing of them in the waste receptacle meant for biohazards.

Aidan nodded. "You know that song 'I'll be home for Christmas'? Well, that's what I'm trying to do. Trying to get there. Though, with the way things are going, it'll be Christmas 3006 before I make it home."

"Don't know if you've been told yet, but they've been rerouting traffic off the spur into White Wolf through Cut Bank. That's why it took so long for us to get here."

"Why?" Aidan asked.

"What's going on?" Darion added.

"A slide took out a good section of road about fifteen miles up the road from here. Happened about four hours ago. Believe it or not, somebody must've been watching out for you folks. If you hadn't been delayed by *this* accident, you probably would have been caught up in that slide. I hear as many as six other vehicles got up in it. And we ain't found a survivor yet."

Aidan felt the air squeeze from her lungs. She was dizzy, disoriented and desperately needed to sit down. She leaned on Darion for support.

He wrapped his arms around her shoulder, drawing her close.

"No, sir. Not the night to be traveling, is it?" the paramedic went on conversationally.

"No," Aidan murmured. "I guess not."

"But you guys made it all right. If I were you, I'd count my lucky stars and get the heck off the road!"

Chapter 14

Aidan had her doubts about the kind of roadside motel that intentionally misspelled *road* in its name. She supposed that if she weren't so completely exhausted, she would have pointed out that fact to the night manager.

She stood next to Darion, bleary-eyed and ill-focused, as the desk clerk interrogated them, his questions thinly disguised as friendly chatter. He paused long enough to compare the scrawl of Darion's signature on the motel guest card with his driver's license, and the signature on the back of her brother's credit card. It was obvious the signatures didn't match.

"I had a cousin who worked out at the Holling's Way ranch once. His name is Wayne Quincy. You know him, Mr.…er…" He consulted the driver's license again. "Mr. Haddock."

Wearily, Darion leaned his elbows on the front desk and massaged the bridge of his nose with his thumb and index finger. "No, I can't say that I do. People kinda come and go often."

"Yeah, I imagine that they do. Seasonal work and all," the night manager said. "We get that same thing around here…college kids looking for a quick buck. Single parents trying to make ends meet. Me, I've been working the desk for almost four years. Seen a lot of people come…seen them go. Yes, sir. All types. But I suppose it takes all types to make a world, doesn't it?"

Darion made a noncommittal sound. It might have been agreement. It might have been him simply clearing his throat.

The clerk looked down again at the credit card. Then he tapped out a couple of items on his keyboard. Over the desk, Aidan couldn't see what he was doing. For all she knew, he could have been playing solitaire.

"No, Cousin Quincy didn't last six months out there."

"It's hard work. Not for everyone," Darion said patiently. At least, on the surface he appeared to sound patient. Aidan would have smiled if the muscles in her face didn't hurt so much with fatigue. If she closed her eyes, she could almost hear her brother talking. Holling sounded exactly like that when he was on the edge of going off. Her brother could always be superpolite, even when he was two seconds away from pounding you to a pulp.

"Me, I like the cushy inside jobs. None of that hard labor for me. The worst I've got to look out for is a paper cut." He laughed, raising a finger wrapped in a bandage.

As tired as she was, Aidan wanted to reach over that desk and slap some sensitivity into that clerk. What was he griping about an insignificant paper cut for? He couldn't have missed the bandage on Darion's head.

"Does that finger stop you from typing?" Aidan asked pointedly. She hooked her arm through Darion's and moved closer to him. She did so as much to prop him up as because she needed support herself. Darion covered her hand with his and squeezed gratefully.

"You folks look like you've been on the road a long time," the clerk commented. "Sorry to keep you waiting for so long. The computers are a little slow tonight."

"We're very tired," Aidan spoke up. "It's been a rough trip from the airport. Maybe you heard it on the news…there were several accidents caused by the weather."

"Yes, indeed. Seems like we just got those roads fixed and now we've got to spend our hard-earned money on more taxes to repair them again."

He pretended to keep his eyes trained on the monitor, his fingers still occasionally tapping on the keyboard; but Aidan saw him lift his eyes to give her a cursory once-over. She could see him mentally checking her image against her own driver's license picture. Her hair was different on the driver's license photo. And she was several pounds heavier in the photo. Who was she kidding? More than several pounds. There might as well have been two people in that photo.

Any other time, the desk clerk's delaying tactics while he verified the credit card would have been amusing. Even self-gratifying. She'd worked hard, extremely hard, to lose her weight, tone up those loose muscles. And though Aidan figured she still had a way to go, the appreciative stares she sometimes received were the extra validation she needed to keep up her efforts. But tonight, she wasn't amused. Now, she was annoyed. She was tired and hungry. Homesick and frightened. Her nerves were worn down to a frazzle. A frazzle of a frazzle. Either he was going to let them have the room or not.

She placed her hands on the top of the check-in desk, and

used the same tone she'd used with that patrol officer when she'd stood in the way of her getting to Darion's rescue team.

"Sir, is there a problem here?" she asked.

"Ma'am?" He looked up from the monitor, with eyebrows raised.

"With us getting a room," she clarified. She didn't know how he had the nerve to look surprised at her tone. If he'd worked there for as long as he'd said he had, he must have known that people only had a certain tolerance for being kept waiting.

"No, ma'am. The computers are slow."

"Maybe it's operator error," Aidan suggested nastily.

"Aidan," Darion said in quiet warning, rubbing her soothingly in a circular motion between her shoulder blades.

"No, don't *Aidan* me!" she snarled, then turned the full brunt of her ill humor back onto the desk clerk. "Look, I know it's late. And I know that you're only trying to do your job. But look at us! Will you take a good look at us? We're filthy, cold, and about two seconds from collapsing from sheer exhaustion. If you had been watching the news, sir, you'd know that it was us who were involved in one of those weather-related accidents. If you're so freakin' concerned about authorization on the credit card, why don't you call the ranch. Ask for my brother Jon-Tyler Holling. His name is on the card. His number is in the phone book. Go ahead. Call him. Or don't. Either you're going to let us have a room or you're not. Either way, don't waste any more of our time!"

The night clerk pressed a key on the keyboard, causing a bill to spit out from a small printer beneath the desk. He pushed the paper across the desk along with a pen bearing the motel's name and logo.

"Sign here, please," he said stiffly, directing the comment

to Darion. "I'm sorry that you've had such a hard time tonight. Were you folks caught in that avalanche?"

"No," Darion admitted. "We were involved in another accident."

"The one with that tanker truck?"

"That would be the one," Darion said distractedly. He picked up the motel bill, scanning it before signing.

The night clerk tsk-tsked, shaking his head. "A shame what happened to that driver, busting through the rail like that."

Aidan's eyes widened, wishing she could do something to shut that clerk up.

"What room number is that?" she broke in, trying to change the subject.

"Room 137." The clerk answered her question and kept on talking without a break. "The reporters say that it's a miracle that his truck didn't go up in flames."

"Yeah, he was pretty shaken up," Darion said.

"Is that room on the ground or on the second floor?" Aidan asked, snatching up the keys that the clerk laid on the desk for them.

"Ground floor. When you go out this door, make a left around the side of the motel and then another left. Room 137. It's about midway down."

"Thank you," Aidan said, nodding once at the night clerk and tugging on Darion's arm to pull him toward the exit. "Come on, Slim. Let's go catch some z's before the sun comes up."

"Hang on a minute," Darion laughed. He waited for the clerk to pass back their licenses and the credit card.

"Shaken up? Mister, you've got a gift for the understatement," the clerk remarked.

"What do you mean?"

"About that tanker accident. Shaken up? Yeah, like a

frog in a blender. They said on the news that poor guy was dead before he hit the ground. Neck snapped like a twig. Chest all caved in, punctured lung, broken leg. He was a real mess."

Darion swiveled a hard glare to Aidan. "You don't say," he said harshly. "No, I hadn't heard that."

"Don't you watch the news?"

"I guess we were too busy ducking news cameras and gore-seeking reporters," Aidan retorted. "Like I said, we were right there when it all went down…er…I mean, when it all happened. Right, Darion?"

Darion didn't respond. He took the bill and the credit-card receipt, folded them slowly, deliberately, glaring at Aidan. He pressed his index finger and thumb along the fold, creating a sharp crease before sliding the papers into his inner jacket pocket. Only then did he follow behind Aidan.

She'd held on to the keys to the truck, after driving from the scene of the accident. Darion had offered to drive back, but she'd tapped him lightly on the forehead, suggested that he probably wasn't in the best condition.

So, armed with the highway patrol's warning and directions to the nearest motel, she somehow made their way into Cut Bank—merely miles away from her final destination. It might as well have been half a world away. After she pulled up in front of their motel room, she rested her forehead against the steering wheel.

"Oh, thank God!" Aidan gave a sigh of relief that she felt all the way down to her toes. Maybe she wasn't home yet, but at least she was off the road. She sat there for several seconds, letting inertia take her over. If she didn't do something fast, she knew that she'd fall asleep right there in the seat, a few feet away from the warmth and comfort of their motel room.

The only things keeping her awake were the waves of white-hot anger she could feel emanating from Darion. Still resting her forehead on the steering wheel, she turned her head to look at him.

Darion sat staring with stony silence straight ahead. He rested his arm on the dashboard. His fist was balled and his mouth pressed against it as if he were, by sheer force of will, keeping the things he wanted to say—and knew that he shouldn't—safely behind clenched teeth.

"I was going to tell you," Aidan said without preamble. She reached out and touched his shoulder. When he flinched, Aidan drew her hand back.

"So, why didn't you?" he demanded.

"It...it wasn't the right time," she finished defensively.

"You shouldn't have kept something like that from me, Aidan," Darion admonished her.

"I know," Aidan said dejectedly. "But you'd already been through so much, Slim."

Darion muttered something under his breath, something she couldn't quite catch. Something that almost sounded like *you don't know the half of it.*

"What?" She prompted him to repeat what he'd said.

"Nothing," he muttered curtly. He closed his eyes and leaned back in the seat. "It doesn't matter."

"If it means anything, I'm sorry," she said.

"It doesn't," he said in a flat, indifferent tone that bothered Aidan even more than his anger.

She threw up her hands, literally and figuratively. There was no placating him. Not while he was in that mood.

Lordy, if he doesn't remind me of my brother, Aidan thought in bitter amusement. Holling and Darion might as well have been cast from the same mold. She knew that they were both grown men, but they could be such babies when they wanted to be! When something didn't go their way, first came the cold, stony silent treatment. The pouting. Yes, she should have told him about his friend. She would have eventually. But it hadn't been the time. She thought she was doing him a favor by not heaping one more pile of troubles on him. And this was the thanks she got?

Aidan managed to dredge up a little righteous indignation of her own.

"You know what, Slim, I don't want to fight with you tonight. Not now. I'm too tired. Can we call a truce, if only for tonight?"

"Only on one condition."

"Fine. If it'll get us inside that room and to sleep that much faster, give me your condition!"

"Your brother trusted me to take care of you, Aidan Holling."

"And?" She made a hurry-up gesture with her hands to make him come to the point.

"I want you to trust me, too."

"You don't think I trust you?" she said in disbelief. "How could you say that? Darion, I let you—a perfect stranger— pick me up from the airport. Then I fell asleep, for goodness' sake, and let you drive me to parts unknown. Do you think I had any idea where I was when you went skidding off the side of the road? That highway wasn't there the last time I was here in Montana. If that isn't trust, I don't know what is."

"That was trusting me to do my job," he clarified. He looked around, as if he were searching in the open air to find the right words. "Like you'd trust a cab driver to get you to your destination. I want you to trust *me!*" he said fervently, tapping his chest with his hand. "Trust the man. If there's something I need to know, you tell me. Don't hold out on me.

Tell me the truth. All of it, whether you think I can handle it or not. Do you think you can do that for me?"

Her eyes widened, then she gave him an affable smile. "I can do that."

"Now we can go inside."

She nodded, then reached out once more. "Before we go in there, Slim, I gotta know something."

"What is it?"

"You're not going to get all funny on me, are you?"

"What do you mean?"

"I didn't ask the clerk if this last room was a single or a double. It's going to be tricky enough if it's a double. If it turns out that it's only a single bed, I'm not going to have a problem with you, am I?"

Darion shifted uncomfortably. "Sleeping on the floor is no problem, if that's what you mean. Believe me. I've slept in worse places."

Aidan lifted her head, burst into laughter. "You are such a nutcase," she teased him. "I wouldn't make you sleep on the floor, Slim. What kind of a person do you think I am? I'm sure the bed's plenty big enough for the both of us." She pinched his arm. "From the look of you, I'm sure you don't take up much room."

"I'll stay on my side," he promised. "Anything else you need to know?"

"Are you a light sleeper?"

"Mostly."

"I snore," Aidan confessed.

"I'll cover my ears."

"And I'm a blanket hog. I like to curl up."

"Then we'll call to the front desk for extra blankets."

"And extra towels. I can't wait to get into a hot bath."

"Anything else?"

"No, I think that about covers it," she confessed.

"Good."

"Good," she echoed.

"One more thing you forgot to add," he reminded her.

"And that is?"

"You wake up grouchy."

Aidan gave him a wide, saucy smile, then winked at him. "Not necessarily. It all depends on how I go to bed."

"That trust thing," he began.

"Uh-huh?"

"Let's build on it a little at a time. Some things I don't want to know. Not until we've known each other for…oh, at least a week."

Darion opened the truck, pulled out her few bags, while Aidan hurried to open up the room. The first thing she did upon entering was to start the heater. She adjusted the temperature to maximum heat, maximum airflow.

As Darion stepped through the door, she took inventory of the room.

"Looks like you're granted a reprieve, Slim," she said, patting him on the back as he passed by her. "Two beds. Sitting room. Kitchenette. I suppose if we have to stay holed up here until the weather and the roads clear, this isn't such a bad place to be."

"Do you think there's anything in that fridge?" Darion asked, nodding at the kitchenette.

Aidan put her hand on her abdomen and squeezed to muffle the sound as the mention of food made her stomach gurgle.

"Are you hungry?" Darion asked.

"I could eat," Aidan admitted. "Why? You've got a T-bone tucked inside your jacket pocket?"

"Nope."

"How about a bologna sandwich. I'd settle for that."

"I'll see what I can do. I might be able to get the desk clerk to open the inn café or even the convenience shop to give us a few things to tide us over."

"I don't know," Aidan said doubtfully. "That clerk didn't seem to be the trusting type."

"Maybe you ought to turn more of your charming personality on him," Darion suggested. "That ought to convince him."

"You think so?" Aidan said, lifting her eyebrows.

"No," Darion replied. "You were a little lacking in the finesse and social graces department back there with him."

"You don't pull any punches, do you, Slim?" Aidan said, plopping down on one of the beds. She fell back, spreading her arms and letting out a contented sigh. "Oh, this feels so nice right now. I want to curl up in the blanket and hibernate like a bear for the next three seasons."

"Before you do, you may want to bathe first."

"Are you trying to say I stink?" Aidan said in mock offense, peeking at him with one eye.

"We're both a little dusty. I'm only thinking about the cleaning staff, who'll have to put the linens in the laundry. You go on and bathe first," Darion offered. "I'll go foraging for food."

"Nuh-uh. You go ahead," she responded through a deep yawn. "I'll just lie here for a minute…just a minute…I'll be up in just a minute…" Her voice trailed off as her breathing deepened.

"Not sure what good taking a shower will do," Darion said aloud to the quiet room. "I'll just have to put on the same filthy clothes."

Aidan propped up her head. "Believe it or not, I might have something that'll fit you. I didn't throw out all of my big-girl clothes. I think I've got a big T-shirt that I use as a sleep shirt."

Darion's mouth lifted at the corner. He shook his head. "You want me to wear your T-shirt?"

Aidan grinned at him. "You sound like you have something against wearing women's clothing."

"Not something I want getting around the bunkhouse boys," Darion agreed.

"Relax, Mr. Testosterone," she said, pulling herself to an upright position. "Your secret's safe with me. Toss me that backpack over there," she directed. Darion scooped it up from the floor where he'd dropped it, then tossed it underhanded at her.

"How much hush money am I going to have to shell out to stop you from telling the whole world that you made me wear women's underwear?" he asked.

Aidan reached into her bag and tossed out an extra-long T-shirt. "It's Hanes. Big and tall for men. Check the label if it makes you feel any better."

Darion caught the shirt in midair. "Thanks."

"I'm the one who should be paying you to keep my secret," Aidan said, giving a self-conscious chuckle.

"Why is that?"

"I'm not ashamed to admit that when I bought that shirt a couple of years ago, it was almost too small for me."

Darion held it up in front of him, raising it high enough so that Aidan's head appeared about where it should have been if she were wearing it.

"Yes, all the big-and-tall shops know my name. That includes women's and men's shops," she said, lifting her chin and staring at him, glaring at him, and daring him to make an offensive remark. "You think I want the whole world to know that I had to buy men's clothing to find something comfortable and fashionable that fit?"

"It doesn't fit you now," Darion observed. "Why do you keep it with you? All that's in your past now."

"Those who don't remember history are doomed to repeat it," she said. "I keep it to remind me where I was and where I am and where I could have been."

"Could have been?" Darion echoed.

"That's right. Could have been. You think it was vanity that made me lose all that weight, Slim," she scoffed. "It was medical."

Darion sat on the opposite bed, facing her, his expression openly concerned.

"What happened?"

Aidan lay down again, staring up the ceiling with her fingers laced across her abdomen. "You don't know what it feels like to be minding your own business one day and the next to find yourself in a hospital. Just *this* close to dying." She pinched her index finger and thumb together. "You know, Slim, I was perfectly fine with my life as a plus-size woman until it almost killed me."

Darion folded the T-shirt and set it on the bed beside him. "I guess everything happens for a reason. If you hadn't kept this shirt with you, I'd be sleeping—"

"Au naturel?" Aidan suggested, with a lift of her eyebrow.

"In the same filthy clothes that I'm wearing now," Darion corrected.

"And you have the nerve to suggest that I reek," Aidan quipped. She pulled a few toiletry items from her backpack, a gray, ribbed, sleeveless T-shirt and lounging pajama pants with tiny Frosty the Snowman images all over it. She started for the bathroom, looking back over her shoulder. "While you're out foraging for food, I'll try to save you some hot water."

"Take your time," Darion advised. "And make sure you use plenty of soap. We could always ask the maid service for more."

Aidan closed the bathroom door behind her, but not before offering her own terse suggestion on what he could do with that soap.

Chapter 15

It took Darion longer than it should have to pick from the limited selection in the motel-lobby convenience store. Vacuum-packed sandwich meat; a small tub of pimento cheese spread; an assortment of juices; sodas and beef jerky; and all of the gum or candy he could want. He supposed he could have waited until the café attached to the motel opened. Yet, the convenience store was open 24-7 and they were hungry now! The food in the convenience store wasn't exactly gourmet, but it would stop the pangs.

Darion almost laughed. When had he become so choosy about where his meals came from? It was barely six months ago when his options had been more limited than this—he could either beg for food or scavenge for throwaways.

His pickiness wasn't as much about hunger of the stomach as it was hunger of the soul. He needed time away from the room, away from Aidan and the thought of her in the shower.

The image of her walking around in men's clothing was enough of a teaser. She'd had to plant the image of her bathing in his head, too.

Darion knew the moment she turned on the shower that he'd better find a way to put some distance between him and Aidan. Through the paper-thin door, he could hear almost every move that she made. He'd heard the shower rings slide against the curtain rod as she'd pushed the curtain back. He heard her sharp cry of surprise and delight as superheated water hit her skin in a massaging spray. Darion had listened for the changes in the water splashes as she'd adjusted the showerhead nozzle.

From that point, he'd let imagination take over where his other senses of sight and smell and touch had been hindered by the closed door. Just as he'd imagined her nearly nude, lying on the beach, coiled around him, he'd had no trouble at all visualizing how the sudsy water streamed down her bronze body, her own hands following in its wake. His undoing had been her singing to herself. He couldn't make out words, but he could follow the rise and fall of notes of a pleasant soprano. A siren's song. Darion had found himself unwittingly, unwillingly standing and walking toward the bathroom door. He hadn't come back to his senses until he'd found himself standing there, his hands on the doorknob, only a half turn away from walking in on her.

When he'd found himself in that position, he'd yanked his hand away and spun around in the opposite direction and started for the door. The door that wasn't as likely to lead him into as much trouble. He'd needed time to clear his head. He hadn't even driven down to the motel lobby, but had rebuttoned his jacket, settled his hat low over his eyes and walked back.

After he picked up a few things that he figured wouldn't give them food poisoning until they could have a proper breakfast, he spent some time lingering by the shelf that offered him more assortments of toothpaste and deodorants than it did dairy products.

He tossed in a couple of items for himself, a toothbrush and disposable razor, and took his purchases up to the register to be rung up.

The little lady behind the cash looked as if she'd only been up for a few hours. Her makeup was fresh but applied as if she'd been still half-asleep when she'd done it. A steaming cup of hot coffee and a half-eaten prepackaged sausage and biscuit sat within her hand's reach.

She ran each item in front of the scanner, dropping them into a plastic bag.

"Nine seventy-five," she said, giving him the total. "Will that be all, sir? Sir?" she prompted, when Darion didn't respond, but stared at the shelf behind her head. "Will that be all?"

"Yes," Darion said, lowering his gaze. He lifted it again, meeting the girl's eyes directly. "No," he corrected himself. "I'll take a box of those."

"These?" She pointed to the box that Darion indicated.

"Yes," he repeated.

She twisted around, reached over her head, dropped the box into the bag and gave him the new total.

"Thank you."

Darion could hear himself speaking to the lady. He could see himself handing over the credit card to pay for the purchases. But he couldn't reconcile himself to the fact that yes, it was him, who had knowingly, willingly, used the boss's credit card to buy a box of condoms that he fully intended to use with the boss's sister.

"Thank you, and come again," the girl said through a barely stifled yawn.

Darion wanted to laugh at her, at the irony and the completely unintentional double entendre her simple salutation offered. He grabbed the bag and started for the exit with a nod at the desk clerk.

Though he'd bought the condoms, he was counting on a different kind of getting lucky. He'd been gone for thirty minutes. More than enough time for Aidan to have showered, changed and climbed into bed. Maybe, if he was lucky, she'd already be asleep, curled up peacefully in that fetal position she seemed to enjoy. If his luck held, he could slip inside, grab his own shower and climb into bed before she realized that he was back.

When Darion made it back to the room, he rapped on the door with his knuckles before inserting the key in the lock and slowly swinging it open.

"Aidan?" he called out to her. "Are you dressed? Can I come in?"

The entire suite was quiet, the lights dimmed. No radio chatter. No muted glow from the television. After he passed through the sitting area to the kitchen, he put the food items in the miniature refrigerator. He entered the sleeping area, pausing in the doorway.

As he'd hoped, Aidan was already in bed. She slept on her side with her blanket pulled up to her shoulder. Somehow, finding her already asleep didn't give him the satisfaction and the sense of relief he'd thought he'd have. Part of him was tempted to make a noise, slam a door, cough out loud, drop a shoe—anything to startle her awake. Darion tried to tell himself that since he'd gone through the trouble of getting her something to eat, she should at least stay awake long enough to appreciate it. But that wasn't the real reason he was irritated. And he knew it. The other, more truthful part of him wanted to be there to watch her come from the shower, her skin glistening with moisture, either from the shower or her body lotion, and climb into bed. Even from several feet away, he could smell traces of her body wash. Jasmine. It was the same scent that had seduced him as she'd rested against him on that grueling drive from the airport.

No sense in bitching about it now, Darion berated himself. He'd had his chance. He could have been there when she'd gotten out of the shower. If he'd pushed the issue, he could have been in there with her, in the shower. Instead, he'd chosen to do the noble, responsible thing and stay out of the room while she'd undressed.

As Darion stepped between the two beds to pick up the sleep shirt Aidan had loaned him, he confessed to himself that he wanted to reach out and touch her hair, to see if it felt as silky as it looked. Of course he wanted to touch her. More than touch alone. Why else would he have bought those condoms? It was in anticipation of doing more than watching her. He stood by her bedside, not speaking, barely daring to breathe, watching over her, and willing his secret desires to make their way into her dreams. He'd done it before. He could do it again.

While she'd slept in the truck and he'd imagined them coiled together on some deserted island, she must have sensed those feelings then. She'd wrapped her arms around him, embraced him, caressed him, and filled the small confines of the truck with the scent of sexual heat. Mental telepathy. Pheromones. Call it whatever you wanted, Darion didn't care what label anyone could put on it. The truth of the matter was he wanted her and she'd responded.

He stood in the space between their two beds, feeling like a total stranger in his own skin as he slowly reached forward and brushed her cheek with the back of his hand.

Who was he? It couldn't be Darion Haddock, who, a few hours ago, had wrestled with his conscience and his commitment to his boss.

I trust you, Darion.

The echo of his boss's affirmation was drowned out by his own voice.

"Aidan," he murmured. "Aidan, wake up. I brought you something."

And it's called gently ribbed and lubricated for comfort. Darion thought about the box of condoms still in the plastic convenience-store bag clutched in his hand.

Aidan stirred slightly, reaching up to touch the hand that brought her gently to wakefulness. Her eyelids fluttered open.

"Hey, Slim," she said, holding her jaws together to keep from yawing in his face. "Where'd you go off to?"

"To the lobby store for a few minutes," he answered.

"Seems like more than a few," she teased him, reminding him of his claim when she'd left him to go back to the truck for rescue supplies.

"Are you still hungry? I can make you a sandwich," Darion offered.

Her eyelids drooped closed again. "Nuh-uh…I'm too tired to eat."

"Well, it's there if you want it."

I'm here if you want me, he added mentally. "I'm going to go wash some of this road dust off me." *Why don't you get out of that bed, Aidan, take off your clothes and join me. You wash my back and I'll take my own sweet time washing your entire irresistible, luscious, make-a-man-risk-a-beat-down body.*

Darion couldn't stop the thoughts from churning in his head. It was only a matter of time before thoughts communicated to action. And action transmuted to trouble. He took his hand away, then backed up a few steps to see if his unspoken wishes stirred a reaction within her.

Nothing. Not even another fluttering of an eyelid. Maybe that dream pipeline only flowed one way, he conjectured. There was no denying that she had the power to affect him, even in her sleep. Even now, as she lay curled and comfortable underneath the covers, he acknowledged that ability. He'd wanted to turn the tables, to make her want him. Yet, he was the one standing there, foolishly agonizing and hoping that she'd wake up and respond to him.

I've got it bad! Darion harshly diagnosed himself. Crush. Lust. Love jones. Whatever it was, he needed to find a cure. Fast! The longer he was out here, alone with this woman, the harder it was going to be to disguise his lack of self-control.

He heard her draw a deep breath, then curl her arm underneath her pillow. Aidan Holling was out for the count, and there was nothing he could do about it other than accept the fact that he might get some much-needed sleep after all.

Chapter 16

Aidan was jolted out of a sound sleep. She sat up in bed, stared around her in total confusion. Her heart thudded in her chest so loudly that, at first, she didn't hear the distraught ramblings of Darion lying in the bed across from her.

She glanced over, squinted in the darkened room. From the crack in the curtains, she could tell it was morning, though it took her some time to orient herself so that she could find the small clock. She fumbled for it on the nightstand and turned it to face her. It was after ten in the morning.

Ten o'clock! How could it be so late so soon? It seemed as though she'd just climbed into bed. She must have slept hard: the bed covers were barely disturbed. That wasn't like her at all. Usually by now, she would be all twisted up in the covers.

Like Sleeping Beauty over there, she mused. Aidan turned her attention back to Darion, watching him writhe on the bed, moaning and swinging out against foes that only he could see trapped behind his eyelids and given extra-menacing abilities by the power of his subconscious mind.

"Slim?" Aidan called to him, unsure of whether she should try to wake him. When he didn't even register her presence in the room, Aidan picked up one of her pillows and tossed it at him. It bounced off his leg and landed on the floor.

"I'm not touching that one with a ten-foot pole," she told herself. She wasn't going to try to wake him up. If she thought she woke up mean, she could only imagine how Darion would be if wakened abruptly from a nightmare.

Aidan pushed the covers back and swung her legs off the edge of the bed. Rather than wake him, she decided to pick up her pillow, grab her blankets and relocate herself to the sitting-room area. She was pretty sure that the couch folded out to a sleeper sofa. Even if it didn't, it looked comfy enough. As long as she couldn't hear him, she could go back to sleep and finish out the rest of her own pleasant dreams.

She scooped it up, whispering and waving at him with thoughts of self-preservation as she headed for the doorway. "Nighty-night!"

Darion moaned aloud—a deep, agonizing, heart-wrenching lament that caused Aidan to turn around. What could make a man, so tightly wound, so intent on being in total control, cry out so? He tossed from one side to the other. Aidan saw that he was drenched in perspiration. His sleep shirt was damp and plastered to his skin.

"Darion…are you all right?" She took a step toward him, her hand outstretched.

"No! Don't!…Darius!"

"Darion? Hey, Slim. It's me, Aidan. You're having a bad dream."

She edged closer to the bed, leaning forward to grasp his

shoulder. The moment her hand touched him, Darion's eyes flew open as he partially raised from the bed. His dark eyes were wide and bugged, but Aidan knew from his expression that he wasn't seeing her. Eyes wide open, he was still asleep. Still dreaming. But that didn't stop him from continuing with the amount of aggression and precision of someone who was fully alert. He grabbed her arm, jerking it so hard that she fell over on top of him. Before she could even cry out, Darion rolled over, pressing his forearm to her neck, squeezing the breath from her. His expression was a twisted mask of fury.

Aidan could barely breathe. Her first instinct was to lash out. Adrenaline shot through her veins, driving her to protect herself. She struggled for a moment, surprised that the man who'd been so mild, so accommodating all night, could be so strong in his ferocity. He pinned her down with the entire length of his body. One hand clamped around her free wrist, holding it on the bed. The other was still against her windpipe. Not crushing, but not relinquishing his hold, either. She expelled a long breath. If he'd wanted to, he could have killed her. But he didn't. Something held him back. Some subconscious part of his mind kept him from following through with the murderous intent she saw reflected in his eyes.

"Darion," she whispered his name. "Darion Haddock. Listen to me. It's me. Aidan Holling. You're dreaming. A nightmare." She chose her words carefully to conserve her air and to get through to him.

He didn't move, didn't blink. Simply stared down at her with glassy, unfocused eyes. Aidan shivered, looking up into two ebony pools that she could easily drown in. If she didn't snap him out of it, those intense eyes would be the last sight she saw.

"You're dreaming," she said with more insistence. "And you're killing me."

Aidan wasn't sure if it was the words or the tone that brought him to full wakefulness. Suddenly, Darion leaped off her as if pulled. He backed away, nearly stumbling over the bed she'd vacated in his haste to put some distance between them. Aidan hauled herself to a sitting position, rubbing her neck. She didn't speak right away, but warily watched Darion as he edged around the bed, feeling along the side of the mattress as the blind might feel along a wall for guidance.

"Darion." She spoke his name again, making sure that he really was awake. She stood, reaching out to him.

"Don't!" he said sharply, pointing a shaking finger at her. "Just…stay…right… where you…are!"

"Do you know where you are, Darion? Do you know who I am?" Aidan questioned. She didn't try to touch him, showing him that she would comply by folding her arms and tucking her hands beneath her underarms.

He shook his head slowly back and forth. Aidan wasn't sure if he really didn't know where he was…or if he was suddenly, painfully aware of where he was and what he'd done. Darion spun around and headed for the restroom. He paused at the double-sink vanity, flipped on the lights and started the water running in the basin. Aidan followed him, but at a respectful distance. She watched in concerned silence as he bent over the sink, splashing cold water on his face.

"Are you all right, Slim?" she asked in open concern.

Darion planted his hands on the counter's edge, looked up into the mirror, meeting her gaze. "Are you?" he inquired tightly.

"Understandably, I'm a little freaked out," she admitted, touching her neck, then jerking her hands away to keep from drawing extra attention to the red marks starting to form at her throat. "But I'm okay," she insisted.

Darion lowered his head, squeezing the vanity so hard that Aidan was sure that he'd break off a chunk. "No thanks to me."

Cautiously, Aidan approached him, pulling a dry towel from the rack.

"That was some dream, huh, Slim?" Aidan tried to sound both sympathetic and mildly amused as she dabbed at his face. But the tremor in her voice and in her hands revealed her true feelings.

Darion took the towel from her, wiped around his neck and beneath the collar of the borrowed T-shirt. Then he draped the towel around his neck, tugging on both ends as he lifted his head to the ceiling. He didn't speak for several seconds, as if he was collecting himself, gathering his thoughts.

Aidan didn't push to make him talk, either. She clasped her hands behind her back and leaned against the wall facing him. She didn't even look at him directly, but stared down at her feet. It was as close as she could come to giving him his personal space without physically leaving the room. Finally, after a few minutes of relative silence, Darion spoke.

"You ever have your dreams come true, Aidan?" he asked in a subdued tone.

"Sure." Aidan shrugged. "Sometimes, if I work really hard at it."

Disgusted, Darion yanked the towel from his neck, balled it up and flung it at the tiled bathroom floor. "Well, I didn't have to work too hard for this one."

"Do you want to talk about it, Darion?" she encouraged him.

"No, Aidan. I don't. I've done all the talking I'm going to do about it." He turned and faced her. "What about you?"

Aidan looked at him, her expression puzzled. "What do you mean?"

"How much talking are *you* going to do? When I take you back to your family, what are you going to tell them?"

"You mean tattle on you to my brother?" she asked incredulously.

Up until he'd mentioned it, the thought hadn't occurred to her. She was still reeling from the fact that he'd performed such a Jekyll and Hyde act on her that she hadn't thought about how or what she should confess to Holling. She knew that Darion hadn't intentionally tried to hurt her. Yet, how could she go to Holling and tell him that the man he'd put so much faith in had turned violent? She had no way of knowing whether this was a one-time episode or if he was prone to violence. Aidan couldn't quite reconcile the image of the man who'd run off into a snowstorm to help a perfect stranger with the man who'd almost choked the life from her.

"I wouldn't expect you to try to keep something like this from him," Darion said. "If I were your brother, I'd want to know."

"Is that what you want me to do?" she asked. "You could lose your job."

"Don't you think I know that? Your brother knows a lot of people. He could make it hard for me to find work again."

"Holling is a hard man. But he isn't vindictive," Aidan said. "If I told him what happened, the whole story, he might—"

"You won't have to tell him. I will," Darion interrupted her. "Are you sure that's what you want, Slim?"

If she did tell Holling what Darion had done, there was no way she could put a positive spin on it. The truth was, Darion had been filled with murderous intention. And whether he'd meant for it to be or not, it had been all directed at her. She wasn't even sure that Darion could promise her that it would never happen again. Whatever was troubling him went deep. Deep into his soul. That kind of trouble didn't go away on its own. For him to try to suppress it was painful. The kind of pain that hurt too much to even think about, let alone talk about.

"So—" She drew out the word by expelling a long breath, then gave him a mischievous smile. "What are you going to tell him? That you and I wound up in bed together?"

Darion slanted a *get serious* look in her direction. "That's not what happened, Aidan," he pointedly reminded her.

"Technically, it was," she contradicted. "The truth is, you and I were both lying right there…in that bed…." She pointed to the spot.

"You think this is some kind of a joke?" Darion snarled. "Lady, I could have killed you."

"But you didn't," she said matter-of-factly.

"But I could have!" he insisted.

"But you didn't!"

When Darion opened his mouth to protest again, Aidan stepped up to him, placing her index finger against his lips. "Shush!" she admonished him.

He tried to speak again.

"I said hush, now!"

"Anybody ever tell you you've got a bossy streak?" Darion said, smiling reluctantly.

"Anybody ever tell you that you don't know when to shut up?" she countered.

This time, to stop his argument, Aidan stood on tiptoe and silenced them both by pressing her lips firmly against his.

Neither of them had really addressed the issue sitting with all the subtlety of the proverbial giant elephant in the middle of the living room. Here they were, two adults, strangers on one hand, yet undeniably intimate with each other on the other hand. Aidan couldn't count the range of emotions she'd shared with Darion since leaving the airport. Suspicion. Fear. Jubilation. Irritation. Confusion. Compassion. This latest one, she didn't have any trouble at all recognizing—or accepting.

Aidan felt the stirring to life of an emotion she had not experienced in such a long time.

Desire!

She'd been alone—and lonely—for such a long time. Did it occur to her that she wasn't acting as wisely as she should? Of course it did. Did it occur to her that she wasn't thinking clearly? Without question. Could this need to be close to him, to want him, even knowing so little about him, be blamed on a touch of the holiday blues? Aidan considered the possibility.

It also occurred to her that this man had had her emotions all aflutter from the moment he'd walked up to her at the airport. The way he spoke, the way he carried himself, the way he had of making her feel that when he was with her she had all of his attention, made her feel as if this were the kind of man she wanted to know. She wanted to know him more than on a casual level. Though experimental, there was nothing casual about the way she kissed him. She kissed him in response to the unasked questions hanging heavily in the air, shrouding them, and binding them so that there was no backing down. No backing away. The longer she held the kiss, the more questions arose.

Could you be the one for me, Darion? Could you? Could you be wanting me as much as I want you? Could you?

Chapter 17

Darion admitted to himself that he'd fantasized about kissing her. He'd imagined more than one scenario when he might have opportunity to do so. The fact that she'd presented the opportunity so soon after meeting him left him stunned. He stood there as Aidan balanced herself on her tiptoes, holding on to his shoulders for support. Perhaps it was only a sympathy kiss. A way for Aidan to show that she'd forgiven him for his much-too-active nightmare.

If he'd only broken it off the moment her lips had touched his, he might have convinced himself—and her—that this might have been a platonic kiss between friends. Friends who'd only just met, but had instantaneously formed that bond.

If he'd reacted differently, perhaps he might have talked himself into believing that his fantasizing about her was far better than the real thing. In his fantasies, her lips were supple and sweet, offering themselves up to him in the perfect kiss.

If he'd reacted sooner, perhaps he might have extricated himself without giving Aidan any indication that he'd ever had inappropriate thoughts about her. One step back. That's all he needed to take to salvage his dignity and his job. Lift his head an inch. A fraction of an inch and that would have been one less thing she would have to run and tell her brother.

But he didn't.

Darion's reaction to Aidan's kiss was instantaneous. Undeniable. He didn't move away from her. Instead, he moved closer. Darion grasped Aidan's arms above the elbows, ran his hands along the backs of her arms, and finally came to rest around her shoulder blades as he drew her closer. He drew her into his chest, bending her head back as he deepened the kiss. Instead of breaking off as he should have done, he lengthened the contact. Deliberately, willingly prolonged it. He savored every moment as he literally retraced the paths his mouth had taken in his fantasies.

He treated the moment like a wondrous journey. Each new turn of his head, each gradual shift of his mouth was a new discovery. A new touch. A new taste. A new tingle of anticipation shooting through him. And Darion took every opportunity to explore. He didn't have to open his eyes, to peek to see if she was enjoying the kiss as much as he was. He knew instantly by the small moan of sensual surrender that Aidan was with him every step of the way. He felt her clutch his shoulders, her nails gently gouging into his skin. She took up the rhythm of his kiss, moving her body against him in perfect time. Darion felt the press of her breasts through the thin ribbed material of her sleeveless T-shirt. The friction alone was enough to make her nipples swell and peak, calling for his immediate attention.

When Darion slid his hand under her T-shirt, cupping the

generous curves, as he'd imagined on their tropical island getaway, he heard the sharp inrush of her breath and felt her teeth gently bite down on his lower lip. A prelude to a more passionate response if he accepted the blatant invitation she offered by lifting her leg and coiling it around his. More friction as Aidan rocked her hips, sealing her pelvis to his. He could tell by the contour of her pajama pants against her body that Aidan wasn't wearing underwear. No bra. No panties. It wouldn't take anything at all for him to pull the waistband down and—

"We're such idiots!" Aidan suddenly turned her head away from him and exclaimed.

"I know…I know…we shouldn't be doing this," Darion concurred, muttering against her mouth as he resumed the kiss. He couldn't stop himself from continuing to pulse against her, making sure that she was acutely aware of what little material separated him from her. Darion shifted his hands, cupping her bottom and lifting her so that her feet almost dangled in the air. He was so ready for her, he knew that with little or no effort, he could penetrate right through her clothing.

"No…no…" Aidan struggled to speak. It was hard to do so through the flurry of intense kisses that covered her mouth, her cheeks, her eyelids, even the hollow of her throat.

This time, Darion used his weight to pin her against the wall. She was still breathless, though not with fear. She was dizzy with total anticipation as she felt Darion shift his feet.

"No?" Darion was coherent enough to recognize the word. He understood *no* when he heard it and didn't take it to mean her offering a token resistance.

"Not like this," Aidan said, then immediately clarified when obvious disappointment turned his expression almost comical.

"We've got two perfectly good beds right over there," she said, tilting her head in the direction of the sleeping area.

"Ohhhh!" Darion let out a breath of understanding. He set Aidan on her feet again, but continued to hold her hand as she led him between the double beds.

"Your place or mine?" she quipped.

"Better make it yours," he said, nodding at her full-size bed. "Bad memories in mine."

Aidan climbed into bed first, then held the covers open for him to slide in next to her. She lay on her side, with Darion facing her.

"Aidan," he began hesitantly.

"You're not going to start talking to me again, are you?" she teased. "Now's not the time, Slim…unless of course, you want to tell me how much you want to—" She leaned forward, whispering a few words to him that momentarily made him lose his train of thought.

Actually, the image she painted for him gave her intentions razor-sharp clarity. And they weren't any less vivid than what he'd imagined. Only, he'd been trying to be too much of a gentleman to repeat what he'd fantasized about. Now that Aidan had put into words what he'd wanted all along, he didn't think any less of her. In fact, it reminded him of something Luke had said to him. Something about liking it when a woman knew what she wanted and could tell him. Darion had to admit that he liked it, too.

"I was trying to say that I hadn't planned on this," he began. "But then I'd be lying. I did plan," he admitted. "Hell, I don't know. Maybe even schemed."

"Schemed?" she said, laughing at his expression and choice of words. "That almost sounds devious."

"When I went to the motel lobby to buy food, I bought condoms. In case you were hungry for something other than food, I wanted to be prepared."

Aidan reached out and placed the palm of his hand over her heart. "Darion Haddock, that's the sweetest thing anyone has said to me…or done for me in a long, long time."

"Then you're not mad at me?" There was more than a little surprise in his tone.

"Mad? What for? Why should I be mad?"

He shrugged. "I don't know. I figured you'd be mad for assuming that you'd want to sleep with me. People who make assumptions usually wind up making an ass out of themselves."

"Did you buy those condoms thinking that I'd be that easy?" She sounded offended.

"No!" he immediately denied.

"Good answer," she praised him. "So, did you go into this thinking that you'd win some sort of achievement badge that you could brag about by scoring with the boss's sister?"

"No, Aidan. Of course not."

Aidan could hardly keep herself from laughing as she continued. "Then, you're saying I should be mad because you looked at me as someone you wanted to share an intimate moment with? Oh, I get it! Maybe you were thinking that after all of the hell we'd been through last night, you thought maybe you could grab a quickie with me and that would relieve some tension and allow you to finally get some rest. Is that it? Because that would make me mad."

"That's not what I meant at all, Aidan."

"Then, I'm having a hard time understanding why you think I should be mad at you, Slim."

"I guess I'm sort of…um…concerned how fast this is all happening for me," he confessed.

"Tell me, Slim. Are you talking about having sex or are you talking about having feelings for me?"

"Both," he confessed.

"Maybe," she began slowly, "you're worried that maybe this isn't real. Maybe you're thinking that we're just reacting, or rather overreacting, to the accident," she suggested. "Or maybe we've been alone for so long, you're thinking that the holidays are as good a time as any to grab some companionship. Even if it doesn't last. Even it's as fake as flocked trees."

"You said it better than I could. That's essentially it."

"I thought about that, too," she agreed. "As far as things happening fast or slow, I don't know. I've never felt like this before, so it's not something I can compare. Maybe it did happen fast. Does that make it any less real? Or meaningful?"

"I want to be sure."

"Of what?"

"That it's real. That it'll last."

"Maybe it isn't meant to last," she offered. "Maybe it is what it is, for as long as it is."

"If I wanted quick and meaningless, Aidan, I wouldn't be here," he assured her. "I've had my chances for cheap and easy. Not what I wanted."

"Then," she said slowly, "I guess how long this…whatever this is we have….is going to last depends on us."

Darion reached out, taking a handful of her hair. He tugged gently, guiding her to lie flat on her back.

"Oh, I can make it last," he promised, his tone tantalizing and taunting.

"Okay, then. Here's a crash course in All About Aidan. What is it you think you want to know about me?" she asked, forcing herself not to smile. This time when he rolled onto her, pinning her to the bed, she didn't resist. She didn't struggle, but opened her thighs to allow him to settle between them.

"Favorite color?" he asked immediately. He started to kiss her again, making it difficult to talk.

"Orange," she responded.

"Hmm…*interesting*." His voice rumbled deeply in his chest.

"Why interesting?" she wanted to know.

Darion shrugged his shoulders. "It just is."

"What about you, Slim? What's your favorite color?"

"Don't have one," he said, distracted by the feel of the hollow of her throat against his lips as he continued to trail a line of kisses.

"Everybody has a favorite color," she insisted.

"Everybody but me."

"What makes you so special," she scoffed, "that you can't pick a color?"

"Well, I can tell you that it isn't my color preferences that make me special," he boasted, shifting his hips slightly, making her give a squeal of delight when she felt Darion's *specialty* press against her thigh.

"Do you have a middle name?" she asked, trying very hard to concentrate on maintaining the conversational flow.

"Lee." He lifted his head to respond before inching farther down to flick his tongue over her breasts.

"Mine's Elizabeth," she offered on exhaled breath.

"I know. Your family calls you Aida Beth. Your brother talks about you all the time."

"See, you did know something about me!" she exclaimed.

"Need to know more," he muttered, pulling on the waistband of her pajama pants with his teeth. He nuzzled the flat planes of her stomach. "Favorite movie?" His question came back muffled.

"My new favorite is called *Crash*. Don Cheadle. Sandra Bullock. That guy from the *Mummy* movies. Have you seen it?"

"Nope," he confessed. "Don't have much time for watching movies."

"It's good," she gave her assessment. As Darion moved lower, she placed her hands on top of his head. Her fingers clenched, grabbing two handfuls of his thick dark hair, and pushed down to guide him farther. "Really…really…good!" she panted.

"I'll have to check it out," he promised.

"Favorite song?" she fired back another question, and could barely focus on his answer. Her back involuntarily arched as a sudden ripple of pleasure coursed through her.

"'I Can't Make You Love Me.' Kevin Mahogany's version."

"Not Bonnie Raitt's?"

"Nope."

"Oh!" Aidan squirmed, bringing her leg up and around so that her heel rested on Darion's back. He kissed her hips, her inner thigh, continuously working his way downward.

"Pet peeves?" he asked.

"Waiting!" she exclaimed. "Can't stand to wait. Drives…me…absolutely…out of my mind!"

Darion lifted his head, grinning at her. "Me, too."

"You've already discovered something we have in common." She sounded very pleased with herself. It wasn't all Darion discovered. He could tell instantly as her breath quickened and her heel dug into his back. She moaned aloud, arching her back, lifting her hips to meet him as he playfully exploited her weakness. He could feel the beginnings of tremors quiver in her legs.

"Where are they?" she cried out suddenly.

"Hmm?" Darion said distractedly. "Where are what?"

"Your little early Christmas packages that we need to unwrap," she insisted.

"In a box…nightstand…bag…" He punctuated each word with a lingering lave of his tongue.

Aidan had gone beyond squirming and was now openly, wantonly writhing against him. She raised her arms above her head to clutch the headboard.

"Get them out," she begged, bending her knees and widening her legs even more.

"In a minute," he promised.

"I told you I don't like to wait," she warned him. "I can't wait anymore, Darion. Please!" She strained toward him, lifting her hips and inviting him to explore more.

Darion tightened his grip on her hips. His long fingers splayed against her sides, but he kept pushing her back into the mattress. Each time she tried to shift her body, to position herself directly under him, he held her down, pushed her back until her breathing reached a fevered pitch.

"Worst party you've ever been to?" he asked, making her focus on his words rather than what he was doing. Or not doing, to Aidan's growing frustration.

"Freshman year at college. Trash-can punch. Lots of throwing up. Name of your first crush?" she wanted to know. "And teachers don't count."

"Dee-Dee Harrison. I was nine. She was thirteen. Yours?"

"Joaquin Vallejo. I was seven. He was twenty-seven. Worked for my father that summer, helping him break horses."

"Is he still around?"

"Why do you want to know?" she asked coyly.

"Gotta check out the competition."

"He's still around," she admitted.

"Are you still crushing on him?"

"I still remember his name. What do you think?" she taunted him. Her getting her jealous revenge on him barely compared to the sweet torture he was putting her through.

"Point him out to me."

"Why?"

"So the next time I see him I can kick his ass."

Aidan giggled, surprised that he could sound jealous even while driving her to distraction.

"He's married now with bunches of kids and several grand-kids…not that I keep tabs on him, or anything. Do you want kids, Slim?"

"Bunches and bunches," he answered. "When the time's right."

Darion didn't need Aidan to tell them that his timing was perfect. He'd taken her to the brink of all she could stand. Reaching above her head, she desperately clawed at the headboard to keep from gouging his scalp. She caught her lower lip between her teeth, trying to keep from crying out. The slow, torturous teasing, advancing and retreating, ex-ploring and exploiting of his skilled kisses and caresses left her twisting and writhing in the sheets. Her heels dug and thumped into his back. When she felt she would scream from wanting, she turned her face into the pillow and bit down into the stuffing. When she knew she would not be able to last another moment, Darion's hands left her. Guided by that nonverbal, but no less intense, signal, Darion rolled away from her.

"No! Don't stop now!" she exclaimed in dismay.

"I'd better stop," he advised. "Or in a minute, there will be more than sweat dampening these sheets." He'd concentrated on pleasuring her, ignoring his own body's responses for as long as he could. But now, he'd reached the point where he wouldn't be able to contain himself, either. He reached out to the nightstand and fumbled for a moment while he yanked on the nightstand handle.

He let out his own muted hiss of frustration when the

darkness of the room and slick, trembling hands kept him from properly putting on the condom.

"Best job you've ever had?" she asked, stroking his back, helping him focus.

"You are talking about work, aren't you?" He kept his back to her so that she couldn't see the grin on his face.

"If you say so." Aidan didn't hide the laughter in her voice.

"Silicon Valley," he answered, but didn't elaborate on the type of work. "Best and worst. Yours?"

"Worst job. Telemarketer for a carpet-cleaning company. Best, and most short-lived job, working at a cosmetics counter for a big department store."

"Why'd you quit?"

"To come home," she admitted. "I missed my family…even my big-head brother."

"I'm glad you did, Aidan," Darion confessed.

Moments later, he took up position over her, staring down into her eyes. He didn't move right away and neither did she. Despite the teasing and the frantic quest for each other's flesh, both seemed to realize the significance of their choice. There was still time to turn back. Still time to change their minds. It was as if, without having to say it, they were giving each other the opportunity to back away. To save face if this was, indeed, a mistake.

Darion stroked her hair, smoothing her dampened skin around her temples.

"I want you," he said simply. There was no denying the fact now. No hiding it.

Aidan laid the palm of her soft hand on his face and caressed his cheek. "Make it last, Darion," she implored.

He lowered his eyes, his eyelids momentarily shuttering away the expression of uncertainty reflected deeply within them. Then, he encircled her, cradling her back as he rested on his elbows. When Darion lifted his gaze again, his eyes glittered with renewed purpose as he thrust deeply into her. He didn't have to worry that she wasn't ready for him. She was. He'd made certain of that before he'd even reached for the condoms. He entered her swiftly, easily, moving his hips in a steady, fluid motion that she could follow. She wrapped her arms around him, pressing her hands against the small of his back. Then she clutched his bottom, squeezing, pulling him closer—increasing both the depth and intensity of his thrusts.

Aidan started to shudder, unable, unwilling to stop the ever-widening ripples of a powerful orgasm. Darion held tightly on to Aidan, breathing with her as her trembling subsided. He collapsed beside her, draping his arm across her waist and drawing her close to him. Aidan snuggled under his arm, turning to kiss him one last time before languor took over.

"So much for making it last," she teased.

Chapter 18

Aidan lay curled in the fetal position with her knees drawn up, resting on her arm. Her eyes were closed, but she wasn't sleeping. That didn't stop her from feeling as though she were caught up in a dream—a bizarre dream state where time stood still and the impossible suddenly became probable.

If anyone had told her a week ago that she'd give her love to a man she barely knew, she would have called them a bold-faced liar and probably would have been ready to fight. Not her. Not Aidan Elizabeth Holling. She was no saint, not by any means. But she was nobody's whore, either. A fact that she'd had to remind a few people of the day she'd left home.

The argument she'd had with Holling was so sharp and clear in her focus. It had been ten years ago, but it might as well have been that very moment, as painful as it still was for her. She loved her brother dearly. But he could be so stubborn. So convinced that he was right, even when he wasn't.

Aidan herself was convinced that she might have handled their sibling rivalry if Holling hadn't been so overbearingly protective of her. He'd watched over her like a hawk, ready to swoop down on any poor soul who got too close to her. Social life? What social life? There had been no such thing as one-on-one dating as long as Holling had had anything to say about it.

She'd tried to understand. Tried to accept the fact that she wasn't going to have the type of freedom that other girls had. She wouldn't go so far as to say he'd picked her friends—as long as they were other girls. But let anyone with a little bass in their voice try to call her up on the phone… And walking around White Wolf, if any boy had even looked cross-eyed at her, Holling had had something to say about it.

She knew that he was afraid that she'd grow up to be like the first woman in his life he'd ever wanted and couldn't have. The one woman who'd repeatedly withheld her love for him. And as hard as she tried to fill that gap for him, to be a positive female source of love and acceptance, she couldn't. There was no substitute for a mother's love. Aidan knew that the older she got, the less and less he saw her for who she really was. She wasn't Aidan Holling. She was an extension of their mother Janeen. It wasn't only Holling behaving that way, either. All of those Holling men had their suspicions about her.

No wonder she'd bolted out of there as fast as she could. She might have even been willing to stick it out, to make them see her for who she was, if it weren't for Holling blowing up one day when he'd found her hanging out with one of the ranch hands.

Okay, Aidan corrected herself, more than hanging out. Making out. But it had been innocent. Oh-so-innocent. When Holling had caught them, they'd still had their clothes on. But

Holling hadn't seen that. All he'd seen was his baby sister flat on her back.

Aidan smiled in bittersweet remembrance. You could have heard the shouting for miles. The accusations. The name-calling. The threats. He'd yanked her by her arm, pulling her upright with one hand, while grabbing that poor kid by the belt and shoving him out in the front yard with the other. All the while, he'd been yelling at her, shaking her and making predictions on her life. All of that drama because of a little kiss.

Well, to be honest with herself, more than a little kiss. She had to be careful about revisionist history. The truth was, she *had* let that boy put his hands on her. And his lips. And his tongue. And his crotch. And his….

And why shouldn't he!

Aidan felt a surge of self-righteous indignation swell up in her breast. Nobody else had wanted to touch her. When you were seventeen and overweight and had nobody around to tell you how beautiful you were or how special you were, you craved attention. Any attention. Even if it wasn't in your best interest. Yet, Holling hadn't seen it that way. As mad as he'd been, she didn't think he could have seen anything but red.

"What the hell's the matter with you, Aida Beth?" He'd shaken her so hard that her teeth had rattled in her head. "Haven't I taught you better than that?"

"He…he said that he liked me!" she'd wailed. It was her only excuse for her behavior. If he'd only known how lonely she'd been, how starved for attention, maybe he wouldn't have been so hard on her.

"What makes you think you can spread your legs to any lying bastard with an itch in his pants? I swear, if you ain't just like *her!* Is that what you want, Aida Beth? To be the new town skank?"

"Don't you dare! Don't you dare compare me to her, Holling. I am not her! I am not like Mama! I am not a whore!"

"Looks that way from where I'm standing!"

"Then get out of my way!" She hadn't been strong enough to push him out of the way. But she had been strong enough to get out of his. Out of his way. Out of his house. Out of his life.

"Where are you going?"

"None of your damned business, Holling."

"Don't you cuss me, gal!"

"Who do you think you are? You're not my daddy. You're not my boss."

"I'm your meal ticket, little girl," he'd reminded her. Other than ranch chores, she hadn't been working. Hadn't started school yet. She hated the fact that he could dangle the family checkbook over her to make her submit.

"No, Holling," she'd shaken her head at him. "Not anymore, you're not."

"Not that you couldn't stand to miss a meal or two, Aidan—"

Cruel. So, so cruel. They'd always argued. Typical brother and sister stuff. Yet, even at their most verbal, he'd never been abusive. He'd never sunk so low as to use her weight against her. He must have been furious at her. Even though she knew they'd both spoken in anger, that brotherly cut had never healed. His words had continued to haunt her for a long, long time.

"You think because you're the oldest that you can boss me around, tell me what to do. Make me jump and dance like a puppet on a string. Yassir, Mr. Big Boss Man. Do whatever you say, boss. I's gon' shuffle on back to the big house now…."

"Stop it, Aidan."

"Yassir, yassir. Whatever you say, suh… Shuttin' up my mouf right away, suh."

"You need to be **worried** about shutting your legs," he'd sniped at her.

"You two-faced, double-standard, chauvinist pig!" Aidan had flung back. "It's all right for you to go dropping your pants whenever you feel like it. Yeah, that's right. I said it. You think I don't know what you're doing when you go off on one of your so-called late-night rides. You think I don't know what you do when you and Red Bone and Matías and Zack go into White Wolf. Come back with your truck stinking with empty beer bottles and used condoms. You're a hypocrite, Holling. You're nothing but a hypocrite."

In her heart, Aidan knew that her brother wasn't as bad as *all* that. More often than not, he was always the designated driver, making sure that his friends got home, safe and sound. Yet, he'd hurt her so badly by accusing her of being a slut. He was her big brother. He was supposed to watch out for her, protect her, take care of her…even if that meant protecting her from himself. He'd been so afraid that she'd turn out like their mother, that he hadn't realized he was driving her toward that very same behavior. He'd yelled at her for wanting to give herself to a boy she barely knew. Ten years' worth of experience later, and what had she learned?

It was no secret why she'd left home. She'd left because of a man. But she wasn't chasing one. She was running *away* from one. From Holling. And from her father. And from Shane. Every time the three of them had looked at her, she could see it in their eyes. When was she going to turn? When was she going to go bad like Mama had? Maybe that's why she'd gained all of that weight. Eating herself sick. They'd said she looked like her. That she acted like her. And soon she would be her. Aidan wasn't going to let that happen. If she could make herself so that no other man wanted her, maybe it would make those three get off her case.

She found it ironic that they kept talking about family. And sticking together. Only part of that fairy tale was true. Those Holling men stuck together all right. The three of them had gotten together and decided that she wasn't going to turn out worth spit. That was why she'd run away...and had stayed away. She hadn't wanted to sit here, trapped for the rest of her life, and listen to them drag her down. They were wrong. She wasn't a whore.... She wasn't easy.... Or was she?

Aidan drew in a shaky breath and turned her back to the door. Here she was, ten years older but maybe none the wiser. How in the world had she ended up here, like this, with Darion? She squeezed her eyes shut and tried to imagine herself having this conversation with Holling. This time, she couldn't even say that the boy had claimed he'd liked her. Darion had said he'd wanted her. Wanting wasn't loving. Wanting was needing. She'd responded to his need. And to her own.

"Who's the hypocrite now?" she whispered aloud.

When she heard the bathroom door open, she closed her eyes, breathing deeply. Maybe he'd think she was still asleep. She didn't want to talk right now. She didn't want him to know how her doubts had suddenly crashed in on her and tainted their last hours together.

Darion didn't speak as he entered the room, simply sat on the edge of the bed. He reached out and touched her hair. The back of his hand was still damp from the shower as he caressed her cheek.

"I saved you some hot water," he said by way of greeting.

"Thanks," Aidan mumbled. She could almost feel him looking at her. She could almost hear the thoughts in his head.

Probably wondering why I'm suddenly acting like such a big baby. You're a grown woman, Aida Beth. You made the decision, now you gotta live with it. Turn around and face the man. Go on... Look at him!

Aidan turned over on her back, but she couldn't quite make herself open her eyes. She squeezed them shut tightly, biting her lip in consternation. She might have drawn blood if she hadn't felt Darion's fingertips softly graze her lips, forcing her to relax and release.

"It's all right, Aidan," he soothed. "I understand."

Aidan's eyes flew open. "No," she contradicted. "I don't think you do."

"You're not the only one with—"

"Doubts?" she offered.

"I was going to say *questions.*"

She blew out an exaggerated sigh of relief. "Whew! As long as it isn't regrets."

He shook his head back and forth, smiling graciously in response to her attempt at humor. "No regrets. What about you?"

"No. Not really."

"Not a very convincing answer. Want to tell me what's on your mind?"

Aidan shrugged her shoulders, looking away. She pulled the covers up closer around her, as if putting that extra layer over herself put more distance between them. "I'm sorry, Darion. I freaked out for a minute."

"About us?"

Aidan then closed her eyes, nodding. "This isn't like me. I don't usually jump in the sack so quickly. I don't know what came over me."

"Sounds like you do have regrets," he observed. Darion turned so that he was no longer facing her, but the opposite bed. He rested his elbows on his knees and leaned forward so that the heels of his hands rested on his forehead.

"Believe it or not, Aidan, it's been a while for me, too. I've had…uh…a couple of rough relationships. Made me want to chill out for a while, you know? Get my head together. Figure out what I'm really looking for."

"I haven't had much luck in the romance department, either," she replied. "Before I lost the weight or after. Before, I didn't have any confidence in myself. Plenty of guys tried to talk to me, but I didn't trust that they were for real. I kept wondering who put them up to it. Who paid them to be with me. Or what kind of prank they were pulling trying to get with Holling's pathetic fat sister. Or, I wondered what kind of a fetish did they have. And after I lost all my weight, well, I didn't have any confidence in you men, either. Sorry, I hate to man bash, Slim, but that's the way I felt. Anytime I hooked up with anybody, I got the sense that they weren't trying to get to know me. Just trying to get into the panties of another big-bottomed sister."

"And here I come along and the first thing I try to do is—"

"Take care of me," she interrupted. "My brother sent you out there to pick me up. You decided to take care of me on your own, Darion."

"It wasn't a hard decision to make. In hindsight, I know we should have waited, Aidan, before we slept together. But I have to tell you, you're the first woman in a long, long time who's made me *want* to try again."

"Come on, now," Aidan said in a disbelieving tone. "There aren't very many single, respectable, good-looking, incredibly fine men in White Wolf. You had to be a prime target for every woman on the prowl."

"Thanks for the boost to my ego. I didn't say that I didn't

have any opportunity. I said I didn't have any desire. That all changed when I saw you, lady."

"Now who's the one boosting egos," she accused.

"I wouldn't lie to you, Aidan. From the moment I saw you, I couldn't stop thinking about you. I tried. You don't know how hard I tried. I gave myself every excuse I could think of why you and me weren't a good idea. It wasn't even a question of lack of self-control. Because I knew what I was doing. Knew that I should stop. But I didn't."

"Don't put it all on yourself, Darion. I think I had something to say about what went on between us."

"So," he said in resignation, turning to look back at her. "What do you want to do?"

"What do you want to do?" she asked, turning the question back on him.

He flashed her a wicked grin.

Aidan laughed despite her misgivings. "That's what prompted this conversation in the first place."

He quickly composed his features. "Sorry. A knee-jerk reaction. I didn't mean to make light of our predicament. This is no laughing matter."

"I know. I'm scared, Darion."

"Of me?"

"No, of course not. It's my brother, Holling," she clarified.

Darion blew out a frustrated breath. "What do you think he'll do?"

"To you? I don't know. Maybe fire you."

"Is this still the making-light-of-things part?" Darion asked hopefully.

Aidan gave an enigmatic smile. "The last boy he caught me with, he tossed him out in the dirt by his belt loops."

"I'm not a boy," Darion pointedly reminded her.

"You don't have to convince me," Aidan said, giving him her own mischievous smile. "Really, Darion. It's not you I'm worried about. It's me. The last time I was home, I didn't leave on the best of terms. Do you know what it's like, Slim, to have a family you love…love dearly…but don't necessarily like?"

"It's not all that uncommon."

"Everybody thinks my brother walks on water. I'm not saying that he's not a good man. Because he is. When it comes to us, there's something broken there. Something is missing. And I don't know what I can do to fix it. It's one of the reasons why I've stayed away so long. There's no fixing it."

"A lot can happen in ten years, Aidan. A man can change."

"I thought I'd changed," she said, lowering her eyes. If she didn't elaborate, maybe he'd think she was talking about her physical appearance.

"Your brother loves you. I know that for a fact."

"You can love a person to death, you know."

"Yeah," Darion replied, his tone full of sarcasm as he said, "I know. Know all too well."

He stood up, readjusting the towel around his waist as he did so.

Aidan rose to a sitting position, one hand pressed to her mouth, the other clutching the blanket to cover herself.

"Darion," she murmured. He turned around, noting her expression as she swung her legs off the bed and slowly approached him.

"Darion?" she repeated his name, questioningly. "Are those…gunshot wounds?" Aidan was amazed. Why hadn't she noticed them before?

She stepped up to him, her finger tentatively reaching for the small puckered circles. Three of them, in a tight spread pattern, to the right of his navel stood out, raised and pale against his dark skin.

Darion didn't answer, but remained motionless as she faced him.

She examined his abdomen and circled around to his back to note where the bullets had exited. When she reached out to touch him, she raised gooseflesh on his arms, back and neck.

"Oh, baby. What *happened?*" she exclaimed in a breathy whisper. "Who did this to you?"

When he spun around to face her, she looked up at him, her eyes filled with questions and concern, seeming to mirror the anguish on his face.

Before Aidan could ask another question, Darion wrapped his arms around her waist and drew her to him. He pressed her tightly against his chest. He lowered his head, capturing her lips, stealing her words and her breath away. How long he stood there, savoring the feel and the taste of her mouth, Darion didn't know. Didn't care.

"Darion!" she exclaimed, trying to tear her mouth away. "I know there isn't a lot we know about each other yet. But you have to tell me how you got shot."

"Shh. Hush now," he soothed her. "We can talk about that later."

"But…"

"No…no buts. Later," he insisted. He pulled at her blanket, removing the physical barrier between them once again.

"You're freaking me out again, Slim," she confessed, but she allowed him to lead her back to the bed.

"Everyone should be allowed a little freaking in their lives," he advised, settling over her.

"Umm," Aidan agreed. "A little freaking. More than a little if you're going to keep doing it like this!"

She arched her back, lifting her hips to meet him. "Promise me something."

"Shh…" he insisted.

"No, seriously….um…yes, well…" Aidan found it hard to keep her thoughts focused. "You promise you'll tell me later?"

"Promise," he echoed.

"I mean it, Darion. And promise me you'll tell me if you ever have one of those freak-out moments."

He lifted his head, staring with unfocused eyes. "You mean waking-up-in-the-middle-of-the-night-to-strangle-you freak-outs? Or those bullet-hole-in-your-flesh freak-outs?"

She grasped his face between the palms of her hands. "I mean one of those you-don't-know-if-we're-going-to-make-it-together freak-out moments."

"Oh. One of those."

"Do you promise?"

Darion laid his finger against her lips to quiet her. "Of course I promise."

"And you're a man of your word?"

"I'm a man of my word," he said solemnly.

"Okay, then promise me that you'll—"

"Speaking of words," he said wryly. "Looks like I'm going to have to find another way to hush you up!" Darion threatened, and chuckled at her resulting cry of pure pleasure.

Chapter 19

"Shh! Be quiet. Mama said don't wake her up, Jay-Jay."

"You be quiet, Sydney. I'm not waking her up."

"Yes, you are! You are waking her up. You're too close. Stop breathing on her."

Aidan cracked open one eye and stared blearily with confusion into the faces of her niece and nephew. For a minute, she wasn't quite sure where she was. She was at home in Florida. No, she was sleeping in her brother's truck. No, wait a minute. The motel. How did the twins get into the motel room?

Darion!

She glanced around, her eyes sweeping the room. Where was he?

"I'm not breathing on her!" Jayden protested.

"Yes, you are," Aidan said, settling the argument between them. "I can even tell that you had bacon for breakfast."

"See, I told you!" Sydney shouted triumphantly. "I told you

that you were making too much noise, Jay-Jay. You're gonna get it for waking her up."

Reaching over and clamping the pillow over her ears, Aidan's voice was muffled as she said, "Both of you need a lesson in whispering. Whatever happened to that old saying that children should be seen and not heard?"

"You can't see us or hear us with that pillow on your face, Aunt Aida Beth," Jayden said matter-of-factly. He pulled up one corner of the pillow and hovered his round face even closer to hers.

Aidan smiled, leaned close and planted a kiss on his nose. "Gotcha, big boy!" she said.

"Yuck!" Jayden protested, slapping at his face. Aidan pretended to grab at him when he slid off the bed, dragging half of the covers with him. Demanding her own share of her aunt's attention, Sydney jumped onto the bed, bouncing up and down as if it were a trampoline.

"Wake up! Wake up! Everybody wake up!" she shouted in a singsong voice. "Come on, Aunt Aida Beth. Time to get up now. You already missed breakfast."

Now she knew where she was. She was home! Finally home. She felt a little like Dorothy from *The Wizard of Oz* as it hit her suddenly, painfully, how much she missed being here. Aidan stood up in the bed, joining hands with her niece, and sang along.

"Wake up! Wake up! Everybody wake up!"

"Ooohhhh! I'm gonna tell Mama. You're not supposed to be jumping in the bed!" Jayden warned them. He looked up at his aunt. "You're too old to be jumping in the bed. You know better than that."

"You know who you sound like?" Aidan asked a little breathlessly. She collapsed on the bed, bringing Sydney with her, cradling her in her lap. "You sound like your father." She paused, staring thoughtfully at her nephew. "You know, you look like him, too. And you…you little rug rat, are the spitting image of your mother," Aidan said, nuzzling Sydney's ticklish stomach with her chin.

"Too old and too big," Jayden continued, encouraged by the comparison to his daddy. He sat up straighter, trying to compose his pudgy face into the same severe expression his father had whenever he was about to hand out punishment.

Sydney looked into her aunt's face. "You're not too big," she said.

"Thank you, Sydney."

"How come?"

"How come what?"

"How come you're not fat anymore?"

"Sydney Rose Holling!" Sawyer's tone was sharp and mortified as she called to her daughter from the doorway. "That's a very rude question. You apologize to your aunt."

"It's okay, Sawyer," Aidan said. She held out her hand, inviting her sister-in-law into her room.

Sawyer stepped into the room, her arms folded across her chest. "No, it's not okay. I want my children to be inquisitive. Not nosy and rude."

"It's an honest question…right from the mouth of a brutally honest child." Aidan's mouth twisted wryly before answering. "I guess I don't look the same as in all of my pictures, do I, kids?"

Jayden and Sydney slowly shook their heads back and forth.

"I had to lose weight, Syd," Aidan told her frankly. "The doctor told me that if I didn't, I could get very sick. Maybe even die."

"So, you went on a diet, Auntie Aida Beth?" Jayden asked.

"No," Aidan said gently. "I didn't *go* on anything…I changed the way that I ate. There's a difference."

"I don't understand." Sydney gave a puzzled frown.

"No, I don't expect that you would. Lots of people much older than you are don't understand, either. The difference is, I had to change a whole lot of things about myself. Not only what I ate, but how I ate, when I ate…why I ate… And then I had to learn how to get off my big butt and exercise."

"Your butt's not big, Auntie Aida Beth." Sydney continued to support her aunt.

"It's big enough," Jayden observed. "Looks like you've still got some more learning to do."

"Jayden Nathaniel Holling." Sawyer turned the full force of her disapproval on her son. "Looks to me like we need another lesson in remembering our manners."

Aidan waved her hand in the air, wanting to laugh so badly that she was afraid to speak. She cleared her throat and tried to make herself sound appropriately serious.

"Never mind, Sawyer. Let him speak his mind. I've finally come to peace with the size of my butt. It is what it is…and nothing short of extreme surgery is going to get it any smaller. And I'm not going to go there. Not yet. If a big butt's good enough for Jessica Alba, it's good enough for me." She winked at Sawyer, then peered over the edge of the bed where Jayden sat cross-legged on the floor.

"I'll take that comment about my derriere as a compliment, young man," she said. "But a word of warning to you. You're too young to be looking at women's behinds."

"What are you two doing in here?" Sawyer chastised the twins. "I thought I told you not to wake your aunt Aidan."

"We're sorry, Mama," Jayden was quick to apologize.

"Not sorry enough. Since you two have so much energy,

you can help Chale with his chores today. Jay-Jay, you help
with putting away the dishes. Sydney, you sweep the kitchen
floor and wipe down all of the counters. When you're done
with that, you two can start in the game room. I nearly broke
my neck tripping over all of the toys you left out last night."

"Come on, Jay-Jay." Sydney tugged on her brother.

"Close the door on your way out, will you, Sydney?" Aidan
asked. "Me and your mama have grown-up talk to do."

"Yes, ma'am."

"Thank you, doll."

Sawyer continued to call out instructions to them until she
heard the twins clamor down to their own rooms. "And when
you're done with the kitchen and the game room, you can get
in that nasty bathroom of yours and scrub off all those toothpaste splatters you left on the sink and on the mirror."

"Way to go, Jay-Jay," Sydney complained. "It's all your
fault that we've got extra chores. You got us in trouble, talking
about Aunt Aidan's big butt like that."

Aidan waited until she could no longer hear the twins
before falling back on the bed. She pressed the pillow to her
mouth and laughed until tears streamed down her cheeks.
Sawyer doubled over, pressing her own face to her knees,
gasping for breath.

"My p-p-poor son! She's gonna torture him for the rest
of the day!"

Aidan sat up on her elbow. "I swear if those two don't
remind me of me and Holling when we were kids. We were
always arguing. And every chance I got, I used to whip up on
him so bad. I was always smacking him upside the head."

Sawyer leaned close and whispered, "All that smacking
around, did it do any good? Shape that boy up?"

"You're the one who married him. You tell me."

A sly smile crossed Sawyer's face as she moistened her top lip with her tongue. "Oh, he's good. He's a very good boy."

"He popped out a boy *and* a girl on his first try. I'd say so!"

Sawyer spun around, crossing her legs and resting her back against the footboard.

"Tell me something, Sawyer. It's been seven years now. Any plans for more kids?" Aidan asked. "You seem to have your hands full with those two."

"Oh, me and Holling, we're always making…uh…plans," Sawyer said delicately. "Always. Every chance we get."

"You must be very diligent planners. Even with that busted knee of his, I thought I heard you two making…plans…earlier this morning."

"I thought you were asleep!" Sawyer exclaimed.

"I was until you two woke me up. Plans in the bedroom. Plans on those hardwood floors. Plans in the bathroom… You can hear the strangest things coming from the connecting vents. I'll bet you didn't know that, did you?"

Sawyer fanned her face with her hand. "No. I didn't know that. Thanks for that warning, Aidan."

"With all of that planning going on, you and Holling should have enough rug rats around here to fill this house to the rafters."

Sawyer and Aidan burst into laughter again. They didn't notice as Nate poked his head in the room, until he coughed once, loudly and deliberately.

"Daddy!" Aidan cried out as she leaped out of bed and ran to her father. She kissed him on the cheek, smoothing her hands over his salt-and-pepper beard.

"Welcome home, Aida Beth," Nate said, his voice choking on unshed tears. "Welcome home, baby girl." He patted her awkwardly on the back, then held her out at arm's length. "It's so good to see you."

"Sorry I haven't been up to see you before now, Daddy. I got in so late last night. It took forever for the roads to clear. Sawyer said that you were sleeping. I didn't want to wake you up."

"Don't let her try to pull one over on you, Nate. Aidan's the one who didn't want to wake up. She was so exhausted when she got in that she went straight to bed."

Nate closed one eye, turned to look at Aidan out of the corner of his other eye. "You're looking—"

"Half the woman I used to be?" she finished the sentence for him.

He nodded, his dark eyes twinkling. "What happened to you? And what's this? When did you do this?" He grabbed a handful of her lemony locks and tugged on them. "This ain't gonna come out, is it? The last time I saw you, you were short and spiky and purple. What did they call that? The funk look?"

Aidan shrugged her shoulders, smiling self-consciously. "Punk look, Daddy. Not *funk*. And it wasn't purple. It was a burgundy rinse. I've been growing it and wanted to try something different. What do you think, Daddy?"

"I think you're looking really good, baby girl."

"Feeling good, too, Daddy!" Impulsively, she hugged her father again.

"You had something to eat yet, Aida Beth?"

"No, sir. Like Sawyer said, I just woke up."

"Then, why don't you get dressed and come on downstairs. I'll have Chale fix you some of your favorites. Fried chicken and rice and gravy with plenty of onions."

"How about grilled chicken? Can you make that rice brown?" she added.

"Only if the little missy cooks it." Nate threw a teasing glance Sawyer's way. "All of her rice comes out brown…whether it started out that way or not."

"Not funny, Nate," Sawyer told him. "I told you that I was practicing."

"Practice at the expense of your own stomach," he said, patting his own slightly protruding paunch.

"I'll be down in a minute, Daddy," Aidan promised. "As soon as I change."

Nate stepped to the door, crooking his finger to indicate that Sawyer should follow him. "No hurry," he said. "I'm so glad that you're finally home safe. You lie there and get all of the rest you need, baby girl."

"In that case," Aidan said, lying down and pulling the covers back over her shoulders as she snuggled into the downy comfort of her pillows.

"I'll have plenty of time later to take a strap to you for having me running like a chicken with my head cut off all around the airport looking for you, gal."

Sawyer and Aidan exchanged glances. Aidan lifted an eyebrow in confusion. Sawyer shrugged her shoulders, then gave a negative shake of her head.

"Get some rest, Aidan," Sawyer murmured. "We'll talk later."

Chapter 20

Darion pulled the covers up over his head, wanting so badly to stay asleep. Yet, common sense wasn't prevailing. When he heard the others stirring around, sometime around six-thirty in the morning, he rolled over and tried to block out the noise. He kept his eyes closed and tried to regulate his breathing. *In. Out. In. Out.* Slow. Rhythmic. Calming. Maybe if he could convince his body that he was at rest, his mind would get the hint and soon follow.

He turned over on his side, lying on his arm. Through bleary, red-rimmed eyes, he watched a small patch of sunlight stretch its way across the floor. Dust particles swirled in the sun ray, reminding him of how the blizzard had swirled for two days, making it almost impossible to see the road as he'd driven Aidan back from the airport and keeping them trapped in the motel for another twelve hours before it had been safe enough for them to drive out. Not that he was complaining about that time in the motel. It was a day he would not soon forget. Yet, the reasons they had taken refuge there continued to haunt him.

Darion grunted, trying to push the memory of the drive from his head. He stared up at the ceiling, not counting sheep but the knots in each of the exposed wooden beams running the length of the ceiling. When he thought his eyelids would grow heavy, droop down until he could almost feel himself drifting off, he was startled back to full wakefulness.

What was it Aidan had said? That she'd had a freak-out moment. He'd convinced her not to worry about that. Yet, he couldn't quite convince himself.

Every time he closed his eyes, he could still see Luke's face. He could still hear his voice. His crusty and crudely lustful sense of humor. His overly optimistic view of life and love. He'd only known the man a few hours, yet Luke's influence would remain with him for the rest of his life. In those few hours, Luke had touched him. Marked him forever. He would not forget that night. Not ever.

That thought worried Darion more than he cared to admit. He'd heard of people who'd witnessed traumatic events and were never the same afterward. Some needed therapy to recover. Some needed drugs. Some never recovered—never got their lives back on track. He refused to be one of those people.

"This is crazy," he muttered to himself, flinging his arm over his eyes to block out the image. What was the matter with him? Why was he lying there? It was obvious that he wasn't sleeping. Even though Mrs. Holling had taken pity on him and had told him that he could sleep in today, the longer he lay there, frustrated and exhausted, the more he realized that it wasn't going to happen. Nothing short of a frying pan to the back side of his head was going to make him pass out again.

The thoughts flying around his mind were a jumbled mess, making him too tense to take advantage of her generosity.

For as long as he'd been up, it should have taken a sonic boom to wake him up again. He barely remembered fumbling his way through the bunkhouse last night, passing the rows of snoring workers and collapsing onto his bed. His jacket and his boots remained in a heap beside the bed. Somebody must have thrown a blanket over him because he had no recollection of climbing under the covers. He'd been out before his head had hit the pillow sometime around four o'clock in the morning. It couldn't have been an hour later when he'd sat straight up in bed, sucking air into his lungs as if he'd just run a marathon. Sweat had stood out on his forehead, collected on his back, making his shirt stick to him like a cold, clammy second skin.

He'd looked to his left, then to his right, feeling icy fingers of panic grip his stomach and squeeze. Nothing had seemed amiss. Just rows of sleeping, snoring hands.

"Damn," Darion had muttered, lying down again. He'd been dreaming again. This time, he was thankful that Aidan wasn't there. In the motel, he'd assured her that his nightmare had been a one-time occurrence. It was the only way that she, herself, would try to rest. When he'd told her that he was fine, she'd acted as if she'd believed him—nodding her head at all of the appropriate moments. But, he could feel her lying next to him, tense and watchful, waiting to see if he would have a relapse. The creative way he'd found to lull her back to sleep had worked them both to exhaustion. She'd finally fallen asleep, laughing, yawning and begging for respite from his hip-rocking lullaby.

As enjoyable as making love to her was, he found equally as much pleasure in her company in an upright position. When the motel café had opened, instead of eating there in the restaurant, they'd taken the food back to the room. Spreading their meal out on the motel towels, picnic-style on the bed, they'd sat cross-legged, facing each other, feeding each other. Laughing. Talking. Sharing.

Darion had taken every opportunity to get to know this new woman in his life. He'd rubbed her back. She'd braided his hair. He'd fixed a broken clasp on her bracelet. She'd given him a manicure. Small, insignificant things that probably wouldn't have meant as much if they'd known each other for years or even months. Yet every moment had strengthened the ties they'd already formed during that brief time together.

During the small amount of sleep he did manage after getting back to the ranch, Darion had dreamed. He knew that he'd dreamed. At the moment, what those dreams had been about escaped him. As soon as things quieted down around there, and he started thinking clearly, maybe it would come back to him. All he had to do was lie here, be still, and let his body do what he wanted so badly for it to do.

"Okay." He gave himself a pep talk. "You can do this. Sleep. Go to sleep. You know you want to. Like that old Nike commercial used to say. Just do it. All you've got to do is close your eyes. That's it…that's a good boy. See? Don't you feel better? Aren't you tired? See how heavy your eyelids are? No, don't open them, you jackass!"

Something crashed to the floor across the room. Somebody's coffee mug? A lamp? One of the other hands must have stepped barefoot on the broken shards. Javier, by the sound of his voice. He was yelling for his brother Hector to bring tweezers, alcohol and the first-aid kit stored in the bathroom medicine cabinet.

Darion ground his teeth, trying to ignore the ensuing argument as Hector yelled back in a profanity-strewn mixture of Spanish and English that he wasn't anybody's slave and if his brother was stupid enough not to go around the spill when he saw it happen, it was his own fault and he should get his own bandages.

Any other day, the typical sounds of the Holling's Way ranch workers getting up and getting ready for the day didn't bother Darion. He was usually one of the first ones up, anyway. He was the one turning on the television to catch the morning news. He was the one cranking up the radio, rousing others out of bed with the banal chatter of morning DJs. Cabinets banging, toilets flushing, starting the day with sounds of men cursing—a typical morning symphony. A predictable and comforting assurance that as soon as the sun rose, so did Darion. In the six months that he'd worked there, it had been pretty much the same thing every morning. Variations on a theme. It was all so familiar to him that it didn't seem possible that he'd ever begun his day any other way.

Only, for some unexplained reason, this morning's familiarity bred contempt. All of it. The whining whir of Frank's electric toothbrush. The fact that Danny wouldn't brush his teeth for another three days. The heavy trod of Eli's unlaced work boots against the floor as he stomped back and forth. The sickly sweet smell of Wade's aftershave. Ramiro's tuneless whistling of that Seven Dwarfs' ditty as he spread up his bunk. Tyrell's clearing of his sinuses. Glenn's breathless count as he completed his two hundred crunches—that morning, all of it irked Darion's nerves.

The longer he lay there in bed, the more agitated he became.

"To hell with it."

Darion finally gave up, throwing back the blanket. He pushed himself up, swinging his long legs off the edge of the bed. He sat there for a few minutes, leaning forward on his knees, staring down at the floor until Red Bone came by, thumping him on the back of the head.

"What're you doin' up, Darry?" His gravelly voice was barely above a whisper. His bunk was right next to Darion's. Red Bone plopped down on his own bunk, facing Darion as he buttoned up his flannel shirt over his thermal underwear.

Darion shook his head. "Your guess is as good as mine, Red Bone."

"Mrs. Holling told me this morning not to roust you out of bed, that you should sleep in as long as you needed to. You sure earned it, son. Two days on the road. Must've been some kinda trip."

Rubbing his hand over his head, all the way down his stubbled, itchy chin, Darion said ruefully, "Can't sleep. Wish I could."

"That wreck got you all twisted up, Darry?"

Darion shrugged, looked off. "Something like that."

"We all caught the news. Hell of a thing, that accident. And you were there? You saw it all happen?"

"I was there all right. But I didn't see all of it. The weather was so bad, I could barely see the road."

"It's a miracle that you and Miss Aidan didn't crash yourselves. Somebody must have been watching out for you, boy. You know, the reporters are calling you and Miss Aidan some kinda heroes for what you tried to do to help that poor bastard."

"Heroes?" Darion's laughter was harsh. "A fat lot a good it did. The man died!"

"Darion!" Red Bone popped his fingers to get Darion's attention. "You need to ease up. You did the best that you could, didn't you? You got yourself and Miss Aidan back with barely a scratch."

"Yeah. Barely."

"There you go. *Barely* is gonna have to be good enough."

"You weren't there, Red Bone!" Darion was abrasive. "If you had, you wouldn't be able to sit there and tell me that what I did was good enough."

Red Bone stood up, shoving his arms into his sheepskin jacket. He settled his battered Stetson at a jaunty angle on his head, pulled the brim down low over his eyes.

"You're right, I wasn't there," he acquiesced. "Nobody but you knows what it was like on that mountain. But I didn't have to be there to know that you did the best that you could, boy. Maybe I didn't look into his face. But I'm looking into yours now. You're here. And you got that gal here. That's enough for me…and I'll bet you dollars to doughnuts that it's gonna be good enough for the boss man, too."

"Keep your money in your pocket," Darion advised.

Red Bone's mouth split open, showing a gap-toothed grin as he got a rusty laugh at Darion's expense. "Better be good enough for the big boss man, boy. Especially since every camera from here to Billings caught you snuggling up close and personal with that gal. Wouldn't be surprised if all of that local media coverage made the national news."

Darion groaned as he fell back onto the bed.

Aidan!

That one name summed up all of the anxiety he was feeling. It wasn't the lack of sleep or the irritating habits of his coworkers. It was Aidan. It was Aidan Holling that had him, as Red Bone had put it, all twisted up inside. When they'd been alone at the motel, away from this place, away from curious eyes and wagging tongues, everything had been fine. Perfect. Yet, the moment they'd crossed underneath the archway leading to the ranch, Darion had felt the seeds of doubt springing up inside of him again.

How in the world had things gotten so crazy out of control with that woman? All he was supposed to do was drive the truck. Get her from point A to point B. That's all he was supposed to do. He didn't remember anything in those instructions about fantasizing about the boss man's sister, nearly getting her killed in a car wreck. He was certain that trusting him didn't include grabbing her butt on national television or spending two days locked up in a motel room going through an entire box of condoms.

"It wasn't supposed to go down like that, Red Bone," Darion declared.

"You don't have to explain a thing to me. Anything you want to explain, tell it to the big boss man."

"I'm a dead man," Darion declared. "I am so dead. And he'll get away with it, too. He's going to make sure that they never find my body."

"Saving his sister's life has gotta be worth a stay of execution for you," Red Bone said hopefully.

Darion raised up on his elbows and glared at Red Bone. "You remember Hugh Tracy, don't you?"

Red Bone narrowed his eyes. "No, I don't imagine that I do."

"My point exactly. You think boss man's got a forgiving heart? This is the same man who sent Hugh packing not two days after he started working here because he stared too long at his wife's legs."

"Oh yeah," Red Bone said, nodding slowly and stroking his beard. "Now I remember. But he shouldn't count."

"Why not?"

"'Cause the boss man didn't like Hugh from the start. He was looking for a reason to sack him. Hugh was stupid enough to give it to him. Difference is, Darion, is that the boss man likes you. And he respects you. Most of all, he trusts you."

I trust you, Darion.

Darion sat up again, hoping that movement would drive the sound of his boss's voice from his head. He walked down to the end of the bed where he kept his footlocker. His movements were quick and decisive as he pulled out his duffel bag and stuffed in it another pair of jeans, more thermal underwear and his shaving kit.

"What do you think you're doing?" Red Bone questioned.

"What does it look like I'm doing?" Darion retorted.

"Looks to me like you're packing," Red Bone stated the obvious.

"Give that man a Kewpie. He's won the big prize."

"Where are you going, Darry?"

Darion said, "You and the boss man have worked up the schedule this week, haven't you?"

"Sure."

"You've got Wade out there, riding the north range?"

Again, Red Bone nodded.

"Do me a favor, Red Bone, and switch us."

"Excuse me?"

"I didn't stutter," Darion said. "I said switch us. I'll go instead."

"That's a lot of ground to cover, son. Don't you think you need to rest up a bit? I mean, you just got in."

"I've got all the rest I'm gonna need today. Give me the keys to the mule. I'm assuming you've already got it gassed up. The line shack's stocked with supplies?"

"You know that it is."

"Then, I don't see the problem. If I head out now, I can be out there by sunset."

"What's your hurry?"

"No hurry," Darion said, avoiding Red Bone's gaze. "Boss man's paying me to do a job. Let me do it."

Red Bone snorted. "I changed my mind. You're not packing. You're running."

"I'm not running."

"Like hell you're not. You didn't talk to him last night after you dropped his sister off, did you?"

"He was asleep when we got in." Darion gave a plausible enough excuse. "If anyone had to wake him up, it was better that his wife and sister do it."

"And you don't think he'll want to talk to you before you take off again?"

"What's there to talk about?"

"That's not for me to say, son."

Darion stuffed the last of his few personal belongings into his duffel bag and held out his hand.

"Are you going to give me the keys to the mule or not?"

Red Bone stuck his hand deep down into his pocket. He pulled out a set of keys to the all-terrain vehicle and handed them to Darion, though not before lowering his head and covering his mouth to cover a sneeze.

Darion glared at Red Bone. It wasn't a sneeze that he heard coming from Red Bone's mouth, but a poorly masked exclamation of *"Chickenshit!"*

"I'll hit the boss man on the cell when I'm on my way," Darion said, slinging his duffel over his shoulder and starting for the door.

"If you ask me, Darry, I think you're making a mistake by cutting out like this."

"I didn't ask you," Darion nastily reminded him.

Red Bone trailed behind him. He reached out, clasped his hand on Darion's shoulder. "Not a way to keep the boss man's trust, Darion," he advised.

Darion whirled around, pushing the hand off. "You don't get it, do you, Red Bone?"

The older man regarded the younger one in a mixture of concern and disappointment. "Why don't you tell me what's bothering you."

"It's because the boss man trusts me so much that I have to get out of here. I don't want to do anything to make him regret trusting me, Red Bone. The last few days…well…" He shrugged, casting around for the right words. "All I can say is that those days shouldn't have happened. Not like that. I need a few days to get my head around what I'm gonna do next. Just for a few days."

"Until when?"

Darion opened the door to the bunkhouse, turning his gaze to the house.

I trust you, Darion.

"Well?" Red Bone prompted when Darion didn't respond right away.

He whispered more to himself than to answer Red Bone. "Until I can trust myself again."

Understanding suddenly dawned on the older man. "It's not the boss man you're running from," he accused Darion. "It's her, ain't it? It's his sister."

"I told you once. I'm not running."

"What's the matter with you, Darry? You think you're the only man who let a pretty woman make him act like a fool?"

"It wasn't an act. I *was* a fool. A stone fool."

"So what?" Red Bone said dismissively. "So you got a little free and easy with your hands—"

"That's not it!" Darion snarled.

"Then what is it?"

Darion shifted uncomfortably, stared down at his feet.

Red Bone dropped his taunting. "Are you trying to tell me that you've got feelings for her, son? Or maybe witnessing that wreck has got you confused?"

Darion dropped his duffel on the front porch and leaned against the split rail banister along the bunkhouse front porch. He sounded weary as he confessed. "It wasn't the wreck, Red Bone. I knew long before then that I was going to be in trouble with that woman."

"Like the first time you saw her."

"I don't believe in love at first sight," Darion said derisively.

"You don't have to...as long as it believes in you." Red Bone chuckled.

"When Mr. Holling hired me, he took me for my word. I told him that I'd work hard for him and that I'd never give him a reason to regret his decision to hire me. I meant that. Mr. Holling never demanded more of me than I wanted to give. Even though he knew that I had some things I had to work on...to work out...he trusted me. I owe him for that. I'm not going to disappoint him by—"

"By hooking up with his sister," Red Bone finished for him.

Again, Darion nodded. "I'm not ready to go there with her, Red Bone. Not yet. I've got some things I have to work out first."

Red Bone put his hand on Darion's shoulder. "Put that duffel away, son. You know you're not going anywhere. You're not the kind of man to tuck your tail between your legs and run."

"You think you know me," Darion challenged. "But you

don't. None of you do. Not you. Not the boss man. And not his sister."

"I'll be the first to admit that you can be a closemouthed son of a cuss when you want to be. But a man doesn't have to talk about himself for anyone to figure out what kind of a man he is. His actions tell the world who he is. If you were the kind of man who would cut out at the first sign of trouble, then you wouldn't have tried to help that tanker truck driver."

Darion hefted his bag as he returned to the bunkhouse. His words drifted back to amuse Red Bone even more.

"I *told* you that I was a fool."

Chapter 21

Aidan was no fool. She knew that Darion was avoiding her. They'd been back for six days. Six days since that terrible night and the seemingly never-ending drive to get her back home. Six days since spending what she considered pure pleasure and bliss in that motel room with him. And in all of that time since returning home, he'd barely spoken as many words to her.

As she and Sawyer sat in the library wrapping last-minute gifts, Aidan twisted her face and mimicked Darion's low tones.

"*Yes, Miss Holling. No, Miss Holling.* And that's pretty much the extent of his conversation with me, Sawyer. What's up with that?"

"Don't take it personally, Aidan," Sawyer said comfortingly. "Darion's not much for casual conversation."

Aidan leaned forward and whispered to Sawyer, "There's nothing casual about that man. Everything about him is seriously intense. And I mean ev-e-ry-*thang!* Including the way he makes love. Umph!" She emphasized each syllable.

"Shh!" Sawyer warned, pointing through the wall to the room next to them. "Nate's over there. You think he wants to hear about his baby girl getting busy with the hired help?"

"Oh, thanks," Aidan whispered, then said loudly for the benefit of anyone eavesdropping, "Pass me that strip of green ribbon over there, will you, Sawyer?"

"Of course," Sawyer also said in a raised voice. She looked around before continuing. "He keeps to himself a lot. Maybe he's looking for the right time to talk to you," Sawyer suggested, passing Aidan the ribbon and the tape dispenser.

Aidan sighed, dropping her shoulders and staring discontentedly at the bow she'd placed lopsidedly on the package. "It's not as if I'm not giving him the opportunity," Aidan protested. "Short of stalking the man, I'm not sure what more I can do to get the dialogue going again."

"You sure it's only the dialogue you're interested in?" Sawyer asked. She grabbed another unwrapped present from the bin on the table and selected a sheet of silver metallic paper to wrap it in.

"I'd be lying if I said that he didn't whip something on me," Aidan confessed. "Try the red and silver trimmed tinsel with that one."

"Lovely," Sawyer agreed, holding the ribbon next to the package.

"We're not children, Sawyer," Aidan complained. "I mean, I knew what I was setting myself up for when I let my proverbial guard down. And I knew he'd probably have second thoughts. But, I thought we'd parted with the understanding that it was okay to have second thoughts as long as he lets me know what he's thinking. Maybe we moved too fast. Oh, who am I kidding? There's no maybe to it. We did move too fast. Not only is he refusing to talk to me, but he's not even letting me know that he's thinking about me! That really hurts!" she exclaimed.

Sawyer wasn't sure if Aidan was talking about Darion's treatment of her or the paper cut she suddenly received trying to wrap an awkwardly sized gift.

"Let me let you in on a little secret. When Holling and I first met, I wasn't so sure about him, either. Though, he seemed to know from the very beginning that I was the one he wanted."

"Goody for you two," Aidan complained, sticking her hand in her mouth to soothe the tiny scratch at the base of her thumb.

"Stop that!" Sawyer chastised, forcing Aidan to take her hand from her mouth. "Your mouth is a breeding ground for all kinds of germs."

"You don't have to tell me." Aidan chuckled, remembering how confused Darion had looked when she'd refused the use of his cell phone.

"What I'm trying to tell you is this…" Sawyer continued. "You Hollings are a very stubborn, very opinionated people. Right or wrong, you make up your minds in a hurry and don't give those who don't think or feel as quickly as you do time to agree with you."

"That's my brother Holling all right."

"And you, from what I can see. You two have the same genes. The same blood coursing through your veins. If it's meant for you and Darion to be together, you will be."

"You believe that?"

"Of course I believe that. So stop chasing the man."

"I'm not chasing him," Aidan said, puffing up with indignation. "I'm only shadowing him. Just in case he turns around and decides that's where he wants me to be."

"Cut it out, Aidan," Sawyer advised. "Give him some space."

"You mean play hard to get?"

Sawyer's smile was smug. "Isn't it a little too late for that?"

"That's catty," Aidan replied. "True. But catty. Okay, Sawyer. I'll take your advice. Obviously, you know what you're talking about."

"Why? Because I'm a renowned romance novelist?" Sawyer asked, waiting for her accolade.

"No. Because you've managed to stay married to that bull-headed brother of mine for as long as you have!"

Aidan tried to follow her sister-in-law's advice. She tried to stay out of Darion's way. It wasn't always easy. Since Holling was still mostly bedridden, more times than she preferred, she was constantly running into Darion either coming to or leaving from the house. She kept the conversation cool, to a minimum, as Sawyer had directed. But that didn't stop her blood from boiling every time he left her with a response so cold, she bitterly joked to Sawyer that she wondered if the man managed to leave any cold for the winter to use.

A few days after her return, when she was out playing in the snow with the twins, Aidan thought she saw Darion literally perform an about-face, turn in the opposite direction, to keep from following the path that would lead him past where they were building their snow forts. She didn't think he would have acknowledged her at all if she hadn't swiftly wadded up two handfuls of snow, packed them tightly and launched it right at the back of his head.

The snow missile struck him below the neck, sending chunks of ice down his collar. Darion spun around, clawing at his back, trying to shake out the snow. It didn't take him long to figure out what had happened.

"She did it!"

Both Jayden and Sydney pointed mittened fingers at her, dropping their own snowballs to the ground as he scowled at them.

"Snitch," Aidan muttered out of the corner of her mouth. With her hands on her hips, she scowled back at Darion, daring him to say something. Anything. Anything would have been better than that wall of silence that he'd erected between them.

But, he didn't say a word as he pulled out a large hunk of ice from behind his collar, hefted it menacingly into the air of couple of times as if considering retaliation then let the clump fall back to the ground.

"I don't think Mr. Darion wants to play," Jayden observed. *Out of the mouths of babes,* Aidan thought. "I think you're right," was what she said aloud, smiling down at her niece and nephew. She stood there, staring at Darion's retreating figure a few minutes before Sydney and Jayden grew impatient.

"Come on, Aunt Aida Beth. Let's play! We want to play."

And so did she. Only, Darion wasn't cooperating. She knelt down, grabbing the small tin pan they'd used to scrape piles of snow, and began to pack more snow onto the low wall. Masking her frustration, Aidan hoped that the twins would see her sharp, stabbing motions as enthusiasm.

If he didn't want to play, she thought angrily, then he shouldn't have started the game. What was the matter with that man? Getting her all worked up and then stepping back as if nothing had ever happened! What did he think she was? A light switch? That he could turn on the juice whenever he wanted and flip her off again? He couldn't play with her emotions like that! Who did he think he was dealing with?

"Aunt Aidan?" Sydney tapped her on the shoulder.

Aidan kept scraping. Kept dumping piles of snow on the fort. Kept punching and packing it down with her fists.

"Auntie?" Jayden addressed her, his voice squeaky with concern. If she kept packing snow like that, it would get too big for them to see over.

Aidan supposed that she should have seen Darion's emotional defection coming. Even as he'd pulled up the drive in front of the house and shut off the engine, she had felt him shutting down on her—shutting her out. It hadn't helped matters that he'd called ahead to let them know that they were only minutes away. The look of relief on his face when he'd spoken with Sawyer, instead of Holling, had been almost comical. Aidan didn't have to look at Darion to see the guilt and self-recrimination on his face after he'd reported in. She had heard it in his voice. Though he'd tried to mask it, she felt close enough to him to know that he wasn't looking forward to facing her brother.

Aidan knew that she only had a couple of seconds before someone would be coming through that door to usher her inside. They only had a minute, maybe less, to say the kinds of things they needed to say, wanted to say, before the moment was gone. Aidan counted the seconds slipping away by the sounds of the keys clicking as they swung against the ignition when Darion had come to a stop. And yet, he didn't say a word to her. Not a single word. If he wasn't going to do something, then she'd have to.

"Well," she said with forced cheerfulness, "we made it."

"Yes, ma'am. We did."

Ma'am? When had she become *ma'am* again? While they'd been making the last leg home, she'd been Aidan. And before then, while they'd made love again and again and again so that she'd soon lost count, he'd called her by secret names meant for her ears only.

As they sat parked in front of her brother's house, he

didn't take her hand, didn't put his arms around her, or try to kiss her—even though she wanted him to. It was worse than being on a first date in high school when Holling and her brother Shane had put the word out that they would stomp any boy in the throat who tried anything "funny" with their sister.

Darion's sudden emotional withdrawal wasn't funny. It was painful. She needed him to alleviate that pain. She desperately wanted him to. She needed him to do something. Anything to show that their time together wasn't a fluke. She needed to know that the things he'd said to her, even the words he communicated with only his eyes, were still true.

She'd openly asked him whether he thought she was easy or was nothing more than a cheap thrill. He'd said no and she'd taken him at his word. All she needed now was a word to make her feel secure in her decision to share her most intimate thoughts and feelings with him. She needed to know that he would still be there for her.

Yet, Darion didn't make a move. It seemed to Aidan that he was putting forth an extraordinary effort not to twitch as much as an eyelash. So, Aidan took the initiative.

She unbuckled her seat belt and turned her body so that she was completely facing him. "Well, Slim. What are you waiting for? Are you going to kiss me good-night, or what?" Aidan asked bluntly.

"Kiss you?"

"Yes," she said, smiling slightly. "Right here." She tapped her lips with her gloved fingers. "Or, if you don't like the taste of my Chap Stick, you can kiss me here," she offered, touching her cheek. She waggled her eyebrow at him and lowered her hand to her left breast. "Or what about here?"

"No, ma'am. I'm not going to do that."

"Are you sure you don't want to?" she taunted, reaching for his hand and placing it over her breast.

"Cut that out!" Darion pulled away from her as if she had suddenly contracted leprosy.

"I thought you might want to, considering the circumstances—"

"Exactly," Darion cut her off. "The only reason I'm here with you now is because of circumstances. Circumstances beyond our control. I lost control, Aidan...Miss Holling...and I shouldn't have."

Aidan paused for a moment, absorbing the full impact of his statement. It hit her hard! She felt like a punch-drunk fighter, having taken too many blows to the head. One fatal one to the heart.

"You mean, if given the choice, you wouldn't have gotten out in the middle of the night, braved a blizzard, hurled yourself down a mountain after a potential flaming ball of diesel fuel, or tucked yourself in a mountain hideaway for a night of free and willing sex?"

"By all rights, I shouldn't be here with you," he told her.

Aidan stuck her tongue to the roof her mouth. The way he sounded, the way he acted, it was as if he were dumping her. Dumping her?! Before they'd even gotten a chance to see if they could make it work between them?

Aidan made one last-ditch attempt to salvage the secret treasure they'd found in each other. "So, what are you trying to tell me, Slim? All that stuff about me...feeling you...putting your heart to mine, getting to know me. What was that? Was that just circumstances, too?"

"Yes, ma'am, it was. If circumstances had been otherwise, you know as well as I do that it would have never happened. If that tanker hadn't wrecked, if the roads had been clear, if

I'd been able to drop you off at your doorstep, no detours, no incidents, and…uh, other things never would have gone that way between us."

"Things?" It was Aidan's turn to sound harsh. "By things, do you mean touching me, holding me and kissing me? Me kissing you…in places you've probably never been kissed before. Are those the kinds of *things* you're talking about, Mr. Haddock?" If he could get all stiff and formal on her, she could, too.

"That's exactly what I mean."

"So what am I supposed to do now? Am I supposed to pretend that it didn't happen?" Aidan used every ounce of her self-control to keep from sounding hurt.

He shook his head no. "No. You don't have to pretend. Just forget that it did."

"Can you? Can you forget?"

"No," he replied. "But I can pretend."

Aidan snatched up her purse and flung open the door. "No wonder you and my brother get along. You're a real piece of work, Darion Haddock." She slammed the door to the truck, loud enough to wake anyone who hadn't heard the truck pull up. "I should have known," she said raggedly. "I'm such an idiot! I'll never learn. You're exactly like all of the other SOBs who wind up here under my brother. You're all losers. Every single one of you!"

He got out of the truck, not responding to her accusation, or defending himself or his actions. He simply grabbed her suitcase and would have carried it up the stairs, but Aidan snatched it out of his grasp.

"Don't bother, Slim," she said. "You did your job. You got me here. If I had a dollar, I'd tip you for the services rendered."

That remark must have stung him. He stepped close to her, his expression pained as if he wanted to explain. "Aidan…"

"Don't!" She stopped him by holding up her hand, much like he'd done in the motel after waking from that nightmare. "Please don't."

Don't say her name. Don't look at her like that. Don't make her believe that it was more than circumstances that had brought them together and forged the kind of bond that would make them risk life and limb for each other.

"Look," he said, trying to sound reasonable as he held up both hands to placate her. "We're both tired. Can we table this discussion until we've both had a chance to catch up on some sleep?"

"If you tell me that things are going to look better in the morning—" she began.

"I don't have to," Darion interrupted. "You know that they will."

But things weren't any better in the morning, Aidan reminisced. If anything, going to sleep made matters much worse. On the fourth day since her return home, he'd performed an about-face to avoid her while she and the twins had played. On the fifth day, he'd turned down an offer to join the Hollings for supper. On the sixth day, she'd had enough. *Throw in the towel. Wave the white flag.* Cry uncle. Darion Haddock had proven his point. There was nothing between them. Nothing more than the stress of a traumatic event to bind them. Now that it was all over, whatever bond they had between them was gone, as well.

She was no fool. She wasn't going to go chasing after a man who didn't want her. Not when it was obvious to her that she could have her pick of any man on that ranch. She was no fool and she wasn't blind. All she had to do was crook her finger and any one of them would fall all over themselves to see to her whims. Aidan quickly figured out that she didn't have to lift a finger if she didn't want to. A simple glance at any one of them was enough to have them following her around for the rest of the day, if that's what she wanted.

Javier and Hector were so cute, with their swarthy Latin looks and their fiery poetic declarations of love and devotion. Glenn had the kind of pectorals that would make any woman drool. Even in the dead of winter, he didn't mind showing them off to her, whenever he could, flexing for her benefit. Frank flashed his porcelain veneers at her, smiling all the time he talked to her. Though she thought it a little creepy that a man could talk even through his smile, she never let it show on her expression whenever he offered to keep her company on some of her horseback nature rides. Eli made up the sweetest songs to sing to her. She never knew the words because they were all whistled. But she was touched whenever she heard him deliberately working under her window, whistling as loud as he could to make the song carry. Aidan knew that it was simply a matter of time before one of them asked her out.

It had been so long since she'd been on an actual date that any of them would have been a welcome diversion. Only, it wasn't a diversion that she wanted. She wasn't about to get a reputation of sleeping through all of her brother's hired hands because she was lonely. She was lonely, but she wasn't desperate. And she wasn't a fool. A reputation like that wouldn't stay on the ranch, but would spread like wildfire through White Wolf. She was already a favored topic of conversation. Black sheep of the family. Standoffish. Oddball. Two tons of fun. Flake. Now that she was back and looking as she looked, she wasn't going to add *town slut* to the long list of names. If she believed any of the gossip, that role was already taken by her mother. She knew that everyone in White Wolf was waiting to see if Janeen Holling's only daughter followed in her footsteps.

Aidan wouldn't give them the satisfaction. What was it her father used to say to her? Don't squat where you live? Or something like that... If she was going to mess around, she wasn't going to do it in her own backyard.

She woke up Saturday morning to the sounds of laughter and engines starting. She climbed out of bed, then pushed aside the heavy draperies to stare out the window. Her brother's employees were piling into their vehicles to make a run into White Wolf. Red Bone. Hector. Tyrell. She heaved a sigh of regret. If she had any sense, she'd be out there with them. What harm would it do if she got a party-girl rep if she went out with *all* of them, rather than singling one of them out?

"More drama than I'm ready to deal with," she sighed aloud. She dressed and went down to breakfast, listlessness making her push her food around on her plate.

Sawyer sat across from her, silently watching her.

"You're not going to eat that, are you, Auntie Aidan?" Jayden asked, pointing to her plate of barely touched English muffins and Canadian bacon.

"No, I'm not. You can have it, Jay-Jay," Aidan said, pushing her plate across the table at him. She picked up her coffee mug, sipping contemplatively.

"Aidan, can you give me a hand with these?" Sawyer said suddenly, rising from the table, whisking that plate out from under her son's nose. "You've had enough, son. You need to work off the four muffins that you've already had."

Picking up the extra dishes, Aidan followed behind Sawyer.

"You need me to do the dishes?" Aidan asked.

"Not really. I only wanted to get you away from the table," Sawyer teased. "If your expression got any more sour, I'd expect you to start mumbling 'Bah! Humbug!'"

"I'm acting like a lovesick teenager, aren't I? Ohh, I hate that about myself!"

"You need something to do to take your mind off of things. When I get upset, too wrapped up in myself, I take the focus off of my problems."

"Do you have any suggestions?"

"I do," Sawyer began. "But I have to warn you, Aida Beth, my motives are purely selfish and self-serving."

"No one can accuse you of having ulterior motives."

"Hey, it's almost Christmas. Can't be telling whoppers this close unless I want to find a lump of coal in my stocking."

"What do you need?"

"I was wondering if you could take the twins off my hands for a little while. I've got a few more presents to wrap. Some for my kids and some for the kids at the women's shelter where I volunteer. I don't want the kids prying and peeking and peeling aside wrapping paper."

"You don't even have to ask, Sawyer. I can keep them as long as you need me to."

"I appreciate it. I love my babies, but I know they can be a handful."

"Can the kids ice-skate? I was thinking about going out on Daddy's lake today to get some exercise."

"Can they skate?" Sawyer scoffed. "Holling strapped ice skates on them before they were barely old enough to walk. Skating. That sounds like a wonderful idea. Nate got them sleds last year. Take that, too. If you cut across the pasture instead of taking the road, you'll cut a mile off the trip. One thing, since Nate had the lake dredged and deepened a couple of years ago, it doesn't always freeze solid."

"Oh, well, maybe I won't go, then," Aidan hesitated.

"No, it's all right. Holling makes sure to put cones out near the danger zone. Go ahead and take them. Maybe if they skate half the day, they'll be so tired tonight that they won't try to stay up and wait for me and Holling to start putting together some of their presents."

"I remember how me and Holling and Shane used to take shifts, to try to stay awake and catch Daddy."

"I'll bet you three never made plans to jack that old man for his sack of presents," Sawyer said. "Sydney and Jayden have. You know, I've actually eavesdropped on them and heard something about taking the cookies and milk they've set out for him and dumping in the cold medicine."

"Cold medicine?" Aidan repeated.

"Yes, cold medicine. It made them sleepy," Sawyer explained. "I guess they figured that if they put enough in there, Santa will fall asleep while they pilfer his presents."

"They can't be that bad!" Aidan laughed incredulously.

"Love them dearly. But don't ever let your guard down around them."

"I'll make up a lunch for you and pack some hot cocoa and marshmallows while you get the twins geared up."

"You don't know how much I appreciate this, Aida Beth."

"Don't say another word about it, sister. I've got six years of being the favorite auntie to catch up on."

"You might not say that after you've spent the entire day with them," Sawyer warned. "I told you, they can be tough. Especially that Sydney. She's sweet, but she's sneaky. Watch her closely. Make sure she doesn't talk Jay-Jay into doing something boneheaded."

"I'll treat them like they were my own," Aidan said solemnly.

Sawyer saw a look cross her sister-in-law's face. The look that she read immediately. The look that wondered whether there could possibly be a family of her own in her future. Oh, how

Sawyer knew that look. Before she'd met Holling, after seeing all of her cousins—as close as sisters—happily paired off, she wondered whether anything that special was waiting for her.

"I'll be ready in fifteen minutes," Sawyer promised. She went back into the breakfast nook, crooked her finger at the twins. "Let's go, you two. Get your snow gear on."

Chapter 22

Holling had his game face on. He clenched his teeth, sweat poured from almost every pore as he cautiously made his way from his room. Nate was behind him, giving him his own brand of encouragement.

"Of all the boneheaded ideas," Nate berated him. "You need to put your stubborn, mule-headed butt back in that bed before you do some real damage to yourself. It's not like you're sixteen anymore…or even twenty-five and can heal fast. You've got old bones now, Holling."

"I told you, Pops, that I can't stay in that bed another minute," Holling ground out, sliding his leg without the cast in front of him. Working the crutches and the cast he got through the first set of rooms, and had to lean on the padded arm of the crutch to catch his breath.

Darion was in front of him, walking backward, ready to spring if Holling suddenly became unsteady on his feet.

"As soon as the little missy catches you..." Nate let his voice trail off.

"I'm not worried about that. I wear the pants in this family," Holling said offhandedly, ignoring the scoffs from both Nate and Darion.

"That may be true, boy. You may wear wear them. But since your accident, she tells you when and how you should wear them," Nate pointedly reminded him.

"Okay...okay...I am worried about what that wife of mine will say and do. But, if we hurry this sideshow along, by the time Sawyer figures out that I'm not in bed, it'll be too late to do anything about it. Besides, I figure Sawyer will be glad that I'm outta bed. Maybe now she'll be able to get some rest."

Holling gave Darion a sly look and would have nudged him if it weren't for the fact that he was afraid he'd lose his grip on the crutches and go tumbling to the hardwood floors. He drew a deep breath and said, "Okay, I think I'm ready for that final push. You got everything set up in my office for me, Darion?"

"Yes, sir."

"Good."

Darion had spread out pillows and extra blankets on the couch. He'd moved the desk closer to the couch set up with Holling's laptop computer and cordless phone. Sawyer had not allowed them to bring the computer to the bedroom, saying that the bedroom was for sleeping...or other private activities that didn't involve computers or cell phones or printers or fax machines.

Holling figured that he'd been out of commission long enough. His knee was busted. Not his hands. Not his ears. Not his mouth. He didn't need full use of his leg to get back to work. Maybe, in a few days, if he could convince Sawyer that he could work without reinjuring himself, she wouldn't object to letting him get outside, overseeing work with the livestock.

Though Darion had brought back favorable reports, he wanted to see to matters for himself. He could no longer ignore the nagging sense of urgency to get fully plugged in to his work again. He trusted Darion to do his job. He wouldn't have put him in charge if he didn't. But a feeling deep in his gut told him that he had to get out of that bed. Though he tried to push it to the back of his mind, the longer he lay there and pretended that he was relaxed, the more agitated he became. He had to be involved again. If anything had been seriously wrong, he knew that Nate or Sawyer or Darion would have told him. As much as they wanted him to relax and recuperate, they had better sense than to keep ill news from him. No, it wasn't what they told him that made him anxious. It was what they *didn't* tell him. He might not have ever had an inkling that anything was amiss if it wasn't for a chance encounter with him, Darion, and of all people—Aidan.

She'd burst into the room without knocking to let him know that she and Sawyer were going out. At first she hadn't seen Darion over in the corner. She might not have ever known that he'd been there if it hadn't been for Darion suddenly dropping his coffee mug, sending steaming hot liquid splattering down his shirt. He'd leaped up from his chair, knocking it to the floor as well.

Aidan had tsk-tsked, rolled her eyes, and then had closed the door behind her. Moments later, she'd returned with a couple of towels.

"Here you go, Slim," she'd said as she'd approached him. "Déjà vu, huh?"

Darion had taken a step back as if she'd been holding out a grenade to him.

"Take the towels, Slim. I'm not your mama," she'd quipped. "You'll have to clean up your own mess."

He'd taken the towels from her, practically snatched them from her hand. "Thanks," he'd muttered.

"Don't mention it." She'd smiled at him, but it had been icy. Oh-so-icy. It had given Holling the chills, and it hadn't even been directed at him.

Holling didn't talk to his sister often. But he knew a pissed-off tone when he heard one. There was an undertone that he couldn't mistake. Couldn't ignore. It made him anxious to get back on his feet to get fully involved with his work, with his family again. Because, unless his instincts were wrong, the two had become intricately connected through Aidan and Darion.

Though he desperately wanted to, he'd resisted the impulse to interrogate Darion about his time with Aidan. It was enough for him to know that he'd trusted Darion with Aidan's return and he'd kept her safe, despite the weather conditions, despite the road hazards, despite the perils of the drive from the airport. Aidan had not complained of Darion's treatment of her during that time, so he could only assume that she'd been treated well. He would have gone on believing that all was well if he hadn't caught that look between them. A look that had said nothing, yet had conveyed everything. If he'd had a butterfly net, he could have scooped up all the tension flying in the air between them.

"Take it easy, boss man. Ten more steps to go," Darion encouraged. He checked over his shoulder, making sure the path was clear. No stray kids' toys left on the stairs or on the path to Holling's office to cause him to trip. At the bottom of the stairs, he'd parked Holling's wheelchair. Holling had insisted that he wouldn't need the chair, but Darion knew by the time he'd reached the bottom of the stairs that he was glad to have it. Even now, he could see the strain on Holling's face. Strain and determination. He wouldn't give up. Couldn't, even if he wanted to. He'd made it this far. It would cause him more pain to turn around and go back.

"Easy…easy…six more to go… Make sure you lean on that crutch, boss. Let it do the work for you."

"You're not much help, Darion, encouraging him," Nate chastised the younger man.

"He was going to try it with or without us," Darion surmised.

"You got that right," Holling huffed as he made it down the last stair.

Nate took his crutches as Darion eased him into the chair.

"Whew!" Holling breathed a sigh of relief, wiping his forehead on his shoulder. "I didn't know walking could be this hard."

"You think this is bad, wait until you start physical therapy," Darion advised.

Holling looked up at him. "You know something about reconstructive knee surgery?"

"No…not exactly," Darion hedged. "But I've spent some time in therapy. I'm telling you, sir, it's no joke."

Holling nodded his head, though he knew he couldn't appreciate the full extent of Darion's experience. Even after six months, there was much about the man's past that he didn't know.

Every now and then, Darion let something slip out. Though Holling suspected that it wasn't a casual slip of the lip. There was nothing casual about Darion. Everything about him was deliberate—from his choice of words to his mannerisms to his clothes.

Holling wasn't taken in by the simple way Darion dressed. Darion's clothes were well-worn even though Holling knew that he could afford better. For reasons of his own, Darion chose to dress that way. He'd come to Holling's Way looking for work. Laborer's work. Laborer's wages. Yet, Holling knew from the moment he'd opened his mouth that Darion was well educated. It wasn't a question of putting the *G* at the end of certain words or clearly enunciating others. Holling knew plenty of people who were educated, but didn't have a lick of sense. He'd also had dealings with people who'd barely made it out of high school but could calculate the price of beef on the hoof almost to the dollar by looking at the animal. They could do it all in their heads—without fancy calculators or spreadsheets.

There were other clues Holling picked up on that let him know there was more going on inside of Darion's head than he let on. When Darion had applied for the job, he'd completed the short application quickly, efficiently. Maybe it was because he'd completed many before and knew the answers to the questions without having to refer to a résumé or a cheat sheet. Without letting on to what he was doing, Holling had watched Darion as he'd completed the application. Darion's answers were concise, but directed, almost manipulative, as if he knew what kinds of answers would appear favorable to a possible employer. Again, it could have been because he'd filled out so many of them himself. Or, as Holling suspected, it was because Darion could have once been in a hiring position. He knew the answers that would impress an employer because he could have been one.

Even Darion's nervous habits hinted at the less-than-casual nature of the man. When he was sitting, supposedly relaxing, he gave the impression of being the kind of man who was always active. His mind. His thoughts. His potential. Fingers drumming. Knees bouncing. He was a man used to action.

And not being able to act, for whatever reason, was worse than having shackles.

Despite all of the conflicting signals that Darion sent out, Holling still had a sense about him. Call it a sixth sense. Call it instinct. But he knew that Darion was the kind of man he wanted working for him. And with him by his side.

"Did you pull those figures from last month?" Holling asked.

"The spreadsheet is queued up on your laptop. I also merged the data for the past six months, dropped them into a pivot table so you could see past trends," Darion responded as he wheeled Holling into this office. "If you want to project the numbers out for the next three, six, nine or twelve months, all you have to do is use that macro I built for you. Right on the toolbar."

Holling was visibly impressed. He could probably count on one hand the number of workers who could make a computer dance and sing as Darion was able to do.

"Good. Good," Holling responded. "Move me right up there. Yeah, that's close enough."

Darion pushed him close to the desk so that he could reach the laptop. Holling adjusted the screen, staring at it for a few minutes. His fingers tapped on the keyboard, calling up the files that Darion had created, while Darion stood by.

"Go on and take a seat, Darion. I won't keep you long," Holling promised.

"As long as you need me, boss," Darion said, pulling up the chair that he usually sat in when he faced Holling across the desk.

"It's Christmas eve. I'm sure you've got places to go. People you want to spend your time with. You don't need to spend it here working."

"I'm where I need to be," Darion replied. He sat silently, expectantly, while Holling flipped through several papers in a manila folder, comparing the printed copy to the figures on the screen. "You're one to talk. What are you doing working when you could be spending it with your family?"

"Sawyer says I'm thumbs when it comes to wrapping presents. Believe me, I'm doing her a favor by staying out of her hair. This is her big push to get everything done. I should be able to get a lot of work done since the twins aren't around," Holling said aloud, more to himself than for casual conversation. "Those two certainly know how to stir up a ruckus."

Darion made a noncommittal sound, neither agreeing nor disagreeing with him. Holling almost laughed out loud. He knew that Darion was following the cardinal rule of the non-parent to the parent. Never comment on how "bad" a parent says their kid is. His kids could be setting a fire right in front of him. Darion would never verbally correct them, but would simply do what he thought his boss would want him to do. Put out the fire.

Holling was grateful that he'd never commented about his badass kids, even when he could have. He'd never muttered a disparaging word about Jayden's judgment, or lack of it, when he'd found the boy with his tongue stuck to a metal pole. He'd simply gotten the warm water he'd needed to free him and had brought him inside, shivering, crying and thankful that someone had rescued him from his sister's relentless pranks.

"Aida Beth took them out to let off some steam. And to give their poor parents a break from all of that pent-up energy."

"I saw them leave a while ago," Darion replied. He sat across from Holling, toying with the fringe on one of the accent pillows that Sawyer had tossed all around the room.

"Speaking of letting off steam. What about that Appaloosa mare, Darion? Have you been working her?"

"Not today. But I will if you want me to."

"Actually," Holling said glancing up, "I believe I do. Since the weather's been so bad, she's been cooped up for too long. I don't want her to start cribbing, taking out chunks of the stall because she's bored."

"Fine. As soon as we finish up here, I'll take her out and give her a good run. She's certainly got spirit," Darion agreed.

"Yep. Gotta treat her right so you won't break her spirit."

"I'll be gentle," Darion promised.

"But consistent," Holling added. "I don't want her getting confused and picking up bad habits because her handler isn't consistent. That's why I've only allowed you around her, Darion. I trust you to do what's best for her. I want to know, did I choose the right man for the job?"

Holling looked up, meeting Darion's gaze head-on. By now, Darion should have picked up on the fact that he wasn't necessarily talking about that horse anymore. Darion was an intelligent man. An intuitive man. Holling watched as Darion shifted in his seat, though not from nervousness or discomfort. Darion settled himself in the chair, collecting himself and his thoughts. If he didn't know by now, he was being interviewed, evaluated, much the way he had been on the day he'd come up there looking for a job. Only this time, they both knew that there was something more at issue here than gainful employment. From the look on Darion's face, Holling knew that Darion was giving this interview the proper amount of serious consideration.

"I want to believe that you did, boss man," Darion said. "I want you to know that I'm doing the best that I can with her."

"Is there a problem that I should know about?"

"No. Not really." Darion shrugged.

Holling leaned forward, pinning him with a hard stare. "Would you tell me if there was?"

"If I thought you could help solve it," Darion admitted without flinching.

"So, tell me, Darion, exactly what have you been doing with my…mare," Holling asked bluntly. "Riding her?"

"Taking care of her," he countered. "As best I can. Why do you ask? Have you heard otherwise?"

"Horses don't talk."

"No, they don't," Darion agreed.

"That's why I'm asking you. I want it—"

"Straight from the horse's mouth, so to speak."

"So to speak," Holling echoed, giving Darion the impression that it was better to talk now than for Holling to find out about him later, from someone else, from Aidan, if he'd mistreated her.

Darion clasped his hands in front of himself, leaned forward, but he didn't speak right away. He fidgeted with a bracelet dangling from his wrist as Holling waited for him to tell his story in his own way.

"What do you want to know?" he finally asked.

"What do you think I should know? What do you want to tell me?"

"In a perfect world, I'd tell you what you wanted to hear." Darion laughed, then quickly cut it off. Affairs of the heart were no joking matter. Not when it came to boss man Holling and his sister.

"But this world isn't perfect…and neither am I. I make mistakes like anybody else. Sometimes, boss man, something you think is the right way to go isn't. And you have to make corrections before you, as you say, teach some bad habits. Or cause confusion. I've given your…mare…all of the care and consideration I could. But maybe I wasn't the right man for the job. I guess I'll leave that up to you to decide."

"Darion," Holling said in a tone that indicated all pretenses were set aside, all gloves were off, "I don't know what went on between you and Aidan. Maybe I do and I really don't want to. She's a grown woman, capable of making her own decisions. But she's also my sister. As much as we fight and squabble and have our differences, she's my *sister*." Holling emphasized the word. "Do you understand what that means to me?"

"That if I hurt her, you'll hurt me," Darion finished for him.

"No," Holling contradicted with a calmness that might have sent chills down the spine of any other man. "I'll kill you."

"Been there, boss man. And I've done that," Darion said with equal intensity.

"You know good and well that you can't drop a statement on me like that and not let me know what's up, Darion."

"You'll have to trust that I know what I'm talking about."

Holling pursed his lips, rubbing his hand along his jaw before responding. He'd often advised Sawyer not to pry into the man's business. He didn't want anyone to know. He didn't *want* to be known.

"I like you, Darion. I like you a lot, though I'm not always sure why I do. You don't make it easy for a man to get to know you. You've got more walls around you than a Greek labyrinth."

"I'm not trying to win a popularity contest," Darion reminded him. "You don't have to like me for me to do my job."

"I know…I know that. And if you were any other employee, we wouldn't be having this conversation."

"Then why are we?" Darion challenged.

"In a word…Aidan."

Darion sighed, squaring his shoulders, giving the impression of a man who was facing the inevitable.

"And…" Holling continued, "because I see things in you that

you don't see for yourself. I see you going down a road that isn't going to lead you anywhere. Not anywhere pleasant, anyway."

"My road, my way," Darion said offhandedly. "Shouldn't make a difference to anyone else what I decide to do with my life…such that it is."

"Maybe that was true six months ago. It's not true anymore. Maybe you were traveling alone then. Not now. Not when we've all put so much effort into making sure that you knew you were part of something here. You and I both know that I've given you way more latitude than someone who was only punching a time clock, putting their time in. We…I…have invested in you. Invested more than training. More than time."

"I know," Darion reluctantly admitted. "What I can't figure is why. What's your angle, Mr. Holling? What do you want from me?"

"When I look at you, I see myself. I used to think that I could go it alone. I thought that's what I wanted. And then I met Sawyer. And like that, it was all over in an instant!" Holling snapped his fingers for emphasis. "Almost scared me to death how fast my life changed. I can see that same potential in you, Darion."

"You've got some sort of powerful crystal ball or juju, boss man, that you can see all that?"

"From the minute we shook hands about the job, I knew you were where you were supposed to be. Ever feel that way, Darion? That you just *know* when something's right, right off the bat?"

"You mean like fate?"

"Something like that."

"I don't believe in fate," Darion said dismissively.

"Do you believe anything? Or in anyone?"

"I believe in myself," Darion said harshly. "Because in the end, when the end comes, that's all there ever is. Only you."

Lonely you is what Holling heard. He shook his head. To be so bitter, something traumatic must've gotten ahold of that young man, twisted him, warped him so that he couldn't see a way out of that confusing maze of loneliness even when it was being openly offered to him.

"You don't have to be alone," Holling said. "It's a choice we all make."

"Did you try to make that choice for me, Mr. Holling? Did you set me up to get with your sister?"

"No," Holling returned. "To be honest, the thought never entered my mind."

"Why not?" Darion asked, and Holling could tell in his tone, his tight-jawed expression, where this line of questioning was going.

"First of all, I couldn't imagine the two of you together because I couldn't imagine her coming home anytime soon. In all the times we'd talked, she never gave us an inkling that she wanted to come home…or that she wanted anything to do with us."

"She's here now."

"I know…and now that she is, and I've seen how you are around her… I didn't think Aidan was your type. Not that I knew for a fact what your type was since I've never seen you with a woman…or anyone, for that matter."

"You don't think I'm good enough for her?" Darion asked, deliberately sidestepping Holling's implied question regarding his sexual preference.

"Not what I said, Darion. I said she wasn't your type. I'm not sure if she's anyone's type. Aidan doesn't have a good track record when it comes to dating. She's too damned particular. Too hard to please."

Holling ignored the visible signal of Darion trying very

hard not to comment as he clamped his mouth shut, practically biting the inside of his cheek.

"Man-to-man, Darion, even if we weren't talking about Aidan, even if we were talking about you, I'd wouldn't want to see you end up all alone. But I didn't think about you and Aidan being together because I didn't know if it would work. Not with you looking like you could walk off at any minute, and Aidan has already proven that she'd do the same."

"Are you saying she'd leave me?"

"It's happened before. She walked out that door ten years ago and never came back."

"Until now," Darion reminded him. "She's here now. And she didn't leave me stuck out there after that tanker crashed," Darion said. "She could have. Easily."

"I'm not surprised that Aidan stayed. She isn't cruel. But she does have an uncommon instinct for self-preservation."

"We all do, when it comes right down to it. We protect what's most important to us. Isn't that why you called me in here? To let me know what you'd do to protect Aidan?"

"Yeah, I'm worried about her. And I'm worried about you. I'm worried about both of you. Together. And what that means for all of us."

Darion stood as if to leave. He circled around his chair, clutching the back, his fingers digging into the padded leather. "You don't have to worry about me. I'm not going to hurt her, boss man."

"I don't know, Darion. Something tells me that you already have."

"What has she told you about…us?"

"Nothing that she's said. Just a feeling I have. I know my sister. Even if I don't know everything I want to know about her, I know that she's a Holling. I know how we think. And how we feel. And when something's not right with us. She's putting up a good front. But I can hear it in her voice. See it in her eyes. And, whether you believe it or not, I can see it in yours."

"And you trust your feelings," Darion said, sounding more as if he were making a statement than asking a question. "I wish I could do the same. You don't know how much I want to trust those feelings!"

Holling thought he detected a weakening in the chink of Darion's emotional defensive armor. It was the first time he'd ever heard the man sound so desperate, so lacking in his usual iron-clad control. There was only one reason he could imagine for Darion's uncharacteristic behavior.

Aidan!

She'd gotten to him somehow, made him doubt even his simplest beliefs of himself.

"The funny thing about trust," Holling said soothingly, "is that once you begin, it's hard to stop. Even when all evidence points to reasons why you shouldn't."

"I guess you can say the same thing about love," Darion ventured. "Once you start, it's almost impossible to stop."

Holling sat back in his chair, expelling a long breath. So…there it was. The *L*-word, hanging out there in the air like a glaring, flashing neon sign.

"Are you in love with her?" he asked, his prying question widening the gap in Darion's armor. "Are you in love with my sister?"

"That all depends."

"On what?"

"On whether or not, boss man, you really want me to trust my feelings."

Chapter 23

Sawyer had warned her not to trust little Sydney. And Aidan had intended to follow through with that admonition. Still, Sydney had seemed like such a darling on the trek out to the lake. Dressed from head to toe in her faux-fur-lined pink snowsuit, she sat on the sled with her brother Jayden, singing Christmas carols in her seven-year-old treble with a purity and enthusiasm that made Aidan wonder how Sawyer could have planted such unfavorable images in her mind. From Sawyer's laundry list of things Aidan should watch for, you'd think that she was sending her imps-in-training, rather than the sweet little darlings they appeared to be as they stood with eager, shining faces.

"Don't be such a grinch!" Aidan had chastised as Sawyer had given the kids one last warning glare and a wagging admonition of her pointed finger.

"You say that now," Sawyer had said, waving goodbye as Aidan had started off across the yard.

Sydney sang at the top of her lungs, laughing and squealing with delight when her voice echoed, sometimes making clumps of snow land with a *plop!* from low-hanging branches as they passed underneath the trees.

"Come on, Jay-Jay," she urged. "Sing with me. You, too, Auntie Aida Beth!"

Aidan sang along with them, though she was a little breathless, having to drag the sled laden with the two of them, their skating gear and their snacks. Thermoses contained their hot soup and their cocoa. Aidan figured that they had a good hour before they would have to worry about their lunches losing their warmth.

She followed the trail that Sawyer had given her, breathing deeply in the crisp, cold air. How could she have left all of this behind? Fort Lauderdale was beautiful in its own way. Yet, it was quickly becoming a tourist trap. The influx of visitors was great for the economy. Yet, there was a price to pay for all of that free-flowing cash. Heavier traffic. Increased crime. Higher taxes. It was as if every extra body added to the area seemed to suck up the brisk ocean breezes, making the area where Aidan lived feel closed in, cloying and claustrophobic.

As Aidan stood outside, ankle deep in snow, with her nose tingling and her eyes tearing, she wondered how she could have let ten years fly past her without coming home to recharge her soul's batteries.

"Faster, Auntie Aidan," Jayden urged, when she'd slowed down to admire the sights of winter in White Wolf.

"You're supposed to say 'mush!'" Sydney informed her brother in a bossy tone.

"Mush!" Jayden complied.

"I'm going! I'm going!" Aidan huffed, dragging them up to the fence that divided the yard from the beginning of the pasture. The planks of the fence were spaced wide enough for her to easily climb. The twins scrambled off the sled, lay down on the ground and squeezed underneath the bottom plank.

"Here, Sydney, grab the rope," Aidan directed. They pulled as she pushed the sled through. Aidan climbed on the fence and swung her right leg over the opposite side, followed by the left leg.

"Jump!" Sydney encouraged.

Aidan planted her hands on the top rail, swung her legs out, pulling her hips forward, and landed solidly on the other side of the fence. She flung her arms up in the air, imitating the dismount by Olympic gymnasts as she cried out so that her voice echoed.

"Struck the landing. Perfect ten. U.S.A. takes the gold and the crowd goes wild." Cupping her gloved hands to her mouth, Aidan mimicked the roar of the crowd. When she looked down into the confused faces of her niece and nephew, she made a face and said, "So much for my gold-medal hopes and dreams. Back on the sled, kiddies."

As they approached a gently sloping, snow-covered hill, Aidan told the twins, "I am not hauling you two snow bunnies up that hill. We're all going to walk now."

"Yes, Aunt Aidan," Sydney said sweetly. Aidan should have sensed something was wrong right then and there. They were being too good, too compliant. Especially after she'd told them that she wasn't going to pull them anymore. They'd barely gotten halfway up the hill before Sydney let out a shout…something that sounded like "Jack and Jill!" and pushed her brother in the back. Before Aidan could catch him, Sydney launched herself down the hill, rolling end over end after her brother.

Aidan watched with a mingling of amusement and annoy-

ance as Sydney became a rolling pink blur. Her brother's dark
blue snowsuit was a dark blur as he made it to the bottom of
the hill before his sister.

"Come on, Auntie. Let's make snow angels," Jayden suggested. Lying flat on his back, he spread his arms out and
dragged them up and down, from the height of his shoulders
down to his hips. His chubby legs slid open, then closed,
open, then closed, pushing snow out of the way.

"Very funny!" Aidan stood near the top of the hill, hands
on her hips. "Now come on up here."

"My snow angel's better than yours, Jay-Jay," Sydney
taunted him.

"It is not."

"Yes, it is."

"Is not. Tell her, Auntie."

"Both of you are perfect angels," Aidan said, then grimaced
against that small stretch of the truth. "Now, come on up here
so we can get to the lake."

But they weren't budging. In fact, Jayden started to cry. "I
don't want to go! I don't want to walk anymore."

"I'm not coming down there to get you," Aidan warned
them. "It was funny going down. Let's see how funny it is
climbing back up."

She pretended to turn her back on them, to keep going up
the hill. But then Sydney started to cry, too—large blubbering and wailing that contrasted with the sweet singing Aidan
had heard from her a few minutes ago.

"Oh, all right!" Aidan relented. She let out a breath, could
see puffs of air in front of her face as she followed in their
tracks down the hill. By the time she got to the bottom, Aidan
couldn't help but notice that their eyes, their faces were re-
markably dry. The little thespians. What crocodile tears!

"You two need to take that act on the road," she remarked.

"The road's that way." Jayden pointed out the path to the lake. They piled back onto the sled. With a muffled grunt, Aidan tugged on the rope, starting back up the hill again.

"We're almost there," she panted. "Do you remember the skating rules?"

"Don't go on the ice without you," Sydney piped up.

"Stay away from the warning signs," Jayden continued.

"And the most important rule?" Aidan prompted.

"No making fun of you when you fall down flat on your rear," the twins answered, practically in unison.

"That's right. It's been a while since you're auntie's gone skating. I might be a little rusty."

Once they'd made it to the top of the hill, she said, "Skooch closer together, kids. Auntie Aidan's gonna ride down the hill with you on the sled."

"There's not enough room for you," Jayden complained.

"Sure there is," Aidan said. "All you have to do is get in close to your sister."

"He'd better not put any snot on me!" Sydney threatened. "You move up to the front, Jay-Jay."

Aidan got them to move as close as they could. Jayden sat in the front with the thermal food keeper in his lap. Sydney sat in the middle. And the plan was Aidan would sit in the rear. She would give the sled a running shove, then leap on at the last moment.

"Hang on tight!" she encouraged the twins, making sure they had their hands on the rope. Aidan leaned forward, placing her hands on the rear of the sled. She started to churn her legs, building up momentum. Faster. Faster. In a second, she would leap on and—

"Hey!" Aidan cried out in dismay.

Just when she was about to jump on, Sydney hollered, "Now, Jay-Jay!" and jerked with all of their precocious might. First with their right hands, then their left hands, causing the rear of the sled to fishtail.

Aidan couldn't keep her grip. She sprawled, face forward, with a mouthful of snow as the giggling, squealing twins went careening down the far side of the hill.

"Whee!" their voices echoed back on the wind, mocking her.

Aidan lifted her head, spitting out snow and frozen pine needles. "You little…! You wait until your mother… I'm telling!" she finally shouted in frustration. She lay there for another second before she realized that her threats weren't stopping them. They weren't even slowing down.

"No…. Oh, no!" Her frustration quickly turned to fear.

Aidan had flashbacks of watching that tanker truck careening over the edge of that highway guardrail. Even though she knew there was no mountain nearby for them to fall off, it didn't ease her mind. She watched as the sled whooshed down the hill, out of her sight, through a circular cove of pine trees and low-growing, ice-covered shrubs. According to Sawyer, beyond the grove of trees was the lake.

"Sydney!" Aidan leaped up suddenly, panic gripping her. They hadn't stopped when she'd called. Maybe they couldn't stop. Maybe they'd keep on sliding right onto the lake itself. "Jayden, stop!" she screeched, her voice echoing on the crisp air.

"Sydney!" she cried out again, running full tilt down the hill. "Jayden! Stop that sled right now. Do you hear me? Don't you *dare* go out on that ice without me! Don't you dare!"

Aidan had never run so fast. Never in all her born days. When she was younger, she'd been too heavy to run. After she'd lost her weight, she was too cute to run. Now wasn't the time to worry about her form. She had to get to the twins. Had to!

She tore through the brush, ignoring how the ice-covered branches whipped at her face and left stinging welts.

"God, no! Please no!" she prayed as she sprinted, wiping at her eyes as they began to tear. "Please don't let them be on the ice without me. Please don't…please!"

"Auntie Aidan! Auntie Aidan!"

She followed the sound of their voices. It was Jayden, waving at her with both hands. He stood at the edge of the lake, covered from head to toe in powdered snow.

"Jayden!" Aidan cried in relief, dropping down on her knees and clutching him.

"I fell off," he announced, swiping at the thin trail of blood streaming from his runny nose.

"Where's Sydney?"

Wordlessly, he pointed out to the center of the lake. Sydney sat there, with the steering rope still in her hands, facing them.

"Sydney Rose Holling!" Aidan scolded, sounding very much like the child's mother. Even from that distance, Aidan could see the look of dismay on the child's face at the imitation of her mother's voice. The look of dismay turned rapidly to open terror as the right rear runner of the sled suddenly dipped. Sydney's screech of fear mingled with the unmistakable sound of cracking ice. It cut through the air like a gunshot.

"Come get me, Aunt Aida Beth!" Sydney called to her, dropping the rope and holding out her hands as if asking to be picked up.

"No, Sydney! Don't move! Keep still," Aidan pleaded, hoping that the panic in her own voice didn't cause Sydney to respond to her with equal panic. She leaned down to Jayden. "Jayden, listen to me. Listen to me very, very carefully. I need you to run home. Run home now. Go get your mommy, can you do that? Or Grandpa Nate. Can you do that?"

When Jayden started to blubber again, Aidan shook him roughly by the shoulders. "Jayden! I need you to be a big boy. I need your help. Your sister needs your help…. Do it, now! Follow the trail back. You know how to get back home, don't you?"

This only caused him to wail even louder, causing Sydney to mimic her brother's terror. Sydney screamed when the ice cracked again. Aidan wasn't even sure if the other cracks in the ice were anywhere near the child. It didn't matter. Sydney was afraid. That was what mattered.

"Never mind. Sit there and be still. Don't you move! Not one inch!" She forced him to sit down on the frozen ground, then turned her attention back to Sydney. "Hang on, baby! Auntie's coming. Just stay there, okay? I'm coming."

Slowly, cautiously, Aidan stepped out onto the ice. She clenched her teeth, trying to concentrate on keeping her footsteps slow, steady.

"Light as a feather. Light as a feather." She willed herself to feel weightless. "The lake doesn't even know I'm here. I'm just…a…snowflake…another pine needle blown onto the surface."

She got within three feet of Sydney, heard the ice crack again. This time the entire right runner dipped into the ice, throwing Sydney off the sled.

"No!" Aidan sobbed, forgetting caution and launching herself at her niece. She reached out, grasping Sydney by the coat sleeve. Her forward momentum took them away from the sled, but not any closer to the banks of the lake. Aidan slipped and slid, feeling sections of the frozen water beneath her feet turn to slush as she tried to get from the center of the lake— the deepest section, but also the weakest point where it hadn't completely frozen.

"C'mon, Syd," she panted, grasping Sydney's hand. "Skate with me! Left foot slide. Right foot slide! Do it exactly like your daddy taught you! That's a good girl. Come on. Keep going."

There was no sense in trying to run on the lake. They wouldn't be able to keep their footing…but maybe they could glide. Maybe they could! A few feet. A few feet more and they would be on more shallow, but oddly enough, firmer footing.

"That's a good girl! Don't look back. Keep going!"

When they heard the ice crack again, Sydney screamed, clutching on to Aidan, throwing off their rhythm. Aidan gasped in pain as she came down hard on her knees. She still held tightly on to Sydney's hand.

As she tried to stand again, Aidan felt her left leg slip into ice-cold water, up to her thigh. She bit down on her lip to keep from crying out in both pain and fear. She wrenched her leg out of the water, took another step and stumbled again. Down again, this time both feet as their combined weight and churning feet made the ice weaker. Aidan knew if she went down again, she probably wouldn't be able to get up. Acting purely on instinct, she grabbed Sydney by her jacket and snow pants and shoved as hard as she could.

"Slide, baby!" she urged as Sydney, lying prone on the ice, held her hands in front of her, sliding forward as if reaching for home base. Aidan couldn't see how far she'd actually shoved her. Couldn't see anything at all but darkness as the weight of her own wet clothing dragged her down. Down. Down beneath the surface of the lake.

Chapter 24

"*Aidan!*"

Darion lay on the ice, groping, grasping for the gloved hand floundering mere inches out of his reach.

"Get her, Mr. Darry!" Sydney stood on the shore of the lake, yelling and pointing. "There she is! There she is! Grab her!"

Aidan bobbed out of the water like a cork, sucking air into her lungs. She was almost within reach, and then sank again as the weight of her own clothing dragged her down.

Darion gritted his teeth, straining against the rope tied around his waist. He couldn't help remembering how Aidan had sent a length of rope down to aid him when he and Luke had been stuck out there on that ledge. It hadn't seemed long enough then. Yet, somehow it had reached them, bringing that much-needed blanket and medical supplies. She'd helped him. He really would be a sorry son of a if bitch he couldn't do the same for her.

"Come on… Come on… Reach!" he muttered. "Stretch!"

The other end of the rope was tied to the saddle of the boss man's Appaloosa mare. He was afraid to bring the mare any farther onto the ice. Afraid that they would all fall through.

He saw Aidan trying to reach for him, disoriented by the reflection of the ice and the rippling water. She reached up, pounding with frustration when, instead of reaching his hand, she hit solid ice.

"Come on!" Darion called out to her, hauling his body even more than he dared onto the ice. "Reach, Aidan. Take my hand!" He reached for her but there still wasn't enough slack in the rope.

A few more feet. All he needed was for the mare to move up a few more feet. Close enough to give him the slack he needed to dive in after Aidan, but not close enough that they would all go through the ice and drown.

"Do you want me to bring the pony to you, Mr. Darry?" Jayden offered.

"No!" Darion turned his head and shouted over his shoulder. "You two stay right there."

Though the twins had been raised around horses, at their young age, they were only allowed to handle their own ponies. Shetlands. Child-size ponies for child-size abilities. But even they were not allowed to handle them alone. The last thing Darion needed was for Jayden to try to handle a horse that even he had to take extra care around. Darion knew that if the kids started the horse, they wouldn't be able to stop her before she came out too far. He was pushing the limits of her training, as it was, expecting her to stay where she was by the edge of the lake. She wasn't tied down. She wasn't hobbled. If she got the urge to wander, her attention snatched away by the sight and smell of fresh greens she could munch, or scared away by an unfamiliar noise, there wasn't much he could do about it.

Darion fought against that cruel, sinking feeling of helplessness and despair. He hadn't been able to do anything to help Luke. He couldn't fail with Aidan. He wouldn't let her down.

Even as he resolved within himself to help her, he felt the faith in himself waning. He couldn't see his way through. For all of that big, bad talk about not needing anyone else, relying only on himself, Darion knew that it wasn't the complete truth. He couldn't do it on his own. He needed help. Somebody had to come along. Anybody!

Please! Let someone hear them yelling. Let someone realize that Aidan and the twins have been out too long without checking in. Let that miracle happen. Let someone come!

"Go on, boy! What are you waiting for? Go after her. Get in there! You go in there and get that gal!"

Darion looked back over his shoulder at the shouts of encouragement. It wasn't either of the twins yelling to him. It wasn't Red Bone. Or Mr. Nate. Or the boss man.

"I said, what are you waiting for? I've got this filly. You go get yours."

Darion mouthed a word, a name that he hadn't expected to utter for the rest of his life.

"I won't let you go. I won't let you fall in!"

Luke! He stood there beside the lake, waving that ratty brown cap of his to get Darion's attention.

It couldn't have been. They'd said he was dead. Never made it out of that wreckage alive. Yet, there he was, standing on the shoreline next to that mare, waving that greasy, battered cap of his.

"The rope's too short!" Darion called over his shoulder. "I need more slack. Ease the mare onto the ice. Easy now. A little more."

Darion sucked air deep into his lungs and allowed himself to slide into the lake, past his head, past his shoulders, up to his waist. It was cold. So, so cold. It almost burned. He grasped Aidan around the wrist, knowing deep in his heart that if he hadn't caught her that time, it might well have been too late. He pulled her toward him until he could encircle his arm around her waist. As he pulled her away from the thick section of ice that they could not punch through, he felt himself being dragged back. Slowly, steadily, he was hauled across the ice with Aidan wrapped possessively, preciously in his arms. He didn't check that she was breathing until she was nearly on the shore.

"Aidan!" He leaned over her, calling her name. When he didn't get a response, he tore open her jacket, put his ear to her chest to check for a heartbeat. Darion leaned close, turned his cheek to her mouth and tried to feel for the slightest breath. Nothing. He then pressed his index and middle fingers to the pulse point under her slender jaw.

"Is…she… Is…" Jayden and Sydney crowded around him. They wanted to ask if their aunt was dead, but couldn't make themselves say the words. Instead, the twins hugged each other, starting to wail.

"Shh!" Darion waved them to silence. "I need you two to stand over there and be quiet, now!" He sent them back over to the spot where Aidan had had Jayden wait, out of the way.

"Is there a pulse?" Luke asked.

"I…I don't know. I think so," Darion said frantically. He untied the rope from around his waist to give himself more freedom of movement. He pulled his gloves off with his teeth and pressed his fingers to her neck. "I think there's a pulse."

"You sure it's not your own pulse you're feeling, son?"

"What do I look like? A doctor? Of course I'm not sure."

"Check again," Luke insisted.

Darion reached for the small, candy-cane-shaped buttons at the scooped neckline of Aidan's sweater, then hesitated.

"What are you waiting for?" Luke noticed his reluctance.

"She's...she's not wearing a bra," Darion said, noting how the cashmere material molded to the swell of her breasts.

"I don't think she's in a position to argue with you. Go on, son."

"Turn your back," Darion directed Luke. He'd heard one too many cracks about his view of a woman's body from that old man's lips. Darion wasn't about to give Luke the opportunity to talk that way to one of his trucker buddies about Aidan.

"I don't think Aidan wants the whole free world looking at her breasts. Now, turn your back!"

"You think I came all this way to ogle your woman?" Luke asked incredulously. But he humored Darion and turned around.

"How am I supposed to know why you came back?" Darion muttered. "I don't even know who you are."

"You don't know that lady lying there, either...but you're here for her, all the same, aren't you?"

It was a question that needed no answer. This was no time to question Luke's motives. He was there when he was needed. That's all that mattered to Darion. That...and the woman lying before him, fighting for her life.

Blowing out a deep breath to steady himself, Darion unbuttoned one button, then another, then peeled aside enough of the two halves of her sweater. Enough to expose smooth, bronze skin. He placed his ear against her skin, remembering how good it had felt when he'd lain on her heart, listening to the rapid beating after he'd made love to her. It was too painful to believe that this was the same woman. Now, she was cold to the touch and caused him involuntarily to suck in his breath. He listened hard, tried to concentrate on finding the slightest hint of a heartbeat.

"Got it!" Darion's head jerked up, grinning with unrestrained relief.

Luke turned his head, looking back over his shoulder. "But she's not breathing on her own, is she? Do you know CPR, Darion?"

"Yeah, I took a class a long time ago," Darion said with waning confidence. "A long, long time ago."

"It'll come back to you," Luke encouraged him. "Go on, son. Do what you gotta do for that gal."

Darion tilted Aidan's head back, exposing her throat and allowing her full lips to part slightly on their own. Again, memories of a week ago flooded in on him. He'd seen her like this, head thrown back, mouth parted. But she'd been breathing on her own. Panting. Nearly breathless as wave after wave of pleasure that he'd given her had made her tremble.

Aidan! How could this be you? Darion silently lamented.

How could this be that same vibrant, expressive woman who'd given herself freely, openly, honestly and passionately to him?

Darion felt his heart harden. This wasn't the first time that love and life had collided, causing him this intense agony. The boss man was right. He'd had more than his share of experiences. Up until now, he'd been able to keep the lessons he'd learned from those experiences to himself. But it was times like this that he wished he didn't know as much as he did.

Luke reached out, squeezed his shoulder. "Go on, son," he urged. "Don't you lose her. Don't you give up on her. She didn't give up on you."

Nodding, Darion forced his mind back to trying to remember his CPR training. From what he could see, there was nothing in her mouth. No debris. Nothing that would stop air from getting through to her lungs. He pinched her nose closed, then sealed his mouth to hers for two slow breaths.

"Turn her over," Luke directed. "Get some of that water out of her lungs."

"No," Darion objected. "When she starts breathing, she'll spit it out on her own."

"She won't start breathing until you get the water out, Darion!" Luke insisted.

"Will you let me do this?" Darion responded, trying to get a firm grip on his fear.

When she didn't show signs of reviving, he breathed twice more into her mouth. This time, the rise to her chest was noticeable. Again and again, he continued to breathe life into her. Every so often, he checked her pulse. It was getting stronger. But she still wasn't moving. No sign of life other than the faint heartbeat.

"She's not breathing!" Darion ground out. "I've done everything I can but—"

"Then it's out of your hands," Luke proclaimed.

"No!" He wasn't giving up. Not yet. It was the one thing that had been stressed in that CPR class—don't give up too soon. Though he was starting to feel light-headed, he continued to fill her lungs with air from his own.

"Come on, Aidan. Come on, baby!" he chanted. He sealed his lips to hers, breathed again. "Come on, Aidan. Don't leave me here like this. Don't you leave me!"

Luke knelt down beside him, tsk-tsked in sympathy. "This is your boss's sister. If you let her die—"

"You think I care *who* she is?!" Darion raged. "It's *what* she is that matters…what she is to me… I don't want to lose her."

"There's nothing you can do," Luke stressed. "No skill, no

technique, no power in your hands alone that can save her. You do know that, don't you?"

Helplessly, Darion shrugged. "Then what am I supposed to do? What can I do?"

"You already know the answer to that, son," Luke said, looking down at Aidan. "Like you told her brother, maybe you need to heed your own advice and call on the right one for the job."

Darion blinked, reached at his belt for his cell phone. *Call for help. That's it!* What was the matter with him? Why hadn't he thought about that before?

Luke shook his head, placing a restraining hand on Darion's arm. "There's help for you, son, faster than a phone call away, if you want it."

Darion jerked his hand away, his expression wary and distrustful. What was he talking about? Help from where? From who? Who was this man? This Luke? Some kind of lunatic? Why was he here? How did he get here? From what Darion could see, there was no way he could have gotten here. No horse. No snowmobile. Not even a pair of cross-country skis. What did he want? Was he stalking him? Was that it?

"I'm here because you needed me, Darion. You called on me. I came to help," Luke assured him.

Darion felt a surge of doubt and disbelief rise up inside of him. He balled up his fist, prepared to defend himself against something he didn't understand. Couldn't accept.

A look of pain and sadness crossed Luke's face, as if Darion's reaction alone had physically hurt him. He lowered his eyes, and when he raised them again, Darion saw tears welling in the old man's gray eyes. "Like you, son, I've done everything I can do. The rest is up to you. If you want more help, you'll have to ask for it."

Darion's voice cracked. "I…I don't know how." He pulled the wet knit cap from Aidan's head, smoothed back her drenched hair.

"Yes, you do," Luke contradicted. "You don't want to. You're afraid to. But you do know how. Ask for help, son. I promise you. All you have to do is ask."

Darion closed his eyes, resting his forehead against Aidan's. "Please," he whispered. "Please don't take her."

Nothing more than that. All that he meant to say was conveyed by that single request.

How long he sat there, cradling Aidan, Darion didn't know. He lost his sense of time. He didn't feel the cold and wet. Didn't feel the ice that had started to form on his back and shoulders as he sheltered Aidan in his arms. It might have been mere seconds. It might have been ages. He couldn't trust his ability to reason now. He wasn't thinking clearly.

If he was, he would have called the Hollings the moment he'd pulled Aidan from the ice. Reason should have told him to throw Aidan across the saddle and ride as hard as he could to get her back to her family. Reason should have told him that it was crazy to trust that old trucker, a man he didn't know, and he couldn't explain how he'd appeared to him in this desperate hour.

Then again, Darion reflected, Luke wasn't looking for him to exercise his reasoning ability. Reason had nothing to do with the feelings Darion had for Aidan. There was no rational explanation for why he loved her. But, Darion knew that he did. As crazy as it sounded, he loved her. And in doing so, he had to give up reason for trust—trust that it would all work out. What was it someone had once told him? Step out on faith? That was what Luke had allowed him to do to rescue Aidan. He'd stepped out on faith, trusting that Luke would keep them both from falling through the ice. And to revive Aidan, Darion had to trust that he called on the power to bring her back.

"I did what you wanted, Luke," Darion said.

When Luke didn't answer, Darion lifted his head, looking for that rotund trucker, expecting to see him sitting there with his expression smug and gloating.

"Luke? *Luke?*"

Darion's voice echoed on the air. He could barely hear the whimpering of the twins still sitting by the bushes as he'd directed and the impatient neighing of that mare as she stomped her foot and shook out her coarse, gray mane.

"Jayden! Sydney!" Darion called out, motioning for them to come to him. He intended to place them in the saddle and lead them home as he carried Aidan's body back to her family.

Yet, as he spoke, she stirred. Aidan's body spasmed, followed by a fit of violent coughing.

"Aidan!"

Turning her over, Darion supported her as her entire body shook. "It's all right, baby. That's it. Let it all out."

"Darion!" Aidan clutched him, clamping her stiff, nearly frozen fingers over his forearm. She would not let go. Darion wasn't sure if she could let go, as violently as she trembled. As she doubled over, retching, Darion wrapped his arms around her shoulders to support her.

He placed his hand comfortingly over the one that gripped his forearm and continued to pat her shoulders, smoothed his hand across her back. As the tremors subsided, she looked from Darion to the twins. Her expression was a blend of fear, confusion and gratitude. He saw her struggling for composure. Her mouth worked to form words. She wanted to voice the questions reflected in her eyes, but Darion interrupted. "Don't try to talk, Aidan. Save your strength."

She nodded, understanding.

"Can you ride? I want to get you up to the house."

"I can ride!" Her teeth chattered as Darion swung her up in the saddle.

"Auntie Aida Beth!" Sydney jumped up from her spot and ran toward the horse. The Appaloosa bucked, causing Aidan to clutch the saddle horn to keep from being thrown off.

"Whoa! Easy!" Darion calmed the mare.

"She might be skittish around the kids," Aidan observed. "Maybe I'd better go on ahead?"

"Can you make it up to the house alone?" Darion voiced his concern.

"It's been a while since I've ridden," Aidan confessed. "I don't see any other way."

Darion gripped her hand, squeezed once. His voice choked with emotion as he said, "I'll follow behind you with the twins as fast as I can. We'll be right behind you, Aidan. I promise. I won't leave you."

She smiled down at him. "I know, Slim. I know."

"Get going, now! Yah!"

Darion slapped the mare's rump, sending her at a brisk trot.

Chapter 25

"Nate! Get out here! Get out here, quick! Quick!"

There was no mistaking the urgency in Sawyer's tone. She huddled with her arms wrapped around Aidan's waist as she tried to drag her soaked, frozen sister-in-law up the steps.

"Oh, my God! Aidan, what happened to you? Where are the kids?"

"They're f-fine. Darion's g-g-g-got them!" Aidan could barely speak through her chattering teeth. "He's bringing th-them up to the h-house."

"Nate!" Sawyer screamed again. She tried to hold up Aidan's weight and pull on the heavy front oak door at the same time.

As she pulled Aidan inside, it wasn't Nate who came to her aid, but Holling. His arms worked furiously, grasping the rubber grips of his wheelchair, yanking them forward as he pulled himself from the study.

"Aida Beth!"

"I'm all right, big brother. D-d-don't panic. It's j-j-just a little water. That'll teach me to try to join the Polar Bear Club." When she set out that morning, she'd had no intention of imitating those who, at the first sign of a good freeze, stripped themselves naked to dive into the nearest unfrozen sea or lake. If she wasn't so afraid that she'd bite her tongue in half from chattering, she'd laugh.

"Jayden? Sydney?" He searched their faces for answers to his dreaded question.

"They're fine," Aidan said. "Darion's got them and will bring them back with the sled."

Aidan was exhausted, too soaked to make it all the way to her room. She collapsed on the bottom step and started peeling away the layers of clothing—her jacket, her knit cap, her gloves. She left them in a soggy heap beside her.

"What happened, Aidan?" Sawyer asked.

Aidan shook her head. "One minute, we were sledding along just fine. Not a problem. We were at the top of the hill, heading toward the lake. But then…then…"

"Then the twins got away from you," Sawyer finished. "I told you to watch out for them."

"I know. I know. I can't believe that a couple of seven-year-olds got away from me. But they did. They took off down the hill without me, heading straight for the lake. I couldn't catch them. I'm so sorry, Sawyer. I should have listened to you."

"They went out on the lake without you?" Holling's voice was stern, as if he were already practicing for them.

"Jayden didn't. He fell off the sled."

"Or Sydney pushed him off," Sawyer surmised.

"By the time I got to the lake, she'd already gone ahead without me. Right to the middle of the lake."

"Past the warning cones that I had put there especially so

they wouldn't go out onto dangerous ground?" Holling's voice rumbled, giving Aidan the distinct impression of a volcano about to erupt.

"You might say that she was testing the waters…and skating on thin ice?" Aidan gave a shaky laugh. When no one joined her, she hastily cleared her throat and continued.

"I have to give Sydney the benefit of the doubt. I know she can be a little…um…energetic," Aidan suggested tactfully. "I don't know if she went out there deliberately to disobey me or if sheer momentum carried her there. One thing I can say for certain, by the time I got there, she was terrified. I had to go get her."

"Why didn't you call someone to help you, Aida Beth?" Holling demanded.

"There wasn't time. Besides, I don't carry a cell phone."

"Something we've got to change immediately—" Sawyer interrupted.

"You know how much I hate those things," Aidan complained.

"If you'd had one, maybe you wouldn't have had as close a call as you did," Holling said, sounding very much like the condescending older brother she'd always known.

"Imagine the trouble I would have been in at my former weight. Huh? Huh? Talk about your icebreaker!" Aidan's head swiveled back and forth, searching their faces.

"How can you still joke? Aidan, you almost drowned!" Sawyer exclaimed.

"You don't have to tell me, girl. I mean, whoosh! Just like that." Aidan made the sound of a commode flushing. "If Darion hadn't come by when he did…" Her voice broke as memories of her fear and desperation suddenly overwhelmed her. Aidan placed her hand over her mouth, stopping her next words and her unspoken thought.

Sawyer draped her arm around Aidan's shoulders, rubbing her to comfort and to ward off the chill. "What is it with you two, anyway?"

"What do you mean?" Aidan snuffled, wiping her nose on the back of her already dampened sweater sleeve.

"Are you two running some kind of contest, seeing who can be the bigger hero? Don't you know that when you save someone's life, they belong to you forever?" She looked over at Holling and winked.

"No, I hadn't heard that."

"I'll go out and wait for Darion and the kids," Holling said, grabbing the wheels of his wheelchair and pushing himself back.

"Don't you fuss at them, Holling," Sawyer warned. "They're probably scared enough as it is."

Holling lifted his hands from the wheels and held them up in a placating gesture for his wife. "I'm not going to fuss," he said.

"Very loud," Sawyer and Aidan said almost in perfect unison. Aidan nodded, then grasped the stair rail to pull herself to standing.

"Come on, girl," Sawyer said briskly. "Let's get you upstairs and out of those wet clothes."

Darion didn't expect to be in the shower for as long as he was. It was such a rare luxury that he ever got the opportunity to take his time that he took full advantage of having the showers all to himself. With most of the other hands heading into White Wolf for the weekend, he didn't expect there to be much hot water left for him. Each time one of the others left the shower stalls and opened the door leading to the common room, a waft of steam misted the air so that it turned the whole bunkhouse into a sauna.

He didn't know how it worked in other outfits, but around there, the unspoken rule was last man in got the last of the hot water. The way Darion figured it, it was quite an incentive to make sure that everyone took care of those hygiene needs quickly. It only took him one time of deciding to hold off on bathing until the next day to figure out that he wouldn't ever try it again. He'd spent the rest of the evening putting up with everyone's ragging. They'd stripped off his clothes and tossed them out the window. Someone had tried to boil his boots. And every time he'd turned his back, someone had been either trying to douse him with talcum powder or body spray. Of course it was a matter of opinion, but he didn't think he'd smelled *that* bad. To hear Red Bone and the others messing with him, you'd think that he'd been rolling around in a field full of cow chips.

Darion was glad that no one was around to fight him for the showers now. After he'd left the twins in the care of the boss man, he'd gone straight for the bunkhouse, peeling off his sodden clothes, leaving a soggy trail from the door to the shower. He didn't want to hear any lip from the bunkhouse boys about his lack of housekeeping etiquette. More than once Red Bone had warned them that there were no mamas around there to clean up after them. No maid service. It was everybody's responsibility to keep the place from becoming a pigsty. Keeping the place neat and tidy had been the last thing on Darion's mind as he'd grabbed his towel, shower shoes and soap. Darion knew that his desire for solitude wasn't as much about the scramble for hot water as it was for a need to be alone with his thoughts.

When he'd been out there on the ice, he hadn't given

himself much time to think. Aidan was in trouble. That was
the only thought he'd needed to galvanize him to action. That
wasn't to say that he'd been completely without some idea of
what he needed to do when he put himself out there. Only
fools rushed in without a clear plan for getting out again. Yet,
absence of a solid plan hadn't stopped him from stepping out
on that thin ice. As he'd taken off after Luke when that tanker
had gone off the road, he'd leaped into motion more on
instinct than careful planning. He'd risked his neck for a
perfect stranger. He couldn't do any less for Aidan.

Now that the excitement was over and he was by himself
again, his thoughts crowded him, coming from all sides. He
thought about all of the things he could have done. Or should
have done. The longer he stood under the stinging spray of
the hot water, he thought about the things that might have
gone wrong.

Closing his eyes, Darion let the water splash over his head,
stream down his face. He planted his palms against the slick
white shower walls, groaning aloud as the water hit that *one*
spot against his neck. He reached up, massaged the spot,
working the knotted muscle loose. His fingers pressed his
neck, then worked their way to the spot where his neck and
shoulder connected. He must have pulled something when
he'd been out there on the ice. Something more than Aidan.

As he stood there under the spray, his mind flashed back
to the night he'd stepped from the shower and found Aidan
huddled alone in bed. Of course she'd been alone. He'd been
the one who'd occupied it. He'd left her to take a quick rinse
off. At least, that was what he'd told himself. Yet, as they'd
lain there, her on her side, him curled around her, even as close
as they were, he could feel her withdrawing from him. Her
thoughts. Her emotions. They'd been side by side, and yet

she'd been miles away. What was it she'd called it? A freakout. Yeah, he could understand that. He was doing a little freaking of his own now as the events of the past few days were starting to sink in.

Images flashed before his eyes. Swirling snow. Flashing lights. The glint of the shiny metal diesel tanker as it slid back and forth over the road. Luke's crinkling gray eyes. Aidan's emergency beacon as it slid down the mountain toward Darion. Road signs. Too many road signs, as a simple two-hour drive stretched on seemingly forever. The generous curve of Aidan's hip. A gloved hand striking against a wall of ice. And Luke.

Seeing that old trucker there really blew Darion's mind. It didn't seem possible. How could it be? No explanation of how he got there. Or how he could just as easily leave without Darion noticing. When Luke had shown up at the side of the lake, Darion had accepted his help, not giving himself time to think through how Luke could have found them in such a remote area. Now that Darion was alone again, he was starting to question again.

More than once, Darion found himself questioning concepts that he'd always taken for granted. There was an order to the universe. He'd worked hard the past six months restoring that order. He strived to remove all sources of chaos and confusion from his life. Back to basics. Giving up his home, his job and too many bad habits to list—Darion erased all traces of his former life. He'd shucked himself of the people who were intent on stealing that peace from him. With them out of his life, gone was the stress. No more tension headaches. No more stomach ulcers.

Unconsciously, Darion's hand smoothed over a section of his stomach. The physical wounds were healed over. A few scars remained to show how messed up his life had become.

The physical wounds might have healed, but it had taken more than six months for the emotional ones to do so.

For a while, his defection from his former life had seemed to work. Relinquishing all of his responsibilities for his new, uncomplicated life brought him a peace he'd forgotten that he could have. A new life. A new home. He was finally starting to feel whole again. At least, he'd thought he had everything that he needed. Everything he wanted to call his life complete.

Who was it who'd said that ignorance was bliss? Who was it who'd said you can't miss what you've never had? As part of his past, he'd had women. Some who'd belonged to him. Some who hadn't. Some he'd had a right to be with. Some he hadn't. Some he'd loved. Some he hadn't. Some he'd made love to. Some he hadn't.

None of them had touched him as Aidan had. Though, he had to admit, some of them had been pretty damned good. Enough to make him forget, if only for a little while, that he probably shouldn't have been messing around with them. It was all part of his own private chaos. When he'd come upon Aidan in the airport, old habits had risen up again. He'd been attracted to her physical form. Her lips. Her hips. Her legs. Instant attraction. Old-fashioned lust. He'd be a liar if he said that he wasn't turned on by what he saw. She was one beautiful black woman.

Darion continued to massage his shoulder, harder, more insistently, as if he could press away the memory of Aidan's head where she'd once rested. For a moment, it wasn't the scent of his soap that was in his nostrils, but the tropical, exotic scent of Aidan's perfume. Her scent was all over him. As the water splashed and slid across his skin, he imagined that it was Aidan's fingertips, trailing over every inch of his body.

He followed in the path that he imagined Aidan would

take if she were there with him now. He brushed at the water streaming from his shoulders and over his arms. Both hands covered his pectorals, fingers splayed, almost as if counting each rib as he moved over his abdomen. Lower. Lower. Until the thought of Aidan's hands cupping him, fondling him, easing the tightness of his groin caused Darion to snatch his hands away.

Was it simply physical attraction that drew him to her? He had to ask himself that question. Was it merely physical attraction that made him face her brother down? Was it physical attraction that made him step out on the ice? He knew the answer to that. No. What he felt for her was more than physical attraction. He'd had enough experience being led by what was behind the zipper to know what that was all about.

He was almost afraid to ask himself the question that would naturally follow. If his feelings for her were more than physical attraction, what exactly were they? Friendship? Could friendship describe the intense feeling he had whenever he was around her? At the mention of her name? At the very thought of her? Could friendship describe the pain he'd felt when her brother had threatened to separate them? Could he even imagine being separated from her?

He'd tried to do it. He'd put distance between them, thinking that if it was only a desire to sleep with her that he felt, that would soon cool.

As he made his way back to his bunk, he pulled out more clothes. He sat on the edge of the bed, tugging on boots. He sat for a few minutes, collecting his thoughts.

Were they friends? Yes, he could say so with confidence. Were they more than friends? Were they in love? He knew how he would answer that question. What he needed was an answer from Aidan herself.

Chapter 26

"They are *so* in love," Sawyer announced without preamble. She sat in bed, with her back propped up by several fluffy, frilly pillows. She licked her thumb and turned another page of the magazine she was reading.

Holling lay next to her, resting on his own favorite pillow. Not quite as frilly as his wife's, but in his opinion more comfortable. He was doing some flipping of his own, breezing through channels so quickly, the images were practically a blur. He'd paused in midflip, turning half of his attention to Sawyer's declaration.

"What are you talking about, baby? She's about to suck the life from him." He pointed at the television with the remote as the camera zoomed in on the mating ritual of the black widow spider.

Sawyer glanced up. "Not that!" she exclaimed laughing, then gave a disgusted shudder. "Ugh! How can you watch that, Holling, right before you go to bed? It would give me nightmares."

He leaned over and read the title of his wife's magazine article. "Now here's real nighttime entertainment value for you. Sixty sexual positions to drive your partner insane."

"That's not what it says!" Sawyer said, slamming the magazine shut.

"A man can hope," he returned, then went back to channel surfing. It was a full five minutes before he asked, "Who's in love?"

"Darion and Aidan, of course."

"What makes you think so?"

"I don't think so, I know so," Sawyer said smugly.

"Because you're the world's foremost authority on love," he challenged, reaching for her magazine again.

"Yes, I am." Her tone was snide, then quickly turned wistful. "You can tell by the way they look at each other, Holling. Did you see how Darion looked at her when he came to check on her? I'll bet if we weren't in the room, he would have kissed her." Sawyer raised her hand, patting her heart. "When those two are in the same room together, you can almost see the sparks flying between them."

"You know who you sound like?"

"Who do I sound like?"

"You sound like those nosy, matchmaking cousins of yours."

"Shiri, Essence and Brenda?"

"Yeah, the Gleesome Threesome."

"We only come by it naturally." Sawyer laughed. "The aunts in my family have been playing Cupid for generations."

"Cupid? Who are you kidding?" Holling snorted in derision. "Cupid uses a bow and arrow to get his victims to the altar. Your family uses a cattle prod."

"All the better, since we're right in the middle of cattle country," she said, smiling sweetly at him. She readjusted her pillows, turned on her side to face him.

"So, how do you feel about Aidan and Darion as a couple, Holling?"

"How do I feel about it? Why are you asking me?"

"Because Aidan's your sister. And I know that you're not going to let anyone near her, if you have any say in the matter."

Holling shrugged. "She's my sister. But like I told Darion, she's a grown woman. She can make her own decisions."

"You've already had this conversation with him?" Sawyer accused him.

"Not so much a conversation as a simple statement of the facts."

"Holling," Sawyer said, her tone mildly chastising as she snuggled closer to him. She draped her arm across his torso, drawing lazy circles on his chest with her fingernail. "You threatened the man, didn't you?"

"Of course not."

"Let me rephrase that. You made him a promise. One that he couldn't mistake."

"Uh, something like that," he admitted reluctantly.

"You're a hopeless, consummate bully of a big brother."

"And you're a hopeless romantic."

"Lucky for you that I am," she reminded him. "Otherwise, we wouldn't be lying here like this." To emphasize her point, she unbelted her robe.

"Do you think they're really in love, Sawyer?" Holling asked, frowning so that his brows knitted together. "Just like that?"

"It only takes a split second to fall in love, Holling. You of all people ought to know that," she reminded him as she reached for the buttons of his pajama top. "All the work is in staying in love."

"Not all work," he insisted, pressing the button on the remote to turn off the television.

"Downright drudgery," she returned, flipping the switch on the nightstand reading lamp. "I should get extra compensation for all the things I do for you, my dear!"

"I'll take it up with management," Holling promised, carefully lifting his hips and tugging at his pajama pants.

"She could do worse, you know," Sawyer said. "Darion's a good man."

"Um…very good," Holling echoed as Sawyer moved to straddle him. He grabbed the hem of her nightgown and helped to lift it over her head. He sucked in an eager breath as she settled herself comfortably over him.

"I say we stay out of their way," she suggested, rocking her hips to punctuate her request. "If we get in between them, we'll only mess things up."

Holling uttered a response, incomprehensible as he lost all focus and desire—to argue, that is.

"I'm glad you agree." Sawyer giggled. She leaned forward, cupping her breasts as if presenting an offering to him. He gladly accepted her offering, and might have completely forgotten that he was supposed to be concerned about his only sister's whirlwind romance if he didn't know his wife as well as he did.

"Wait a minute! I think you're trying to blackmail me," Holling said suspiciously.

"Is it working?" Sawyer whispered, then kissed him on the tip of his nose.

"Lady," Holling said huskily, massaging the back of her neck and drawing her closer to him, "keep loving me like this, and I'll give you anything you want!"

Chapter 27

Aidan couldn't find anything she wanted in the first three shops where she'd stopped. Only a day before Christmas, and she was still scrambling to find that perfect gift for the special people in her life.

Each time she entered a store, her MO was the same. She'd walk in, walk around, pick up items without much interest and set them down again. A list of excuses why she shouldn't buy was as long as the list of people she needed to buy for.

Too expensive. Too cheap looking. Too ridiculous. Nothing was striking her fancy and she was starting to get frustrated. Aidan tsk-tsked aloud. Served her right for waiting until the last minute to try to find a bargain this late in the game.

And now that her list of special people had grown by one, she felt extra pressure to find something that would please Darion. Kind of hard to do when there was still so much she didn't know about him. Part of her was tempted to buy him a gift card and let him choose his own gift. Nothing said from the heart when it was his own heart doing the choosing. But that seemed so impersonal. That might work for people she barely knew and had no intention of getting to know. It wouldn't work for her now. She was trying to get up close and personal; Aidan wanted a gift that said how hard she was trying…how much she wanted to know him. Yet, the harder she tried, the more frustrated and discouraged she became. Frustrated. And tired.

I should give up, go home, bake him a batch of sugar cookies and call it good enough, she thought to herself. Yet, as she linked arms with Darion, walking down Main Street and peering into different festively decorated storefront windows, she looked over at him and gave him an encouraging smile.

Trouble was, she couldn't bake from scratch and the sugar cookies from prepackaged dough tasted like cardboard if you didn't eat them right out of the oven. No, there had to be something out there that would express how deeply her feelings for him had grown. She wasn't even expecting anything in return. The best present he could have given her was doing something with her that he wouldn't have chosen to do on his own. To be honest, something he would have done only after being dragged kicking and screaming, leaving deep gouges in the earth for his resistance. Yet, here he was. Doing his best to hide the fact that if he had to listen to one more version of "The Little Drummer Boy" one more time, in one more store, he'd probably go stark-raving mad.

Aidan knew that he might not have come on his own volition. Not that he didn't want to spend time with her. The past few days, they'd spent every moment they could together. The moment she'd mentioned shopping, however, she could see the love light in his eyes go dim.

"All right. I'll spare you this time," she'd relented. But Holling wasn't having it. In hindsight, he might have been doing his part to play matchmaker for her. Yet, somehow, the conversation didn't quite match the intention. After Darion had begged off, she'd gone to her brother with a simple request. The clanging of the Salvation Army's Santa's bell reminded her of the conversation she'd had that morning with Holling.

"I was wondering if I could borrow the keys to your truck."

He hadn't responded too kindly to the request. Perhaps she should have waited until after he'd taken one of his "happy pills," as he called them.

"Borrow the keys? Hell no." His response had been automatic. Then, as an afterthought, he'd asked, "What for?"

"So I can shake them to the tune of 'Jingle Bells.' What do you think I want them for?" Her tone had been equally sarcastic. In hindsight, probably not the best way to sway her brother. But, old habits died hard.

"No, you can't borrow the keys to my truck."

"Why not?"

"Because I don't want you to wreck it, that's why."

"I'm not going to wreck your truck, Holling. I've been driving since I was fourteen."

"But you haven't driven in snow in over ten years. I'm not letting you behind the wheel on your own until you've had some time to practice."

She'd tried a different tack, hoping to appeal to his weakness at the very mention of his better half. "You let Sawyer drive your stupid truck. And she's barely tall enough to see over the steering wheel."

When Holling had grinned, Aidan had known that she hadn't really changed his mind. He'd been reliving some private, happy moment between him and Sawyer. A moment he wasn't going to share. For which Aidan had been grateful.

"My baby may need a stack of phone books to sit on when she's driving, but I taught her myself how to drive on the ice. I know she's not going to get out there, panic and wind up wrapped around a tree."

"Holling, I'm not used to having to ask permission when I want to come and go."

"Get over it, gal. I'm not going to let you drive my truck. But I'll tell you what I will do…"

He'd barely gotten the words out of his mouth before he'd flipped open his cell phone. Ten minutes later, Darion had been knocking at the door and she had her personal driver back again. Her brother Holling had done his usual job— made a request of Darion that wasn't really a request. Aidan had felt guilty for all of thirty seconds as she'd watched Darion heroically form his lips to tell his boss man that he'd love to take her shopping. Now, as she dragged him from store to store, she was starting to feel a twinge of responsibility for his discomfort.

"I told you, you don't have to shadow me, Slim," she said as she pushed open the door of the fourth shop. "If you've got anything you want to take care of while you're in town, I could meet up with you somewhere."

Aidan had the feeling that she was going to be in this store longer than she'd been in the others. Unlike the others, when she opened the door to this one, it didn't give her an electronic buzzer to let the management staff know that someone had entered. This one had actual bells. A string of small, copper bells hung from the top of the door and tinkled delicately as she stepped inside. "If you've got something to do, go on. I'll be fine."

Darion didn't respond, but moved to a corner of the store

where he could watch and wait for her without getting in the way of the other shoppers.

Not that there were many, Aidan noted. She could count the number of patrons in this shop on one hand. Even though the prices seemed, in her opinion, to provide better bargains than the other stores she'd visited. Here, the merchandise was a hodgepodge of one-of-a-kind items. Dresses. Jewelry. Scented candles. Even framed art. Yet, the more she browsed through the various racks and shelves, the more impressed she became. The last couple of shops had left her uninspired and unimpressed by the overpriced and boring—almost homogenized—goods. Items she could have found in any store and in any city.

"Can I help you find something?"

A heavyset woman in her midfifties with naturally auburn hair streaked with gray addressed her. As the woman approached, Aidan could hear the loose-fitting, lime-green Asian-style tunic and trousers she wore *swish* in the near silence of the boutique.

Aidan gave an insincere smile, trying to give off the don't-bother-me vibe. "Oh, I was only browsing."

"For anything in particular?"

"Last-minute gifts," Aidan confessed. "For my brother and his wife and…" She indicated with an almost imperceptible nod of her head to where Darion stood vigil in the corner.

"I see. Well, why don't you look around some more." She gestured with a broad hand; each stubby, squat finger was filled with rings. Some were simple bands. Others were adorned with large, semiprecious stones. Amethyst and amber, turquoise and garnet. She was a walking rainbow.

"If you find something you like, dear, I'll be right over there." She pointed back behind the counter.

Aidan lifted her eyebrows in amazement. No high-pressure sales? No carefully guided suggestions? This went against all of the little training she'd had back at that department store in Florida.

"Thank you," Aidan said gratefully. She wasn't quite sure what she wanted for Holling and Sawyer. She was hoping that inspiration would come to her. Somehow, she would know she'd come across the right gift as soon as she saw it.

Not unlike coming across a certain man she knew.

As Aidan moved behind a rack of evening dresses, from her position, she could see Darion still waiting near the door. He stood with his hands clasped behind his back. From the slight movement of his shoulders, she knew that he was probably tapping one hand against the other. She wondered if he was even aware that he was doing it. The first time that she'd seen him stand that way, at the first store they'd visited, she'd taken the stance as a subtle gesture to hurry her along. She'd almost laughed at the thought. The subtle signal hadn't bothered her. Not a bit. She hadn't been having much success finding anything she wanted to purchase, anyway.

After they'd reached the second store, she'd encouraged him to look around as well. Maybe, if his mind was engaged in some activity of his own, it would take the attention away from her and her lack of purchases for the amount of time she was spending. In the hour that she'd wandered around the store, he'd come out with a new baseball cap and she'd picked up a couple of games for the twins. By the time they'd reached the fourth store, he was losing his ability to hide his impatience.

As she began her present hunt again in this fourth store, her eyes met his briefly to send him the "be patient" message, before she quickly lowered them. She started to slide the hangers over the metal rack, admiring each dress. Each one was more exquisite than the last. Yet, the prices were extremely reasonable—as if the merchant was more concerned about getting those delicate creations of gauze or raw silk or taffeta into the hands of some lucky woman than making a measly dollar off them.

She'd originally gone into the store thinking to buy something for Sawyer. But her hand kept straying to the side of the rack that held her sizes. Her hand paused in its riffling, landing on a moss-green, spaghetti-strapped silk-and-velvet dress that felt so good to the touch of her searching fingers, she couldn't help but wonder how it would feel against her skin.

She pulled the hanger off the rack, without checking the price tag. She wasn't going to buy it, Aidan told herself. She only wanted to see how it looked on her. Now that she'd lost some weight, she wasn't as fearful of trying on clothes.

"Especially ones as delicious as this one," she murmured to herself. She turned toward one of the walls. A mirror, trimmed in shells, more stones and dyed ostrich feathers was hanging against it. She held the dress up against her body, covering up the jeans and leather jacket.

"Be right back, Slim!" She gave Darion warning before asking the woman who'd approached her, "Do you have a dressing room?"

"Right through those doors." She indicated a pair of swinging, louvered doors toward the rear of the boutique. "If you're trying that on, you might want these."

She gave a huff, easing herself off a padded stool and made her way to a shelf lined with shoes. Glancing down at Aidan's feet, she said with certainty, "You're a size nine."

"Sometimes," Aidan admitted. "Sometimes a nine and a half, depending on who made the shoes."

"Try these, hon. They're like walking on clouds." She

pulled down a box and slid off the lid. Inside, a pair of shoes, dyed moss-green to match the dress, lay in the box surrounded by standard white tissue paper. Aidan lifted one shoe and examined it. It was a sling-back kitten-heeled shoe. The toe came to a narrow point. The same crushed stones were sprinkled over the shoe, matching the sparkling stones following the curve of the dress's plunging neckline.

"They're exquisite," Aidan murmured, holding the shoe up to the light of the store, turning it this way and that, watching it glint. "Looks like something Cinderella would have worn."

"That ungrateful wench wouldn't have gotten her foot in one of my creations," the woman said in derision. "Now Imelda Marcos, there's a woman who knew how to appreciate a good shoe."

"You designed these?" Aidan said, impressed.

"Everything in here is mine," the woman said proudly. "Didn't you notice the sign over the door? Kiara's Kreations. That would be me. I'm Kiara."

"A pleasure to meet you, Ms. Kiara," Aidan said earnestly. "You do wonderful work."

"Thank you." She sighed and looked toward the door as yet another shopper left the boutique. "Wish I had more customers in here like you."

"You mean someone with taste other than in their mouths?" Aidan quipped. "I've seen what's been flying off the shelves in some of those other stores around here. Low-quality, high-cost crap that'll fall apart with the first washing. Don't get me wrong, Ms. Kiara. I'm not a label snob. I want a bargain as much as the next woman. But I don't want to spend money to be looking like everybody else."

"Don't get me started!" Kiara exclaimed, herding Aidan

toward the dressing room. As she did so, she reached for a faux-fur wrap, dyed in a contrasting color, to go around Aidan's shoulders; two more dresses; and another pair of shoes.

"You might as well make yourself comfortable, young man." Kiara gave Darion fair warning as she ushered Aidan into the dressing room. "We're going to be here for a while."

Aidan could almost see the thoughts running through Darion's mind.

"Why don't you come back in an hour, Darion," she said, granting him reprieve. "I should be done by then."

"Are you sure?"

"Are you asking me if I'm sure I'll be done in an hour, or are you asking me if I'm sure you should leave?" Aidan asked.

"Both."

"Yes. To Both," she promised.

"I'm going to pop down to the hardware store." He pointed his thumb in the direction down the street. "Won't be twenty minutes. Thirty minutes at the most."

"Fine. Fine. Go ahead," Aidan said distractedly, draping the wrap over one shoulder and admiring the effect in the mirror.

Darion pulled on the door handle, stepped outside. He took a moment to pull up the collar of his coat, pull the brim of his new baseball cap low over his eyes before starting down the street. As he passed in front of the large display window, he peered inside, checking on Aidan one last time.

She waved her hand, shooing him off. Then, on impulse, touched her fingers to her lips and blew him a kiss. Aidan wasn't sure, but she thought she saw him grin before turning away.

"That young man works for the Holling family, doesn't he?" Kiara asked conversationally.

She stopped at the jewelry counter, pulled out a choker

made from emerald-colored beads and gold links, and green velvet ribbon with matching earrings.

"Cutest little bride that man finally landed for himself."

Aidan blinked. "Bride?" The word caught in her throat as she glanced back to where Darion had stood.

"Um-hmm… Some little Southern girl from Birmingham. I heard she used to ride motorcycles, or some such nonsense."

Aidan stepped behind one of the curtained-off stalls and started to peel off her clothing.

"Oh! You mean Holling!" Aidan's voice flooded with relief. "Yes, Darion works for my brother."

She shrugged out of her jacket, sat on the small bench inside the dressing room and tugged off her boots.

"You're a Holling, too? I thought I noticed a family resemblance. I'm glad to finally see Darion with someone," Kiara commented. "Anytime I've seen him around town, he's always been by himself. Looked so lonesome sometimes. You can actually feel waves of sadness coming off him. I'm very in tune with that kind of thing, you know."

"No, I didn't know," Aidan said conversationally.

"That man has had some drama in his life."

"Haven't we all?" Aidan replied. What she thought was, *Not anymore if I have anything to say about it.*

Part of her was wishing she'd found this dress in a slightly larger size. Even a half size would have helped. As she slid into it and reached for the back zipper, she found herself having to hold her breath and draw in her stomach to make the zipper come all the way up to its final resting position between her shoulder blades.

Aidan finally smoothed the dress over her hips and derriere, then pulled the shoes' straps over her heels. When she stepped out for Kiara's approval, Kiara grinned back at her. Her wide, bloodred lipstick split across her face, showing small square pearly white teeth. "That little number was made for you...Ms. Holling."

"Call me Aidan," she said amiably. This time, the smile she returned to Kiara was genuine.

Aidan pulled her locks back over her shoulder, then twisted them on top of her head as Kiara clasped the choker around her neck.

"There now," Kiara said in a breathy whisper. "Perfect. Why don't you come outside and take a look at yourself in the mirror."

"But there's a mirror right over there," Aidan objected, pointing to the one on the far side of the small dressing area. She couldn't wait to try on some of the other items she'd picked out.

"Do me this one favor and walk around the store for a while. If someone sees you strutting around in this sleek little number, maybe it'll entice them to buy."

Aidan put her hands on her hips, turned her back and looked over her shoulder at the mirror to admire her reflection.

"You've already sold me on this," Aidan said. "Man, this makes my butt look good."

"Good. Now get out there and let someone else admire the view."

"What's my modeling fee?" Aidan teased.

"You get someone to buy it and I'll knock ten percent off the price," Kiara offered.

"Deal," Aidan said, reaching out to shake Kiara's hand. "You really have a sweet setup here."

"You like it?"

"I love it. I used to be in sales."

"Did you really?"

"Briefly. Very briefly," Aidan clarified, not wanting to mis-represent the truth.

"Oh."

"Why? Are you looking for seasonal help?"

"Are you kidding?" Kiara scoffed. "It's the holiday crush. This place should be packed."

Aidan looked around the store, absorbing the emptiness of the boutique and Kiara's disappointment in the lackluster sales.

"For a little more than ten percent, I might be able to help you."

"Twenty percent?" Kiara asked dubiously.

"I'm thinking long-term," Aidan said, thoughtfully tapping her index finger above her upper lip. "What would you say if I told you that I could increase your sales and I only wanted a percentage of that increase?"

"If you're anything like your family, I'd say that you aren't talking smack. The Hollings have a good reputation around here. If you've got an idea brewing, I want to know about it. I can...I can... Can I help you, miss?"

Kiara's attention shifted as the copper bells above the door jangled for her attention. Aidan moved easily from the rear of the store where the dressings were located to a more central location. She strolled up the aisle, as Kiara had suggested, pretending to leisurely browse more dresses on the rack.

A woman, in her mid- to late-thirties nodded at her, barely giving her a second glance. She scanned the floor, obviously looking, but not to buy. She stood on tiptoe, craning her neck to see above some of the racks, around some of the displays.

"What are you looking for? Maybe I can help you find something?" Kiara offered.

"Sorry," she said, her voice husky. "I was looking for someone. I was told he might be in here."

She reached her hand into her cashmere coat pocket and

pulled out a Polaroid snapshot. Approaching, she held the photo toward them.

"Have any of you seen this man?"

Kiara took the photograph from the woman, glanced at it and then handed it over to Aidan. Her expression was unreadable as she waited for Aidan to take in the image.

Aidan congratulated herself on keeping a steady hand as she passed it back to the woman.

"Who's looking for him?"

"I told you," the woman smiled, but with thinly disguised irritation. "I am."

"Why? Is he dangerous or something?" Kiara asked. "He's not wanted by cops, is he? Is he some kind of fugitive?"

"Have you seen him or not?" she demanded, shaking the photograph at them. From the look of the crumpled, cracked image, it seemed to Aidan that she'd had plenty of opportunity to flash that photo around.

"We might have," Kiara placated her. "It's been so busy around here. Everybody out trying to buy those last-minute gifts. Isn't that right, Aidan?"

Aidan nodded wordlessly in agreement.

The woman sighed, lowering her shoulders in an obvious display of dejection.

"If he should come in here," Aidan asked, "we'll tell him that you're looking for him. How can we contact you, miss— what did you say your name was again?"

If this was official police business, she would show a badge. Pass out a business card. Something.

"I didn't say." She looked Aidan up and down with open contempt. The woman then turned her back on Aidan and addressed Kiara.

"If you see him, you tell him that his wife is looking for

him. Tell him that he *needs* to bring his narrow ass on home and take care of those snot-nosed kids. You tell him that if he doesn't contact me in twenty-four hours, I'll have his trifling, low-down, on the down-low, whores-on-the-side behind in court for all of that back child support he still owes. Do you think you can remember that? Do you?"

Her jaw was clenched so tightly, Aidan was certain that she'd crack a molar.

"Certainly," Kiara said smoothly. Aidan could tell by her tone and nonthreatening movements that she'd dealt with irate customers before. "*If* he comes in here again, we'll pass on that message. Word for word."

"Thank you," the woman said. She turned up the collar of her coat, wrapped her Burberry scarf around her neck and tucked the loose ends in the opening at her throat. Aidan waited until the woman had cleared the door and the wide display window before grabbing on to the circular rack holding a collection of holiday blouses. She grasped the rack with both hands, breathing deeply.

Wife and kids? Wife and kids! Unpaid child support! Now it all made sense, why a man as intelligent, with as much obvious potential as Darion had, was living so far under the radar. He was a deadbeat dad, trying to get out of paying for his mistakes. Of course he had nothing to lose by jumping into bed with Aidan. If things went sour, he could always move on, leaving her wondering where he was.

Aidan squeezed the metal racks until her fingernails gouged into her flesh. She growled, shaking the rack until the metal hangers clanked. Kiara came up behind her, rubbing her between the shoulder blades to soothe her.

"How could I be so stupid! So gullible!" she shouted, thankful for the fact that the store was empty now.

"It's going to be all right, honey," Kiara soothed.

"No. It isn't," Aidan said in a tone so crisp that she imagined icicles hanging in front of her mouth as she spoke.

"You think you're the first woman who ever lost her head over a man?" Kiara offered.

"I didn't know he was married," she protested. "I didn't know!" Her laughter was harsh, bordering hysterical. "You know, Kiara, what I don't know about the man could fill a football stadium."

"Oh, dear…oh, dear…you poor, poor dear. What are you going to do?"

"Not to sound like a broken record, but I don't know."

"If you want my advice, for whatever it's worth since you only walked into my store less than an hour ago…"

"Sure. Go ahead," Aidan said without enthusiasm.

"Before you do anything, Aidan…and I mean anything, give yourself a moment to think about it. Then give yourself another minute. Don't do anything in a hot split second that will take you a lifetime to pay for."

"You mean, don't wrap my hands around the lying son of a bitch's neck and try to strangle the life from him?" Aidan said sweetly.

"Something like that."

"Don't tempt me," she said aloud. Immediately, the image of the three gunshot wounds in Darion's side came to mind. Obviously, someone had tried to beat her to the punch.

"I can't believe he played me like that," Aidan murmured.

"Then, don't," Kiara said, shrugging her shoulders. "There's nothing that says you have to believe that."

"You heard the woman! She's going to haul him into court. How can I be with a man who can't live up to his obligations?"

"You don't even know who she is. How do you know she's the one telling the truth?"

Aidan caught her lower lip between her teeth. "I don't know who to believe."

"Another piece of advice for you. Take it for what it's worth. If you can't trust your man, honey, then you shouldn't be with him. I don't care how good you *think* he makes you feel."

"The least I can do is warn him," Aidan murmured. "I owe him that much. Do you have a phone, Kiara?"

"In the office," she said, nodding toward the rear of the store. "You sure you want to do that?"

"The man may be a snake. But he saved my life. If she is out to get him, I would feel like the lowest of the low if I didn't give him a running head start."

Chapter 28

Darion stood at the cash register, feeling pretty pleased with himself and his purchases. He hadn't expected to find anything. Not so soon, anyway. The fact that he'd gotten in, found a present for Aidan and was up to the register in less than an hour's time was making him feel pretty good about himself.

He unfolded his wallet and counted out several crisp one-hundred-dollar bills. He didn't even flinch when the cashier rang up the purchase and passed back a couple of dollars in change.

"Would you like for me to wrap that for your, sir?" the cashier offered, pulling out a small decorative box and coordinating tissue paper. "Only three dollars," she gave him the additional service charge.

"Sure. Why not," Darion said amiably. He looked back over his shoulder at the line of people still waiting for their turn at the register. He could almost feel the collective wall of impatience pushing at his back.

His smile broadened. "A gift for my lady," he said, pointing his thumb at the sales clerk.

He felt goofy for saying it. But as foolish as he felt for explaining why he was holding up the line, he felt equally as wonderful for being able to do it. Like everyone else crammed in the store at the last minute, he'd done his share of browsing and putting up with pushy sales clerks, all trying to make their quotas before the registers closed out for the day.

He'd braved all of that, barely mumbling a word, his spirits buoyed by the thought of Aidan's expression of joy and adoration when he presented the gift for her. No doubt about it. He was certainly feeling that woman!

He'd thought about all of the reasons why he shouldn't feel as he did about Aidan. He kept coming back to the one reason why he did. She made him feel good. Not only physically. But emotionally, as well. She made him feel good about who he was. When he was around her, his life *felt* right. For the first time in what seemed like forever, he'd gotten it right. That was a feeling he hadn't had in a long time. Much too long. Life was too short to go through it not feeling right. So, let him feel foolish for once in his life. As far as he was concerned, he'd earned it.

"Here you go, sir." With two hands and a smile pasted on from plenty of practice, the sales clerk passed the festively wrapped package back to him. "Happy holidays."

"Same to you," he said, feeling about as light as his wallet. He gave a cheery wave to the customers still standing in line as he weaved his way back through the store. Past the tinsel and the lights and the displays promoting this year's musthaves. Darion grinned to himself. This year, the only musthave he was concerned about was Aidan. Aidan Holling.

Darion checked his watch. By now, she should have gone

through at least fifty of those outfits. Time to collect her. It was late in the afternoon and the meager breakfast he'd gulped down that morning had long since left a hole in his stomach. Maybe they could grab a bite to eat before heading back. He'd heard of a new restaurant on the other side of White Wolf. Supposed to serve a really mean steak.

He tugged his cap onto his head and passed through the revolving doors of the department store. Yeah. A steak was sounding really good right about now. Or, Darion amended, as he bent his head to a sudden gust of wind driving snow flurries into him, a steaming hot bowl of chili. He imagined him and Aidan sitting across the table from each other. Or better, sharing a booth, sitting right next to each other, doing the unthinkable—cuddling in public and sharing a meal, eating from each other's plates. Cuddling, of all things! The *C*-word.

The thought of it made him laugh at himself. Man, was he far gone. Public displays of affection had never been his style. Then again, neither was braving the worst of the winter crowds on one of the busiest shopping days of the year to find that one special gift for that one special someone in his life. That was something the old Darion would have never done. But he'd made the choice to let the old Darion fade away. He'd made that decision long before he'd met Aidan. Finding her was affirmation that he'd finally gotten his life going in the right direction. Finding her made him resolve that he wouldn't go back to his old life, not for anything in the world. No sir. There was nothing back there for him. And if he never had occasion to think about the man he used to be, the life he used to have, it would be too soon for him.

Wrapped up as tightly in his thoughts as he was in his winter coat, Darion stepped out into the crosswalk without checking traffic. He was shaken out of his reverie by a white-gloved hand reaching out to grab his shoulder and suddenly yanking him back to the curb. He stumbled back against a heavily padded body dressed in a red suit with white fur trim.

The sound of his own exclamation and the clang of a dropped bell was lost as the driver behind the wheel of a car speeding through the parking lot lay heavily on the horn to warn him. Darion turned his head, making eye contact with the driver as the car continued on. His goodwill was instantly damped as he saw the driver's expression and read his lips. Darion was certain that the driver's two-word greeting starting with *M wasn't* "Merry Christmas."

"You angling to become a human hood ornament, son?" Darion's rescuer addressed him.

"Sorry, Santa." Darion reached down to retrieve the fallen bell for the storefront Salvation Army Santa.

Santa dipped his head, peering out from underneath pasted-on bushy eyebrows. Gray eyes crinkled at the corners as he tugged on his beard, revealing his face beneath the fleece.

"Looks like I got to you in the nick of time, if you'll excuse the pun."

"Luke?" Darion mouthed the word. He took several steps back, nearly colliding with the bright red collection kettle tied to a wooden tripod. The coins in the kettle rattled as it leaned precariously. It was him, all right. From his booted feet to his snowy-white hair tucked underneath that grimy trucker's cap.

Where had that donation kettle come from? Darion wondered. He didn't remember passing it on the way out of the store. Then again, he thought ruefully, he hadn't seen the car that had almost mowed him down, either. Darion grabbed the kettle, settling it back into place with an apologetic pat.

"What are you doing here?" Darion asked. "You can't say that I called for you this time."

"But you do need me. That much is obvious." Luke gestured at the steady flow of traffic moving through the crosswalk.

"I guess I do." Darion chuckled reluctantly. "What are you? My own personal bodyguard, or something?"

"No. Not yours personally. I'm a very busy man. Got places to go. People to see."

"So why are you always up under me all the time? Looks like every time I turn around, there you are."

"For some reason, son, for now, you seem to need my help the most."

"Yeah?" Darion's tone was mocking. He hadn't forgotten how Luke had helped him rescue Aidan. But, it was also painfully fresh in his memory how alone he'd been when he'd been desperate and in need, with no one around to help him. When he'd been homeless and hungry, or when he'd been lying injured, near death, where had that self-proclaimed very busy man been?

"If that's the case, where were you a year ago? Where were you then? Huh? I don't know how you know me. But you do. And if you do know anything about me…and you're always talking like you do, you would have been there when I really needed someone. Some serious help."

"I do know you, Darion. More than you know yourself. So, you think back on it. A year ago, you needed me…but you didn't ask for me. Not once."

Darion opened his mouth to protest, then closed it again with an audible click. A year ago, he hadn't been asking much from anybody. Too much of a badass. Anything he needed or wanted, he'd taken. And he hadn't cared if it belonged to him or not. Wanting was reason enough to go after it. Trouble was, more often than not, he'd been wanting the wrong things. And the wrong people. Funny, in giving up so much, how much he'd gained over the past year.

Luke reached out and clasped Darion's shoulder. "What you gave up doesn't compare to what you have now," he said solemnly. "If I were you, son, I'd make sure that she knows that."

Darion was too concerned for Aidan to realize that he hadn't voiced those thoughts aloud. Somehow, Luke had plucked them right out of his brain.

"She? You mean Aidan?"

Something cold twisted up inside Darion. The last time he'd seen Luke, Aidan had been in trouble. More trouble than he'd been able to get her out of on his own.

"What about Aidan? Is she all right?" Darion asked, clamping down on Luke's arm.

"She hasn't fallen into another lake," Luke assured him. "But she's in trouble and she needs you to be there for her."

"Then why didn't she let me know? Why didn't she call me?" Darion said, frustrated at the way Aidan could be so willful sometimes. Every day, she exercised and flexed her independence muscles when she didn't need to. Didn't she know that he was there for her? If she needed him so much, why didn't she call him?

Luke patted Darion's arm comfortingly before extricating himself. "Why didn't you?" he asked Darion and took a step back, resuming his position at the donation pot.

The sound of the Luke's bell ringing could barely be heard over the throng of shoppers threading their way through the maze of stores, the loudspeakers blaring their holiday music to entice the last few dollars out of the hands of willing participants in the holiday hustle, and the rumble and purr of engines crisscrossing the parking lots.

Why didn't you? Luke's question echoed in Darion's head as he dug deep into his pocket, searching for his keys and wallet. The old trucker had given him something to think about; the very least he could do was give something back. He opened his wallet, plucking out his next-to-last C-note, more than glad to add it to the coins in the donation kettle. He certainly would have, Darion noted with a frown, looking around as the crowd seemed to have swallowed up the man and his kettle.

"Luke?" Darion called out, craning his neck to see above the passersby. *Luke?*

"Guess it's not my money he wants," Darion surmised, as he checked for oncoming cars before stepping once more into the road.

Chapter 29

Aidan was already waiting for Darion by the time he pulled into a parking spot at the front of Kiara's boutique. She stood at the display window, her arms folded resolutely across her chest, watching him as he climbed out of the truck. He took a moment to adjust his coat and settle his cap on his head before starting for the boutique door.

For a moment, Aidan forgot herself. She set aside her anger and humiliation at the thought of being used by him. It amazed her how the simple things he did could make her stomach flutter. The simple act of putting on a hat caused her to lose her train of thought. Even from several feet away, she imagined that she could see Darion's eyes. So dark and full of mystery. Mystery and pain. Sometimes, when he didn't think she was watching him, a look of such dejection would cross his face that it tugged at her heart, making her want to take him in her arms and soothe that pain away.

She wasn't foolish enough to believe that simply being with her was enough to solve all his problems. What she did expect was for him to share some of that burden with her. To confide in her so that she wouldn't be blindsided by one of those problems suddenly walking through the door and knocking her flat with the severity of it.

Kiara moved around the store, attending to a couple of potential customers who'd wandered in. She edged close to Aidan.

"Take it easy, now, Aidan," she whispered out of the corner of her mouth. "Don't reach through the glass and strangle that man."

That was when Aidan realized she was gripping her arms so tightly that she was cutting off her circulation. She forcibly lowered her arms to her sides.

When Darion passed up the parking meter without dropping in coins to add more time, she tapped on the glass to get his attention.

"Parking meter," Aidan mouthed, then pointed to a meter reader several cars away from where he'd parked. He was dutifully checking the meters and issuing citations for violators.

Darion grimaced, making a comic show of turning out his pockets to prove how broke he was. Again, Aidan felt some of the ice melt around her heart. Darion was not a man for playing the clown. Sawyer had once remarked that when Darion had first arrived to work for Holling, she thought she'd have to hog-tie the man and tickle torture him to get a smile out of him.

What a difference six months and finding a good woman to loosen him up had made.

Loosen him up is right, Aidan thought reluctantly. If Darion was married to that woman, she would have to cut him loose. That was no laughing matter. Yes, she was lonely out there on her own in Florida. Yes, she could have used a little male companionship on more than one occasion. But she wasn't so bad off that she had to take up with another woman's husband. She was Aidan Holling, not Janeen. She was not her mother. If Darion was married, she'd give him up. Not matter how much he made her smile….or any of those other secretly wonderful things he did for her.

By the time he approached the door and tugged on the antique handle, she'd gone through a complete cycle of emotions—from tenderness, to despair at the thought of having to let him go, to complete resolve. She would do what had to be done, no matter what.

Damn you, Darion! she silently raged.

Damn you for putting me in the position of having to choose between my love for you and love of myself. Why couldn't you have told me about your wife before? Before you came up to me, looking at me with those big, soulful eyes, talking to me with those sexy lips, the first thing out of your mouth should have been, "Don't even think about it. I'm taken."

Aidan anxiously gnawed on a fingernail, caught in a cycle of swirling emotions. Fear. Doubt. Anger. Disbelief. Shame. Compassion. She was on an emotional roller-coaster ride. The kind with no operator and no brakes. She was left all alone to experience the highs and the lows. The sharp dips, the wrenching turns and the stomach-churning loop-de-loops. Aidan was so unsettled that she wasn't sure what she'd do once she saw him again. What should she do? Do her level best to knock him flat on his behind or grab him by the hand and run until they'd left all of that babies' mama behind?

"This is crazy. I don't have to put up with this!" she declared. "I'm young, single, intelligent. Fine. Yes, I said *fine!* I don't have to waste my time with some—"

"Hey," Darion greeted Aidan with a kiss the moment he walked through the door.

"Where the hell have you been? I've been trying to call you!" Aidan whispered tightly, mindful of Kiara's customers, who'd wandered in to browse. He'd come up to her at the wrong time. At the time when the emotional wheel had turned to ultra-pissed. Her expression was strained, but softened as soon as he brought his hands from behind his back and displayed a small package wrapped in red-and-gold paper and metallic-red ribbons.

"The battery went dead on my phone," Darion explained. "I left it in the truck to charge it."

"Oh..." she said, some of the heat taken out of her argument. She felt the click of the wheel go from pissed to curious. "What's this?"

Darion shrugged. "Oh, it's a little something I picked up while I was out."

"Is that for me?" she said eagerly.

"I don't know." Darion smiled at her. "Have you been naughty or nice while I've been gone?"

Aidan grinned at him, leaned closed and whispered. "I've been nice," she assured him. "But I can be naughty later, if that's what you—"

Wait a hot minute! She quickly withdrew her affection. It wasn't supposed to be that easy. She immediately threw up her defenses. Did he think he could walk up in there and pacify her with pretty gifts? Aidan Holling wasn't going to sell herself that cheap. Not this girl. That was probably how he'd tricked that person. The more she thought about how he might have kids somewhere, going without because their daddy was out buying her presents, the more infuriated she became.

Though they hadn't known each other very long, they were in tune with each other's emotions enough to be able to read them. She was furious and he was confused. Or was he? Maybe he was good at playacting and could put on the innocent act whenever it suited him.

"Aidan, what's wrong? What is it?" Darion massaged her shoulders, but she jerked away from him.

"Darion, you and I need to talk," Aidan said somberly. He ought to have been in enough relationships to recognize those code words. She didn't really want to have a conversation. She wanted to vent her frustration and she wanted him to sit there and take it.

"Sure. Why don't we go and grab a bite to eat and then we can talk all you want. I don't know about you, baby, but I'm starving."

"We don't have time for that. When that woman comes back looking for you—" Aidan looked anxiously over her shoulder, as if she expected her to show up at any moment.

"What woman?" Darion asked, frowning. There were a couple of women in the store; they were already at the register paying for their purchases.

Aidan lifted her chin, her jaw clenched tightly as she enunciated clearly. "Your wife."

"My what?" His exclamation brought curious stares from several of Kiara's customers.

"You heard me." Aidan deliberately dropped her voice to make him do the same. "I didn't stutter. I said your *wife* came looking for you. Looks like you've got some unfinished business back wherever it is you came from, lover."

Her tone couldn't be any sharper if she'd dragged it against a whetstone.

Darion reached out to Aidan again, but she wasn't having any of it. She held up both hands, warding him off. "You'd better take your hands off me, Darion. Don't you touch me. Not now."

"Aidan, you're not making any sense," Darion said, though he wasn't sure whether she was listening to him while she was in that mood. He hadn't seen her this furious since he'd spent that week ignoring her. Then, she'd thrown snowballs at him to get his attention. Now, she was throwing daggers at him. Icy-cold daggers shooting from her eyes.

"Let's go," she ordered as she shoved her arms through her jacket sleeves and pulled her knit cap over her head. "Take me home."

"Sure. Are these yours?" He pointed to a couple of boutique bags sitting near the window where Aidan had stood vigil like a wounded lioness, waiting to lash out and pounce on him.

"Yes, they're mine."

She had found a few items. One, she sadly reminded herself, was for Darion. She'd known it was the gift for him the moment she'd seen it in the display case. At Kiara's suggestion, she'd chosen a hand-stitched leather wallet monogrammed with the letter *D*.

Aidan had laughed out loud, remembering how he'd pulled his wallet out to show her his identification before she'd left with him from the airport. The old, beat-up thing looked as if the cow it had come from was the scrub of the bunch. The wallet was well-worn, falling apart, barely enough stitching to keep the thing together. She wondered why Darion still carried it. Maybe it had sentimental value. Or maybe he was the kind of man who didn't want to spend money on himself.

Or anyone else. Like his own kids!

She dragged herself back from that mental stroll down memory lane. She had to keep reminding herself that she really didn't know the man that she'd fallen in love with. And now that she'd gotten a glimpse into this well-kept secret of a past, somehow she had to make herself fall as quickly out of love. She couldn't see herself prolonging their relationship, making it painful for both of them. It was better to end it now. At least, that was what she had to tell herself to keep her resolve.

Aidan didn't look at him as he held the door open for her. When he unlocked the truck for her, she made sure to keep her eyes trained straight ahead. If she looked at him, stared up into the eyes of the man who'd saved her life, who'd touched her heart, she'd start to cry. She knew she would.

Though she could almost feel him wanting to, he didn't say a word as he unlocked the truck and held the door open for her. He didn't even bother turning on the radio. Aidan was glad. She didn't want to hear any sickeningly sweet songs about how good it was to be home for Christmas or how wonderful it was to share this time with family and friends. She would rather make the entire trip home in silence, no matter how uncomfortable it was. Maybe that was her problem. She'd gotten too comfortable, too fast, and now she was paying for her gross error in judgment.

Keep your mouth shut, Aida Beth, she warned herself. *Don't say a word. Don't you dare give him an inkling of how messed up this situation is. Don't let him know how much he hurt you. Don't let him know how deeply you still care for him, even knowing that he isn't the man you thought he was.*

Fifteen minutes into the ride, with her face turned to the window, Aidan was tired of silently, sullenly watching the landscape roll by. It was all so picture-perfect. Too perfect. The sight of her own home was starting to depress her. In the distance, the mountains rose up tall and majestic. They were as strong as she felt she ought to be. It was starting to snow again. Thick flurries swirled all around the truck. As much emotional turmoil as she was going through, she felt trapped in a snow globe. One that someone had vigorously, viciously shaken, leaving her feeling disoriented. Time to settle this.

"Who is she, then?" She broke the silence with more of an accusation than a question.

"You tell me," Darion countered nastily. "You were there. You have all the facts."

There was no mistaking Darion's tone. He wasn't contrite. Not a hint of conciliation. This wasn't the tone of a man who'd been found out and was trying to hold on to Aidan at any cost. This wasn't the way a man should sound if he was going to try to wheedle and cajole, to convince her that everything was going to be all right despite all appearances. He was angry. So angry that she could hear his teeth click together as he clamped down on each word.

Aidan recognized that tone. It was the same tone he'd used when he'd found out that she'd withheld Luke's death from him. He'd asked her to trust him then, and she'd promised that she would. She bit her lip in consternation. She'd promised him and at the first opportunity what had she done? She hadn't even given him the benefit of the doubt. She'd immediately assumed he was a dog, like all of the others she'd avoided. In her heart, she'd thought Darion was different. But she'd let that woman mess with her head, and now she wasn't so sure about him. She wanted to take back her anger and her mistrust. But she wasn't ready to go there yet. If he was a dog, a player, then he'd have that innocent act down pat. He'd know how to turn it around so that it looked as if she were the crazy one for her suspicions.

"She said she was your wife," Aidan began to explain.

"Then she's a damn liar," Darion retorted. "And you bought it."

Aidan winced. Yes, she'd bought it. As quickly as she'd snatched up that green dress of Kiara's. "What was I supposed to think?" Aidan protested.

"You were supposed to trust me," he reminded her.

This time, Aidan knew the pain in his voice was genuine. She didn't know how she knew. She just did. Like she knew the moment she'd met him that this was a man who would significantly touch her life. Like she knew when she couldn't leave him out there on the ledge alone that this was a man she wanted, and needed, by her side. She knew when she and Darion had spent those days cocooned in the motel, they were binding themselves to each other, exclusively, inextricably.

She also intuitively knew why the appearance of that woman had hurt her so much. If her time with Darion had been only about sex, she could have shrugged it off. Oh well. What was that old eighties song? Simply physical? Nothing but a *thang*.

Yet, what she felt for him was so much more than that. And no one could tell her otherwise. Some people searched a lifetime looking for what she and Darion had found. Some people called it a soul mate. Maybe that was it. Maybe it wasn't. But he had touched her. Not only her body, but her spirit as well. Her very soul. She'd let him past her defenses. Taken a chance on him. Aidan admitted to herself that she was afraid to. Afraid to hope that he was the one for her. This woman's sudden appearance spoke to every single one of those fears.

"She had a picture of you…and her…together."

"A picture of her? What did this woman look like?"

Aidan shrugged. "Pretty little thing. About five foot two. Size five. She wore a London Fog all-weather coat and Burberry fedora and scarf."

"That doesn't help me, Aidan," Darion said.

"Short black hair, light brown eyes. Had a serious attitude.

I thought she was gonna claw my eyes out. Does that help you any, Slim?"

Darion sucked in a deep breath and muttered a curse that he immediately apologized to Aidan for.

"No offense taken," Aidan assured him. "She made me want to curse her myself. Who is she, Darion?"

"She sure as hell isn't my wife," Darion ground out. "That you can believe."

"I suppose you don't appreciate her telling everyone that she is."

"I don't give a rat's behind about everybody else. It's you—" Darion didn't finish his sentence. His hands gripped the steering wheel as he drove, clenching and unclenching.

Aidan choked on unshed tears and leaned her head on his shoulder. "Why would she lie about a thing like that?"

"Because she's a pathological liar," he said simply.

"Then you do know her?" she insisted.

"Yeah. I know who she is."

"And?" Aidan prompted.

"She's nobody I want to know."

"Darion, that's about as evasive an answer as you can give me. I want to know who that woman is…if she has the power to do this to us…"

"She doesn't have any power that you don't give her, Aidan," Darion said, momentarily taking his eyes off the road to impress her with his sincerity. Cautiously, he lifted his arm and placed it along the back of her headrest. When she didn't push his arm away, he cupped his hand over her shoulder and massaged gently.

"I'm sorry if she upset you, baby. But you can't believe a word that comes out of that woman's mouth."

"She's not your wife?" Aidan asked, a little less certainty in her conviction of him.

"No."

"And you don't have any kids together?"

"Kids?" Darion's laughter was more of astonishment than humor.

"The thought of having children makes you laugh, does it?" Aidan challenged.

"No," he repeated. "That's not it. I love kids… I love the thought of making babies…with the right woman, that is." Darion boldly let his hand drift so that it rested between the open flaps of her jacket. His thumb casually moved back and forth, stroking her breast.

"Oh," Aidan responded, snuggling closer to him. She hugged him, winding her arm around his waist, and pressed her cheek to his chest.

"She sounded really pissed at you, Darion."

Darion grunted. "I imagine that she does."

"Can you tell me why?"

Darion hesitated. "I want to tell you, Aidan. But I…I can't talk about it now."

"Can't? Or won't?"

"A little of both, I suppose..I know I'm asking a lot from you, but I need you to be patient with me, baby."

"I told you I wasn't a patient woman," she reminded him.

"Then, I'm asking you to trust me. Can you do that?"

"We've talked about that, too. I do trust you, Darion. At least…I thought I did until this woamn showed up."

"I'd hoped it was the last time I'd ever hear her name."

"What does she want with you?"

"You're not going to let this go, are you?"

"I'm not going to let you go," she clarified. "She wants to take you away from me, Darion. I know this may sound corny, but we Hollings won't let anybody take anything that's ours.

We'll fight to the last man, woman and child before that happens. If she thinks she can step up to us and cause trouble, she's got a serious fight on her hands. If you don't believe me, ask Holling. You ask him what he did to that sorry piece of crap who tried to claim Sawyer's babies after he kicked her to the curb and denied it was his."

Darion smiled and kissed the top of her head.

"It won't come to that," he promised. "We won't have to call on your big brother. Between you and me, in case you were ever wondering, that man's behind you, Aidan, all the way."

"I'm sorry I jumped to conclusions about you, Darion," Aidan admitted.

"Don't worry about it. I guess I haven't given you much reason not to."

"No," she concurred. "You haven't. You and I both know that we still have a lot of learning to do before we really get to know…and trust…each other."

Possessively, he squeezed her shoulder. "And we've got a lifetime to do it in."

Aidan settled herself comfortably against him, wrapping her arms around his waist. She squeezed him back, letting him know that her emotional storm had passed. "This sounds suspiciously like the part where we start talking about our future."

Chapter 30

Darion stood at the mirror, staring at his reflection. But it wasn't his own face that he saw; not as it was now. He saw himself as he used to be. Head shaved clean. Face a little fuller. Neatly trimmed mustache and beard. The face of his past. He'd almost forgotten that face. For all his efforts, it had almost faded from his memory until Aidan had brought that image back with crystal-clear sharpness. Like that plasma wide-screen television the boss man had had delivered to the bunkhouse as a gift to the employees.

And with that revived image came the pain. A pain so intense that it made him involuntarily reach up and touch the wounds that had healed physically, but still left him emotionally spent. The memory of where he'd been when he was wounded—and how he'd been—crowded in on Darion. For a moment, he almost forgot that he was a new man now. A man who'd given himself permission to leave the old one behind.

A man who'd found a new life, and a new love. He had become a man who could look at himself in the mirror and not cringe from the sight of himself. Darion had almost gotten to the place where he could feel proud of who he'd become, until Aidan had reminded him that there were still parts of himself out there that wouldn't let him lift his head up.

It wasn't really her fault. She couldn't know how hard he'd tried to forget. But riding back from White Wolf, talking about Joelle, had dredged up memories that he hadn't buried quite deep enough. And now they were back again. Back with a vengeance.

Vengeance was right. Joelle was about nothing nice. She'd hunted him relentlessly. She'd done it when they'd lived together and she was doing it now. Darion fought the urge to do as he'd done before. Run. Run as far as his strength and his funds would allow him to go. He'd done it before. He could do it again. Change his appearance. Change his location. New man. New chance at life. It wouldn't be so hard this time, now that he'd been through it once. He knew all of the pitfalls. He knew how to blend in. To keep himself light, fluid, without entanglements. Living under the radar. He was getting pretty good at it now. Only, one thing stopped him. But it was no small thing. Darion couldn't imagine himself leaving Aidan. He couldn't see himself living without her. He didn't want to.

So, as easy as he made taking off again sound to himself, Darion knew without a doubt that he wouldn't do it. He couldn't do it. He'd let that crazy woman hounding him drive him out of his home once. He wouldn't do it again. No…White Wolf was where he belonged. Here he would make his stand. If he was lucky, maybe Joelle would get tired of looking. Or maybe no one would admit to recognizing that photo that Aidan had said she was showing around.

"Yeah, right," Darion said aloud in derision. She'd come

that close to finding him. It was only a matter of time before she trailed him out there to the ranch. If he'd been thinking clearly, the moment Aidan had mentioned her, he should have gone off in search of Joelle. He should have found her, confronted her and ended this madness once and for all. At the time, it had been more important for him to gain Aidan's understanding and trust. He'd figured with Joelle right there in White Wolf, there would be plenty of time to get involved in the drama that Joelle invoked. If he didn't square things with Aidan right then, right there, there might not be more time for them. As fast as his feelings for her had developed, he knew that if Aidan wasn't handled carefully, it could end as rapidly. These early moments of their relationship, they walked on ice. As slippery and as treacherous as the ice she'd fallen through rescuing her niece, Sydney. Aidan had held on to Sydney, keeping her safe. When it had been Aidan's turn to be rescued, he'd held on to her, pulling her free. He'd keep holding on to her, too, Darion vowed. Literally and figuratively. No one, not her brother, not that woman stalking him, no one was going to separate him from Aidan if he had any strength left in his body.

"Hey, Darry. Get the lead out of your butt, boy! We can't keep the boss man waiting!"

Red Bone strutted to the mirror, peeking over Darion's shoulder to check his own reflection before slapping Darion on the back.

"I'm coming."

Heaving a grim sigh, Darion finished adjusting his silk tie. He lifted his foot, wiping the top of his leather shoes on the back of his wool pants. He'd hoped to have dinner alone with Aidan this Christmas eve. There was so much he still wanted to say to her. Making polite conversation with the boss man and his family and vying for Aidan's attention with some of the remaining guests of the bed-and-breakfast or the skeleton crew who'd stayed on to work the holiday season wasn't Darion's idea of spending a quiet evening alone with his woman.

Red Bone lifted his chin, checking his shaving skill. "This old face is likely to crack the mirror," he commented, tapping the underside of his chin with his fingers to tighten up the loose, leathery skin of his face. He met Darion's gaze in the mirror.

"Boy, you sure clean up good!" Red Bone tugged on Darion's jacket sleeves. "What is this? Armani?"

"Sean John," Darion corrected, adjusting the cuffs of his sleeves by checking his onyx-and-gold cuff links.

"Where did you get the dough to get yourself a suit that fly?" Wade demanded, eyeing Darion with suspicion as he cinched his belt.

"Your mama gave it to him," Red Bone cut him off.

Wade tugged at his crotch, making sure everyone was watching as he gestured rudely at Red Bone. "Got your mama right here, Red Bone. Come on, Darry. Have you been working another job that we don't know about?"

"Leave the boy alone, now. He's trying to look his best for his lady on Christmas eve."

"Guess that's one way to get a Christmas bonus," Wade muttered loud enough for Darion to hear. "Kissin' the boss man's ass and his sister's, too."

Darion turned around, smiling thinly. His voice was as smooth as the spun silk of his shirt. "Makes you wonder if all those years you spent with your head up your own ass was worth the time, doesn't it, Wade?"

When Wade bucked at Darion with fists clenched, Red Bone stepped quickly between them to separate them.

"Easy, boys. It's Christmas eve. No need in getting all riled up before we go have dinner up at the big house with the boss man's family." He patted Wade on the shoulders, brushing at imaginary specs of dust on his suede jacket while using the opportunity to push him back. He leaned over and whispered a warning in Wade's ear. "You don't want to muck with that one, Wade. Darion's not the one."

"He's been walking around here like the cock of the walk since the day he got here, Red Bone," Wade complained. "What chance has a man got with him under the boss all the time?"

Red Bone glanced over his shoulder, watching Darion as he picked up a dark brown wool coat that was laid out on his bunk and set a dark gray-and-brown fedora at a jaunty angle on his recently braided hair. He scooped up a shopping bag filled with presents purchased for the family and nodded at Red Bone before starting for the door.

"Anything Darion's got, he's earned. You remember that."

"You don't think it strange that he's got money for threads like that all of a sudden?"

Red Bone shrugged. "What the boy does with his money is his own business."

"What money?" Wade scoffed. "You remember how he was when he came begging for a job. If that loser had two dimes to rub together it was because someone had given him one of them. If he has anything, it's because he's been giving it up to boss Holling's sister."

"Be careful what you say, Wade," Red Bone cautioned. "And you'd better be careful how you say it and who you say it to."

"I'm only saying what everybody else is thinking."

"Keep those nasty thoughts to yourself. You're gonna be sitting at the boss's table, looking him in the face, taking his money, and all the time, behind his back, you're calling his sister a whore."

"The apple doesn't fall too far from the tree. The gal looks like her mama. Probably acting like it, too."

By this time, some of the other hands who'd stayed behind to work over the holidays had gathered around Red Bone and Wade.

"Don't be a hater, Wade. You're pissed off because Darion got to her first," Tyrell commented.

Wade blew out a dismissive breath. "The fool's just lucky. You mark my words. One of these days, that luck will all play out."

"Why you wanna go and curse the boy on Christmas eve, Wade? Why can't you go to dinner, like normal folks, sit down, enjoy the meal? The boss man invited us into his home to enjoy a peaceful, joyous holiday with his family."

Wade pursed his lips, frowned as he splashed on a third dose of aftershave. "There's nothing peaceful or joyous about that man, Red Bone. He's a coldhearted SOB of the worst kind. You'll see."

Sawyer stood on tiptoe, peering through the frosted-over panes of glass set inside the main entry door for the bed-and-breakfast. Even with the extra height of those exquisite teal four-inch suede heels that Aidan had given her, letting her unwrap her present early to wear for tonight's dinner, Sawyer still couldn't quite see who was at the door.

The grandfather clock in the hall chimed eleven times. Its rich tones echoed, calling to her attention how quiet it was throughout the house.

"This late, it had better be jolly old Saint Nick with a whole lot of presents," Sawyer grumbled.

Their dinner guests had already gone; the last one she'd politely but insistently pushed out the door almost an hour ago. Red Bone, Wade and Nate had hung around, puffing on cigars, reminiscing about Christmases past. She didn't know which stung her eyes the most—the cigars or Wade's cologne.

She'd finally put the kids to bed. Maybe they weren't asleep yet but they were sufficiently warned not to get out of bed to try to catch a glimpse of Santa. The first time they'd tried it, it had been *so* cute. She'd found them sitting in the kitchen in their pajamas with plates of cookies and glasses of milk that they were "testing" for Santa to make sure they tasted right. The second time, they'd wandered to the upstairs guest hall, poking and shaking the complimentary gifts from the B and B left in front of each door.

After that, she'd lost track of the excuses for why they weren't in bed. Sawyer hated to do it, but after the fifth time she'd found them up, she'd threatened her little darlings.

"You get out of that bed one more time, Sydney Rose and Jayden Nathaniel, and I'm going to put the secret sign outside on our door that Santa uses to pass the houses of willful, disobedient children."

"Lamb's blood?" Sydney had immediately piped up, trying to apply one of the recent Sunday school lessons.

"No, they're called return receipts," Sawyer had quipped, figuring that the sarcasm would be lost on them. However, her intention would not be. She was tired and cross enough to make good on her threat. "It's past the time for little boys and girls to be in bed. Now, scoot!"

It had been an exhausting day, with all of those last-minute preparations. Tomorrow promised to be even longer. Sawyer didn't want to meet it with bleary eyes, yawning through the home videos that Nate would be sure to make to catch the spontaneous looks of joy as everyone opened their gifts. With everyone settled in, Sawyer was hoping that she and Holling could enjoy some quiet spontaneity of their own in the privacy of their own bedroom. Time for big girls and boys to be in bed, too.

"Well…almost all," she'd corrected herself. Darion and Aidan had sat in the parlor, enjoying the last embers of the fire. As Sawyer had passed them to answer the door, she'd pulled on the French door handles, giving them their moment of privacy that she knew they'd been yearning for all evening. Though they'd been as discreet as they could be, for the sake of their guests and the two pairs of eager eyes and ears of her children watching every move their auntie made with Mr. Darry, it was obvious that Darion and Aidan were so into each other that, at the first opportunity, they'd be all over each other.

"Don't stay up too late, you two," she'd warned, then wagged her finger. "Remember that you should expect more than Santa Claus to be busting up in here in the early hours of the morning. I mean early," she emphasized. She wouldn't put it past her kids to get up at the first stroke of midnight.

"Good night, Sawyer." Aidan had made a shooing motion with her hand behind the couch.

"Good night," she'd echoed.

Sawyer had paused for a moment with her hands on the door handles, watching the silhouette of Aidan and Darion in the muted light of the room. The overhead lights had been dimmed, and so had the scattered table lamps throughout the room. The glow from the fireplace had cast a rosy halo around their heads as they'd faced each other. As Aidan had snuggled close to Darion, resting her head on his shoulder, he'd draped his right arm across her shoulders, absently, lovingly caressing her.

Sawyer had slowly, stealthily pulled the door toward her, convinced that the heat she'd felt coming from the room had nothing to do with the crackling blaze of the fireplace.

Through the glass, she'd watched as Darion had lifted Aidan's head with his free hand and had lowered toward her.

"Close your eyes, Sawyer," she'd chastised herself. She'd felt guilty, like a voyeur, spying on them as Darion had kissed Aidan. She couldn't help herself. The moment couldn't have been any more pure, more passionate if she'd written the scene herself in one of her novels. She could draw inspiration from a kiss like that. It was the kind of kiss that lingered forever, yet left the eager participants wanting more. So much more. Darion's hand had cupped her at the base of her neck as Aidan had leaned into the kiss. He'd bent her head back with the sheer intensity of it. Sawyer could sense the tension escalating. A prelude to something more.

Sawyer had heard Aidan moan.... Okay, she hadn't actually heard it. Maybe she'd only sensed it. When Holling kissed *her* like that, she moaned all right. Long and loud to let him know that he'd better not stop. It hadn't seemed to her that Darion was going to stop either. The firelight had reflected a shimmer of movement as Darion had edged closer, slid Aidan's dress strap off her shoulder.

Hastily, Sawyer had stepped away from the door. Curiosity was one thing, but she had her own private party to get to. To make sure that other curious eyes, those with less restraint or a respect for their privacy, didn't interrupt them, she'd released the copper-colored tasseled tiebacks to the heavy brocade curtains on either side of the parlor threshold. With the curtains drawn, they completely obscured the doors, a signal to any roaming family member or guest that the occupants of the parlor were not to be disturbed.

How many times, Sawyer had wondered wistfully, had she and Holling sat on that couch, as Aidan and Darion were doing? How many times had Nate had to close the curtains on them? She didn't know. There was no way for her to keep count, so enraptured were she and Holling with each other and engrossed in that moment, that nothing else in the world seemed to matter.

"Like getting up to answer the door," she'd said aloud as the latecomers had rung the doorbell again, insistently leaning on it.

"You gonna get that, darlin'?" Holling had called out from the kitchen where he'd stopped to get a snack before going on to their bedroom.

"I've got it," Sawyer had assured him.

Before opening the door, Sawyer had tried to see who it was. The shoes had given her another four inches to her five-foot-four height. Yet, the frost on the window obscured her vision. She could barely make out two figures as they huddled against the weather under the shelter of the porch. The taller one reached out and put an arm around the smaller one. A parent and child immediately came to mind.

"Who is it?" Holling inquired, as he wheeled himself from the kitchen. His voice was muffled, filled with samples from his snack tray—crackers, cheese, strawberries and the last of the dinner wine.

"I'm not sure," Sawyer returned. She took a moment to adjust the security cameras to get a better view. She didn't like the idea of leaving guests out in the cold. But the idea of being tricked, robbed or even worse because she was too filled with the holiday spirit to take the extra precaution didn't appeal to her, either. As she tinkered with the resolution, she plucked a strawberry from the tray and held it out in front of Holling. At the last possible moment, she withdrew the offer and took the strawberry into her own mouth, making sure to eat it enticingly in front of him.

"Whoever it is," Holling said, catching his lower lip between his teeth, "get rid of them. Fast!"

Laughing, Sawyer reaching for the door handle. "We have to be polite, Holling."

"Not if we don't know them we don't."

"Could be bad for business," Sawyer suggested.

"If I don't get you all alone to myself for some you-and-me time, darlin', that's not all that's going to be bad," Holling predicted.

"The sooner I open the door, the sooner we can be done with them," Sawyer said sweetly. She made a soft sound of irritation. "Temperature has messed with the cameras," she told Holling. "And that porch light is out again. We need to get that fixed. I can barely tell that it's a man and a woman out there. Maybe they want a room for the night?" She sounded uncertain.

"The sign out by the road says No Vacancy," Holling said, letting his irritation show.

"Holling." Sawyer's tone was reproving. "It's late. It's cold. We're not going to leave them out there like that, are we? That wouldn't be right. Not on Christmas eve. You never know. This could be our blessing in disguise."

"All right. Open the door. If the woman ain't pregnant and riding on a donkey, the best we can do is warm up some leftover turkey and trimmings, offer them dinner and wassail, and send them on their way," Holling ungraciously relented.

Sawyer affectionately patted his cheek. "Such the humanitarian." She turned off the security alarm and then unlocked the door. Bending her head momentarily against the gust of wind, she waved the couple in.

"Merry Christmas. Welcome to Holling's Way. Come…this…wuh—"

Her greeting was abruptly cut off as she stared first at the man who stepped through the door ahead of his female companion. Sawyer blinked, as much from surprise as from the wind blowing through the foyer. She did a quick double take, looking from the man, back to the closed curtains in front of the parlor, back to their guests again. She mouthed the word.

Darion?

Even Holling was startled speechless as he looked into the face that was oh-so-familiar to him. Same dark eyes. Same lean face. And he was tall. Very tall. Seemed to be even more so since Holling had to look at him from his wheelchair. He was the same. Yet different. Completely foreign to them both. Though it was the spitting image of him, this wasn't *their* Darion. This wasn't their employee. Their friend.

The woman came inside next, brushing snow from her London Fog trench coat onto the tile floor as she came in. The moment she unwrapped from her head and neck that yellow-and-blue Burberry plaid scarf, Sawyer recognized her immediately from the description Aidan had given her from Kiara's boutique. This was the woman who'd been looking for Darion, flashing pictures and swearing she'd find him and take him to court if he didn't start taking care of business.

Sawyer took an involuntary step back, putting her hand on Holling's shoulder and squeezing to silently communicate her unease. Aidan had made her promise not to say anything to Holling about the incident. Not until she had more proof than accusations. Holling quickly recovered, finding his voice. Though he was sitting in that wheelchair, with this leg brace supporting his injured knee, there was no mistaking the authority in his tone.

"I'm Jon-Tyler Holling. How can we help you folks this evening?"

The man linked arms with the woman. "Pleasure to meet you, Mr. Holling. My name's Darius Haddock. I heard my brother's been staying out here with you. I've come a long way to bring him home."

The Chief's Christmas Lover

Too bad she'd stuck. Darion straddled of hotel they had...

Chapter 31

"We can't stay here," Aidan insisted. Yet, she'd relented as Darion had guided her to recline on the couch, his long, lean frame covering hers. He skimmed his hand along her outer thigh; the roughened callous of his palms snagged on her thigh-high stockings. But, he didn't stop until he was stroking the bared skin at her hip.

"What are you worried about? Hmm? Nobody's around. Everybody's all snug in their beds. Visions of sugarplums dancing in their heads!" He was laughing as he nuzzled her neck.

Aidan snickered. "You know you're only saying that because you want to stuff my stocking with your sugarcane."

Darion's shoulders shook with laughter. "I've been a good boy all evening, Aidan. You ought to be congratulating me. I didn't try to grab you once. Though you don't know how much I wanted to. That dress, woman, and the way you wear it, makes a man crazy."

"I do know, Slim," she contradicted. "Believe me, I know. You looked so good tonight."

"You sound surprised."

"I am," she confessed. "Where'd you get those threads?"

"What? This old thing? It was something that was hanging in the back of my closet that I threw on," he said casually.

"It looks good on you, Slim," she complimented.

"Looks better off." He made the proposition by reaching for the top buttons of his shirt.

Aidan placed her palm on his chest. She stroked him, then her mood shifted as she thumped him on it.

"Now, what was that for?"

"It just occurred to me. That's not the first time I've heard that tonight. That big, bucktoothed lady, the one who's staying in the Rosewood room, kept following you around all night, checking out your butt, trying to get in between us. She had the nerve to ask me for your number!"

"Are you jealous?" Darion said incredulously.

"As green as Sawyer's dress tonight," Aidan confessed.

"She could have set herself on fire, I still wouldn't have noticed," Darion promised her.

"Good answer." She praised the response.

"So, what about it, Aidan?" he suggested, slowly, sensuously rotating his hips. His voice was low pitched, husky with desire.

"What about what?" She tried to play the innocent.

"Are you gonna get me out of this monkey suit or not? Underneath, I've got a special present, made only for you. And I want to give it to you, too, Aidan."

Aidan pressed her lips together to keep from panting like a playful puppy. She breathed rapidly through her nose, figuring that she'd be better off if she had the strength of will to keep her legs pressed together, as well. Cross her ankles. Think pure thoughts. He wasn't making it easy. Through the fabric of his pants, she felt him swell and lengthen. All heat and hardness.

"I want to, Darion." She used his name to let him know how sincere she was. "But not here. Not under Holling's roof."

"Let me take you to my place, then," he offered.

"To the bunkhouse?" Aidan couldn't see the logic in that. There was even less privacy there. Especially with that Wade. She'd had her own bothersome shadow that night. A loud-mouthed, odorous shadow. As much as he was able to hound her, she wondered if he and the lady from the Rosewood room had made a deal to keep her and Darion separated.

"No," Darion said. He sat up, pulling her along with him from the couch. He stood for a moment, holding her hands in his. He used his thumbs to massage her. "I've got a place of my own."

Aidan shook her head in wonder. "I didn't know."

"I didn't want anyone to know. I've been working on it during my days off. It's not exactly finished yet. I've still got a ways to go before I can really call it home."

"So, where is this place, Slim?"

"On the other side of Weeko Canyon. There's a small lake sitting in the middle of about a hundred acres. I bought the land as an investment. When the prices went up high enough, I was going to sell it. But then, I changed my mind and a few months ago, I started to frame out the two-room cabin. Like I said, it's bare bones. And when I'm out there, I'm really roughing it."

"Has it got four walls and a door?" Aidan asked eagerly, tugging him toward the parlor doors.

"At least that."

"Good enough," she said unabashedly. "Let's go check it out."

"It's lightly stocked," he said, setting up the expectations.

"I'm not hungry for food, Slim." Her expression left him no doubts what she was hungry for. "If we have to, we can raid the pantry and take what we need with us."

"You'd better get out of that dress."

"What do you think I'm trying to do?"

"I meant dress warm! The only heat is from the fireplace that joins the main room and the bedroom."

Aidan stood on tiptoe, her lips hovering provocatively in front of his lips. "Sounds cozy. If it's not good enough, Slim, we'll generate our own heat."

Darion sucked in an anticipatory breath before encircling Aidan in his arms. "Before you go, why don't you leave a note for your brother and his wife," he advised. "I don't want them to wake up, find you missing, and come hunt me down."

"I may not have to if you can get me back before the entire house wakes to open their presents."

"Don't count on it," Darion retorted. "Once I get you out there, lady, I don't plan on letting you go for a while. Grab a change of clothes and whatever else you need, Aidan. I'll have you back in time to share most of Christmas Day with your family. You've been too long away from them for me to try to take that away from you. But, after that, you and I are going to—"

"Sorry to bust in on you two."

There was a brief tap on the glass doors before Sawyer called out apologetically. She gave a single warning knock then pushed open the door, carefully averting her eyes as she entered.

"It's all right, Sawyer." Aidan and Darion exchanged amused glances. "We were only making plans."

Sawyer uncovered her eyes, grinning foolishly at Aidan.

"What did you need, Sawyer?" Aidan asked.

"Oh…yes. Darion. I came for Darion." Sawyer delicately cleared her throat.

"Yes, Ms. Holling?"

"You…um…have someone out in the foyer…they want to see you."

"Awful late for visitors, Ms. Holling." Darion sounded apologetic and suspicious at the same time.

"I know. But they were insistent. Very insistent. I couldn't turn them away. I think you should talk to them, Darion."

Instinctively, Aidan edged closer to Darion. He squeezed her waist reassuringly, then kissed her on top of her head.

"Do you want me to show them in?" Sawyer asked.

Wordlessly, Darion nodded, then said, "Them?"

"Yes. A couple. They said they were your brother Darius and his…wife?"

"Joelle." The word came out of Aidan's mouth, sounding almost like a curse. She and Sawyer had talked earlier about that incident in Kiara's boutique. The dinner, enjoying time with family and friends, had almost made her forget the ugliness of it.

Sawyer pointed her thumb back over her shoulder. "I'll show them in." She backed up a couple of steps, pulling the doors closed once again. As she did so, Aidan turned to Darion.

"So, Joelle's your brother's wife?"

Darion nodded.

"Why'd she say that she was yours?"

"I told you," he interrupted. "Because she's a liar."

"And your brother?"

"I don't know. Maybe he's one, too. I guess I'll find out in a minute." He looked toward the doors as he heard the sound of voices approaching.

Delicately, Aidan cleared her throat. "I'll go upstairs and pack some things for tonight."

The look he gave her was a mixture of gratitude and disbelief. "You still want to be with me tonight, Aidan?"

"I know I had one of my freak-out moments, earlier. I should have trusted you before jumping to conclusions. I'm all right now. And I'm here to tell you. That woman hasn't changed my mind about how I feel for you, Darion."

"Maybe you will after you hear what Darius and Joelle have to say."

"I didn't think you wanted me to hear," she confessed. "Family reunion and all. I was going to leave so you and your brother could talk in private."

Darion grasped her hand, holding it tightly as he raised it to his lips and kissed it. "You made a choice to give yourself to me, Aidan, before you had all of the facts. That wasn't fair to you. I don't have a right to ask, but I'm going to anyway. I want you to stay. Stay with me now for a few minutes more. I...I need you with me. I need your support. My brother and his wife and I don't really get along. That's putting it mildly. They make me lose control. I need you to keep me from jumping off the deep end."

"I'm here for you, Darion," she said fiercely, then added, "no more slides down the mountain for you."

When Sawyer drew the curtains aside and opened the doors again, she found Darion and Aidan standing before her, Aidan's right hand held firmly in his left. She looked back at Holling, trailing behind. Sawyer didn't miss the look of curiosity on his face. Not as he watched Darius and his companion, but as he witnessed the staunch display of solidarity between Darion and his sister.

"Right this way," Sawyer said, ushering Joelle and Darius

inside. "Can I get you anything? Coffee? Tea? I think we still have some eggnog from tonight's dinner."

"Don't trouble yourself, Ms. Holling. They won't be staying long," Darion said with finality.

"I'll take coffee," Joelle said, dismissing Darion's implied request for them to leave.

She sauntered into the room, making herself comfortable in one of the oversize leather armchairs. Joelle deliberately placed her hands on the cushions of the armrest, stroking the butter-soft leather, leaned back and crossed her legs. "Cream and sugar."

"Give me a hand, Aidan?" Sawyer asked, a discreet way of granting Darion time alone with his family.

Aidan looked to Darion, not asking permission to leave, but silently promising him that she'd return.

He nodded. Then, to make sure there was no doubt of who she was, and what she meant to him, Darion leaned down and kissed Aidan fully on the lips. Maybe he held the kiss longer than he should have. Holling raised his fist to his mouth, giving a less-than-subtle cough.

When Aidan broke away, she gingerly touched her lips. Her eyes glittered brighter than twinkling lights on the Christmas tree.

"I'll be making instant coffee," she said so that only he could hear. Darion smiled, despite the apprehension she saw reflected in his eyes.

As soon as Aidan, Sawyer and Holling left him, Darion whirled on his brother. All pretenses of civility dropped.

"I don't know what you two are doing here. To be honest, I really don't give a damn. But I want you out of this house by the time they get back. They're making it instant coffee. None of that long-brewed stuff. So say what you want to say and then hit the road."

Darius spread his arms wide. "What? No greeting for your brother? Do you know how long we've been looking for you, Darion?"

Joelle massaged her chin with her index finger and thumb. She scrutinized Darion, openly appraising him.

"Damn, boy, you're looking good these days. All this fresh Montana air is treating you right. I don't blame you for staying away from us for as long as you have."

"I don't think it's the air that's got my brother hanging out here in the sticks," Darius observed. He bent down, picking up the decorative silk scarf left behind on the couch. The scarf that matched Aidan's holiday dress. He lifted it to his nose, sniffing the delicate perfume. When Darion snatched it out of his hands, Darius laughed.

"I was just playing, bro!"

"I didn't know you went for blondes, Darion. I should have known you and she were together…the way she turned green when I showed her that picture of us."

"That wasn't us," Darion said knowingly. "You mean a picture of you and Darius."

"It might have been us," Joelle returned, a hint of wistfulness in her voice. "If I hadn't gotten drunk and wound up in his bed instead of yours, hadn't gotten pregnant, things might have been different."

"Drunk? Who are you trying to fool? Why don't you tell it like it was, Joelle. You were high. You stayed high… Both of you." Darion cut his eyes toward his brother.

"That's over now, Darion," Darius assured him. "I've been clean for almost a year now. Ever since that night—"

"Oh, please. Don't hand me that crap!" Darion stalked across the room, turning his back on his brother. He stood at the fireplace, his hands gripping the mantel with both hands.

If he'd been that character from the comic books, Darion was certain that he would have turned green before now, busting out of his clothes, tearing up the house on a rampage.

"I'm telling the truth!" Darius shrugged out of his coat, then began to unbutton the cuffs of his shirtsleeves. "I swear before God, I'm clean!"

"I don't want to hear it, Darius." Darion closed his eyes, his ears and his heart to his brother's claims. "I don't believe you."

"Look at me, Darion. Would you just look at me? I came all this way. The least you can do is hear me out."

When Darion turned around, Darius stood in front of him, with his shirtsleeves rolled up. Darion's eyes involuntarily strayed to the crooks of his brother's arms. Only the faintest scars from repeated needle pricks could be seen.

"That doesn't mean a thing," Darion quickly declared. "You could still be shooting up. Behind your knees. Your ankles. Inside your lip. We've been through this before, Darius."

"Not like this time," Darius insisted. "I told you. I checked myself in. Got some help."

"Once a junkie, always a junkie," Darius said, his tone frigid and unyielding.

Joelle reached into her purse, pulled out a slender cigarette and platinum lighter. "That's not necessarily true, Darion. You kicked it," she reminded him, raising her cigarette to her slick, raspberry-tinted lips.

"You can't smoke in here," Darion said automatically.

"Then, let's you and I step outside," she offered.

"I don't smoke…anymore."

"You've stopped smoking, too?" She lifted a professionally arched eyebrow in mild surprise.

"Sort of had to after I found out that somebody was lacing my smokes with that junk."

"One of these days, I'm going to quit," Joelle predicted. She gave a mock sigh. Her slender shoulders lifted and fell dramatically. "But today won't be that day."

"What do you want, Darius?" Darion asked, pointedly ignoring her.

"What makes you think I want something? How do you know that I don't want to see you because I haven't seen you? For God's sake, Darion. It's Christmas. Can't a brother want to be with his family during the holidays?"

"I'm not going to ask you again. Tell me what you want, then get out."

"Tell him, Darius." Joelle waved her hand toward him. "He's not thinking about you. He's got his mind on little miss rich bitch out there." Joelle lifted her chin, using it to point beyond the parlor doors.

"All right, that's it." Darion whirled around, starting for the exit. "You two, get out. Stop wasting my time."

"Come on, Darius. We'd better leave before Darion's lump of coal in his crotch burns a hole through that suit." She dropped her eyes, intentionally focusing on evidence of Darion's erection. "And here I thought it was I you were so pleased to see."

"Shut your mouth, Joelle," Darius warned.

The more she talked, the angrier, the less patient Darion became. In a moment, he wouldn't ask them out. He'd physically escort them to the door.

"Wait…wait a minute, bro. Just hear me out. Five minutes. That's all I want."

"That's not all you want." Darion's eyes narrowed. "You knew where I was. Anything you had to tell me, you could have called."

"I told you. I wanted to see you."

"See if I was still alive?"

"That's not what I meant."

"Then, what is it?" Darion said in exasperation.

"Joelle and I…that is…uh…we…"

"Spit it out, Darius!"

"We need some more money from you, Darion," Joelle said bluntly.

Darion shook his head, laughing. "I knew it. I knew it had to be something. Did you two blow through that insurance money already? I thought I'd left you pretty well situated before I left."

"We do need money," Darius admitted. "But that's not the only reason why we're here."

"It's the only one that matters," Joelle snickered behind her hand.

"I said shut your mouth, Jo!" Darius pointed at her. He entreated his brother. "I'm not asking for much, Darion. Fifty G. That's all I need. I swear. Loan it to me and I swear that I'll never ask for another dime again."

"Fifty thousand. Oh, is that all?" Darion said condescendingly. He folded his arms across his chest. "I'm almost afraid to ask what for."

"Why should it matter? I'm your brother and I told you I need it. Isn't that enough?"

"No, Darius," Darion said flatly. "It isn't."

"Tell him, Darius," Joelle encouraged. "You don't have anything to lose…except maybe your life."

Darius sat down on the couch with his legs spread, his elbows resting on his knees. He clasped his hands in front of him, rocking back and forth in agitation. He opened his mouth to speak, then quickly closed it when Aidan returned to the room with a serving tray.

Her eyes on Joelle sitting with practiced calm in the armchair, Aidan set the silver tea service on the coffee table between them. Neutral territory, Aidan thought. Because if Joelle didn't quit eyeing Aidan as if she wanted to slap her, Joelle was going to find out what hot coffee could do to that pretty pout.

When Aidan set out several cups, pouring the coffee, the silence in the room was almost deafening. It was so quiet that Aidan thought she could hear the steam rising from the cups as she poured.

"Cream and sugar?" she offered, feeling as if her voice sounded strained and unnatural.

"The perfect hostess," Joelle mocked as she took the cup from Aidan.

"You'd better be careful, Joelle." Aidan smiled through her animosity. She slid a stirring spoon across the tray toward her. "I wouldn't want you to burn your tongue."

Their gazes locked, silent communication flying through the air between the two of them. Aidan wasn't warning her about the coffee and everyone in the room knew it.

"I doubt it's all that hot," Joelle replied, flicking a dismissive glance over Aidan.

"No?" Aidan challenged. "Why don't you try it and see." She turned her attention to Darion's brother. "Coffee, Mr. Haddock?"

"No…no, I don't want anything," he refused.

"Except fifty thousand dollars," Darion said in derision. Darius glared at him, tilting his head slightly in Aidan's direction as if to chastise his brother for putting his business out there in front of strangers.

Aidan didn't react as she continued to pour. Didn't even bat an eyelash. "How about you, Darion?"

"Naw…I'm good."

Darion crossed the room and took a seat next to Aidan.

"Maybe we should talk about this family business another time," his brother suggested.

"Nope. This is the only shot you'll get. Oops. My bad. Did I say *shot?* Poor choice of words. Freudian slip. Shooting must be on my mind."

Aidan watched as Darius visibly cringed. He was openly wringing his hands now, swaying back and forth. "I told you for the thousandth time," he said raggedly. "I don't know who shot you, bro."

"Tell me again for the fifty-thousandth time," Darion flung back. "Tell me why I wound up, my life leaking out of me, right after I refused to loan you the money the first time, *bro.*"

"Darion, on our parents' grave, I don't know who shot you. We were all strung out that night. The party got way out of control. Folks coming and going…half of them I didn't even know."

"Oh, you knew them all right," Darion said raggedly. "You had to. There were only three of us who knew where that safe was. You. Me. And you," he said, indicating Joelle. "Only you and I knew the combination to the safe. One of you gave it away. Gave my money away. My life."

"It's your own fault, you selfish bastard!" Joelle leaned forward. "You knew we needed the money! You were a tight-ass then and you're a tight-ass now. Come on, Darius. We're wasting our time. He's not going to loan us that money."

"Hell, no, I'm not going to loan it to you," Darius agreed. He leaned back against the couch cushions, tapping his thumb against the wooden frame "You don't want a loan. You want a tax-free, no-strings-attached gift. I know I'd never see that money again."

"Darion, if you don't, you'll never see me again! Do you

understand what I'm saying?" Darius covered his face with his hands. His shoulders shook, openly weeping.

Aidan looked to Darion with concern. "Darion," she said, laying her hand on his thigh. It had started to bounce, either from habit or nervousness. That was the effect his family had on him. One moment, he was a loving, caring individual. The next, the calluses on his hands covered his heart. Darion pursed his lips, looking off. He wasn't buying his brother's sorrowful act.

Joelle got up and, for the first time that evening, displayed more than sarcasm or indifference. She sat on the couch that faced Aidan and Darion, next to her husband, cradling him as she made soothing noises. "Sh…it's all right. It'll be all right, baby."

"No. No, it won't." Darius looked to his brother. "Darion, please! These people don't play. If I don't get it to them by the end of this week, they're going to kill me! They've already tried. It's only a matter of time before they do it. They know where I am. They'll come after me!"

"Don't you understand!? He can't help you!" Aidan was stung into saying. Her heart ached to see the terror on his face, a face so similar to the man who had her heart. "He doesn't have that kind of money."

Joelle stared with incredulity at Aidan, then suddenly threw back her head and laughed. She laughed so hard, tears squeezed from her eyes, causing her mascara to streak and run down her cheeks. Not the reaction that Aidan was expecting from someone who'd seemed so desperate a moment before.

"Are you insane? Or are you just stupid?" Joelle took the small linen napkin on the service tray and dabbed at her eyes. "No, wait. You're neither. You're both. You really are in love with Darion, aren't you, to be so blind? She doesn't know, does she? You haven't told her, Darion?"

Aidan had too much pride to ask what had suddenly put her in a position of ridicule. She picked up her coffee cup, taking a sip, to keep herself from asking the obvious questions.

Joelle tsk-tsked. "Shame on you!"

Aidan didn't know whether she was talking about Darion for keeping an important secret from her or Aidan, for supporting a man she knew nothing about.

"Go on, player," Joelle urged. "Tell your woman the truth."

When Darion didn't speak up, Joelle threw her cup across the room, shattering it against the fireplace as she shrieked at him, "Tell her, Darion! Tell her. No? All right, then. I'll do it, since you don't seem to have the balls."

Joelle stood, staring disdainfully down her nose at Aidan. "You didn't know, honey? Your man's loaded. Got more money than he knows what to do with it. Got all kinds of accounts. Onshore. Offshore. Swiss. You name it. He's got it. Stocks. Bonds. He probably wipes his narrow ass with hundreds. For the life of me, I don't know what he's doing out here, shoveling cow crap. How do you earn a living, Darion? I know you can do better."

"Where did you get…how do you make…what do you…" Aidan could barely frame her mouth to ask the questions. After hearing about his lifestyle—wild parties, drugs and women—she didn't know what to think. The pieces didn't match up. How could Darion be that person that Joelle described? This man, so considerate of others, so willing to selflessly risk his life to save strangers…the man who watched out for children, who gave to the community, who valued the work of his hands over the trappings that money could buy for him…how could that be him? Who was this man who wore the same pair of jeans five days out of the week and could break out in expensive suits the next? Her hand reached up and touched the diamond solitaire necklace that he'd given her. She'd felt so guilty for accepting this gift from him, knowing that he'd probably used most of his savings to get it. Obviously, that wasn't the case. The man who gave her this necklace, evidently, could have afforded to buy one for all of White Wolf. Who was he? Who was Darion Haddock?

She closed her eyes, centering herself. *I trust you, Darion.*

"I know you help manage the ranch for my brother. You're his ramrod," Aidan began, then ignored the suggestive sniggers from Joelle at the term. "But what else are you doing, Darion?"

"What I do is all legal, Aidan," he told her. "And classified."

"Classified?" She could feel herself going to that freak-out place in her mind. Like those women who find out their husbands are leading double lives, keeping two wives, two families on opposite coasts. Or who go and conduct secret military espionage missions on the weekdays, to be back in time for barbecues and baseball games on the weekends.

"Don't look like that, Aidan," Darion soothed. "It's not what you think."

"I don't know what to think!" she exclaimed.

"I helped develop and maintain software to prevent hackers from bringing down military installations. I'm nothing more than a computer geek who likes to play cowboy." He shrugged. "Only…after I got out here, I wasn't playing anymore. The more I saw, the more I liked. This life that I've made here is more real to me…more satisfying, than anything else I've ever done. I'm not going back."

"Get this! The computer nerd got paid for designing what-if scenarios," Joelle explained. "There hasn't been such a loaded geek since Gates and Microsoft. And he gave all of that up for what? For you?" She gestured at Aidan. "You two loonies deserve each other."

"He's sitting on all that money and he won't lift a finger to write a check to save his brother's life," Darius grumbled.

Darion watched as Aidan carefully kept her hands from shaking as she set the coffee cup down on the tray. He silently congratulated her when the cup barely rattled on the tray despite her trembling.

He placed his hand on her shoulder, then instantly removed it when he felt her stiffen, actually pull away from him. Darion didn't know if she was more upset with him because he hadn't confided in her or because of his callous disregard for his brother's troubles. A little of both, perhaps. The former, he could not change. He'd withheld information for her for reasons that didn't seem important now. With Darius before him, moaning and rocking and wringing his hands, it was impossible for him to remain unmoved.

"What happens if I do?" he finally asked. "What happens if I give you the money, Darius?"

"What you should be asking is what will happen if you don't," Darius responded, wiping his face on the back of his hand. "They'll kill me, Darion. Like I said, they know where I am. The know I'm here in Montana. Maybe they won't stop with me." He glanced meaningfully at Aidan, then at the Christmas tree with gifts that were obviously meant for the children in the house. Bikes. Rollerblades. A model-size kitchen set with plastic pots and fruits and vegetables waiting for some pint-size cook to explore.

Darion leaned forward, his voice filled with deadly promise. "If anything…I mean anything…happens to anyone in this family, Darius, I'll make you regret you ever set foot in White Wolf. They'd better not get as much as a splinter or I'll be all over you!"

"Give me what I want. I'll leave. I'll go away. You'll never hear from me again."

"That's what I'm afraid of," Darion snorted. "I'm not going to give you the money, Darius. I know you. I know what you'll do with it. Smoke it up. Snort it up. Shoot it up. That money will never see your…associates."

"Then, I'm a dead man. I hope you can live with yourself, Darion. Because you've killed your own brother."

"Welcome to the club. The doctors told me I died twice on that operating table, bro." He held up two fingers, forming a V sign. "Twice."

"The third time's the charm," Joelle retorted. "I'm willing to bet that you haven't cut your brother out of your will yet, Darion. Montana's a dangerous place. Accidents happen out here all of the time. All we'd have to do is wait for one…and then collect. The wait might not be as long as you think it'll be. We know people who for a fraction of what we're asking will help us."

Aidan's blood boiled at the blatant threat. "You bitch!"

"Say whatever you want," Joelle returned with equally as much venom. "I've come all this way, I'm not leaving without that money."

"Yes, you are," Darion said, standing.

"No…" Aidan said slowly, reaching out to take Darion's hand and pulling him back to the couch. "No, they're not."

"Aidan," Darion said in a voice that wouldn't accept argument.

"You know you're not going to let your brother die. Would you do any less for him than you'd do for Luke? Or for me?"

"You don't understand—" he began.

"And who's fault is that?" she demanded.

Joelle sat up straighter, her interest piqued. "Ooh? Is there trouble brewing in this mountain paradise? Maybe I was wrong about the two of you. Maybe you're not as in love as I thought you were."

Aidan squeezed Darion's hand, letting him know that she would address that assertion.

"Lady, I don't know you and you don't know me. But you wouldn't be out here, begging, threatening, risking a serious beat down from me and the rest of my family, if you didn't love that man," she said, gesturing toward Darius. "Or his money."

Joelle stared hard at Aidan, then lowered her gaze in acquiescence.

Aidan continued. "For the record, you are wrong. So incredibly wrong about us. Darion and I are very much in love. The kind of love that won't let somebody like you come between us." She swung her gaze from Darion to Darius.

"I don't know what happened to you. Sounds like you people were really living the life… Until it almost killed you, Darion…and you, Darius, don't seem to be far behind. Got yourself a real mess. A stinking pile that you've dropped on our doorsteps. But that's all right. We've been ranch folk for generations. We know how to clean up crap. Since you've dragged me into this, I'm gonna tell it to you straight. What you're arguing about is crap. You two are family. Brothers. Twins, for heaven's sake. Tied together in the womb, you should be tied together in life. You're responsible for one another. And you're going to let something as ridiculous…as fleeting…as ultimately meaningless as money come between you?"

"Aidan," Darion began again, and again she cut him off.

Aidan stood up, crooked her finger at Joelle, a look on her face that said, *You and me. Outside.*

Joelle hesitated for a moment, giving the appearance of a woman who wasn't sure if she should be pulling off her heels and earrings getting ready to throw some blows, or making a prudent dash for the front door.

"Joelle and I are leaving this room," Aidan announced. "And when we come back, there had better be either a check on the table for fifty big ones or a plan for getting one. Do I make myself clear, boys? The only word I want to hear from either of you is *yes*. If you don't want to say it, nod your heads. Shake them up and down so that I know that you understand me."

She looked back and forth from Darion to his brother when they didn't respond. "Do you understand me?" She enunciated each word clearly, her voice growling with intention.

"Now who's the bitch?" Joelle said aloud.

Ultimately, reluctantly, Darion and Darius made sounds of acquiescence.

"Is she always that pushy?" Darius asked his brother.

"You don't know the half of it," Darion said. His somber acknowledgment of Aidan's take-no-prisoners attitude was a connecting point between him and his brother. Something they had not shared in a long while. Darion visibly relaxed. He and his brother shared a name and physical features. And now they could relate to something else. The love of a woman. Whether he liked Joelle or not, whether he approved of her as a choice for his brother, it didn't matter. As Aidan had said, she was here, standing by Darius. Standing up for him, no matter what the challenges. Reminded him of another lady he knew. A lady he loved. One who would not leave him alone, despite his own reckless, life-threatening behavior.

"Good boys," Aidan said, pleased with her efforts to unite them. "Now get to planning."

Chapter 32

Five o'clock in the morning. Aidan hadn't planned to be up so early. Then again, many things she'd planned over the past twenty-four hours hadn't gone as expected. She yawned, stretched, careful not to fall off the couch or jab Darion in the ribs as she lay curled with him in the parlor. Aidan shivered, suddenly realizing that the fire had burned low and the small woolen throw that she'd taken from one of the other couches left her stocking feet exposed.

Even in deep sleep, Darion sensed her distress and shifted to curl his arms around her.

She snuggled closer, lifting her head enough to kiss him on the bottom of his stubbled chin. When Darion's dark eyes fluttered open, he had to scrunch his neck to look at her.

"Good morning, sleepyhead," she hailed him.

"Good morning," he returned. "Merry Christmas, Aidan."

"Are you sure?"

"Sure that it's Christmas? Or sure that it's morning? Man, I'm so tired!"

"Are you sure it's going to be a merry one? You didn't look too happy when I made you promise to give that money to your brother last night."

"I'm not giving it to him," he corrected her. "I'm giving it to the folks he owes."

"Do you have to get involved, Darion? Why can't you let the police handle it?"

"If the police get involved before they get their money, there's no telling what they'll do to Darius. You heard him. Those folks don't play. I don't want to do anything to have them coming after him…or you. I won't allow that, Aidan."

"You're a computer geek, Darion. Not a superhero. As much as you like to play one."

"I won't take any chances."

"How do you know that after they get it, they still won't try to kill him? Or you? You could get caught in a crossfire. I don't want you to go, Darion. I know I wanted you to give your brother that money…but that's because he's your brother. A part of you. And I couldn't stand to watch him in so much pain."

"You've got a soft heart, baby," he acknowledged. "But I don't have a soft head. I'm not stupid, Aidan. It won't be a face-to-face drop. Darius told them where the money would be. And then I told the police. Neither one will make a move until we're out of the area."

"So, what are me and Joelle supposed to do while you two are off dropping money around like a reformed Ebenezer Scrooge?"

"Sit back, sip eggnog and open presents," Darion teased her.

"I'm serious, Darion!" Aidan insisted. She raised up on one elbow to look at him.

"I know you are. You won't have to wait long. I'm not comfortable with the idea of leaving you and Joelle alone."

"She doesn't frighten me."

"I was more concerned about what you'd do to her. I thought for a moment that you were going to take that woman down."

"You know, that Joelle is a piece of work. She was still complaining about the accommodations even though we told her that there would be no charge for the night's stay."

Darion rolled his eyes. "That's the way she is. Champagne taste on a gimme-gimme-gimme-for-free budget."

Aidan made a face. "Can I ask you something, Darion?"

"Sure."

"Were you and she ever—"

"Never," Darion said heading off that line of reasoning before she could go there. "She's Darius's type. Not mine."

"If she could have, she would have. She made that no secret. I don't get her. She's married to your brother. Why does he let her get away with talking to you like that? Her eyes were all over you. Like she owned you. Or had you, if you get what I mean."

"That's just the way she talks. She's that way about every man she meets. Like they're hers for the taking. I wouldn't be surprised if she didn't make a play for your brother."

"Sawyer won't let that happen. Besides, Holling is so blinded by love, Joelle wouldn't stand a chance. Still, why doesn't Darius put a stop to it? Why is he still with her?"

"I don't think he has the confidence to think he could keep her," Darion surmised. "Or that he doesn't deserve better. I sorta know how he feels. I wasn't sure I was the kind of man who could hold on to you, Aidan."

"You don't have to worry, Slim. You've got me. I'm not going anywhere." She paused, then laughed softly.

"What?" he asked, noting her amused expression.

"So, you're stinking rich."

"Mostly stinking," he confessed. "After I got shot, I realized all the money in the world wasn't making me a happy person. It couldn't stop my brother from going on drugs. Couldn't stop him from hanging out with the kinds of folks who'd kill for less than what he was flashing. Couldn't stop a bullet from tearing into me. Cost me a near fortune recuperating. I almost went through all of my savings on hospital fees. And when I got out, I spent way too much time trying to figure out who shot me. When the police couldn't do anything, I hired private investigators."

"And you still don't know who did it?"

"I have my suspicions. Nothing I could prove. Or anything the investigators could prove. Like Darius said, everybody was high that night. I'm ashamed to say even I was. I couldn't even focus when I walked in on someone going through my office. The next thing I knew, I'm being wheeled through the emergency ward. Someone's shouting my name, asking me how many fingers they're holding up. Found out that I was overdosing and bleeding out at the same time. A helluva mess to be in, Aidan. I don't recommend it to anyone. Not even my worst enemies...or my closest brother."

"Darion," Aidan began.

"I don't do that stuff, Aidan. I told you, it was never my choice. And by the time I found out what Joelle and Darius were doing to me, keeping me out of my head, making me sign crap so they could get to my money, I was already making plans to cut them out of my life."

"That wasn't what I was going to say," she said sheepishly. "But I'm glad you told me."

"Then what was it? What do you want to tell me?"

"I'm sorry we didn't get the chance to go to your place last night," she said, lazily drawing patterns over his chest bared by the open buttons. "I really wanted to."

"I know you did, Aidan. I suppose it was for the best. The first time we were together alone, it was good...let me rephrase that...it was *damn* good...but it wasn't the right time. We should have waited. Now that we have plenty of time, I want to take it slow."

"Ooh!" Aidan said, imitating Joelle. "You sound so noble."

"Really? That wasn't my intention. I was just thinking about the long-term."

"Long-term?" she repeated.

"Yeah, you know. That time that comes the day after the day after the day after the day after tomorrow."

"You're talking about the future again, aren't you?"

"Yeah. I'm talking about the future. Funny, I didn't used to think like that. When I was making all of that money, I was always living for the short-term. What could I get now. Now. Always now. Even last night, I was all about what I wanted right then. If you hadn't reminded me where we were, it would have been a repeat of the hotel room. Long-term, I don't want that from you, Aidan."

Aidan's voice caught in her throat. "What do you want from me, Slim?"

"First of all, I want you to stop calling me Slim," he teased her, knowing she wouldn't do it.

"What else do you want?"

"Well," he admitted, "when I first met you, I wanted to take you away on some deserted island. Sip tropical drinks and become a beach bum. Spend my days and my money in total slackerdom."

"Been there. Done that. I'm telling you, it gets old after a while," she said as if bored with the idea. "I thought you wanted to spend your days playing cowboy?"

"I'm done playing, Aidan," he said thoughtfully. "I came out here to heal. Heal my body and my spirit. It wasn't easy taking the road I took. And I'm not just talking about finding my way out here to White Wolf. I'm talking about finding myself again. I was so lost," he confided.

When his voice cracked with emotion, Aidan laid her head against his heart. She didn't press him to speak, but let him tell his story in his own way. "Shh…it's all right, Darion. You don't have to go on if you don't want to."

"I want to," he insisted. "This is what I should have told you first before I made love to you. I wanted you to know that kind of man I had been. Because I could see it in your eyes when I first walked up to you. You were afraid of me."

"I wouldn't say *afraid*," she hedged.

"I would. You took one look at that raggedy bum coming up to you and you wanted to fight me…or run. I understand, Aidan."

"But I got to know you, Darion. Know the kind of person you are. The kind of person who would drive through a blizzard to see a perfect stranger home. The kind of person who cared that I was freezing my tail off. You put your arms around me to make it better. You're the kind of person who would risk his life, throw yourself down a mountain, dive into a freezing lake… Money doesn't make you a hero, Darion. Your heart does."

"I came to that conclusion, too. That's why I put my money where I couldn't get easy access to it. I wanted to make myself become the man I should have been. Strong. Self-reliant. Even sympathetic. Because I wasn't feeling much of that after what happened to me. I had to unlearn a lot of bad habits. And renew some better ones. Your brother helped me more than he thinks he did. Taught me what it means to trust. And to be trusted. Now that I know that this is the type of life I want, this is the type of man I want to be…I know what it takes to get it…and keep it.

"I'll do anything to keep it, Aidan. Keep us. What I really want is for us…you and me…to get old after a while. I want to do it together. I want to sit out on the front porch of the house that I built with my own hands. I want you to be with me when the sun sets, watching it melt across the lake. I want warm summers watching the wildflowers bloom, chilly falls beside the fireplace. I want to wake up on Christmas morning, waiting for our own kids to come down."

Aidan's throat hurt so much, she could barely speak. *Don't cry. Don't cry. Don't cry,* she repeated, though she could feel tears of joy stinging her eyes. "No wild parties?"

"Nope."

"No strange women roaming through your house, trying to get into your bed?"

"Not a one."

"Sex, drugs, rock and roll?"

"I want you, Aidan Holling. I want to hold you. To take care of you. To keep you. To marry you."

"Darion, are you sure? Like you said before, this is happening too fast!"

He kissed her gently on the forehead. "Life is fast," he told her. "And it's frighteningly short. Nobody knows that better than I do."

"Baby, I'm so sorry you had to go through that," she commiserated.

"Don't be. Everything happens for a reason. If I hadn't gone through that, I wouldn't be here now with you, would I?"

"Are you sure you want to marry me? I'm not the world's best cook, you know."

"I'm not always hungry for food," he reminded her of her own words from the night before.

"And sometimes I get moody," she complained. "Sometimes I wake up ready to fight."

"With a hundred acres to roam around on, there will be plenty of space to take what you need. We'll just go to neutral corners until we're ready to kiss and make up."

"My family's intense. You have to get through them to get to me."

"I've worked with your brother for six months. I know how he is…and he knows me. You might say I've given him six months to get used to the idea of me being around."

"Sounds like you kept that hardheaded brother of mine in check," Aidan laughed. "Seriously, Darion, you think he'll believe we're in love, that we're meant for each other?"

"He doesn't have to…as long as you do. I want you, woman. You don't have to give me an answer right now. Take your time and think on it."

Aidan sat up, pulling her hair back over her shoulders. She looked out the window, watching the early morning light filter through. She watched the snow falling fast and thick, settling onto the ground below. Again, she was living a moment in a snow globe. Only this time, Aidan told herself, there was no chaos. No turmoil. For the first time in years, she felt settled.

"I will," she promised.

"Think on it?" he clarified.

A tender smile lit Aidan's face as she shook her head back and forth. "I *will*," she said, changing the emphasis of her words so that he knew exactly what she meant. Darion shot up from the couch, tumbling Aidan to the floor in his haste.

"Are you sure?" he asked excitedly. "I mean, really, really

sure? Don't play with me, Aidan. I'm not playing house with you. If we're going to do this, it's going to be real."

Aidan was laughing as she took the hand he offered to help her off the floor. "I wouldn't do that to you, Slim."

His whoop of joy was overshadowed by the sounds of twin seven-year-olds barreling toward the parlor with high-pitched squeals. They burst into the parlor, nearly dragging the curtains and curtain rods down in their haste.

Still dressed in pajamas and robes, Sawyer soon trailed after them, pushing Holling in the wheelchair. Nate was calling out orders like a movie director as he caught the first moments of Christmas morning in the Holling household with the video camera. As Sawyer walked into the parlor, she commented on Darion and Aidan holding hands.

"Didn't I leave those two last night standing there, just like that?" Both Aidan and Darion were still in their holiday clothes, looking a little worse for wear, crumpled from sleeping on the couch.

Grinning foolishly, Darion rubbed his hand over his chin. "Maybe I ought to go change."

Aidan flounced for the benefit of the camera. "Not me. I paid a pretty penny for this dress and I'm going to get every ounce of wearing out of it."

"You're going to look mighty funny trudging around in the snow when you take the twins out to test the new sleds I've got them," Holling told her. "Get a shot of that over there, Pops."

Sydney and Jayden had piled onto the new sled, swaying back and forth as they pretended to slalom down a hill.

"Oh, no!" Aidan groaned. "You are not going to get me out on the ice again with those two. It'll be Christmas 3006 before I do!"

Darion walked up to Holling. "Merry Christmas, sir," he said.

"Same to you, Darry. You're looking well rested for some-one who spent the night on a narrow, itchy couch…and with my sister!"

"On a couch. Not a bed, Holling," Sawyer muttered out of the corner of her mouth. She waved to get Nate's attention. "Make sure you edit that part of the tape out, Nate."

"Sure thing, little missy. Just like I'll be editing out the smoke detector going off when you and Holling try to cook us breakfast this morning."

"Are you, your brother and his wife joining us for break-fast, Darion?" Sawyer asked.

"I expect they'll want to," Darion said, trying hard to sound civil despite his misgivings.

"You go on ahead and change, Darion," Holling advised. "You've got time. We'll all still be here going through mounds of wrapping paper before you get back."

"Yes, sir," Darion said, starting for the door. He paused, then turned around. Darion should have spoken loudly to be heard over the sound of Jayden strumming on a miniature acoustic guitar, trying to follow notes from a book and warbling "Jingle Bells." Instead, he dropped his voice, making sure Holling was paying complete attention.

"When I get back, when you've got time, there's something I want to talk to you and Mr. Nate about." He glanced invol-untarily at Aidan, sitting in the middle of the floor with Sydney, reading from a boxed set of books.

"I imagine that you do," Holling replied seriously. Inside, he was shaking with laughter at Darion's serious expression. Poor soul. He had no idea what he was getting himself into. Maybe he didn't care. Holling thought back to how he'd rushed headlong toward Sawyer, ignoring all of the advice from family and friends that told him why he shouldn't want her. He could see the same look of determination in Darion's eyes.

"Don't you worry, Darion. You go on, grab yourself a shower and shave. You'd better change into something you'll be comfortable in all day. Something tells me you'll be here for a while."

"I'm planning on it," Darion agreed, knowing by now that Holling understood the nature of the conversation he intended to have.

"Like I said," Holling continued. "We'll be here. *She'll* be here. Whatever it is you want to say, I promise you. It'll keep."

Darion held out his hand, giving Holling's a firm shake before heading off to the bunkhouse. He took a moment to glance up the stairs to where his brother and wife lay sleeping in comfort. Comfort that, once again, they'd somehow wrangled out of him. Same old Darius. Same old Joelle. Always trying to get something for nothing. And now, here he was, bailing them out again.

"Hold up there, Slim!" Aidan rushed to greet him, peeling aside tinsel and wrapping paper that had somehow gotten stuck to her dress.

"Something the matter?" Darion asked, trying not to sound irritated.

She paused, giving him a tentative smile. "I got lonely," she confessed.

"Even with all of that going on in there?" he said incredulously, covering his ears against the din of noise that both twins raised.

"Even with."

She ran up to him, flinging her arms around his neck. "I missed you, Darion Haddock. I love you!"

Darion squeezed her tight, closing his eyes. "I love you, too, Aidan Holling," he whispered against her hair.

"Hurry back," she told him.

"I will."

As he opened the door, shielding his eyes against the dazzling sun bouncing off fresh Christmas snow, Darion put his hands in his coat pockets to warm himself. His hand brushed against something crumpled. For a moment, he thought it was the scarf that he'd snatched from his brother. But it didn't feel like silk.

As he pulled it out, he stood in the doorway, laughing softly to himself.

Aidan joined him at the door, peering around his arm. "What is it?" she asked. "What's so funny?"

"A present from an old friend," he said. Aidan looked with some misgiving at the brown, oil-stained cap that Darion held reverently in his hands.

"You asked for this?" She raised her eyebrows at him. She knew that Darion often wore ball caps. She'd even considered buying him a new one if she had an inkling if he enjoyed sports or knew what his favorite team was.

"Is this supposed to be some kind of inside joke?"

Carefully, Darion folded the cap, Luke's signature trademark, and put it back into his pocket.

What was it Luke had once told him? He could almost hear that old trucker chiding him.

Giving up never gets you anywhere. You spend half of your life giving up and you wind up with half of your life with nothing in it.

Luke had been wrong. Darion had finally let go. Letting go was exactly what he needed. All of it. Darion had let go of his bitterness and his disappointment at how his life had been. Yes, Darius and Joelle had hurt him. And maybe he'd hurt them, too, by not sticking around to support them. By taking off on his personal quest to renew his life. Now that they'd found him, he had to let go of his suspicions and fear that they'd drag him back to a place he didn't want to go.

Let them have it, Darion thought. His brother and those goons he ran with. Let them take the money from him. He didn't need it. He didn't even really want it. If giving up meant giving a new life to his brother, so be it.

Maybe that was what Luke had been trying to tell him all along. To get, he had to give. To keep what he needed, he had to relinquish what he didn't. Even as Darion held tightly to Aidan, hugging her, loving her, he realized that he had given up, and because of it, found his arms, his life and his heart fuller than ever.

Dear Readers

The inspiration for *Her Brother's Keeper* came when I asked myself—what does it mean when someone, a total stranger, crosses your path more than once? Is it mere coincidence? Or is it fate? Is it just the random churning of the universe? Or is there a grand design, a divine plan at work? These questions are at the very core of *Her Brother's Keeper*.

For this tale, I've taken you back to White Wolf, Montana—my idyllic fictional world where, in the season of *Joyeux Noël*, not-so-ideal, real-life issues threaten the fleeting chance at love for my characters. We meet Aidan Holling and Darion Haddock, seven years from the events of *Unconditional*. In telling Aidan's and Darion's story, I've crafted a string of unrelated coincidences and chance meetings.

What would have happened if Nate *had* found Aidan at the airport? What would have happened if Aidan and Darion *hadn't* been delayed by the diesel truck crash? What would have happened if Joelle *hadn't* stopped by Kiara's boutique where Aidan shopped? Random choices by self-determining characters. Or were they? Were Darion and Aidan always meant to be? Would they have eventually found love without Luke's aid? I'll let you be the judge, Dear Readers.

Until we meet again, keep reading, and keep looking for those seemingly chance opportunities to love and be loved.

geri_guillaume@hotmail.com

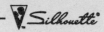
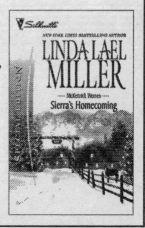